ENDORSEMENTS FOR STAGGERWING

What a great book! It reads with the intrigue of a Louis L'Amour novel and the introduction into the aviation world of Ernest Gann. I read it cover to cover in two sittings. Great insights into the emotions and adrenaline of the air race. Pushing the engine past 100 percent, temperatures high, and flying fifty to a hundred feet off the ground. Wingtip to wingtip with another plane is the greatest adrenaline rush I know.

Of all the planes I have flown, the Staggerwing is second only to the P-51 Mustang in the challenge and sheer joy of flight. The Staggerwing is light on the controls and very powerful. It is short on rudder and disability. It demands the full attention of the pilot on takeoff and landing.

John Bagley
Reno Air Race pylon pilot

To someone who loves sleek airplanes with round engines, *Staggerwing* is like chocolate cake and vanilla ice cream. A great read!

Col. Scott Lyman
Six thousand hours of combat flying
Recipient of Distinguished Flying Cross, Air Medal (three), Bronze Star, and Purple Heart

I found *Staggerwing* to be a riveting love story, packed with adventure and intrigue. I was very impressed with all the detail and accuracy, especially with reference to the flying stories. I flew rag-covered tail-draggers in the fifties and Alaska bush in the sixties before becoming an airline captain. Bob Wells was able to take me on a nostalgic return trip to my past with this wonderful novel. It was quite gratifying to this old aviator.

Capt. Alan Leineke
Pilot for Pacific Northern, Western, and Delta

First, *Staggerwing* is a delightful love story of two young, strong-willed, talented people falling in love, each challenged by the different dreams, aspirations, and goals of the other. Each demonstrates strength of character and strong family relationships while being willing to change, forgive, and make sacrifices.

Second, the flying aspects of the novel deal professionally with the technicalities of flight both in the pylon race and the New York–to–Los Angeles, cross-country air race. Maggie flies one of my all-time favorite airplanes at that early era of aviation, the Staggerwing.

Bob Hosking

Twenty-five thousand hours of flying
Stunt pilot in James Bond and Indiana Jones movies

In a day when a woman was expected to stay in her place, Maggie found hers—racing an airplane! Staggerwing was a plane that marked a turning point in the history of aviation. Maggie also represents a turning point for women everywhere. She is bold, independent, and capable. She balances education, work, and family, all while pursuing her dreams—amazing aspirations that were once well out of reach for females. Readers in today's world will appreciate the spirit and fire she showed at a time when such characteristics in a woman were not always admired. Wells shows a similar spirit in his writing, and the reader will sense his passion for airplanes, education, Argentina, and dreams. The author's writing reflects his own life full of love, adventure, and flying high.

This book is a movie in the making!

Brad Wilcox, PhD
Author, lecturer, Brigham Young University professor

STAGGERWING

A NOVEL

ALSO BY ROBERT E. WELLS

Trust
(Salt Lake City: Bookcraft, 1983)

We Are Christians Because . . .
(Salt Lake City: Deseret Book, 1985)

The Mount & the Master
(Salt Lake City: Deseret Book, 1991)

Hasten My Work
(Salt Lake City: Bookcraft, 1996)

New York to Buenos Aires in 16 Days: The Daring Adventure of a Young Family's Intercontinental Flight in a Single-Engine Plane
(Salt Lake City: Patagonia Press, 2021)

Adventures of the Spirit – Personal Experiences with Prophets, Apostles, and Other Church Leaders
(Salt Lake City: Patagonia Press, 2023)

STAGGERWING

A NOVEL

AUTHOR OF *NEW YORK TO BUENOS AIRES IN 16 DAYS*

ROBERT E. WELLS

Cover design by Armen Osipov
Interior layout and design by www.writingnights.org
Book preparation by Chad Robertson
Edited by Elayne Wells Harmer

ISBN: 979-8-9912584-0-1
Library of Congress Cataloging-in-publication Data:
Names: Wells, Robert E., author.
Title: Staggerwing – A Novel.
Description: Patagonia Press, Salt Lake City, Utah, 2023.
Identifiers: ISBN 979-8-9912584-0-1 (Perfect bound) |
Subjects: Aviation | Fiction
Classification: Pending
LC record pending

Patagonia Press
Printed in the United States of America
Printed on acid-free paper

24 23 22 21 20 19 18 17 8 7 6 5 4 3 2 1

To the memory of all the great aviators, designers, engineers, manufacturers, investors, and race promoters who advanced the science of aviation through dangerous air racing in the 1930s. Many took great risks, some made the ultimate sacrifice, and all loved aviation with devotion and pure passion.

Pilots are drawn to flying because it's a perfect combination of science, romance, and adventure.
—Charles Lindbergh

Flying isn't just about controlling the machine; it's about understanding and controlling yourself.
—Amelia Earhart

CONTENTS

FOREWORD

This novel is loosely based upon the cross-country Bendix Trophy Race on September 4, 1936, when female aviators challenged the male aviators and the women won. Louise Thaden and her copilot, Blanche Wilcox Noyes, flew a Beechcraft C-17R "Staggerwing" from New York to California in 14 hours, 55 minutes, with only one fuel stop. They also set the speed record in the history of the Bendix race by a woman unaccompanied by a man. In fifth place was Amelia Earhart, with copilot Helen Richey.

Some sources report that an unknown aviator bought the winning Staggerwing and flew it off to Central America; another source says that a wealthy Latin American bought it and flew it away to parts unknown.

This book takes great liberty with the facts of the race and adds the mysterious legend with some romance mixed in. Any resemblance to persons, living or dead, is unintentional. I have made no attempt to be completely accurate in historical details, and I apologize in advance if my romanticizing and fictionalizing of the story offends any who know and admire the pilots and the classic airplanes of the 1930s.

But although the characters are fictional, the Staggerwing airplane is absolutely real. It is an actual airplane whose allure and reputation among pilots cannot be exaggerated. The model flown in the 1936 race was powered with a stock 420 hp engine; one year later, two Staggerwings flew in the cross-country race, one with a 450 hp engine and one with an enormous 700 hp engine.

I hope that you, the reader, will enjoy the combination of Hollywood glamour, galloping polo ponies, Latin American culture, streaking airplanes, roaring engines, and the courageous pilots who flew these ground-breaking aircraft. In the air, these men and women were giants and pioneers of aeronautical science. On the ground, they fell in love, were disappointed in romance, ran out of gas or money, and made mistakes, just like you and me.

Robert E. Wells
Salt Lake City, Utah
September 2024

ACKNOWLEDGMENTS

FIRST AND FOREMOST, I wish to thank my late wife, Helen, for her invaluable contributions and talents when I wrote the first edition of this book in 1988. She was a sounding board as I mused about content, did all the computer programming, formatting, and typing, and encouraged me when I hit obstacles in writing and publishing.

I also thank the many friend and family members (listed in alphabetical order) who provided proofreading, editing, printing, plot and character adjustments, constructive literary criticisms, and encouragements: John Bagley, Joseph Bishop, Mark Coleman, Chris Harding, Elayne Wells Harmer, Dan Hogan, Bob Hosking, Alan Leineke, Scott Lyman, Joseph Meier, Douglas Stewart, Mark Swint, Stan Walser, and Sharlene Wells.

In 2024, my daughter Elayne, an attorney and editor, decided it was time for an upgrade. She spent many, many hours editing and polishing the text, tightening the narrative, re-writing dialogue, and working with an artist to design a cover. I am grateful for her expertise and tireless work in making this second edition better than the first. Thank you ever so much, Elayne.

CHAPTER 1

THE WINDS OF FATE

September 1935

IN OUR LIVES, and in our affairs, for good or ill, the winds of fate will inevitably blow. On this particular day the wind itself was not merely symbolic—it was real. It was gusting too hard to film a very important scene, although Eric Von Steineman, the German director, was not about to give in to Mother Nature. His reputation—and his bonus for finishing on time—were on the line. His crew, however, felt otherwise. The dust was an impediment for the cameramen, the gusts were strong enough to tip over a camera and tripod, and the pilot essential for the success of this last major action scene had backed out and refused to fly.

Luke Whitney was an experienced stunt pilot, a highly respected race pilot, and a WWI combat veteran. In his opinion, the wind was too squirrelly, too unpredictable. With unmistakable emphasis he had insisted he dared not dive low over the stunt girl on the horse for fear of hitting her with his whirling propeller.

Maggie Rockwell, the stunt girl, was dressed in Western gear and standing alongside Luke by his plane, watching the tumble weeds roll by. The gusts rocked the plane on its wheels. The chocks blocking the wheels might as well have been cardboard in this wind, so the crew added tie-down ropes to secure the plane.

"Luke, what's the forecast for the wind today?" Maggie asked, not particularly worried. "Do you think it will calm down soon?"

"Can't tell," Luke replied, shrugging. "It should calm down some, but unless it drops to a light breeze with no gusts at all, it would still be too dangerous to try. Let's go over to the car and wait it out."

On their way over to her car they passed by Maggie's palomino tied to the back end of its trailer, all saddled and anxious for action. Maggie patted her photogenic mount.

"Steady, old boy," she cooed. "We might work you a bit or we might not. Just rest and relax."

The horse lifted his head, nodded as if understanding her words or her attitude, and shifted his stance a little.

"Freddy?" Maggie called to her stablehand. "Could you please put Roamer in the trailer and give him some hay to entertain him? This wind won't calm down for a while."

Maggie and Luke walked over to her car, a two-year-old, two-door Chevrolet convertible with a rumble seat, dark green with black trim. The top was in place, the windows rolled up, so they were comfortably out of the wind once they were inside.

This was their first movie stunt together. Maggie had been taking flying lessons for more than two years, but her original instructor had left to fly airmail over the Rockies. Luke had agreed to take over as her new instructor of advanced aviation, and as a mentor of sorts.

Luke was not dressed in the nonchalant manner typical of pilots of the

1930s. Instead, he always wore a full dress uniform of his own design. He was very meticulous with his appearance, and each day wore a freshly ironed khaki shirt, knotted tie, and neatly creased gabardine trousers. To complete the ensemble, when not flying, he would sport a sharp, military-type belted suit coat decorated with numerous shining brass wing and propeller emblems on the cuffs of the sleeves, lapels, and breast pockets. When he flew, he exchanged the suit coat for a leather jacket and the trousers for cavalry breeches with over-the-calf high leather boots. He was the perfect image of an adventurous yet well-dressed pilot.

His flying was as precise as his dress, instilling confidence in all who sought his services. He was warm, friendly, generous, and kind. Everyone loved Luke and sought his company. He and Maggie developed an instant rapport based upon mutual respect and admiration.

Settling into the car seat, Luke spoke first.

"Maggie, everyone notices how much you love your horses. You pet them and look after them with real affection. How long have you been riding?"

"All my life!" Sensing Luke's curiosity, Maggie launched easily into her family history. "I was born and raised on Dad's cattle ranch, so we always had horses. I had a colt or a pony of my own as I was growing up. When I was little, my folks insisted that I ride bareback, Indian style, because one of Mother's brothers had been thrown off. His foot caught in the stirrup, and he was dragged by the frightened horse. His head bounced on the rocks and he almost died. Mother saw the whole thing and wouldn't let me ride with a saddle and stirrups until I was well into my teens. But the good thing is that I learned to be balanced at any gait or any speed just like the Indians!"

Intrigued, Luke questioned further.

"So that's where you got your training for the trick riding you do so well?"

Maggie laughed and responded modestly.

"Yeah, I guess," she said. "My brother and I both rode bareback all the time. Some of Dad's Indian cowboys taught us their style, and we picked up some other tricks along the way."

"You sure did!" Luke exclaimed, nodding vigorously. "I saw you two perform at the Las Vegas Helldorado rodeo and then again at the Laramie Roundup. Great shows, both of them. I was very impressed. In fact, I've been following you since those days, and when you showed up at the airport to do those stunts for the movies, you really made my day!"

The two continued exchanging stories about their youth and interests for some time, as the wind whistled around them, dust filling the air. After about half an hour, the wind seemed to calm down. The director sent a messenger to tell Maggie and Luke to get ready to perform the stunt.

Luke answered quickly. "Tell him not yet. It's still too dangerous. *We'll* tell him when it's safe."

Maggie was keenly aware that, although Luke was about twenty years older than she, he had clearly become interested in her in a personal way. Her prior instructor had always been very professional in teaching her to fly and helping her do wing-walking and parachuting stunts for the movies. She suspected that Luke, on the other hand, had more in mind than just a casual instructor-and-student relationship. He had never done anything overtly, but still, she sensed that he really liked her. On her part, she admired him and respected his flying ability, but never thought of him as a possible suitor.

Maggie took advantage of the delay to change the conversation to the coming air races.

"Luke," she asked. "Do you think I can fly well enough to enter the races this year?"

Luke paused for a minute and thought carefully before he answered. He felt protective of Maggie, yet he knew what an excellent pilot she was, and he knew how important air racing was to the future of aviation. It was a showcase for improvement in engine reliability and stronger, lighter structures of more streamlined, faster design. At the same time, increased speed and longer range was the goal in order to match the progress of military designs in Europe, where war was again looming on the horizon. European governments were financing the development of military aviation, while in the United States it was mostly private financing. The main test bed for these private initiatives was air racing.

"You can fly well enough for the cross-country race," Luke finally responded, measuring his words carefully. "You have a talent for it, and the determination needed for such a long race. Also, I've been impressed that you'll be graduating this year with a degree in aeronautical engineering. You have definitely shown a passion for flying, and your studies have helped you appreciate the mechanics of how these high-powered planes work."

He paused for a moment. "But," he continued cautiously, "as one who has flown the races, I have to tell you that the pylon race is very dangerous, and the cross-country race is only somewhat less dangerous, no matter how good you fly when nothing goes wrong. So, if you were my daughter—or my wife—I wouldn't let you do either one."

Although Maggie was pleased that he thought so highly of her flying ability (and just his saying the word "wife" meant that her suspicions were confirmed about his subconscious thinking), she was very disappointed that he felt it was too dangerous for her. But Maggie was of a contrary nature, and that which a man told her not to do, she had a tendency to want even more to prove that she could do just as well or better. She ignored his answer.

"Luke," she said eagerly, disregarding his concern, "I really want to compete in both the closed-course pylon race and the long-distance cross-country race. Can you help me get the sponsors and planes I need?"

Puzzled over what he considered an overly obsessive desire, Luke couldn't help inquiring further into the impossible dreams of his precocious flying student. That was how he truly perceived her—talented and very competent—but Luke, as most men of that time believed, didn't think any woman should be in the dangerous and even deadly air races.

"Before I answer you on that, Maggie," he responded, "tell me how in the world did a rodeo-performing gal become intrigued with being a pilot and flying in races? Don't you have enough danger and excitement in your life already?"

Happy to share her passion with flying, Maggie began to tell her story.

"When I was about fifteen," she began, "the first airplane I ever saw zoomed over our home, and the roar of that engine was so startling that I ran out of the house to see what it was. It was an airmail pilot forced off course by bad weather in the mountains. He landed in our pasture and rolled right up close to where I was standing on the porch. After he shut down the engine, I ran over to look at that magnificent flying machine that had literally dropped out of the sky. I had never seen anything so peculiar and interesting. I walked all around it very slowly, observing every little detail, touching it to feel the fabric that was stretched tight covering the wings and the fuselage. I knew about engines from our tractors and trucks and was so impressed by this big aircraft engine swinging that huge wooden propeller."

Luke was listening intently, so Maggie took a breath and continued.

"From that day to this I have been hooked on airplanes," she stated emphatically. "I would even make model planes like my brother did. When I started taking flying lessons I met your friend, Mary Jane, who has flown in air races, so I wanted to do the same. She encouraged me to set my goals high and was so supportive and helpful that she has been my idol ever since."

Luke was mulling over in his mind how he should respond to this attractive and ambitious girl's consuming passion to compete in something he considered dangerous even for men—when the director's assistant interrupted again, demanding that they come at once. Reluctantly leaving this conversation unfinished, they agreed to continue discussing the race matter later.

Von Steineman was fuming over their tardiness. He felt he could wait no longer.

In his very thick German accent, he demanded, "You must fly now! Vee cannot stay here all day, and I don't vant to come back out here tomorrow. Vee are over budget already. It costs money to have the people just sitting around all day! Vee are behind schedule and the front office is demanding that vee get this scene filmed because it is the last part of the whole movie and the most important one!"

The director was irate and wouldn't take no for an answer.

"Maggie, you get on your horse!" he insisted, bellowing. "Do your action. Luke, get in your plane, take off, make your dive and pick Maggie up!"

Luke had flown against the Germans in the war, so he didn't like the director to start with. He especially didn't like taking orders from him, and doing something that would endanger Maggie's life was definitely over the line.

"Don't you realize that this stunt requires absolutely calm air?" he reacted angrily. "If we do it right, my propeller is only a few inches above Maggie's head when I pass over her. If a gust drops me ten inches or so it can take her head right off. If a swirl pushes me to the side just as she jumps for the bottom rung of the ladder she will fall into the dirt and could break her neck. Flying in this wind is suicide or murder!"

The German's face reddened. His temper had reached the boiling point, and, as a test of his authority, he fired back, shaking his decorative walking stick for emphasis.

"If you don't vant to fly and if she doesn't vant to ride the horse, I will fire you both and go find somebody else! There are many pilots and girl riders out of verk these days. Take it or leave it!"

Luke, hardly able to control his anger, looked over at Maggie for a response from her. Maggie was actually not as worried as Luke, because the ladder was dangling out the left side of the plane. Luke's prop would be to the right of her head. The big black left wheel in the streamlined pants would be as much of a danger to her head as the prop, and neither worried her as much as grabbing the bottom rung just as it passed over her. Her risk was either having it jerked out of her hand, losing her grip, or missing it altogether and ending up sprawling in the dirt. She did admit to herself, though, that Luke was right. If she landed wrong, she could break her neck.

But, she reasoned to herself, *I have flopped many times off my horse at a dead run practicing stunts with my brother. The dirt where my horse will be running is loose sand. I need the money, and so does Luke.*

"Aw nuts," she exclaimed out loud. "Let's go try it!"

Luke looked heavenward, rolling his eyes in quiet resignation, knowing that mere mortals were helpless to change this unusual woman's mind once she decided something.

Maggie had Freddy pull Roamer out of his trailer where he was feeding, protected from the wind, and she mounted up. She pulled on a long, blonde wig to make her look like the heroine in the movie and rode off to her position far down the dirt road.

Muttering to himself, Luke cranked up the biplane's big rotary engine and took off, trailing a cloud of dust enhanced by the wind as well as his prop-wash. The German director waited for the plane to climb to its position, then quickly fired his flare gun for the action to begin.

Maggie raced her palomino toward the cameras, while actors in dark cowboy hats menacingly fired their six-shooter smoke-blanks at her in the chase. Luke nosed over into a power dive with the ladder whipping in his slipstream. The plan was well-conceived, but Nature had her own agenda.

The wind was still strong enough that Maggie's horse created a rising cloud of dust, making it hard for the bad guys to see, and harder for Luke to see without clobbering her with either the prop or the left wheel. The turbulence caused swirling eddies that rocked the plane's wings and even shifted it from side to side. As Luke got lower, the ride got bumpier and more uncertain, but he did his best to place the ladder over Maggie's right shoulder. He looked down over the cowl of his cockpit and saw the ladder whipping back and forth.

He timed it just right, he thought, but at the exact instant Maggie felt the thrashing vibration of shock waves off the tips of the propeller and knew that the ladder was right behind, a strong gust pushed the plane to the right, forcing her to lean way out of her saddle to catch it. She might have caught it, but Roamer shied left, away from the enormous shape of the plane directly overhead, and she lost it.

She was leaning too far out and was off balance. Knowing that she was going to fall, Maggie kicked her feet out of the stirrups, pulled her arms in close, and rolled off into the dirt in one enormous, upside-down ball to protect her face. She landed, rolled, bounced, and slid, finally coming to a stop in a huge ball of dirt and dust.

The chasing cowboys were close enough to see her spectacular fall and reached her almost immediately. Luke pulled the plane around in a tight circle to survey the disaster below, which he had accurately envisioned as one of the tragic possibilities. His face was wrinkled in fear and worry—and anger at that stubborn German. Had she survived?

The actors surrounded Maggie, fearing to move her in case of major broken bones or pinched nerves, especially in her neck and back. The cameramen who had been filming the scene came running, and an ambulance doctor raced over to take charge.

Maggie was covered with dirt. She was a mess, and she lay deathly still. The men feared the worst. Slowly she opened her eyes, coughed, and spit out dirt and grit—but no blood.

The doctor knelt at her side. Seeing that she had her eyes open he asked hesitantly, "Are you all right, my dear?"

Her answer was typical Maggie.

"I've tasted better dirt," she announced. "Help me get up and we'll see."

The doctor cautioned her against moving until he had checked her neck and extremities. He asked how many fingers he was showing to check her vision and had her swivel her neck to each side. Finally, he asked those closest to help her stand up. She was shaken from the fall, had a bit of stiffness, and felt some pain in her ribs, but she was able to stand alone. Luke roared overhead. She squinted into the sky, shading her eyes, and waved at him to signal that she was fine.

The crowd laughed with relief, and someone started to sing "Oh, for she's a jolly good fellow" to show their support.

Von Steineman, showing no apparent concern for Maggie, did not even come over to see how she was. The doctor reported to him that she needed to go to the hospital for X-rays, although he could not see anything broken, nor evidence of a concussion.

The director gave up in disgust. He threw his arms in the air, jumped into his car and zoomed off, angry at the failed scene. Luke flew back around and landed. He rushed to Maggie's side, relieved. He hugged her gently, and a bit affectionately.

By now she was feeling somewhat better. After a drink of water and some cleaning up, she felt almost herself again.

Panic-stricken, she suddenly exclaimed, "Good heavens! I have a test at the university! I'll have to rush to make it. Freddy, take care of old Roamer for me, please. I notice that he's limping, and as soon as I finish my exam, I'll find a vet to look at him, but I've gotta get going now. And Freddy, please get Blondie ready for tomorrow's shoot, just in case."

Luke asked if she needed someone to drive her to her exam.

"No, I've fallen off a lot of horses," she reassured him. "I'm really okay. I'm just glad I didn't hang on to the ladder for a few seconds while you climbed higher, and then fall from fifty feet up instead of six. Falling from saddle height is just part of this business."

Luke's mind spun in amazement as he thought, *What an unusual woman! She has spunk and resiliency. Not many of this kind around. She will be bruised tomorrow though, I'll bet.*

As Luke watched Maggie drive off to her exam in a cloud of dust, he thought more about her request that he find sponsors and planes for her to fly in the coming air races. He felt protective of her, yet he could see from her handling of the risky stunt and spectacular fall that she was mature enough to take on the risks of racing against seasoned pilots, even male ones. Still, he did not yet understand the depth of Maggie's competitive spirit, her obsession to beat the male pilots, and the intensity of her passion to fly bigger and faster airplanes than anyone.

Unbeknownst to Maggie and Luke, an important and unusual incident had occurred a month before at the racetrack where Maggie stabled her two beautiful palominos. It involved only two people—strangers—but it was to have a major influence on the lives of this race-obsessed, ambitious, young aviatrix and her race-pilot instructor and mentor.

Sir Douglas Barrington, a British actor knighted for his contributions to the arts, had become very popular in the Hollywood movie scene. Among his many interests was a weekly trip to the Southern California horse races. He was an aficionado, loved the four-footed athletes and their riders, and frequented the pari-mutuel betting windows.

Early one fine morning, as Douglas was driving his open convertible to the track to time a new horse, he passed by a ten-foot-high hedge. From the other side, he heard the distinctive crack of a mallet head on a polo ball. As a former polo player—and not knowing that anyone in California in the mid-1930s was playing the game—he was intrigued. He drove on until he found a driveway leading to the source of the sounds. He parked inconspicuously by the side of the field and watched a single player on a magnificent mount practice some exercises. No one else was around.

After a few simple swings of the mallet driving the polo ball about fifty feet at a time, the horse loping slowly and effortlessly, the rider lined up six balls out at the midfield point. They were spread out in a pattern Douglas remembered from his own years of training. The white balls, about the size of a softball, were placed three on one side and three on the other side of an imaginary line running toward the distant goal posts. The polo player trotted his pony back to where he could look down the open "aisle," then went back out and adjusted the balls so they were equal distance one from the other, and finally returned again to look toward the far goal posts.

He sat still for a moment, patted his horse, leaned forward in the saddle, and with a shout, a quick kick in the flanks, and with a swing of the mallet, signaled the horse to take off with a leap and gallop at a dead run down the middle. The polo player hit the first ball on his right, driving it all the way to the goal posts, twisted in his saddle, and with a mighty offside backhand forward shot drove the first left hand ball all the way to the goal. Still at a breakneck speed, the polo player turned again and hit the next right-hand ball, repeating the same movements downfield until he had knocked all six balls from midfield right through the goal posts. The last one rolled into the same spot as the first five. They made a tight, small pattern.

Douglas was astounded. He had seldom seen such perfect form, such smooth dexterity, and such accuracy even from ten-goal handicapped players back in England. He could not believe his eyes. He wanted to talk to this young player, but at the same time he did not want to interrupt his concentration. Besides, he had an appointment at the racetrack to time a new horse while it was being exercised by its jockey. Reluctantly, he drove away, shaking his head in disbelief. He drove back to the side of the racetrack rail, where the owner of the racehorse was waiting for him. He stopped his engine, got out of his car, and walked over to the man.

Out on the track, a thoroughbred racehorse, young, beautifully proportioned, with strong muscles and a pleasingly wide chest was trotting around, guided by a slender jockey. They had completed their morning warm-up exercises and were waiting for the famous actor to arrive. The owner signaled the jockey to take his position at the starting gate. Both men got out their stopwatches. Douglas had a pair of binoculars in his hand. With the drop of a flag, a timed practice race began.

The horse ran beautifully, poetry in motion, every stride eating up long distances of track. The jockey bent over smoothly, encouraging his flying mount, and the two men at the rail mentally calculated the results at each marker around the track. Douglas peered through his binoculars, looked down at his stopwatch, then back to the glasses. The horse came charging around the last turn and down the final stretch toward the finish line. The scene was thrillingly beautiful to every horse lover, and especially so to the owner who had raised the horse from a colt, trained him carefully, and now saw him ready for entry in his first race. Douglas knew the owner and had been tipped off that here was a one-of-a-kind future Kentucky Derby winner in the making.

The jockey let his pony slow down, then trotted the lathered and deep-breathing horse over to where the owner and Douglas were standing. The rider looked down at the men, grinning happily.

"Didn't I tell you he was in great shape?" he said, chuckling. "I'll bet that was his best time ever! Right?"

Douglas and the owner checked their stopwatches again and read off the time to the tenth of a second.

"I don't think any other horse in the state can beat that time," Douglas said. "However, the track is in perfect condition today. What if we have a wet track or even mud? How much will that slow him down?"

The wiry man in the saddle did not hesitate.

"He'll blow right by any other horse I know of, no matter the condition of the track. He's the best ride I've ever had, and I don't have to use spurs or whip. He runs because he wants to, and he runs even better against another horse. He really wants to win every time."

After a few more comments, the jockey took his mount back to the stables. Douglas returned to his convertible, gleaming in the sun. It sparkled and was extremely impressive. He had brought it from England, and it was so spectacular that the studio bosses wanted to feature it with Douglas in publicity photographs. But it had a problem.

Douglas closed the door, enjoying the sound of a solid *chunk* like a vault door closing, denoting a massive amount of thick, high-grade steel and a quality locking mechanism. With trepidation he turned the key, pressed the starter button, and listened for the electric motor to crank. Nothing happened. He stopped, turned the key off and then on, and tried cranking again. It had been slow starting ever since he got it off the cargo ship. In England, it had started perfectly every time. He was worried and perplexed. It was one of the most expensive cars in the world and should start up easily and quickly.

Unnoticed by the actor, a young man leading a polo pony happened to be passing by. He had slowed down to admire the enormous automobile and had heard the failed cranking.

"Excuse me, sir, but I see you have a problem," the young man called out impulsively. "Might I be of help to you?"

Douglas turned, and saw a tall, handsome, very athletic-looking fellow dressed like a polo player—certainly not the mechanic he needed at the moment. He recognized him as the polo player he had watched earlier, but at this moment he was more concerned with his car.

"Thanks very much," he responded, "but with this car I only let a factory-trained mechanic work on it. I don't want to affect my warranty, you understand."

The young man smiled.

"I know I don't look like it now," he said politely, "but I once worked for a Rolls Royce agency. I suspect you have a relatively new model and I guess it must have recently made a long sea voyage from England. You probably have some saltwater corrosion in the distributor rotor points. There should be a small tool for just that purpose in the tool kit in your boot. It comes with all export models because they don't have metric sizes over here. If you will let me, I can get it out, open the bonnet, and I can have it fixed in a few minutes."

The world-renowned Shakespearean actor hesitated for a moment, but the young man's distinctly British accent—along with the words "boot" and "bonnet," not used in the United States—gave him a feeling that he could trust this stranger with his prized car.

"All right, go to it," Douglas said. "Let's see what you can do."

After a few minutes, the young polo player said, "Try it now." The big automobile started immediately. Douglas was most grateful and offered to pay him.

The young man smiled and said, "No, thanks. It was my privilege to tend to a great machine like this."

The actor was intrigued with this stranger.

"Sorry, but I did not introduce myself," he apologized, extending his hand. "I am Douglas Barrington. May I ask what your name is, and where you are from?"

"I'm Fernando Underwood." He grasped Douglas's outstretched hand and shook it firmly.

"I live here," he explained, pointing toward the polo stables. "I work at the polo field while I study at the university."

Douglas, still curious, remarked, "I saw you practicing polo. You are an incredible player. Also, you know this Rolls Royce so well—you must be from England, am I right?"

Fernando's explanation was quick and somewhat hesitant.

"Yes, thank you, sir. I did study at Cambridge for a while. Sorry, but I have to be going. I've got an appointment I need to get to."

With that, he turned and left, taking quick long strides, rounding the corner of the grandstand of the racetrack and disappearing from view with the polo pony in tow.

Douglas was left with a lot of questions. The more he thought about what had just transpired, the more puzzled he became. For the next few weeks he could not get the boy out of his mind, and he became more and more eager to investigate this polo player/mechanic/student. He became obsessed with the mystery and began to ask questions.

The results would turn out to be both good and bad, favorable and unfavorable—for Maggie, for Luke, and for Fernando himself, just like the variable winds of fate.

CHAPTER 2

A MYSTERIOUS POLO PLAYER

THE SOUTHERN CALIFORNIA Polo Club was teeming with people, and the visitors were alive with excitement. The razzle-dazzle speed, flashing color, and beautiful horses of a polo game had attracted an elegant, sophisticated crowd—avid fans, as well as curious newcomers were in attendance. The large green playing field was as smooth as a billiard table with its close-cut, rolled, and manicured lawn grass. The field itself was surrounded by landscaped shrubs, flowers, and carefully chosen full-foliaged trees. A short, foot-high white fence marked the sides of the playing ground, and set back from the boundaries were stadium stands for the spectators.

The umpires were just getting ready to start the first chukker when two large and unusually flamboyant cars entered the already-full parking lot. At the same instant, eight prancing, high-strung horses were moving onto the field, each ridden by a well-tanned, muscular, athletic player. Four of the riders were wearing red polo shirts and the other four wore white, denoting the two competing teams. All eight players wore white cork helmets with white riding breeches and tall leather boots.

As the two fancy cars entered the spots reserved for special dignitaries, the umpire threw the white wooden ball between the two opposing sides now lined up facing each other. An immediate scurrying and scuffling ensued. Each team fought for control, dervishes swinging mallets at the ball on the ground. The lacquered willow sphere abruptly shot out from the melee of legs and mallets. The horsemen whirled to follow it up the field.

The ponies' flashing hooves dug into the green turf and kicked up sod divots the size of dinner plates, their legs bound in colored bandages to protect them from the swinging mallets. Their tails were also tied up to keep long hair from tangling with the sweeping arcs of the bamboo-shafted mallets.

The thoroughbred horses gleamed in the sun as they galloped up field at full speed, only to instantly reverse their direction to follow the ball back toward the opposite goal. The horses wheeled and charged, pivoting and dashing off again in multiple directions like flocks of birds at sundown darting here and there for no reason. The polo ponies followed the erratic path of the white ball up and down the field, played first by one team and then intercepted and controlled for a while by the other.

The two late-arriving cars pulled alongside each other. The parking lot housed the usual assortment of vehicles at a polo match: wood-sided station wagons loaded with saddles, mallets, and riding gear of the players; late-model convertibles driven by young ladies of fashion, there to admire and cheer on the young men on the field; and large limousines driven by chauffeurs hired by the very rich—older parents of players and fans of the game.

Nevertheless, even amidst the fanciest vehicles of the most affluent, the two new cars caused bystanders and other late arrivals to turn and watch with curiosity. The lead car was a four-door orange Rolls Royce convertible called the "Torpedo Phantom II." The second car was even longer—more impressive but less colorful. It was a Rolls Royce "Silver Cloud" limousine, silver with black trim, flying two flags of the British Empire, one on each front fender, flapping smartly in the breeze, announcing that the passengers were official representatives of His Majesty the King of England.

Two official-looking gentlemen descended from the passenger compartment of the chauffeured limousine, distinctly non-Californian in dress and demeanor. Another equally impressive-looking gentleman, wearing a tailored tweed jacket, gabardine trousers, and aviator sunglasses stepped out of the convertible.

"I say, old boy, it is a pleasure to see you again," remarked Lord Charles Jockham, who was wearing a diplomat-style gray homburg hat and smartly dressed in a gray flannel suit. His red-striped school tie sported a large diamond stickpin.

"Bit of all right to see you out here in the West, old chap," Douglas, the convertible's driver, responded as he removed his glasses and placed them in his coat pocket.

They shook hands warmly, right hand gripping right hand, left hand grabbing each other's forearm, and then they embraced in continental fashion with a familiarity known only to intimate and longtime boarding school friends meeting after a considerable absence from each other's company.

"Thanks for waiting for me to lead you in," remarked Douglas to his distinguished friend.

Charles graciously acknowledged the courtesy and turned to introduce his companion, who was his vice-consul and secretary.

"This is Edward Williams. He gets all the work done at the office. Edward, this is my friend, Douglas."

The two men shook hands.

"How is the consulate business getting on these days?" Douglas asked the consul, more formally attired than his much more sportily dressed friend.

"Just so-so, I'd say," Charles answered jovially. "Not much of a post for me after being in India so long. But I guess the home office thought that Hollywood and all you actors from London needed me to look after you."

That brought a chuckle from Douglas, who looked very much the part of the British actor he was.

"By the way," the consul continued, "how is your career going over here? Do the Colonies appreciate your finer talents?"

The actor smiled broadly, his thin, wide moustache emphasizing the famous grin he was so well known for in the movies.

"Well, they pay me a lot more here than at home and they like my dueling abilities," he responded. "I'm writing fencing scenes into the scripts, and they even like my accent! They think I am better suited for the talkies than their own actors. I do think it must be the Shakespearian training. By the way, have you seen my latest on the silver screen?"

Charles broke into his widest smile, exposing a full set of perfect white teeth offset by a thick and bushy moustache.

"Most certainly, my dear friend," he said. "Although we have not seen each other much the last few years, I never miss you on the screen or the stage, and I carefully read every article about you in the magazines. I have been an admirer of yours since we did Shakespeare in school together. I must say I prefer your art on the stage, but if they pay you more for the movies, your loyal theater public back home will just have to suffer!"

The banter continued until the consul asked the actor, "Tell me, what is all this about anyway? Why have you asked me to meet you here at a polo game with no explanation at all—just saying it would be terribly interesting? I didn't know anyone knew how to play polo out here in California. What are you up to, my old friend? I was so intrigued that I came directly from the consulate."

Douglas leaned in and lowered his voice.

"Well, I don't usually go in for cloak-and-dagger mysteries," he said conspiratorially, "but I found something here the other day that absolutely intrigues me. Then I heard just yesterday the most welcome news that you had moved here to open a consulate office, and I said to myself, *Aha, here's a chance to kill two birds with one shot.* I wanted to welcome you to California anyway, and old Jock is the one to solve this thing as quickly as possible! I need help back in England, and it occurred to me that perhaps you might be the only one I know who has the connections to do it. Besides, I thought that we might renew our old friendship and polo rivalry by watching a few chukkers together at the site of the mystery. Let's go up to our box and I'll tell you all about it."

On their way to their box, they paused occasionally to observe the game in progress. They noted that there were many missed shots, some confusion, and the score at the end of the second chukker was a disappointing zero to zero. During the rest period between the second and third chukkers, while the players were mounting up on fresh horses, the two friends arrived at their box.

"This is a lovely afternoon and I am very happy to see you again," the consul said, "but this is not the best game of polo I have ever seen. You and I, even at our age, could easily saddle up and take on all eight of them and still beat them by ten goals to zero rather quickly. Neither side is passing to the open man, and they are missing most of their shots completely or else topping them or hammering them into the turf!"

Douglas smiled knowingly and nodded.

"Right-o, Jock. Elementary polo, I do agree. The university started a polo class and team three years ago, but this is a kind of exhibition game between the students of the man I want you to see. I think he will take the field to demonstrate faster play this next chukker. Polo is very new out here and they are trying to build up interest in the sport. The man I want you to observe is the polo instructor, who is also a university student here. He is their team captain when they play anyone else. The university owns this polo field, including the stables to put up their players' ponies.

"Over there is the big racetrack and other stables for racehorses and private owners' horses," he explained, pointing off in the distance beyond the polo field toward the racetrack.

Charles stood to look in the direction Douglas was pointing and saw the major facilities visible through the trees. The polo stadium and stables were close to but totally separate from the other large complex.

"This polo teacher gives classes and runs the whole installation here for the university," Douglas continued. "I think he is hiding under an assumed name, and I also suspect that he may be from some important family. However, no one knows anything about him. He just showed up one day over at the racetrack doing a very menial job. When they found out that he played polo, they gave him a job over here. The university will not disclose anything about him. I think they know but are simply not telling anyone anything."

Douglas lowered his voice even more, almost to a whisper.

"One day when I was passing by on my way to the racetrack I heard the distinctive crack of a hardwood mallet head on a willow polo ball and came over to look. Just couldn't resist, you know. This boy was lofting shots half the length of the field or more. I had never seen anyone like him. He is a ten-goal handicap player if I've ever seen one!"

Charles had been listening to Douglas's quiet background explanation with nonchalance until now, but the claim of a ten-goal handicap player out here in the western part of the United States was preposterous. Few men in the world deserved that lofty acclaim and honor. He interrupted so loudly that heads turned.

"Aww, come on, me laddie!" the consul exclaimed. "That is impossible! The only top handicappers like that are well known and are all at home in England. There is one player on the East Coast—a Mr. Hitchcock, I believe—who is coming along fine, but you know there could not be a ten-goal handicap way out here in the West!"

Douglas looked intently at his friend and continued, keeping his voice low.

"Jock, just wait a minute. I have watched him play! You have never seen anyone with the precision of this boy. He can pass to any of his team anywhere on the field, dropping the ball right where they can pick it up, and if no one is open he will take the ball the full length of the field himself, as if there were no defense. He is like a phantom on a horse!"

Charles scoffed.

"But more than that," Douglas continued enthusiastically, "one day, just after my new Rolls Royce convertible arrived, I was out here at the stables and it wouldn't start. Only one day off the boat, as a matter of fact. This polo player came by leading his horse and asked if he could help. I told him no and explained that only a factory-trained representative would be allowed to open the hood of a Rolls."

Douglas recounted his conversation with the young man and the astonishing result.

"I asked him where he was from since I could detect a British vocabulary with a Spanish accent in his speech," he continued. "He told me that he had studied at Cambridge, but I don't think he meant to tell me that much because he quickly changed the subject and tried to modify his accent. It has become obvious to me that this boy is well-educated, and I'll bet he's from a home where one or both of his parents speak the King's English all the time."

Douglas had not finished his account when the play began again, so he quickly interjected his request.

"Jock, old buddy, for old time's sake, can you get your people to find out about a top polo player about twenty-six to twenty-nine years of age, interested in engineering, who disappeared about three years ago? He is studying aeronautical engineering here. He receives no money and no mail, and he sends no mail. He lives here in the stables, supervising the stablehands and the horses. They say he is also a superb vet. Some of the racehorse owners bring their problems over to him. His clothes are made by as fine a tailor as we have on Saville Row in London, although they are starting to show some wear. He once had a very privileged situation, I dare say."

Some clamor from the playing field caused Douglas to turn to observe the play. In so doing, he spotted the mystery man he had been telling his friend about.

"Jock, watch number four of the red team—he's just come in. There—that's our man!"

The distinguished consul took his prized Leitz binoculars out of a finely tooled leather case and focused on number four red.

After a few seconds of play, Charles said casually, "Yes, he sits very well, handles his mount smoothly . . . uses balance and his knees and very slight pressure from the reins, knows how to make his horse change hands . . . hmmm."

Interrupting his friend's musing, Douglas said, "Just keep watching and you will see what I mean. He seems to loaf along letting the others play, but every now and then he will effortlessly explode with something magnificent."

Suddenly the white team made a good charge down the field on the far side, crossing to within striking distance of a goal. One of the white forwards was not being guarded closely enough by his red opponent. The white player had a clear shot at the goal, and he lofted a superb shot well into the air with perfect line.

Normally it would be impossible to stop a shot like that but, with seeming ease, the mystery player caused his pony to explode into runaway speed, stood up in his stirrups, and raised his mallet head high enough to intercept the ball mid-flight. The ball dropped to the grass just ahead of him in front of the goal line. He made a mighty shot under the neck of his mount that rifled the ball thirty feet into the air, all the way back up to midfield, precisely where his own unguarded forward number one could take it and drive off for an unexpected goal at the far end of the field.

The crowd was stunned and silent at first, but those who knew a spectacular polo play when they saw one jumped to their feet, applauding vigorously and shouting, "Good job! Great shot!"

Following their cue, everyone else leapt to their feet and roared their approval. Whether they understood the fine points of polo technique or not, the fans all sensed they had seen something unusual and spectacular.

Charles turned to Douglas, lowered his field glasses and exclaimed, "Incredible! I haven't seen an interception like that in twenty years! The only player I ever saw with that kind of skill was old Whitey from the cavalry. You remember him, don't you? Whitey Summers—colonel with the regulars—played until about sixty, I think. One of the greatest we ever had. Dead now, may he rest in peace."

Douglas bowed his head and held a moment of silence for the legendary man.

"But I now see what you mean, Douglas!" the consul continued energetically. "Remarkable, absolutely remarkable. It looked effortless. He wasn't even in a hurry! Just picked that ball out of the air and sent it whizzing above both teams to midfield. By Jove, if he can make that kind of a play, he indeed has the potential to become a ten-goal handicap!"

After a few more minutes of routine play with no one making another goal, Charles, watching again through the binoculars, whispered to Douglas, "Uh-oh—our mystery man is up to something. He just motioned to number three to take his place guarding the goal on defense and he is moving up to forward one or two position. Let's watch and see what he is up to. Hmmm . . . he stole the ball from the white forward. He's taking it into their territory—white two is riding him hard with a faster horse—oh—oh—hey! Will you look at that!"

The crowd erupted with a roaring "Gooooaall!" accompanied by exuberant applause.

"Did you see that miracle shot, Douglas?" Charles exclaimed, lowering the glasses in amazement.

"No, tell me! What happened?" Douglas responded innocently, pretending he hadn't seen the play.

The consul, hardly containing himself, put aside his dignified persona.

"Let me show you!" He stood up and acted out the shot with exaggeration, twisting his upper body to the left, and, reaching his right hand high, still holding the binoculars, swept down and hit forward with a backhand offside shot, shouting "Gooooaall!" to all around him. Other fans laughed good-naturedly at the re-enactment.

"He was moving down the near side of the field kind of dribbling the bocca along when white two caught up with him—faster horse by far," Charles said enthusiastically. "But all our man did was pass the ball from his own right side to the left side of his horse. White two tried to push him off the line so he could get to the ball—rode his horse over hard into our man, almost a foul I'd say. Our man normally would have lost the ball since white two has a bigger and faster horse, but that mystery man of yours simply twisted into one gigantic offside, backhand, forward shot and made a goal from an impossible distance!"

Douglas acted amazed, as though he had missed the action.

"He blasted that ball like a bullet the rest of the length of the field and the goal umpire signaled a goal," Charles continued, still looking astonished. "That was a one-in-a-million shot with his opposite riding him that hard—and with a better horse and from that distance—*and* an offside forward backhand shot!"

He finally sat down and Douglas patted him on the knee.

"Sorry, old chap, but that was no miracle shot," the actor said with a smile. "He does that more often than not. In practice or in competition, no matter how hard they ride him or how close they guard him, or even if he's surrounded by all four of the other team, he repeatedly pulls out one of those 'miracle shots,' as you call it. He is the best polo player I have ever seen, and no one knows who he really is. I made it to a seven-goal handicap when I was playing with the Prince of Wales almost every day, but never in my wildest dreams could I play like this fellow plays. Take my word for it. I have never seen the best Englishmen or even players from India play any better. Have you ever seen anyone this good?"

Despite the consul's enthusiasm, he was cautious about using that superlative.

"Well," he responded, "I have seen the most outstanding players of all time and with a stable of top-quality horses better than any on the field today by far, so I might not be ready to say your player is the best in the world. You know that they say the mount is 51 percent of the play and the rider is 49 percent or less, but I guess I would have to agree with you that your man is exceptionally talented. If he can play consistently in good competition with good mounts and do what he just did several times in each chukker, he could indeed be a ten-goal player.

I sure would like to know who this boy really is! Tell me, what else have you dug up about him?"

"Well, I have been a bit of a Sherlock Holmes," Douglas admitted with a sly smile. "I have learned that he is a brilliant student pulling top honors. He has absolutely no social life—as celibate as a priest. Never dates any girls and seems to stay away from them. I gather there are many who have tried to stir up some interest on his part but he never goes for their bait. He doesn't seem to have any friends in particular, yet he is very friendly to everyone. He's very likeable and pleasant to be around. Smiles easily, but he just won't talk about himself—"

Charles interrupted. "You say he just walked onto the scene here about three years ago?"

"That's what I've been told," Douglas replied. "He had just been hired over at the racetrack as a stablehand. One of the regents at the university was leading his lame polo pony around looking for a vet when he saw this young man—Fernando Underwood is his name, he says—and the regent asked him where he could find a vet. Fernando turned around, examined the horse, and said, 'You don't need a vet. That is only a mallet bruise. I can have him healed in a few days' time.'"

Douglas recounted the rest of the story to his friend. Although the horse's owner had not mentioned it was a polo pony or what had caused the lameness, Fernando had known it immediately. The regent let the young man treat the horse, and three days later the horse was ready to play again. The owner was so impressed, he invited Fernando to change to the university's polo stables, and he captivated everyone so much with his expertise that they quickly put him in charge of all the grooms, the stable boys, and exercise jockeys—and finally in charge of the whole polo program. Of course, along the way they also discovered that Fernando was an incredible polo player.

"The regent is Dr. Reinhart, a famous neurosurgeon and the founder of the polo club, the team, and the courses in polo at the university," Douglas explained. "He worked out a scholarship deal so that Fernando could become a full-time student in the aeronautical engineering program, which would also allow him to be the coach, trainer, team captain, and head man at the university's polo facilities."

"But how does he pay for his expenses?" Charles asked.

"I understand he gets room and board and tuition, plus a little spending money for incidentals," Douglas replied. "I have tried to get more information from the doctor, but he is almost as close-mouthed as young Fernando. They say the boy speaks Spanish like a native with a South American accent, and he is fully conversant in French and German as well. Sharp as a whip, but I dare say he is hiding something about his background. Well, that's all I know."

"That's quite a chunk for starters," Charles remarked, smiling. Lord Charles "Jock" Jockham, Earl of Wittingham, retired colonel of the famous cavalry regiment from India, and now His Majesty's consul for the entire western part of the United States, turned to his vice-consul.

"Please cable the London office to the attention of Mr. Durham," he said crisply. "You know his full name and title. Ask him to check on the Underwood family of Dorchester and London. They played a lot of polo some twenty-five years ago, back before the war. One of their daughters, who also played good polo after women were allowed to ride astride, married into a very wealthy family from someplace in Latin America. This boy might be tied in there somehow and using his mother's maiden name. In fact, he even resembles other members of that family. All the men were very athletic and tall, and had muscular builds."

He turned to Douglas.

"You say he speaks Spanish? Do you know if there is any indication that he might be from Argentina or Cuba?"

Intrigued, Douglas responded, "I'm told he listens to Cuban-type music on the radio or his record player, but it might be music from some other Latin country, for all I know. But he seems so distinctly British that it threw me off. Besides, they don't play that kind of polo in Cuba. Farther south maybe. I'll be anxious to see what turns up."

After the match was over and farewells extended to those around them, the three British gentlemen made their way to their vehicles.

Douglas bid the consul and vice-consul goodbye as he climbed into his open car, enjoying the late afternoon Southern California sunshine and the perfume of eucalyptus in the air. *Delightful day*, he thought to himself. *Old Jock will figure this mystery out. I'll bet on it!*

CHAPTER 3

MAGGIE ACES THE STUNT

VERY EARLY ON the morning of his Strength of Materials exam, Fernando assigned chores around the stables and grounds. He also posted the exercise program he had worked out for each horse on the polo facility's bulletin board.

One crew was to work on the main polo field to fix the divots created during the exhibition game. Another team had the assignment of mowing and trimming the landscaped area surrounding the playing and practice fields and exercise area, the stables, and the other buildings that were part of the complex. The grooms were to take the horses out for their daily exercises, including walking, trotting, galloping, and a short dead run. Other business matters occupied Fernando's mind: ordering more bales of hay, bags of oats, medicines, and other items.

A few of his students came by unexpectedly, asking for pointers on physical exercises that would strengthen their onside backhand shots and offside forehand and backhand shots, all of which Fernando performed brilliantly. Attempting to execute such shots after the game the day before, they realized that some actions required the development of specific muscles and skills.

Thinking there was plenty of time before he had to leave for his exam, Fernando had a mount saddled up and joined his students with their ponies on the practice field. As usually happened, several horse owners and student riders stopped whatever they were doing to watch Fernando.

After about an hour of demonstrating and watching the students practice, he was about to go back to his quarters and change out of his riding clothes, but when he dismounted, a stablehand came running to tell him there was a sick horse in the stables. The man told Fernando what he had observed of the mare's condition, but when they entered her stall, Fernando sensed that the problem was even more serious than the stablehand had thought.

"Go call Dr. Bell!" he exclaimed urgently. "This mare has a temperature, and he will have to prescribe some medicine to bring it down. In the meantime, please bring me some eucalyptus bark from a tree. Don't pick up any from the ground."

He also asked for items that would allow him to prepare and boil the liquid that would give off a vapor that would permeate the stable stall of the sick animal. Fernando knew what he should do, but he was also aware that a registered and licensed veterinarian was required to order the medicine this valuable mare needed.

By the time the vet came, discussed the treatment, prescribed the medicine, and explained what he wanted done, Fernando suddenly realized that his margin of time for leaving for campus had completely evaporated. He was not worried about the requisite knowledge—he knew what he needed to know—but the time of the test had simply gotten away from him.

"Dr. Bell, I've got an emergency," Fernando said. "I'm due at the university in fifteen minutes for an important exam. Could you please drop me off over there on your way?"

The good doctor was more than happy to accommodate Fernando. This would give him an opportunity to get to know this unusually talented young man better. He had come to like and appreciate Fernando more and more as they took care of these beautiful polo horses together. Unlike previous occasions when he had wanted to ask Fernando personal questions and either fear or propriety had dictated that he keep them to himself, he began their conversation with a flattering comment.

"Say, you seem to know as much about horses as I do!" the doctor said. "I am amazed at your practical knowledge in spotting that mare's problem and diagnosing it so accurately. Where in the world did you learn so much?"

Fernando was always uncomfortable when people asked direct questions about his past, and he was evasive as usual.

"Oh, I grew up around horses and I guess I just kind of absorbed what others did to take care of them," he said quickly.

This time, Dr. Bell dared a more specific tack.

"Fernando, just where did you grow up?" he asked. "How do you know so much about racehorses and polo ponies? You've either had a lot of education in a classroom on veterinary science or you've had the most extensive practical experience I can imagine—or both."

Fernando accepted the compliment but evaded the answer.

"Well, I've lived all over and I have a couple of friends who are vets who loaned me books to read. It's just a hobby of mine I guess." Then he subtly changed the focus of the conversation. "Where did you go to school, Dr. Bell?"

The doctor realized that he was not going to get any more information than anyone else had been able to glean from this young man over the last three years. *Best to just let it be and continue to build confidence and trust in our relationship*, he thought.

"I went to the Veterinary Science School in Colorado," he answered. "It has an enviable reputation, and my parents live in the mountains on a ranch near Denver. The tuition is low for residents, and besides, I was close enough to home to be able to visit my family on weekends."

Fernando followed that up with another quick question.

"And did you practice anywhere other than Colorado or here in California?" he queried.

By keeping the vet occupied answering his questions, Fernando was able to avoid further interrogation.

With just a few minutes to spare, they drove up in front of the broad steps of the very impressive building where the engineering exam was being administered. Fernando asked to borrow a pen from the vet, and he realized he would have to find one of his classmates who would give him an extra blue book in which to write his test answers. He thanked Dr. Bell and whirled around, bounding up the steps two at a time.

His Strength of Materials class was one of those subjects required of all aspiring aeronautical engineers. The students had learned during the course of this demanding class that, in the beginning, aircraft had been built of bamboo covered with linen cloth tightly stretched over the frame, then waterproofed and shrunk with a special varnish called "dope." This was the lightest structure the earliest aviators had designed. Subsequent engineering progress was made with wooden frames, still covered with linen cloth; after that, plywood was tried as both part of the structure and part or all of the covering.

Hollow steel tubes, welded together like a bicycle frame, were also tried and proven to be very strong and light at the same time. These were covered with cloth or with aluminum, and sometimes even with polished steel as thin as tin plate to conserve weight. Next, the engineers experimented with all-aluminum frames and aluminum-skin coverings riveted in place. All of these materials had their limits, and an engineer had to know everything about them.

Fernando had studied the properties of every possible material that could be used in the construction or manufacture of an airplane, including wood, steel, and aluminum. Possessing a keen analytical mind and almost photographic memory, he knew the relative elasticity, hardness, and stiffness of each material, and he knew how much stress on a material would produce strain or distortion or actual breaking of that material. He knew all the variables of tensile stress (pulling), compressive stress (compression), and shearing stress (cutting action) for various kinds of materials and shapes, such as hollow-tube, solid-rod T-, I-, and U-beams. He was especially interested in new ways to extrude aluminum, and how to force the hot metal through a die that produced a specific shape for building lightweight but strong airplane structures.

As he ran up the stairs, Fernando felt very much out of place and self-conscious in his white riding breeches, sweat-stained and smelly from the flanks of the horse he had just ridden hard. He was also wearing tall black riding boots and a red polo shirt, cutting a striking figure. He was aware that his hair was tousled from the helmet he had worn while riding, but he didn't notice that the insteps of his boots were carrying a smelly smear of manure from the stall of the sick horse.

At the exact same time, from the other side of the wide steps leading up to the entrance of the vine-covered university building, a beautiful, willowy young woman was also dashing up the steps two at a time. Maggie too was late for the same exam. Like Luke, she was also wearing riding gear, but in cowgirl Western attire: plaid shirt, neckerchief, Western-cut trousers, Mexican hand-tooled belt with a silver buckle, and high-heeled Western boots. She was tall, athletic, and lithe with a strong grace in her running.

Like Fernando, Maggie was sweaty and dusty and showed the effects of having spent the morning in a corral around horses and the appearance of one very thorough dumping in the dirt. Her waist was slender, and the tailored trousers revealed strong muscles in her hips and legs. Neither she nor Fernando realized that they both carried the distinct, strong, and unpleasant odor of manure from the instep of their boots.

Maggie Rockwell and Fernando Underwood noticed each other simultaneously, almost colliding as they hurried for the door that led to the foyer inside—both breathing heavily from the running, both dressed for the corral and not for the university class, and each representing totally different cultures and styles of riding.

Fernando quickly pulled the door open for Maggie, mumbled an almost inaudible "hello," and smiled—a flashing smile so captivating that it caught Maggie off guard and almost took her breath away. She remembered seeing this young man in classes and around the campus, but she was not aware that he was interested in horses, nor had she noticed that he was so broad-shouldered, well-developed, and utterly handsome. His tight-fitting polo shirt practically rippled with well-defined muscles.

For his part, Fernando remembered seeing this attractive girl in some of his classes, but since he carefully kept his distance from women, he had never spoken to her. As they hurried to the room where the examination was taking place, he suddenly realized he hadn't brought his test materials. He slowed his pace and thought quickly.

"Miss, do you happen to have a spare blue book?" he asked Maggie. "I left a sick horse at the stables too late to pick one up in my room, and . . ."

He knew he didn't have to give a full explanation, but it seemed appropriate given her attire. She looked like she would understand problems like sick horses.

How beautiful she is! he thought, wondering why he had never noticed her before.

"Sure do!" Maggie replied with a smile, fumbling through her books and papers. "Here's one. By the way, that's a coincidence, you mentioning your sick horse—I have a lame horse!"

She looked down at herself self-consciously and laughed.

"I had an accident this morning," she confided. "That's why I look so awful!"

Fernando noticed the twigs and dust still in her hair and on her clothes. She did indeed look like she had been through a spill, but they didn't have time to talk further as the assistants were just about to close the doors of the test room. The two slipped through with just seconds to spare. An assistant handed them the test, then wrinkled his nose and made a face.

"Boy!" he exclaimed. "You two must have your horses hitched to the post just outside. Or did you bring the barn in with you? Better sit here at the back—one or more seats between you as usual."

Maggie was a good student, but she tried to keep a low profile and did not volunteer to participate in the aeronautical engineering classes. She was working full-time at her profession, supporting herself and sending money home each month, aware that her dad was having trouble making loan payments at the bank because cattle prices were so low. She didn't mix much with the other students because of a lack of time and common interests, and also because she felt they might not accept her rather humble origins.

Maggie assumed that all the students at this upper-class and expensive private university were of prominent families, so she concluded that this horseman with the fancy riding clothes also came from some elite, prominent family of society. She was earning very good money, considering it was right in the middle of the Depression, but she knew it was nothing compared to her classmates' trust funds.

The senior class was not too large, having lost some by attrition, so she figured that this new male acquaintance must have seen her before. He was ruggedly handsome and there was something different about his way of speaking that reminded her of a British accent, but with some other indefinable ingredient that added a distinctive quality to his speech. *South American?* she thought. *Or maybe Cuban?*

Before she was able to focus her mind on the test, Maggie wondered what this young man would think if he knew that she had just been filming a very difficult and risky movie scene for a major Hollywood studio. Sure, she wasn't an actress herself, but she was a stunt rider standing in for the leading lady, a famous movie star whose name appeared almost daily in the newspaper gossip columns that enjoyed reporting on the entertainment industry's personalities.

A former rodeo trick rider, Maggie Rockwell had turned to stunt riding in the movies, and from that had picked up an interest in flying and aeronautics because so many of her scenes were closely related to airplanes, parachuting, fast cars, and horse stunts—all very much in vogue in Hollywood at that time. She had specialized in both horseback stunts and flying stunts so she could have more jobs: kind of a two-for-one offer to the major studios that hired her. She was dependable, capable, and created a good impression because of her thoroughly professional work.

After the fiasco on location this morning, Maggie did not have time to return home to wash up before the test, although she had beaten most of the dust out of her clothes and face after the spill. But worse than that, she hadn't noticed that she had stepped in a horse pie with one boot before leaving the movie location site.

Her wandering mind was brought back suddenly to the test at hand and she began reading the printed questions, but not before stealing an admiring glance at this attractive man sitting a few feet away from her.

It might be interesting to get to know someone involved in both aeronautical engineering and horses like I am, she thought. *And besides, he's better-looking than anyone else I've seen here at school! I wonder why I haven't noticed him before? Did riding clothes make the difference?*

Once again, her mind was jolted back to the test and she tried to catch up with the other students, noticing the clock ticking away the allowed minutes. Two hours later, the bell rang and the professor's assistants began collecting the blue books.

Maggie and Fernando stood up at almost the same time and walked out of the room without saying a word, waiting for the other to speak first. A few of the students passing the two of them looked at them disapprovingly, noticing the unusual way they were dressed. Those closest to them stayed their distance, smelling the odor of sweat and manure, leaving the two to walk alone.

Fernando was hesitant to speak, although he did owe this girl another thanks for giving him the blue book required for the exam. He just didn't quite know how to say it.

Maggie took the initiative and broke the silence.

"Well, tall cowboy in English breeches, how did you do on the big test?" she said with a grin. "By the way, my name is Margaret—my friends call me Maggie. And what do your friends call you?"

"Fernando," he replied with a shy smile. Hoping to not have to answer any more questions about himself, he quickly asked, "And where do you call home, Maggie?"

"I'm from a place you've probably never heard of, unless you know where the best cowboy movies are filmed," she replied.

Fernando was so intrigued by this unexpected reply that he wanted to know more, which was exactly what Maggie had hoped. It always worked.

"Oh?" he said, raising his eyebrows. "And where do they film the best cowboy movies?"

"Kanab, Utah!" Maggie said proudly. "Do you know where that is?"

She could tell by his bewildered face that Fernando had no idea.

"It's just north of the rim of the Grand Canyon," she explained. "The South Rim is in Arizona, and access to the North Rim is through southern Utah. It's the most beautiful place on earth—red cliffs, cedar and pine tree forests, snow-covered blue mountains, desert areas with cacti and sand dunes, and old abandoned mining towns that are perfect for movie sets. We even have native Indians for those cowboy movies, since the Navajo reservation is close by."

Maggie did not usually talk so openly about herself, even to strangers. She quickly turned the questions around to Fernando.

"What about you? Where are you from?"

Both were walking quickly in their nervousness, but she had no trouble matching his long-legged strides step for step.

This direct and talkative girl fascinated Fernando. She was clearly different from other girls he had known. Deflecting her question, he asked to know more about the Grand Canyon and Kanab as they walked past the entrance gate of the university.

"Well, this is where I turn off," he said. "I'm going back to the stables over by the polo field. Where are you headed?"

"To the stables by the racetrack," Maggie responded, smiling. "Say, I have my car parked right over here. Would you like a ride? My horse went off alone this morning, a bit spooked after my spill, and when he came back, reins dragging, he had a limp and his left front fetlock seemed to be swelling a little. Do you know anything about fixing a lame horse?"

Gosh, why did I just ask him for help? Maggie thought, mentally slapping her forehead. *I just met the guy!*

Perhaps it was because she didn't have the money for a vet's fees and needed to ask someone for help—even a new acquaintance. Perhaps it had something to do with his sincere smile and dazzling good looks.

"I certainly do," Fernando replied quickly, pleased that she had asked him. "I'm taking care of my own sick horse. I'd be happy to look at yours."

He usually used a bicycle to get from the polo stables to the university or jogged the distance, but right now he had neither the bike nor the shoes. He gratefully accepted Maggie's offer of a ride.

They walked to her car, a '34 Chevrolet convertible roadster with wire-spoke wheels, two side-mounted spares embedded jauntily in the front fenders, and a rumble seat in back. Fernando opened the door for her, closing it carefully before taking his seat on the passenger side.

Maggie was very impressed with his gentlemanly manner. *What planet did this Sir Galahad come from?* she thought. *Or maybe I should ask myself, where have I been?*

"Fernando, why haven't I seen you at the stables if you're boarding horses there?" she asked.

"Oh, no, I work over at the polo stables on the other side of the racetrack," he explained. "I don't own any horses—I just take care of them and the stables. Some of the owners let me use their polo ponies, though."

Maggie had two matching palominos with long blond manes and tails that her father had raised and sent to her from Kanab. They were in top condition, adept at rodeo roping and cutting, fast enough to be in quarter-horse races and long since thoroughly trained for her trick-riding stunts. They were sought after for movie stunt work because they were so alert, obedient, spirited, and photogenic. They were dramatic and showy, especially when ridden well by an attractive girl with a matching long blonde pony tail whipping in the breeze. When Maggie was decked out for a parade in her full dress outfit with the silver-mounted Mexican saddle, bridle, and martingale, she and her palominos were spectacular. With her gracefulness, outstanding horsemanship, and beauty, Maggie always stole the show. It was no surprise that she and her horses were in so much demand for the movies, which paid much better than the rodeo and parade business.

Although Maggie lived alone, she was so busy with school and movie jobs that she was seldom lonesome. She had friends, but no young man had yet been able to keep up with her fertile mind, strong character, and lofty ambitions.

"Fernando, how did you do on that test?" Maggie asked, changing the subject. "I thought it was kind of tough. The professor had covered the material all right, but I think some of the questions were pretty vague."

Because Fernando had no social life to distract him, and also because of his interest in just about every subject related to aviation, he had done a lot of extra reading on this particular subject. His special project involving new and better techniques to extrude aluminum had earned him plaudits from some of the more progressive thinkers in the industry, which was a most unusual accomplishment for a mere student.

"Yes, I agree," he answered, not quite truthfully. "Those tricky questions were covered more in detail in another textbook I've read. The professor doesn't use it in our class, but I came across it at a university on the East Coast, and by accident happened to find it in the library here. It covers the same material but from a more theoretical point of view and in more depth than the text we are using. That reading helps me answer those ambiguous questions you refer to. Do you recall the questions that gave you problems?"

Maggie immediately realized that Fernando was way ahead of her. She had never thought of looking in the library for other textbooks to supplement her class reading.

"Well, the ones on the elastic limits stumped me," she said. "I know that elasticity is the point to which a solid material can be deformed by a force without changing it permanently, but I had no idea about the relative elasticity of wood and steel rods versus glass. Surely no one is going to make a glass airplane!"

"Yes, you're right," Fernando said with a smile. "It was just a trick question."

Fernando gave a full explanation of the principles involved in stress and strain of different materials, then answered more of Maggie's questions. He told her what he had learned about the "ultimate strength" of materials before breaking and clarified some points about metal fatigue, flutter, vibrations, and so on.

Maggie was impressed with the wealth of information Fernando had just taught her. She imagined what a great help it would be for her to review subjects with him before future tests. He had just explained some of those concepts better than their professor ever had in class.

When they arrived at the stables, Maggie parked the car and they walked over to the stalls where Maggie's horses were housed. Her stablehand had brought her injured horse back from the movie location in the horse trailer pulled by Maggie's old but faithful Ford pickup.

The movie studios rented her animals, paying well enough to cover the costs involved, but she still had to be frugal. There usually was some profit left over after expenses, but she always sent that home to her father, who had given both ponies to her in the first place.

When they arrived at the stall, Fernando took the rope tied around the palomino's neck and led the horse in a circle, closely observing the walk and the obvious lameness. The lower leg was now swollen even more than when Maggie had first noticed the problem. He lifted the affected leg carefully, examined the hoof, and expertly felt around the nearby joint tenderly, watching the animal's reaction. As Fernando listened to its breathing and checked the heart rate, he was aware that Maggie and some of the men who had gathered were observing carefully what he was doing.

"What do you think?" Maggie asked.

"Well, there are two problems, not one," he said, patting the horse affectionately. "He must have hit something after you fell off, which is causing the swelling, but he also has laminitis, which can cause swelling too. I suspect he had the laminitis before your fall, but you wouldn't have noticed it."

"What's laminitis?" Maggie asked, concerned. "I've never heard of that before!"

"Oh, forgive me," Fernando said quickly, shaking his head. "You call it 'founder' here. It is an inflammation of the foot. Notice the hot feel of the foot and the increased heart rate while resting? And over here you can see the bump, but it alone is not sufficient to cause the problem. He has both an injury and a laminitis—or founder—problem."

"Well, I know of 'founder,' of course," Maggie said, "but isn't that related to the horse getting into a new pasture and eating too much lush green feed?"

"Yes," Fernando answered, "but founder is really caused by stress in the digestive system, which in turn comes from too much water, too much grain, or, as you mentioned, too much green feed. That stress or acid situation in the digestive tract causes dilation of the blood vessels in the foot. The dilation causes pressure, swelling, and pain, so the horse limps. Now, we must cause the blood to leave."

"And how do you do that?" Maggie asked, amazed at the wealth of Fernando's knowledge.

"In the mountains we have the horse stand in a very cold running stream of water," he explained. "Here in California, we must get ice, crush it, and apply a pack to the swelling. I'll show your stablehand how to do it so it won't slip and how often to change it. Give your pony three days' rest and after that begin normal exercise. I'll look in on him every day, if that's okay. And don't feed him too much. Keep him on short rations, and not too much water, either."

Fernando also checked on the other palomino, a mare, and declared her to be in excellent health and condition. Maggie was duly impressed and very grateful. In this very short time she had gained complete confidence in her new friend.

"I'm relieved the mare is fine," she said. "I have to use her early tomorrow morning for a retake of a movie scene we ruined today."

Fernando had no idea what she was talking about.

"Oh, I'm sorry," she said. "I didn't tell you. In my spare time I do stunt work for movies, usually involving horses, airplanes, or both. The pilot for this scene told our stubborn German director that it was too windy this morning to film a difficult scene and that we should shoot it tomorrow earlier in the day while the wind is calm. But he was behind schedule and wanted to catch up. He insisted that I do the stunt anyway, but I sure ate a lot of dust when I missed the jump to the ladder!"

Fernando was puzzled at the partial explanation, but made no comment, waiting for more of the story.

She paused, thinking about an idea that just popped into her head. She had never invited anyone to watch her before, but maybe Fernando would like to see how movies are made. That would be a fun way to thank him for his help with her horse.

"Say, would you be interested in seeing how we do the movie stunts and filming?" she asked. "The location is about thirty miles from here and I'll be going there directly from my apartment, but you could ride over with Freddy in the pickup from here. And after the shoot we can come back together in my car—or you could come in your own car, if you prefer."

It was an innocent assumption on her part—that he owned a car—but she secretly hoped that he would choose to ride back with her.

"Well, I don't have a car," Fernando said, a bit embarrassed. "I'm going through school the hard way—working at the polo stables plus some scholarship money, but no car. I would be very happy for a ride. I would be interested in seeing what you do in the movies and also how you are going to make that jump you talked about."

"Wonderful!" Maggie exclaimed, delighted.

"My only conflict is that I do have some polo classes to teach tomorrow morning about ten," Fernando said. "Would we be back in time? I can't miss them."

He was hoping it would be possible to fit in both activities—Fernando had a very acute sense of responsibility to his students, but his natural curiosity to learn new things, augmented by this unusual woman, also intrigued him.

"Oh, we'll be back in plenty of time," Maggie reassured him. "You should leave here about six and arrive there around seven, just after sunrise. It should be calm at that hour and there'll be enough light for the filming. We'll be through before eight and back here by nine. I think you'll enjoy it! And I promise I'll be a lot cleaner and smell a lot better than I do now!"

She grinned and gave him a little wave goodbye. All the stablehands turned to watch her go. Fernando was surprised that he felt a bit jealous that other men looked at and admired the way this girl handled herself. But he also recognized that here in the stable environment, men could have respect and admiration for a competent rider—as well as feeling attracted to a beautiful woman who was refreshingly natural and open in everything she did and said.

Fernando walked back to his own side of the race track and polo complex, absentmindedly kicking at clods in the dirt and smiling to himself. It had been a very long time since he had felt attracted to a woman. He had distanced himself on purpose since the accident, but he had never met a girl like this before—an authentic Western cowgirl who also possessed intelligence and an interest in aviation. This was certainly an unusual combination in a woman.

He had quickly become aware that Maggie was elegant and attractive, and, without makeup, her hair windblown, and even in dusty clothes, she exuded self-confidence. He had noticed her well-formed figure, her wide smile, full lips, a square jaw line denoting character and determination, well-arched eyebrows, brilliant clear green eyes, and her classic Grecian nose. Her shapely long legs reminded him of the chorus girls he had known in Paris.

The slight freckling of her complexion, probably caused by spending a lot of time in the sun riding horses and flying airplanes, added the final touch to the all-American, well-rounded young woman. Yes, Maggie had definitely made a profound impression on him.

Questions and doubts raced through Fernando's mind. He had a strong desire to be friends with Maggie, but felt restrained at the same time.

Can I let this attraction develop into a friendship without getting into the same old problem? he thought, conflicted. *Women have always been my downfall. Every time I have had a problem it was because I was trying to impress some girl. Can I keep control this time?*

Fernando decided he would go watch Maggie the next day, but on the way back he would tell her that he didn't have the money or time to date. They could be friends—but nothing more.

As he approached his quarters above the stable offices, he continued thinking about her. She is so unusual—she seems so down to earth and practical, not like the society girls of Buenos Aires or Paris or London or New York.

He was surprised at his own feelings. A few years ago he was attracted to that kind of stylish, flirty woman. But now that he was working on his own and not spending his family's money, reality had caused him to feel differently about the society rich.

I sure hope Maggie is as solid a person as she appears to be, he thought. I really like her.

Before sunup on Saturday, Fernando helped Freddy, the stablehand, load the bridle, saddle, and other tack items into the horse trailer, and finally Maggie's horse, Blondie. Her palomino was well trained and walked up the ramp and into the trailer with no balking or hesitation. They fastened the tailgate securely, slapped the horse affectionately on the rump, and climbed into the pickup's sturdy cab.

There was only light traffic on the highway. Freddy and Fernando chatted amiably about the work around the stables and the horses. The stablehand had heard about Fernando and was well aware of his competence in caring for, grooming, and training thoroughbred horses. Curiosity about Fernando's personal life got the best of him.

"All the men at both the racehorse stables and over at the polo stables say you know more and teach more about horses than anyone they have ever known," Freddy said. "Fernando, everyone really likes you, but no one knows anything about you. You don't talk about yourself much. Where are you from? Are you in some kind of trouble or something?"

Freddy kept his eyes straight ahead on the highway, his questions spilling out like machine-gun rapid fire.

"Please don't get annoyed with me or the other guys," he said apologetically. "It's just that we all like you and want to help if we can—if you will let us."

Freddy stopped talking, not knowing what to do now that he had blurted out his thoughts—and Fernando, too, did not know how to handle the innocent questions and sincere offers of help from this kind man he had just met. However, he knew it would only make things worse if he sidestepped all questions about himself. After a moment or two, he finally spoke.

"No, Freddy, I am not running from the police or anyone or anything," Fernando said with a soft chuckle. "No one is looking for me, as far as I know. It's just that I want to have a private life with no complications and with no connections to the past. Thanks, anyway, for the offer—and your interest."

Fernando looked over at his new friend and smiled.

"But it is nice to know that if I needed help, you fellows would be available."

Fernando leaned his head back and closed his eyes for a moment, hoping this conversation was over. Freddy sensed his feelings and remained silent the rest of the way.

When they arrived at the location for the movie filming, the sun was just peeking over the horizon. There was absolute calm, not even a slight breeze. Freddy knew where to park the trailer from the previous day's experience. Fernando opened his door, stepped down, and looked around. He could see several small groups of men setting up tripods, big cameras, and reflector equipment at various locations. A few trailers were parked close by, and men were saddling horses and adjusting costumes.

With its slightly rolling, grassy hills, clumps of low trees and green brush here and there, the picturesque valley glowed in the light of the early-morning sunrise. One could see a hill topped with big boulders in the distance, and to the other side of the valley the tall mountains rose majestically. A winding dirt road came up from the fields below the colorful valley, and the paved highway was close but hidden from view by the trees. Fernando had to admit that it looked like an ideal place to make a movie.

The two men unloaded the palomino, bridled and saddled her, and walked her around slowly to make sure she was in good shape after the transport. As they moved toward the dirt road that seemed to be the gathering place, they heard the sound of an approaching airplane. Fernando located it quickly and pointed it out to Freddy. They watched it draw closer and lower until Fernando could see that the pilot was going to land on the part of the dirt road that had no curves or trees close by.

He could hear the pilot reduce his power, increase the pitch of the propeller, and noticed him slip down slightly in order to see over the round engine and long nose of the aircraft. He admired the perfect three-point landing after the slip. The plane taxied toward them, a plume of dust trailing. Fernando recognized that it was a Waco biplane with streamlined wheel pants used to increase the speed and greatly improve the looks of the plane.

Luke shut off the engine and climbed down from the cockpit. A few of the men who had been waiting walked over and helped the pilot turn the plane around by hand so that it pointed back the way from where it had come.

Fernando loved everything associated with aviation and looked wistfully at the Waco and its pilot. He missed flying. It had been over three years since he had been at the controls of an airplane. Fernando noted that the pilot was a tall, good-looking man, though rather weather-beaten, and perhaps about forty-five years old. The pilot pulled off his helmet and goggles, revealing wavy brown hair. He had a wide bushy moustache, typical of many pilots of the World War I era. He wore a leather jacket, a long, white silk scarf around his neck, and military riding breeches with tall leather boots. He was the epitome of the handsome, adventurous, experienced aviator of the mid-1930s.

Wondering where Maggie was, Fernando looked at his wristwatch. It was two minutes to the time she had said she would meet them. *I wonder if she is the type to arrive late, or if she is punctual for her appointments?* he thought.

Someone else was concerned with the same question. Hollywood moviemaking was a real circus with outlandish characters, and the director of this movie was right out of central casting. He was brilliant, no doubt, but he was just as eccentric as he was talented. Furthermore, Von Steineman was an import from Germany, and not all the wounds had healed since the war less than twenty years before. The film crew called him "Herr Direktor" with an exaggerated accent. Behind his back, at times, it was changed to "Herr Diktator."

The great director looked the part: big and stout, a monocle over his right eye, polished boots, waxed moustache, and a florid red face. He was becoming more and more irritated, convinced that Maggie was going to be late and put him even further behind schedule.

"Verr is that girl?" he shouted to no one in particular. "She ees impossible! Vee are behind schedule and she vill make it vorse!" He turned to an assistant, impatient. "Are the men ready on the horses? Are the cameramen in their positions? Ees the film loaded and ready?"

The aide calmly assured him that all was ready, and pointed to the men and equipment in various positions scattered amidst the scenery. The director insisted on more details.

"And the airplane—ees it ready to take off when she arrives?" he demanded.

Again, the assistant reassured the irate director. He showed him that the plane was ready and also showed him that Maggie's horse was saddled and was now being held by Fernando.

Moments later, Maggie's convertible was spotted coming down the lane from the highway, clouds of dust trailing behind. She pulled up beside the pickup and horse trailer and jumped out, her long blonde ponytail swinging back and forth as she strode to where Fernando and her horse were standing.

Fernando smiled, handed her the reins, and held the stirrup while she mounted. As Maggie settled into her comfortable Western saddle, "Herr Direktor" stormed toward her, ready to call her to task for almost being late.

Maggie leaned down toward Fernando and whispered, "Good morning, Fernando. Watch this scene with the director. Right after I do the stunt and climb the ladder, I'm going to teach him a lesson he'll never forget!"

Fernando had no idea what she was referring to, but her warnings intrigued him.

"Verr have you been?" Von Steineman barked up at Maggie, towering over him in her saddle. "You are almost late! Vee are ready and waiting! Vee could have started earlier. Yesterday you made us lose von half day with your mistake!"

Maggie's mouth dropped open and she stared at him in disbelief.

"*My* mistake? *My* mistake?" she retorted indignantly. "*You* are the stupid one who made the mistake yesterday! Luke told you it was too windy to do that stunt and you almost killed me! It was entirely your darn fault. You'll get your picture today if we hurry and start before the wind picks up instead of standing here wasting time with your absurdities!"

She wheeled her horse around and galloped over to where Luke was waiting beside his plane.

"Good morning, Luke!"

She was cheerful now, already calm despite her exasperation with the director.

"Wow, you really let him have it—and deservedly so!" Luke said with a smile and a wink.

Maggie smiled back at him but then got serious.

"Luke, it's calm enough this morning to do the transfer, but please keep that prop out of my ear," she said, furrowing her eyebrows. "That sudden gust yesterday almost made mincemeat of me, and when I tried to jump for the rope the wind jerked it right out of my grasp."

Luke grinned widely and agreed.

"Yeah, Maggie—you sure got a mouthful of that dirt! Sorry about that, but we'll do it right today. By the way, how are you feeling after yesterday?"

His concern was real—she had really taken a bad spill.

"No problems," she assured him. "I've taken worse dumpings than that when I did rodeos. It was good clean dirt. I hope so, anyway! It was just plain dumb for that kraut to insist on the jump so late in the morning yesterday with those gusty conditions."

Maggie had one last comment for him before she rode off.

"By the way, Luke, your timing was perfect yesterday. I'll see you in the air," she called back.

Maggie rode over to Fernando, and, with her back to the director, explained, "I'm still angry and not as mean as I wanted to sound, but I'm going to get even with that dumb 'diktator' today. When we come back, be sure to duck. We'll give him a buzz job he won't forget!"

Fernando was confused. He did not understand what a "buzz job" was, but he knew she was very unhappy with the German movie director. He also sensed that Maggie was a complex woman who usually got her way.

Feeling competent despite her accident, Maggie rode down the dirt road to her marker, the place where her run toward the cameras would start. Once there, she sat poised on her horse, sitting sideways in the saddle like a resting cowboy, very much at ease on her obedient palomino. She could see the "bad guys" farther down the road away from the cameras. They were the villains who were after her character. She was going to escape by having the hero appear out of the air above and drop a rope ladder from the plane, then she would jump from her horse to the ladder at full gallop right in front of the main cameras. Other cameras, strategically concealed at various points along the route, would also film the dramatic stunt.

The plane would slow down to sixty miles per hour, and the palomino could gallop at thirty miles per hour for a short distance. The slack in the rope ladder would have an elastic effect for two seconds, so the stunt was possible without pulling her arms out of their sockets. Afterward, the film would be sped up to make it look like the plane was diving much faster and the horse running at an impossible speed. In the industry, this is called "trick photography."

Luke cranked up his engine as soon as Maggie left him. The engine was still warm from his recent arrival, so with no delay he took off and climbed for altitude. As soon as he was over the pre-arranged position, he rocked his wings as a signal to those on the ground and circled over the bridge he used for his starting point.

The director, standing on a raised platform, noted the rocked wing signal, waved a flag for attention, and brought it down smartly in a starting motion. His assistant fired a red flare from a Marine Very pistol. The brightly burning flare arched high, glowing clearly against the blue morning sky, and the action started to unfold.

Maggie had pulled on a platinum blonde wig with long flowing tresses. When she saw the flare, she dug her heels into the flanks of her horse, who jumped to an immediate dead run toward the camera positions. The bad guys pulled their black cowboy hats down hard on their heads, tightened the chin straps to keep the hats in place, and began their pursuit. They pulled their guns and fired blank smoke cartridges at her. According to the script, Maggie's character had discovered their dastardly plan to rob her father's bank. The mean-looking and unshaven motley crew was gaining fast on the lady in distress when the biplane appeared, diving from above and right behind her.

Maggie and Luke had timed their convergence to coincide at a wide point on the dirt road. On film it would look like Luke had the plane in a power dive, but in reality he was controlling his speed to approach the running horse as slowly as possible. He was looking out over the left side of the leather cowl around the open cockpit toward the flowing platinum wig. The rope ladder he had thrown out was whipping back and forth like a giant snake in the rushing wind of the slipstream.

Maggie felt the throb of the big prop above her head and knew that the rope ladder was just behind it. She turned her head and saw the streamlined wheel pants pass over her with the ladder twisting behind the left one. She guided her horse a bit to the right. Luke was in perfect position. Maggie grabbed the bottom rung of the ladder with her gloved right hand, turned in the saddle, dropped the knotted reins on the neck of the horse, and with her left hand reached higher for the second rung. With both hands firm, she kicked her boots loose from the stirrups and started to climb the ladder, hand over hand, her feet dangling and twisting in the wild wind. As soon as her feet found the bottom rung, she clambered up toward the plane.

Her well-trained horse, saddle empty and stirrups flopping, ran straight ahead according to plan, and then slowed to a trot and then a walk. Freddy was waiting to go after Blondie.

The plane climbed slowly, wings level. Maggie struggled in the wind, thinking, *This is a wild and risky way to make a living, but it sure is fun and it pays better than anything else I know how to do!*

Soon she had a foot on the bottom wing and from there on, up to the cockpit was easy. She was well aware that any slip meant sudden death, since she wore no parachute. Once she was safely in the cockpit, Maggie breathed a sigh of relief, pulled in the ladder, took off the platinum wig, and stowed it. She dug in a pocket inside the cockpit for the helmet and goggles she had placed there earlier and put them on over her ponytail.

She tapped the top of her head with the flat of her gloved hand three times, which signaled to Luke, "Give me the controls." Expecting the request, he nodded, smiled, removed his hands from the stick and throttle, and took his booted feet from the rudder pedals.

You've got it, girl, he said to himself. *You deserve your victory roll and your revenge after that successful and dangerous stunt!*

Maggie was now in another of her favorite elements. She reflected on how quickly she could change from loving her palomino galloping at the touch of her reins to being in the air at the controls of a big, tough aerobatic biplane. She loved the plane as much as she loved her horse.

They were by now some distance from the camera crews and the director on the ground. Maggie made a climbing turn to the right and came back toward her audience on the ground. She had enough altitude by the time she was directly over them. Maggie checked her belts again, and rolled upside down for a few seconds. Next, she pulled through a split-S maneuver into a power dive directly at the men below, who were still in their original positions.

The wires of the wings began to vibrate in the increasing wind speed and the engine was at maximum revolutions, screaming. Maggie pulled out of the dive right over the site and started a high-speed pull-up climb before going vertical. At this point, she started her victory roll—with elegance. Fernando didn't know Maggie was flying, but he did know good aerobatics. What he saw was a perfect four-point vertical roll, with hesitation points, pulling over at the top to inverted flight.

This time, Fernando noted the plane went farther away than before, prior to starting a second dive. The plane rolled upright, still at full power, turned back to face those on the ground, and started a power dive at a forty-five-degree angle toward them. The plane seemed to be zeroing in on a ground target just to Fernando's right. To him, it looked like the pilot was now making a classic military strafing run. Finally he understood! This was the "buzz job."

Maggie looked over the long nose of the diving biplane and spotted her target. Von Steineman was still standing on the raised command platform where he had started the scene. She smiled mischievously to herself and pointed the plane right at him. Everyone else had been tipped off, including the assistants, so they had all run for cover. Only "Herr Diktator" was out in the open on his raised perch.

By the time he realized the plane was not going to pull up as it had before, it was too late. He saw the shining chrome spinner of the prop pointed at him and it was obvious that it would drill him if he didn't hit the dust.

He dove headfirst into the dirt and the prop went by overhead with barely a few feet to spare. The director jumped to his feet as the plane sped past, shouting obscenities in German, shaking his fist, determined to tell the studio bosses that this crazy pilot had flown a plane right at him. He would force them to cancel Luke's contract before he killed them all.

Maggie brought the plane back around to a perfect three-point landing every bit as good as Luke's landing earlier. In fact, Fernando thought it was Luke. She taxied to where the men were waiting, followed by billowing clouds of dust. The director had driven off in a dusty huff—anger mixed with embarrassment.

Maggie pulled the mixture back, and as the engine clanked to a stop, she cut the switches, undid her seat and shoulder straps, and stood on the seat to swing out onto the wing. Luke offered a hand so she could make the long jump to the ground. Fernando and Freddy came over and stood near the wings, smiling and marveling at this extraordinary horse-to-plane feat that Maggie had just accomplished, wrongly assuming that Luke had done all the flying.

Luke, sweeping his arm in an arc-like movement in front of Maggie with a Sir Walter Raleigh gesture of courtesy, remarked, "My dear, you treat my plane real sweet like that, you can fly it anytime you like!"

"Why, thank you, Luke," she responded with a big grin. "You are a true friend, a gentleman, and a great pilot. And thanks for putting that rope right where I could get it! And for letting me scare the wits out of the old director."

"Don't thank me," Luke responded admiringly. "You did the hard part. No way could I ever grab a rope ladder while galloping at breakneck speed. You were absolutely superb! And the buzz job on 'the diktator' was well done and totally deserved."

Maggie looked admiringly at this legend of a man before her. Luke was an idol in the flying community and to her as well. Not only had he flown in the war, he had also flown for gold miners, bankers, oil executives, and anyone else who wanted to hire the best pilot in the world to get an important job done. He had also flown in air shows and still entered most air races where the purse was attractive. Now he had a steady business doing executive charter for the movie studios as well as stunt work for them when the job was tricky or difficult or both.

In his younger days, Luke had also been a circus lion tamer, and he still kept one or more lions at his hangar in place of guard dogs. For sure, no one ever entered his hangars when the lions were loose. He was a colorful character but also the flying fraternity's best friend and a soft touch when any were in need.

Maggie was anxious for Fernando to meet Luke. She noticed him standing at the tip of the wing and motioned for him to come over.

"Luke, this is my friend, Fernando Underwood. He is a future aeronautical engineer. He is also an expert on horses—and polo. Fernando, this is Luke Whitney, the best pilot and friend anyone could have in the whole world. He is also my flying instructor."

"Aww, thanks, Maggie," Luke said appreciatively. "Fernando, what did you think of Maggie's buzz job on the director? She sure made him eat the same dust he made her eat yesterday!" Luke laughed at the memory of the director sprawling in the dirt.

Suddenly it dawned on Fernando that it was Maggie diving the biplane at her tormentor. Now he understood her suggestion that he watch what she was going to do. A wave of admiration swept over him as he began to realize that this pretty young woman was not only an expert rider and acrobat on the "flying trapeze" but was an accomplished stunt pilot, too. He could also see that when insulted unjustly, her anger could move her to revenge. That four-point hesitation, vertical victory roll was a beautiful maneuver to behold, but now he was more concerned for Maggie's safety.

"Luke," Fernando advised, "if it were my plane, I don't think I'd let her get that low again—you've got brush in your wheels!"

They all looked under the wing at the wheel pants, and sure enough there was brush stuck in one wheel. Fernando climbed under and pulled it out.

Luke was doubly stunned. First, he did not like an upstart young student telling him anything about flying, let alone warning him that his prize student had come dangerously near to the ground. But second, he was chagrined and somewhat embarrassed that he had let Maggie get that low without noticing. He too had been caught up in the spirit of her revenge to the point of almost letting an accident happen.

Maggie, sensing that Luke might have a negative reaction to Fernando pointing out the obvious, quickly changed the subject, calling out to the head cameraman, "Harry, did you get it all on film?"

Laughing, Harry answered, "Sure did, sweetheart. I'll get a copy for you and print up some eight-by-tens. And thanks for the call last night to tip me off. I warned everyone to get out of the way. The crew will laugh for weeks! That was a classic comeuppance."

Maggie wasn't usually vindictive or prone to any kind of unnecessary risk, but this time the director's attitude had really gotten to her. She felt she had to give Fernando some background, but everyone else understood.

"Fernando, I just had to get back at him," she explained. "His insisting yesterday that we try that stunt in the gusty wind was really wrong. He showed me in our contract where I have to try the stunt if the director so mandates. In the future, I will have my lawyer add a clause that those at risk decide if conditions are safe for the stunt or I won't do it. Anyway, I feel okay now. It worked out better than even I expected. Wait till you see the films!"

Maggie waved to the other horsemen—the "bad guys"—who were now guiding their horses into the trailers, and shouted, "Good ride, guys. Thanks for the help and support. You timed it perfectly."

She also had some friendly compliments for the camera crew. They all liked working with this unpretentious, attractive cowgirl. She always did something special to show her appreciation. Sure enough, she pulled out a basket of homemade cookies from the rumble seat of her car and invited them to share.

"Sorry I couldn't find a cow to bring for milk!" she joked.

Everyone laughed and hurried over for the treats, while Maggie turned back to Luke.

"Say, friend, don't forget that we're going to talk about getting two planes to fly in the races this summer, and sponsors to pay for them," she said eagerly. "I understand that five or six women have already signed up and I don't want to be left out. When can I come see you at the hangar?"

Luke looked at his wristwatch.

"How about this evening?" he replied. "I have another flying job at noon but I'll be through about sundown. By the way, I have a new Ryan Sportster to show you. You know—that new low-wing job with the inverted in-line engine. Real sleek. All-aluminum body—cute little aerobatic plane. You'll love it."

He took a good look at Fernando standing beside Maggie and figured that maybe this know-it-all youngster needed a lesson in humility. He admitted he was jealous. He knew he was somewhat older than Maggie, but he had become more and more enamored of her after he started giving her private lessons in aerobatics, cross-country navigation, all-weather flying, and the fine points of air racing. He found her enchanting, smart, and competent. Now this young Fernando was riding back with her, while he was flying back all alone. Luke didn't like the idea of Fernando moving into his territory—or what he would *like* to be his territory. He would think of something.

As though a light turned on in his mind, a perfect idea occurred to him. Luke called out to Fernando, "Come on over, too, young man, if you like. Anyone who is Maggie's friend and is interested in aviation is sure welcome."

Fernando had no idea that a jealous Luke believed he had suckered him into a trap, and he happily hollered back to Luke as he help Maggie into her car, "That Sportster sounds really unique. Thanks for the invite. I accept your offer."

Here I go three years without seeing or talking alone to a girl or flying a plane, and now in two days I am seeing a lot of Maggie, enjoying her company, and have a chance to see a new plane! Fernando thought, shaking his head. *But never have I seen a girl that flies well, rides well, is intelligent—all rolled into one very captivating lady! Why not be fascinated by her and a new plane?*

Fernando looked at his watch and exclaimed, "Oh, Maggie, I've got a polo lesson shortly and a game to play after that. I'm going to have to hurry."

They waved goodbye to Luke as he climbed into his plane, fired up the engine, and taxied down the dusty dirt road.

Maggie had told Freddy to take the pickup and trailer back to the stables and she would drive Fernando to the polo area in her car. As he climbed into the passenger side of the car, he picked up the package of cookies and started to hand it to her.

"Oh, I kept those out just for you, Fernando," Maggie said, smiling. "I knew the men would wolf the others down before you could get one."

He thanked her profusely after he finished the last one, almost inhaling it, savoring the last morsel, and congratulated her on making such a mouth-watering delicacy.

As Maggie pulled the convertible onto the highway, Fernando's thoughts were a confused mixture of how to look to the future without entanglements. He was extremely attracted to this young woman beside him, her hair blowing in the wind, yet he dare not make the mistakes he had always made in the past. Perhaps it would be safer to talk to her about her flying, which had in fact truly surprised and amazed him.

"Maggie, I had no idea you flew aerobatics—and to do so with such spectacular skill!" Fernando exclaimed. "Wow! That was a great four-point hesitation vertical roll. And your jump from the horse to the ladder? I have never seen that done before. I am impressed beyond words—*fantástico*! *Espectacular*!" Fernando was so carried away that he inadvertently lapsed into Spanish.

Smiling a bit self-consciously, Maggie responded with a compliment in turn.

"I heard through the grapevine that you ride very well yourself, and I know what you can do as a vet," she told him. "Freddy tells me my lame horse, Roamer, is already doing better. And the word is that you are amazing on the polo field. I have to admit, though, that I have never seen a polo game, so I don't know what 'amazing' would have to be."

She went on rambling, making small talk.

"I guess it always seemed to me a bit pointless to chase a little white ball around the lawn. I'm a working gal and I'm used to using horses to round up cattle or do some kind of work, not just for fun. Perhaps I need to be educated about the game to appreciate it."

In his disappointment that so intelligent a girl would belittle his favorite sport as nothing more than "chasing a little white ball," Fernando completely missed the hint that she wanted an invitation. Instead, he became a bit defensive.

"Well, let me explain. Compare polo to golf. In golf, the player is standing still and the ball is lying still. That is easy compared to polo, where the player is galloping his horse up and down the field and the ball is usually not still either. It's always bouncing along the turf. The hand-eye coordination required to hit that erratic ball consistently is quite difficult."

Fernando looked at her to see if she understood. Maggie considered that for a moment and admitted that she had never thought of it that way.

Fernando drew similar comparisons with ball/stick-type games, such as baseball, tennis, and cricket, intentionally weaving in the horse's role in polo, knowing Maggie's love for horses.

"The polo pony is at least 51 percent of the game, and many times the horse is even more important than that," he explained. "Frequently, good players just never get to be part of the game because their pony is not fast enough to keep up with the play. Sometimes the horse is too timid and will not ride the other one off the line. You can't attack another horse from an angle of more than forty-five degrees, because that would cause too many dangerous collisions. It is a foul with a penalty. But you can ride alongside another player and move in at a lesser angle to push him off from the line of the ball. And all the time both you and your opponent are swinging your mallets around the two ponies' heads so the horse has to be trained to not be afraid or distracted but to follow the ball also."

Fernando took a breath and realized Maggie was listening intently.

"A polo pony has to be extremely well trained and very obedient," he concluded. "He should be as fast as a racehorse or a quarter horse over short distances, quick and maneuverable as a cutting horse, surefooted, and long-winded."

"Okay, okay, I apologize," Maggie said, chuckling. "I'm beginning to understand. Forgive me. I really would like to see how this all works out on the playing field. May I watch today?"

Fernando had to admit he liked the idea of showing off a bit.

"Sure, come on over," he said, elated to be able to spend more time with her.

They drove in silence for a few minutes. Eventually, Fernando knew he had to say something about the two of them. He could not hide behind horses and airplanes much longer. He enjoyed her company, but he didn't understand this unsettling feeling he had. All he knew was that he had to clear the air and let Maggie know that he was not in a position to enter into any kind of a relationship.

With new courage and determination he began.

"Maggie, I think you should know that I haven't dated for over three years. I don't like the social crowd because I don't drink or gamble or keep late hours as so many do."

There! He had said it all. Maybe a bit too direct and perhaps she would never understand his complex feelings, but at least he had given a clear signal. Now the big question was, how would she react?

Maggie was taken completely off guard. Why did he think that he had to explain or apologize for not wanting to date? Maybe she had been too forward by inviting herself to the polo match. Nevertheless, she decided to match bluntness with equal bluntness. She could be just as candid as Fernando had been.

Without turning to look at him, she responded, "Fernando, I don't know where you are coming from. In fact, I don't know anything about you except that you are into aeronautical engineering, so I presume you like airplanes as I do. And you have a reputation as a horseman and I like horses. I'm not wealthy, either, nor am I into the social scene nor do I drink or gamble or stay out late, as you put it. With my work and studies I don't have time for much dating. I see a few old rodeo friends now and then but that's all."

She was silent for a moment and then continued.

"My only interests right now are to graduate and to fly in the air races next summer. I do admit I like the company of a young man who loves horses and airplanes as I do. But please understand that I am not interested in romance right now either. No seriousness, and no hidden agendas, okay?"

Fernando, though surprised with her directness, was relieved to hear Maggie's response. Fernando had glanced at her as she spoke, her rigid body language leaving him somewhat confused, but her attitude could not have suited him more, from his point of view. To him, it meant that they could freely enjoy horses and flying—their passions—without any entanglements of any kind. That was better than he had hoped for.

They drove into the polo stable area in awkward silence, still very much attracted to each other. Fernando's mind returned again and again to the spectacular scene at the movie location. He had gone there knowing she was involved in movie stunts using horses and airplanes, yet he felt foolish for not having understood that Maggie was a real performing star in two separate worlds—superb horsemanship and outstanding aerobatic piloting.

He could only shake his head, smiling, remembering this lovely, slender, and attractive girl galloping down the road wearing a platinum wig chased by several "bad guys," followed by the jump to the rope dangling from the plane sweeping by overhead—and the aviation aerobatics done by the same girl.

He had never met a woman like this before. Not one of his female acquaintances in Argentina, England, Europe, or anywhere else came even close to this remarkable Western cowgirl named Margaret Rockwell. What an explosion she would create in the Paris, London, or Buenos Aires ritzy social circles! He smiled as he contemplated the probable reaction among old school buddies or stuffy wealthy friends were he to take her to their very selective events or dinners. He was sure that she would more than hold her own and probably dazzle them as she had him. It seemed to him that this girl was a combination of the lady markswoman Annie Oakley of Buffalo Bill fame and saloon owner Minnie in Puccini's opera *La Fanciulla del West.*

CHAPTER 4

A SURPRISING AEROBATIC PILOT

AT THE PONY STABLES, Fernando was in his element. He could take charge now. He had been quiet at the movie location, but here he was home. He introduced Maggie to his waiting polo students, then escorted her to a shady spot in the spectator stands. She looked sharp in her Western outfit, yet very different from all the others dressed in English riding boots, white breeches, brightly colored polo shirts, and white cork helmets.

Maggie was intrigued as she watched Fernando instruct his beginning students. These students sat astride foolish-looking, barrel-like, wooden "horses" with saddles on them. The stablehands tossed polo balls on the ground to the side of them, and the students swung their mallets trying to hit them squarely. The mallets made a distinct *crack* when they connected. They worked on forehand and backhand shots off the right side—called near-side shots—and after a while Fernando had them change to practicing the much more difficult forehand and backhand shots off the left—or far side—of the horse.

Fernando took his more advanced students to the practice field, where he instructed them to work on shots and plays using their own ponies. He walked around observing and giving instructions for almost an hour. Finally, he blew his whistle to get the entire group's attention.

"Let's all go to the grass practice field and play a couple of chukkers," he told them.

With his natural gentlemanliness and courtesy, Fernando accompanied Maggie to another covered place halfway up the stands near the midpoint of the field. He dusted off the seat for her and, as she sat down, explained what they would be doing. As he left to get his horse, Maggie was joined in the stands by a group of interested students, both young men and women.

The frivolous comments of a few of the girls amused Maggie.

"Isn't Johnny handsome on his horse? He rides so well!" said one.

Another admirer exclaimed, "My James is good, too! Look how well he sits in his saddle and how smoothly he handles his horse. He used to ride Western style but now Fernando is teaching him to ride English style!"

Something that caught Maggie's interest even more was a comment made by another girl: "Look, there's Fernando! My boyfriend says he's one of the best polo players in the world, but no one knows anything about him except some of the regents of the university who have arranged his scholarship. A couple of my friends have tried to attract some interest on his part, but he won't give any of them the time of day."

Maggie pondered on what she had just heard. Who was this mysterious young man with whom she had spent the morning? Where was he from? Why couldn't others get him to pay any attention to them, but she clearly attracted him? Was it the combination of her interest in aviation and horses, or was it deeper than that?

Fernando put on a seminar in polo for Maggie's benefit. He chose one companion to play with him against four players on the opposing side. They lined up, two against four, for the line judge's throw-in. Fernando did not have the fastest horse but he was more than a match for the entire opposing team.

Out of the melee came Fernando with the ball. When an opposing player charged in from the right, Fernando passed the ball under his horse to his left side and continued toward the goal posts. The other players ganged up on him from both sides, all at full gallop, but Fernando dodged this way and that, dribbling the ball, passing back and forth, outmaneuvering the other players until he was close enough to the goal, where he fired one long shot so fast it whizzed past the defending goalkeeper.

The next time the ball was thrown into play, he lofted the ball high over the heads of the astonished students. Previously it had been a lesson in driving the ball along the grass, but now it was an air game. Usually the faster horses caught up with the ball before Fernando, but he finessed the ball away from them and took it toward his goal. Again he had a point for his team.

Maggie sat in the stands watching and trying to follow the flow of the game. She noted that Fernando never missed a shot, never failed to steal it from the other team, couldn't be stopped, and rode beautifully. It seemed that he was glued to the horse by the way they moved together, never off balance, as though they were one. To Maggie, the smooth riding was almost like a ballet dance in slow motion. She marveled that Fernando did not appear to guide his horse with reins, whip, or spur. Instead, it seemed as though this animal did what Fernando was thinking.

The movements Maggie enjoyed the most were when Fernando made a backhand shot to take the rolling ball away from the other team, then would wheel sharply to reverse direction back toward his goal. He did backhand shots off both sides of his mount with equal facility. She could see how difficult these shots were because no one else tried them. It was beautiful how he raised up in his stirrups, twisted in the saddle, and crossed his mallet over to the far side of his horse to hit the ball without losing his balance.

After the seven-minute chukker was over, Fernando came off the field to get a fresh horse. When they were about to start the next period of play, he divided the players into two equal teams of four. He stayed on the sidelines coaching from the saddle, riding slowly outside the low white border fence. Fernando shouted instructions to both sides, guiding the play.

Suddenly a horse went down, throwing the rider. The player sprawled on the ground. The horse scrambled to its feet, but the rider lay there writhing in pain. In a flash, Fernando was off his horse and kneeling beside the injured player. He performed a quick but thorough triage and concluded it was just a painful sprain. He helped the player to his feet and assisted him slowly to the side. The frightened riderless horse had raced back to the stables, so Fernando sent in a substitute player and the game resumed.

After two more chukkers, Fernando called it a day for practice. He spent some time making suggestions to the assembled players, teaching some specifics, and congratulating them for what they had done. He also took time to get a report on the student who had fallen.

"Bill is okay. No broken bones—just a bad sprain," he announced.

Maggie remained in the stands after the other spectators had left. She was enjoying the quiet and the lingering memory of the beauty and drama of watching fine horses and their riders maneuvering on a smooth, green playing field.

Maybe there is something to this game after all, she mused. She had to admit that. After seeing just a little of it, she really wanted to play—no matter how many lessons it took. She wanted to be able to play and ride like Fernando. He was classy all right, although she would remain loyal to the Western style of riding.

She concluded that Fernando was right—it was a challenging game that would improve the horsemanship of the players. The thunder of the horses' hooves as they charged by the stands excited her, and she imagined it would also be exciting to anyone who loved horses or a fast-paced sport.

Fernando looked up to the stands to be sure Maggie was still there. As soon as the students left, he ran up the steps two at a time toward her.

"Well, my movie stuntgirl, now what do you think of this game called polo?"

Maggie, a bit chagrined, smiled and took his arm.

"I see that it really is an awfully lot more than just chasing a little white ball down the field!"

Fernando responded with a quick, "Good thinking!" Looking at his watch, he said, "You must be hungry. How about something to eat? There's a hamburger place still open over at the racetrack."

Starved, Maggie accepted his suggestion. While they ate, she commented approvingly on the little bit of polo she had seen.

"And on top of that, Fernando," she added with a smile, "you have quite a following among the co-eds whose boyfriends are studying with you. They think you are really special."

Fernando had the poise and self-assurance to handle compliments easily, but his response surprised Maggie.

"And what do *you* think?" he asked.

Blushing slightly, Maggie replied, "Well—I think they're right. It's very beautiful to see the way you ride and the way you dominate the playing field and the game. I can see what they mean. Some of the girls said their boyfriends insist you're the best polo player in the world!"

Fernando was truly surprised this time but quickly brushed aside the praise.

"Oh, no! I am not that good," he said, shaking his head. "I have seen ten-goal players in England and Argentina who are much better than me."

He seldom, if ever, mentioned Argentina, his homeland, for fear that someone might try to connect him to his family there. Inadvertently he had made a slip, but he hoped she had not noticed. Fernando was modest enough that he did not realize how much his polo skill had improved these last three years. He was now at his prime and playing on a level with the very best in the world—but he didn't even recognize it because he was not in a position to compete with them.

After finishing their hamburgers and milkshakes, Maggie and Fernando strolled over to the stables where her two matched palominos were boarded and cared for.

On the way, Maggie asked, "Do you think my horses could be trained to play polo?"

"By all means!" Fernando exclaimed. "There is no secret to it. Only lots of training. Training and practice and more training and more practice by both rider and horse. Your palominos are strong and obedient animals, but I don't know if they are fast enough or maneuverable enough for the starts and stops and quick turns. All I have seen in action is the one you were riding this morning, and I presume she has more speed than I saw. Would you like me to try them out?"

"You bet! I would love that!" Maggie responded immediately. "They are both faster and more maneuverable than you think. They can hold their own in quarter-mile races with the best. And you ought to see how they work cattle as a cutting horse! Both are trained ropers too—fast start outta the gate and a fast skid to a stop as soon as I get my loop over the steer's head."

Fernando was charmed by how Maggie adored her horses, and the way he looked at her while she talked made her lose her concentration. She switched topics quickly.

"Fernando, have you ever seen a Western rodeo—a real rodeo?"

"No, not really," he confessed. "I guess I know as little about Western rodeos and riding as you do about polo."

They both laughed and agreed that each could have a try at educating the other in their respective specialties.

"There's a rodeo coming up soon," Maggie said. "I can get free tickets. I'll let you know."

They looked in on Roamer and found the swelling much reduced and the lameness less noticeable. The treatment seemed to be working well.

"Your pony will be all right in another day or so," Fernando announced.

They discussed their various interests—horses and their training, veterinary medicine and its applications, different kinds of exercising, breeding and the merits of various blood lines when combined for one purpose or another. They wandered about the stables looking in on several prized animals out of mutual curiosity.

Eventually Maggie and Fernando strolled out onto the infield of the racetrack where some long-legged, pink flamingos made their home in a mirror-like, shallow pond. Flower beds arranged artistically and interwoven betwixt the landscaping were in full bloom, and the sun was warm. Even while they tried to dampen their feelings of attraction, the two seemed oblivious to the passage of time. Their conversation changed from talking about horses to a rambling discussion, learning more about each other's feelings and impressions.

They both felt that they were kindred spirits but would never have dared say it loud. Maggie had never known anyone with whom she shared so many common interests. Fernando was cultured, polite, considerate, intelligent, and a fascinating conversationalist. Likewise, Fernando had never spent any time with such a charming, beguiling woman, so well-rounded and informed in a variety of areas. Yes, he was still impressed with her early-morning stunt riding and flying, but she was also very intelligent and unique. The time sped by quickly until they realized they had to leave if they intended to make it to Luke's hangar by six.

Fernando stopped by the stables to give some instructions to the boys who worked under his direction. The stablehands had only seen him at the stables or at the university, so they were very surprised when Fernando told them he was leaving for the night. Also, it was the first time he had been seen with a woman in more than three years. The boys eyed each other while grinning, each of them deciding that Fernando was normal after all. They presumed he must simply have very particular tastes in feminine companionship.

Fernando and Maggie drove up alongside the big hangar at the airport where Luke had his office. Outside the hangar were a number of beautiful planes, and Fernando let out a low whistle.

"Those are some real beauties," he said. "Who do they belong to?"

"Those over there are Luke's fleet of planes for charter or rent," Maggie explained, pointing. "In the second line are planes for sale, and the third row of planes belong to clients who use Luke's mechanics for regular maintenance. Inside the hangar he has his own race planes—the ones he's used before and the new one they're putting together for the cross-country race later this year."

"Is he flying in the pylon race?" Fernando asked.

"Not this year," she answered. "He can't afford it. Everyone thinks Luke is wealthy, but the truth is he is in debt and in trouble with the banks. He's too generous with his friends—you know, other pilots who are down on their luck, have wrecked their planes, flunked their flight physical, can't find work, and so on."

They entered Luke's office through the door marked "Employees Only" and found Luke sitting at a large rolltop desk covered with scattered papers.

Fernando noticed the impressive trophies on stands, the pictures on the walls, framed newspaper clippings recounting Luke's rescue flights or race exploits, and autographed pictures of famous movie actors and other well-known celebrities Luke had flown in his planes.

"Hello, kids," Luke said. "Don't mind Gertrude, she won't bite. But best never to turn your back on her."

He was looking down at a large lioness lying on the floor beside him. When he stood up, the lioness stood up, so Fernando and Maggie backed away cautiously. Luke gave a hand signal to the beautiful animal, who immediately laid back down on the floor.

"Best watchdog I have ever had," he said proudly to his visitors. "Come with me. I want to show you the new Ryan Sportster."

As they walked out into the hangar, Luke thought, *This kid seems more mature than a typical student, but he has probably never been through a real aerobatic wring-out. He's probably just a spoiled rich kid from back East. I'll bet he'll get sicker than a dog with just a few stunts upside down or a two-turn spin. That might teach him to give me advice on flying matters! And when Maggie sees him upchucking, she'll lose interest in him real quick.*

They walked by several exotic race planes sheltered carefully inside the hangar, and Fernando noticed that the floor was spotless, certainly unusual for a typical flight operation. Normally there was grease and oil dripping from the planes and dirt on the floor, but not here—everything was very neat and tidy. That meant that Luke ran a tight shop and that the engines were probably in tip-top shape also. The cement floor was painted a military gray and shined from frequent sweeping, mopping, and cleaning.

The three of them walked through a small door situated in the large hangar door and out into the late afternoon sunlight. Right before them was a mirror-polished, aluminum, two-place, low-wing monoplane.

"Look at that little beauty!" Luke exclaimed. "Ryan has produced a real winner again. That's a fine factory down in San Diego that made Lindbergh's *Spirit of St. Louis.* Why don't you both go fly it? I know Maggie likes to practice aerobatics, and I assume Fernando can handle it?"

Luke had anticipated that Fernando would not dare chicken out in front of Maggie.

"Over there are the parachutes and two sets of helmets and goggles," Luke said, pointing. "I think they'll fit."

He led them over to the bright silver plane. On the leading edge of the wing were two parachutes with the harnesses hanging down, and on top of each parachute was a canvas summer-weight helmet and quality goggles. Luke was surprised that Fernando seemed to know what to do with the gear.

Donning a helmet and goggles is rather straightforward. However, one measure of a pilot's experience is how familiar they are with the procedure of getting into the complicated system of straps and buckles of a parachute required for serious aerobatics. Fernando and Maggie had automatically turned their backs to the wing, picked up the shoulder straps, slipped their arms into the right places, and stepped forward so that the parachute pack dropped from the wing and hit them in the back of the knees. Each had reached down to pull the dangling lower straps under and between their thighs and up in front to buckle up properly with the shoulder straps and belt.

Luke's face fell, and he started to think that maybe his dirty trick on Fernando would backfire.

Maggie tried a helmet first and then handed it to Fernando.

"I think this is more your size," she said, laughing.

Soon both were ready. Fernando was still in his polo clothes and Maggie in her Western outfit, but now both looked like veteran pilots ready for serious aerobatics.

Luke knew Maggie was an experienced pilot, so he was not hesitant to let her take the plane, but he still gave them a series of instructions.

"There's no way to communicate except by the usual hand signals and wiggling of the stick," he told them. "Stalling speed is sixty-five. Red line is two hundred. It's stressed for 6G positive and 3G negative, so it will take anything you want to try—except for an inverted spin. Nobody's tried one in this baby before, so we don't know how she'll behave. Stay above two thousand feet."

I sure hope Maggie will pull enough Gs to upset Fernando's stomach! Luke thought.

"It has gas for an hour and a half, and you've got about an hour of sunshine left," he said. "The electric starter is on the left of the panel and the master switch and magnetos are right beside it. Primer and fuel selector are on the floor to your left. Trim tabs are in the usual place and set for takeoff."

"Okay, okay," Maggie said, teasing him. "Can we go have some fun now?"

"Aww sure," Luke said, relaxing. "Just don't wreck it, y'hear? You know where the restricted aerobatic practice area is between the airport and the river alongside of us right here. We'll watch you do your stuff over there!"

He waved to an area of sky to the side of the airport, and called out, "Oh, check the mags at 1500 rpm on this engine. I'll pull your wheel chocks when you give me the signal."

Luke walked to the end of the wing while the pair climbed into the smart, sporty aircraft. As they were climbing in—Maggie up front and Fernando in back—Maggie said softly so Luke could not hear, "Fernando, you do have a pilot's license, don't you?"

He nodded.

"Any aerobatic experience?"

"Yeah—some," he said with a little smile.

She had noted the ease with which he put on his parachute, showing some familiarity with it.

"How many hours do you have?" she asked, expecting him to say maybe two hundred or so.

"Over a thousand with multi-engine and commercial carnets," he answered casually.

Maggie noticed that Fernando slipped occasionally into words with which she was unfamiliar. She didn't know whether "carnet" was French or Spanish, but rightly assumed it to mean "license" or "rating." In any case, she was impressed. As far as she knew, very few pilots had that many hours unless they were fully immersed in aviation on a high level.

The next hour was one of sheer delight for the two pilots. Neither had ever had so much fun wringing out a new plane. Each was respectful of the other, and they shared equal time alternating stunts. No one else was in the air this particular day and there was no traffic at the airport.

The mechanics and line boys from Luke's hangar and others nearby heard the engine laboring in climbs and racing in dives. Sensing something unusual was happening, they all came out to watch. These were complex maneuvers being performed as though they were in an air show. The loops were perfectly round, the rolls were quick with no loss of altitude, and the spins started and ended in exactly the same direction, showing that the pilot had not lost orientation in the spin. There were hammerhead stalls, tail slides, snap rolls and hesitation rolls, Immelmann turns, and even Cuban eights. A few of the men laid down on the grass looking up so they had a better view of this display in the sky without getting a crick in their necks.

The sun finally dipped just below the horizon, and Maggie pointed to her watch, signaling that the hour was over. Fernando wiggled the stick from the back cockpit to indicate that he would like to take the last turn and make the landing. Maggie let go and sat back, hands on the cockpit edge, waiting for whatever surprise he had in mind.

Fernando made the traffic circuit at higher-than-normal altitude and instead of lowering his nose at the runway, he stayed high and level. He flew toward the runway, showing no intention of landing. Maggie wondered what in the world he was thinking of doing. She had never seen a landing approach like this.

When he was almost over the end of the paved runway, Fernando pulled the nose up into a full stall, kicked hard rudder, and put the plane into an intentional spin. One turn, two turns, and finally full recovery followed by a violent slip toward the runway, first on one side and reversing to the other in a controlled "falling leaf." Fernando bled off the excess speed smoothly and kicked the plane straight for a perfect three-point landing almost vertically under the point where he had entered the nose-up stall. Maggie was speechless—not to mention breathless!

When they pulled up on the apron in front of the hangar, Luke and the other spectators came running toward them. Fernando cut the mixture, the prop wound down, and after a little delay he turned all switches off. He finished the cockpit procedures for shutting things off and putting everything in place—common pilot courtesy to accommodate the next pilot. The engine silenced and the crowd burst into applause.

Maggie was already out and on the ground before her companion stepped down, unbuckled his chute straps, and flipped the chute over his right shoulder, holding it by the short crotch straps.

Luke thought, *That boy handles a chute like he was born with one!*

He walked over to them and spoke only to Maggie.

"Sorry you had to quit, Maggie!" he said, awed. "That was quite a show! We haven't seen anything like that for a long time. If I had known you were going to do all that I would have had more gas in it. When the heck did you learn to do that two-turn spin to a falling-leaf slip?!"

"That wasn't my doing—that was Fernando," Maggie quickly

admitted. "I've heard of that kind of stunt, but I've never seen one, let alone been on board when it was performed. For a moment there, the ground looked awfully close over that nose!"

Luke was annoyed that his attempt to embarrass Fernando hadn't worked, and he was very surprised that Fernando was such a competent pilot.

"Okay, well, then, uh, which one did the eight-point hesitation rolls?" Luke asked.

Now laughing, Maggie pointed to her companion.

"Fernando did those too!"

Luke was beginning to get the drift. His impatience for, and dislike toward, this interloper began to show around the edges.

"And who did that perfect tail slide?" he asked hesitantly.

Maggie started to answer, but Luke cut her off with a question for Fernando.

"What kind of aerobatic plane do you usually fly, young man?"

"A 240 hp German Jungmeister," he responded modestly.

Luke couldn't help but whistle.

"I hear that is the best aerobatic plane ever built," he said. "Perfect balance, perfect response. How do you think it compares with the Ryan?"

Fernando did not want to offend Luke. He had enjoyed the flight very much, but he also wanted to be honest.

"Well, the Jungmeister is the better of the two for pure aerobatics, but the Ryan, with an experienced pilot, can do everything the Jungmeister is capable of," he said, choosing his words carefully. "I do like the looks of the Ryan better—the aluminum fuselage is perfectly molded, and the monoplane picks up speed faster than the biplane. But the Ryan needs more horsepower to compete directly with the German plane."

Reluctantly, Luke managed to demonstrate a new respect for Fernando as though he were listening to an equal, not just another upstart young pilot. *Where did Maggie find this kid?* he thought. He knew the Jungmeister was a precision-made, custom-built plane and there were only two in the United States. They were incredibly expensive and hard to come by. And that show-stopping spin to a landing!

Luke was the picture of chagrin. His dirty trick had not worked, and Fernando probably had made a lot more points with Maggie after this demonstration.

Well, Luke thought, *maybe I'm the one outclassed. She probably thinks I'm too old for her, especially if she starts to compare me with this kid.*

After the trio rolled the Ryan into the hangar, and while Maggie was talking to a couple of Luke's mechanics, Fernando pulled Luke aside and asked, "Maggie says she wants to fly in both the coming air races. She is very hopeful and excited, and she is intent on wanting to fight to the front of the closed-circuit, tightly grouped planes doing pylon racing. She also wants to enter the daylong, cross-country race. Do you think she is ready?"

Luke assured Fernando that Maggie could handle weather, navigation, pylon racing, and cross-country racing challenges as well as any of the other women who would be flying.

"All right. Is it possible to get two good planes for her?"

Luke looked over his shoulder at Maggie, still talking with the men.

"Well, she's safe and capable, but, between you and me, I don't like the idea of women in air racing," Luke confessed. "I guess I'm just old-fashioned. She has talked to me about it, so she knows how I feel. Maybe I'm the one who'll have to change."

Fernando was quiet, giving Luke space to express his feelings.

"Anyway, the problem is that no one I know has the money to sponsor one race plane, let alone two," Luke admitted. "I don't even know if *I* will have enough money to be in both races. I'll let you know if a sponsor for her turns up, but don't let her get her hopes too high. I know her well enough to know she doesn't like to be disappointed."

CHAPTER 5

TANGO IN THE BARN

A THOUSAND MILES AWAY, two brothers were discussing their dilemma at an empty airplane factory. Not one plane was under construction. No employees on site. A large empty wooden box sat on the cement floor beside a brand-new radial engine just removed from the box by an overhead hoist. Some wing panels were hanging from the rafters above, but they were just the skeleton rib structure, uncovered. The floor was clean, but it was obvious that no project was underway.

Roy and Oscar Butterfield, owners of the small factory, were at a crossroads.

The taller one, Roy, drawled, "Well, we have a little bit of cash in the bank, one new engine on the floor, a few pieces of steel pipe we could weld into an airframe—but no orders. Should we build another plane like the last one and hope for a buyer to appear, or should we experiment with something new? Whadya think?"

The shorter and younger brother, Oscar, was chewing on a stick of gum, nibbling a little bit at a time. He stopped and considered Roy's assessment of their predicament.

"Ya know, you're the businessman here," he said, shrugging. "I don't know if you can find the money. Times are difficult. But if you can figure out how to finance it, I'd like to try out some new ideas and see if it'll sell. We know we can build good, tough, working airplanes that will stand up well and do the job, but I think this is a good time to build something bigger, faster, and rather revolutionary. I know it's a bad time to take a risk, but I've been a-thinkin'. Why not try it?"

Roy leaned on the engine box and smiled.

"Okay, little brother, you're the engineer. Just what do you have in mind? I already know you want to use this bigger engine we splurged on. It's a beauty, all right. We've never built a plane that could take advantage of something like this. We've made a business out of work-horse, open-cockpit biplanes. But now you want to make sump'n fancy. Have at it. I'm a-waitin'."

"Okay, Big Bro," Oscar replied. "So, we've got this big, round engine. Let's draw a plane behind it. Big and round enough to seat four people, two plus two. But not too big. Just kind of imagine four people sittin' right behind this engine instead of two up on top of the fuselage with their heads sticking out of little holes. They are all four enclosed in a cabin with windows so they can see out, and a little bit of forward windshield. They don't have the wind in their faces or the roar of the engine in their ears. It won't be too cold in the winter or too hot in the summer. We'll give 'em a heater in the winter and a shot of cool air from outside in the summer. Behind, the cabin will taper down to a very slim tail section where we mount the rudder and the elevators. Get the picture?"

Oscar was sketching on a piece of paper all the while he was talking.

"Yea, I can see that," Roy said, nodding. "Great ideas. Not many planes on the market with a good cabin arrangement. But what kind of wings ya gonna have and what will ya do to make it go faster?"

Oscar was ready with answers for all of Roy's questions. He had obviously thought things through long beforehand. Oscar began to lay it out.

"I didn't tell ya, but this here new engine is not only bigger but it is better. It has what they call a supercharger to compress the air at altitude for more oxygen to make bigger explosions in the cylinders. Some superchargers run by exhaust gases, but this one has an impeller run directly off the crankshaft. More power for the same displacement. But I've got another idea. Ready?"

Roy felt they were getting down to the specifics, and he needed to plan a sales strategy.

"Sure I'm ready and I'm all ears, but it better be as good as your enclosed cabin. But let me guess. I'll bet you're gonna go with aluminum skin instead of fabric. Right?"

"Wrong!" Oscar said, smiling. "I think we better stay old-fashioned with the fabric over a welded steel tube structure—and I'll tell you why. The aluminum is new, you have to rivet it together, you have to bend it very carefully, and you need trained workers and equipment to cut and trim and rivet it."

Roy nodded his head in agreement and waited for some other shoe to drop.

"Thanks for being willing to stick with fabric and techniques we are used to, but first let me tell you about the wings we can use," Oscar continued. "We have some wing panels already in process hanging from the rafters. We can try a single wing on top or a single wing on the bottom. Or we can stick with our tried and proven system of a biplane. There are benefits for each. Most engineers are going with the monoplane, single-wing approach. I still like the biplane, but this time let's make the wings shorter for less drag. Also, I want to try retracting the wheels inside the lower wing for less drag."

Roy had heard enough to pique his interest.

"Okay. Go ahead. Draw up some plans. Do the engineering on stresses. Give me some figures on cruising speed, rate of climb, landing and takeoff distances for ground roll, etc. I think the market will go for a four-place cabin. But please make it pretty! The world needs prettier airplanes. Lately, a lot of planes look kind of boxy and old-fashioned, especially the biplanes. How soon can you give me some drawings of both inside and outside?"

The two owners had no idea how much their original idea would evolve and change nor how well their final concept would be accepted by the market, but they forged ahead, enthusiasm sweeping them along.

Driving toward the polo stables, Maggie ventured to ask Fernando a few questions, but all she received were evasive answers. Instead, he responded by asking about her family or her life, and she gave honest straight answers.

Finally, Maggie had had enough of his secrecy.

"Fernando, you don't give me the same kind of answers about yourself that you expect—and get—from me!" she blurted out. "You seem to be holding back something. Can't you tell me what the problem is—if there is one? We've only known each other a few weeks, but in the last two days we've flown together, driven together, you've watched me film a movie stunt, and I've watched you play polo. I have flown with you, and you are an outstanding aerobatic pilot. And you have nursed my horse to health."

Fernando remained silent, trying to figure out how to respond.

"I like that you're involved in equestrian and aviation matters with a very high level of skill in both," she continued. "But I still don't know anything about you. If we are to be friends, I think I deserve to at least know where you are from or where your family lives or what makes you tick. I like to know those things about a young man—um, a friend—I am seeing."

They weren't dating, but down deep in her heart Maggie knew she wanted to see a lot more of him. She stopped her rapid-fire talking, expecting him to elaborate. She was accustomed to being direct and frank, giving her opinion and dealing with men as equals since she worked with them so often in her areas of expertise. But perhaps in this instance she had said too much and been too inquisitive.

Fernando struggled. *Should I tell her or not? Would she judge me harshly? What difference would it make? Would she feel differently toward me? Would I lose what I have gained these last three years?*

"Maggie, I can't tell you everything you want to know just yet. Please let me take my own time. Things are complicated right now. We'll get to it one day, but not right now. Let's just treat each other as we have been and be friends. Let's leave digging things out of the past, at least for now. Can you accept that?"

She was quiet for a moment, considering what he had just expressed. *Well, at least he is courteous about it. He could have said that it was none of my business. I enjoy his company and I think he enjoys mine. There is no one else on the horizon at the moment. In fact, after seeing him ride and fly and explain aeronautical engineering principles to me, I'll have to admit that he may be the most fascinating man I have ever met!*

Her thoughts were mixed up and confused and she was very slow to answer Fernando's question. Maggie was not one to fall in love easily—she was far past that vulnerable stage of her young life. Now, very few men were intelligent enough and strong enough of character to attract her. In prior years, many young men had disappointed her. They had not been able to measure up to what she expected in a suitor.

She had heard her father say that to trust a man you had to measure his character, his capacity, and his capital.

"Character," he had told her, "is an unblemished moral code and integrity. Capacity is intelligence or proven skills sufficient to make a living and support a family. Capital is collateral in reserve for emergencies."

Her father had said that, to a banker, "capital" for emergencies meant additional assets to pay the loan, not just the project being financed, in case of unexpected need. However, to a daughter measuring a man to marry, he taught that she should look at his reserves of emotional stability to handle disappointments likely to occur, his investment in his education, his commitment to his God, the way he treats his mother and other women, and other qualities that would see him through the challenges of life. Her father had added that the best spiritual treasures a man can have are the wife and children he loves and looks forward to being with in the life to come.

No one had ever passed the test her father had outlined for Maggie. However, here was a mature, talented, handsome man with many hidden qualities combined into one six-foot two-inch athletic frame. He was quiet, but whenever someone like Luke asked a question, this "mystery" man seemed to have a very knowledgeable answer. He was obviously intelligent, had depth, competency, and a world of experience. She hoped that he would pass her father's entire three-part test.

Who would have imagined that this fellow student had so many flying hours and credentials to prove it! *Well,* she thought, *I will have to play it his way for now. Just friends—no digging into the past. Maybe there's a character flaw there to be found or maybe there is no capital in reserve for emergencies. I just won't fall in love till I know more.*

"All right—it makes sense," Maggie said with a small sigh of resignation. "No more digging—just friends." She noted that Fernando was still deep in thought and was not smiling. Did her answer disturb him?

When they arrived outside his stable office, it was almost dark except for the dim lights at the door of each stable. There was no one around, and everything was very quiet—even the horses. A brilliant idea occurred to Fernando.

"Maggie, before you leave, would you like to hear some popular music from my country?" Fernando asked impulsively.

"Yes, I would!" Maggie answered quickly.

"Wait right here while I bring my record player and records," he said, motioning for her to sit down on a chair that was against the wall near where they were standing. He bounded up the stairs that led to his quarters, turning on the porch lights as he went along.

In less than a minute Fernando returned with his record player, records, and a long extension cord. He put the player on a table beside Maggie and made the connections.

The yellow lights along the corridor created a soft glow. The block-long porch was lined, full length, with brick arches that held up the roof. It shaded the long row of horse stalls that were part of the extensive stables. The area in front of the office where they were now standing was paved with large Spanish tiles, making a nice, polished floor. Back in the darkness were other rows of stalls just as long. An occasional horse would whinny or neigh.

"This is tango music," Fernando explained. "It is my country's most popular music."

Maggie had no idea where the tango came from. It sounded kind of French, yet he once slipped and mentioned Argentina. That would explain his Latin name, "Fernando," but did not explain the English name "Underwood."

"This is romantic dance music," Fernando continued. "In fact, it used to be so romantic that it was banned for a time."

He laughed without explaining.

"But that attitude changed and it is now socially acceptable all over the world. Our tango has been very popular in Paris, London, and Europe in general because it is so sensuous. Here in the States—at least in the East—the famous dancers Vernon and Irene Castle have made the tango quite popular."

Maggie loved dancing very much. She enjoyed square dancing, waltzing, fox trots, Latin-type dancing, but she didn't know the Argentine dance.

"Is the tango anything like the rumba?" she asked. Maggie had learned a few steps of the rumba and loved its fascinating new rhythms.

"Yes and no," Fernando responded. "The rumba is four-four time with a quick-quick-slow step rhythm. The tango borrowed some of the accentuation from the rumba, or maybe the rumba borrowed it from the tango. But the tango has a two-four time with an irregular accented beat; the steps are slow, slow, quick, quick pause. We think the tango started with an Argentine native dance called the "milonga" and someone added some features of the Spanish tango—that's where we get the name—together with some bits of the Cuban *habanera.* The milonga style is characterized by a very close embrace, small steps, and syncopated rhythmic footwork."

"Do you think I can pick it up?" Maggie asked.

"Oh of course. It is not too hard to learn, especially when the woman has long legs like you do," Fernando said, demonstrating the steps as he explained.

He quickly felt embarrassed for having mentioned her legs, and Maggie lowered her head to hide a self-conscious smile the moment she perceived his discomfort. She was pleased he had noticed them.

Fernando turned back to the record player and put on the first record—Carlos Gardel, the Bing Crosby of Argentina. The sensual beat had a stirring effect on both of them. Maggie looked up from where she was sitting. Fernando stood tall, towering over her. She did not understand a word of the lyrics but the rhythm was so different, so inviting, and Fernando seemed to know all about music and dancing, which delightfully impressed her.

"Please, go ahead," she said. "Start with the simple, basic steps."

Fernando waited to be in rhythm with the music, then started dancing alone with his arms out as if holding a light-footed, wispy, invisible dance partner. He did the long, stretching, slow steps followed by the intricate, quick-quick, short, twisting steps. The tango can be danced alone, as Fernando well knew, and is very attractive when performed that way. But with two partners in perfect synchronization, it is even more spectacular. It's always a showstopper.

After listening to the beat and seeing a few of Fernando's steps, Maggie could feel her feet wanting to dance. At his invitation Maggie stood and glided smoothly toward his open arms. Fernando immediately drew her to him and did a full pivot, causing her head to whirl. Then he stopped.

"Now, step backward three long steps when I say go," he instructed as they stood very close to each other. He waited for the right place in the music and quietly said, "Go!"

Led by Fernando, Maggie stepped backward to the strong pulse of the music, and waited expectantly for his next verbal command. Instead of talking her through the next part he simply pushed her left hip back with his right hand, and with his left hand in hers, he pulled her right shoulder forward. The twisting movement caused her feet to reverse, and to her surprise his feet entwined with hers in a perfect dance-step turn of the tango.

He stopped right there, smiling proudly at his successful efforts as a tango teacher.

"Bravo! You are good! Now let's do it again, but this time we won't quit. We will just keep going till you get mixed up."

Fernando thought he was teaching her to tango, but Maggie felt it was some kind of magic. She felt that the combination of the new music with the deep underlying beat, the words which she sensed were romantic even though she could not understand Spanish, and the growing pleasure of being held closely by a tall, dark, handsome man were all making her feet and body and soul react in a mystical kind of way that disconcerted yet excited her.

No dance had ever affected her this emotionally. She knew she was not a show dancer like those at the movie studio in the big musicals—at least she had never felt like one before tonight. But now she felt strange and even enchanted—her feet were lighter and more coordinated than ever before. She seemed to be able to anticipate Fernando's movements and be ready to respond before he even gave an indication.

"Maggie, you are a wonderful dancer! It is as though you had danced the tango many times before. Are you sure you haven't?" His question was sincere. "I have never had a better partner."

Maggie reassured him that she'd never even heard the music before. Secretly she was thrilled. Never in her life had anyone complimented her on dancing so well, and here she was at the stables, still in riding clothes and boots.

What would it be like dancing with Fernando in a long flowing gown? she wondered.

Fernando turned the record over and they danced to the music on the other side. They said very little to each other. The music seemed to say it all. The steps became more and more elaborate as Maggie became more experienced. Her efforts were magnified and she became quite swept away with the romance of it all. She had never danced so long or so well. She felt her cowboy boots were Cinderella slippers with fairy godmother dust on them.

Fernando was also under her spell and that of the music and the dance. He marveled that in all his years of chasing after attractive women in the world's great cities, he had never felt this way before.

Is it just the close embrace of the tango steps? he asked himself. He could feel the grace and strength of her body move smoothly under his lead. She was responsive and even eager for his leadership in the dance. She let him initiate every step and turned and followed as closely as if they were tied together invisibly.

They went through all the tango records Fernando had, dancing closer and closer in the twisting whirls and pivots, posing ever more dramatically with Fernando intentionally holding each pose longer and longer as the sense of closeness deepened for each.

Finally, after a long, long statue-like pause where Fernando held Maggie close to him for several seconds, he lowered her gracefully until her long ponytail almost touched the floor, bringing her back up to a standing position with a flair.

The previously unseen audience of stablehands broke into spontaneous applause. Drawn by the music, they had crept quietly out of their rooms, staying back in the shadows, entranced by the fascinating dancing. The mystery of young love mixed with emotions expressed by motion—dancing by a man they admired and a beautiful girl they did not know—had moved them to silent observation. But Fernando's professional finish had sparked spontaneous applause and had given their presence away to the two dancers who'd thought they were completely alone. The scene had been irresistible to these workers. Now the bubble had burst—they were sorry for that but glad they had witnessed the magic of the dance.

Fernando was not embarrassed. In fact, he was happy these men had shared in this sweet experience. He bowed with a sweeping gesture that brought the men out into the light, still clapping enthusiastically.

Maggie, suddenly feeling uncomfortable, did not know where to hide, for she had let the experience turn into sudden infatuation—with the dance or with Fernando, she wasn't sure, but it was new and deeper than any feeling she had enjoyed before.

The audience was unexpected, and that changed the magic slightly for her. She thought that she and Fernando had a right to privacy, yet she felt relieved that Fernando was not embarrassed in front of the men. Maggie sensed that he was used to being in the limelight and was not self-conscious at all.

Concluding that the best thing to do was to follow his example, she curtsied prettily, waved to all, and whispered to Fernando, "I really must be going. Would you walk me to the car, please?"

Fernando gave her his arm, and with the other arm waved to the men, calling to them, "Good night—the show is over. Thanks for the applause." The finality in his tone was enough to send them all back to their own quarters.

"Thank you, Fernando, for two of the best days of my life," Maggie sighed, as they walked to her car.

"Maggie, this may sound strange to you, and I have never said it to anyone else in my life, but you are the most fascinating woman I have ever met. I too feel that these have been the two best days of my life and the beginning of a new life for me."

"Fernando, before I drive off, please tell me who you are and where you are from—just *something* about your life. Please?"

With a request like that and after having danced intimately for a long time, lost in the feeling of closeness only the tango can produce, Fernando could not refuse. He was too much of a gentleman.

"Maggie, I am from Argentina. I do not want anyone to connect me with the past yet. I have to graduate on my own and then I have some fences to mend with my family. There are some serious mistakes I have made which only I can correct. After I have graduated and have erased the disappointment I have caused my parents and family, and only then, can I tell you everything about myself."

He paused, and when she did not react, he continued.

"I have lived and studied in England, on the Continent, in the eastern United States, and in Argentina, of course. I have studied in a number of universities, but I must make it through this university on my own, and then I hope my family will be proud of me again. That is important to me. I am just a few months from graduation, just like you are, so please wait for me to do what I have to do in my way, and after graduation, I will tell you everything."

Maggie did not know what to say.

"Trust me, Maggie," Fernando pleaded. "I haven't broken the law. It is just a family situation that I can't explain right now. Okay?"

Maggie was quiet for a long time.

"Will I see you again?" she asked.

"Of course—that is, if you would like to. I want to very much," Fernando answered. Somewhat embarrassed, he added apologetically, "But, you see, I can't even drive you home. I don't have a car and can't get one under my present circumstances. I won't be able to take you out to fancy restaurants or dancing with an orchestra—or even buy you flowers. But trust me. Someday I will—someday soon."

For the first time in the last three years, Fernando was chagrined and self-conscious about being poor, almost destitute. He had been trying to punish or purify himself in some way by remaining poor. He had asked the university for nothing but bare essentials and anonymity. He hadn't needed a car or cash, but right now he wished he could change some of that for Maggie. No, he would make it on his own. He would stick with the course he had chosen. He had said enough.

"Maggie, please trust me," Fernando said, looking at her intently.

"Just let me do it my way without digging too deeply into the past."

There was one other important question in Maggie's mind that she just had to ask.

"Fernando, please forgive me for asking another question, but I have to know one thing for sure. Are you married? Is there anyone else in your hidden past? I can trust you and not ask anything else as long as I know that."

Fernando had to admit to himself that she was a wise and logical girl. He should have anticipated a question like that.

"No, Maggie, I promise you there is no wife, no girlfriend, no marriage ever, no complications like that. I would ask you to go steady, but that is for younger kids, and besides I can't offer anything but a tango lesson—or maybe horseback riding down by the river." They both laughed.

Maggie knew she could easily fall hopelessly in love with this mysterious man. She was suddenly and uncontrollably infatuated and felt she was truly able to understand him. Fernando was strong but timid in a little-boy kind of way. His pride and relationships with his family had been hurt—deeply wounded—and he was still licking his wounds until they healed.

She could understand that and his need for privacy. Also, she could understand that he felt awkward not being able to take her out on a real date. Again, a matter of pride. Men were funny that way. *Well,* she thought, *I can help more than he realizes.*

"Fernando, I do trust you," she said, putting her hand on his forearm. "You have told me all I have to know right now. We can deal with the rest at a later time. In the meantime, my horse still needs to be checked on, and I want to come over and watch you play polo. Maybe I could even take a few lessons myself! I would like you to train my ponies so they won't spook with the mallets, too. Oh, and I do need help preparing for my exams since you obviously know more about aeronautical engineering than I do! I won't ask for anything else except for a little of your time. If you want to see me, you know some of the classes I am in."

Now it was her turn to be embarrassed. Maybe she was being too forward. She froze, groping for some way to stop herself.

"You do need to know that I broke up with someone who proposed to me, but he still calls me," she said. She just left that hanging out there so Fernando would not think she had never had any romance in her life. She wanted him to think she was somewhat sophisticated in such matters.

Fernando realized things were close to getting out of control. He did not want this evening to end this way—a conversation running out of words. Being the assertive man he believed himself to be, he simply did what he had wanted to do all along.

He gathered her into his strong arms, planted a full kiss on her willing lips, and kissed her thoroughly. Maggie didn't resist, and afterward, she laid her head on his shoulder, enjoying the tender embrace for a long moment.

Suddenly, she said, "I really must go. Good night, Fernando. Thanks for a wonderful day."

"Good night, Maggie—see you soon."

Fernando opened the car door and she slipped into the driver's seat. She drove off almost in a daze, wondering what had just happened. Fernando stood there watching the little roadster's taillights disappear down the lane, knowing full well exactly what had happened.

CHAPTER 6

AN EMERGENCY OF INTERNATIONAL STATURE

LORD CHARLES JOCKHAM scanned the morning mail from England, breathed a deep sigh, and began the laborious task of reading each letter. His secretary had left the correspondence in a neat stack on his desk, each one opened, spread flat, and organized by subject matter. After reading each item, he called in his secretary to dictate concise instructions to each staff member who would follow through with the action needed.

"Please tell Mr. Samuelson to check this insurance claim from Lloyd's through the Los Angeles Port Authority," Charles stated crisply. "There is a man there by the name of William Josephson who helps us. Terrible tragedy to lose that ship, but at least there was no loss of life."

He went on to the next item in the stack of correspondence and gave his secretary more instructions.

"Telephone the Hollywood film company shown here and tell them that London approves their request to film the visit of His Majesty to Australia next year. They wanted a special permit so they could get their news camera closer than usual. We see no security risk. However, they do need to coordinate everything with our Sydney office after they arrive in Australia. Please give them the names of whom to contact."

A set of official-looking papers in front of him caught his eye.

"What's all this?" he asked, more to himself than to his secretary. "Hmmm . . . this is fascinating."

Pondering its significance after glancing through the material, he turned to his secretary, who had pencil and pad poised ready to write.

"By Jove, old Douglas really *was* on to something!" Charles exclaimed. "Will you please give him a call? I will need to set up a lunch with him as soon as possible."

She left to make the phone call while the earl reread the pages of background research in his hands. They had just arrived from the home office in London. He underlined some parts for emphasis and made brisk comments in the margins, then called his vice-consul, Mr. Williams.

"Edward, you remember our friend Douglas and his request that we run a check on that young polo player who seemed so good?"

"Of course!" he responded.

"Well, I have just received an answer," Charles said in an urgent tone. "Come on over to my office and look at this stack of material. We have ourselves one beauty of a mystery to unravel!"

The consul hung up the phone just as his dictation secretary re-entered his office.

"I am so sorry, sir, but they say your friend Douglas is at the studio filming and can't be interrupted," she said. "What shall I do?"

"Nonsense!" Charles responded. "Don't take no for an answer. Tell them that the King of England's representative demands that the call be put through. This is an emergency of international stature. Get him on the line!" His military bearing and tendency to issue orders was still with him.

Douglas was not actually at the studio; he was at the gymnasium working out a scene with two younger actors, giving them specific directions for a particular action.

"Gentlemen, please make me look good," Douglas asked them. "I am not as young as I used to be, but the public doesn't know it yet. I will be forcing the two of you down the stairs with my aggressive sword play until I see your reinforcements coming to help from the far side of the grand hall. They will be rushing across the room toward the bottom of the stairs. Then I turn and see that more of your men are coming to help you from the top of the stairs over there."

The younger actors nodded and agreed they would make him look good.

"At that precise moment I have to jump up on the banister here and keep parrying the two of you," Douglas continued. "I will grab the rope tied to a ring in the wall, and swing over the heads of the crowd below to the other balcony on the far side. My dramatic escape will be spectacular! Now, let's give it a go."

All three men were dressed in white fencing garb with foils in their hands and protective face masks pushed up on top of their heads. They pulled their masks down, and took *en garde* positions. Douglas, above the other two on the steps, began the action. All three were well trained in Olympic fencing but were exaggerating their moves for the scene.

After the first few seconds, it was obvious that Douglas was equal to the task of forcing the two younger men down the stairs. This was furious sword play; Douglas was actually beating the two of them. The two men were doing their best, but with Douglas's expert parrying and thrusting, they were being pushed backward.

Suddenly, Douglas looked across the imaginary great hall floor to the far side; while still defending himself with his sword, he took a quick glance above and behind himself, pretending to see more foes joining the fray. He reacted with an exaggerated expression of fear, seeing himself outnumbered, moments from being overwhelmed—but spotting the hanging rope, he jumped on the banister a prop man had put alongside the long staircase and shouted, "Cut!"

The three men removed their masks, and Douglas smiled approvingly.

"Great job, fellows. Thanks!" he exclaimed. "Now let's do it one more time to make sure we've got it. We seem to be dividing the attention almost evenly from one to the other. But don't you think I should hook one of your foils and flip it away at the last minute? Or is it all right the way we are doing it?"

The perspiring antagonists were bending over, trying to catch their breath. Finally, one spoke.

"Sir, I hope you know that neither one of us is acting," he said, in between breaths. "We are trying our best to get through your defense, but even with two of us, you are beating us soundly. You aren't even breathing hard. How in heaven's name do you do it?"

"Oh, lots of training, my lads," Douglas responded with a smile. "Lots of training. Now, let's do it again and I will see if I can hook your foil and flip it away. That is good for the excitement of the movie, but I won't tell you in advance which one I will take. What say the loser puts up for the drinks?" His good humor and easy way was a delight for all on the set.

Just then a staff member came in.

"The British consul is on the phone, sir. He suggests that you interrupt your rehearsals and take this call from him on a very important matter. Says it's something about international diplomacy and the King of England."

"What in the world is Jock doing this time?" Douglas said under his breath. Turning to the staff member, he replied, "Yes, I'll take the call. These two say they need a rest so they can beat me on the next run-through."

Douglas followed the man into the office and picked up the phone.

"Jock!" he exclaimed. "How in the world did you find me over here at the gymnasium?"

"I called the studio, thinking you might be filming," the consul explained. "They didn't want to disturb you but I threatened them that the king might try to take back his colonies if they didn't tell me your number. It seemed to work—I must try that line more often! Am I really interrupting something terribly important? If so, I will be brief."

"No problem on this end, dear Jock," the actor responded. "What is so urgent that I deserve this privilege of speaking with 'your excellency'?"

"Douglas," Charles said, lowering his voice, "are you interested in hearing some information about that mysterious young polo player you asked about?"

Douglas was instantly alert. He had been wondering what news might have come from Jock's inquiry to London.

"Of course!" he replied quickly. "What information have you found?"

"Douglas, I have in my hand a full set of newspaper clippings and a full dossier on the young man's family!" Charles said excitedly. "We have positive identification and it is all very sensitive. When can we meet?"

"I can cancel my luncheon today and meet you at our usual place in a couple of hours," Douglas said. "The studio bosses only wanted to talk money—that can always wait!"

Douglas is in for a real surprise, thought the consul with a grin as he hung up.

At precisely one o'clock, the two flamboyant Rolls Royce automobiles pulled into the parking lot of a fashionable, exclusive restaurant on Sunset Boulevard in downtown Hollywood. They were ushered in by a uniformed doorman who recognized them as regular patrons worthy of the very best attention. The maître d' led them to a dim, secluded booth and assured the two that no one would bother them.

They ordered quickly, and Charles opened his briefcase.

"Laddie, you have no idea what a gold mine of challenging problems you have dug up!" he said, pulling out a thick file. "Do you remember who the wealthy Underwood family is?"

"Not in detail," Douglas responded, "but I believe they own a major bank and some insurance company—oh, and a shipping line, I believe.

Seems like they have holdings in India and South America or someplace like that. And I seem to recall that they contributed substantially to the Shakespearean arts."

The consul nodded.

"Are they related to this Fernando?" Douglas asked.

"Yes, he is very much related!" Charles responded. "This Underwood family is his mother's. Also, have you ever heard of the Velez-Candiotti Braun family from Argentina?"

Douglas stirred his memory for a moment.

"Wasn't there a polo player by that name who was quite good?" he asked. "I think I lost track of him years ago. Seems he returned to some place in South America to look after his family interests down there. Guess I never paid much attention to which country. What are you leading up to, my friend?"

Charles was hardly able to keep his excitement under control.

"This is a most fascinating story you have stumbled into, Douglas. And you are right about the Underwood fortunes. I have the file from our office covering all the interests you mention and many more not as well known. Very big—very big! Oh, and they have a daughter who married the polo player you mention, by the name of Hugo Velez-Candiotti Braun. Hugo's father is Argentine-born but of old Spanish land-grant aristocracy. Hugo's mother is from the famous Braun family and fortune from Germany. Helen Underwood married this same Hugo and they went off to Argentina to live and work and raise a family."

"Did Hugo continue to play polo?" Douglas asked.

"He did!" his friend answered. "According to these documents, Hugo continued playing polo and became an eight-goal handicap. They happen to have a son named Fernando, so we are sure we have the right man. Would you like to hear about the Velez-Candiotti Braun family?"

Douglas was more than interested—he was almost salivating.

"Get on with it, man. Who are they? Why the mystery?"

"Let me start at the beginning," Charles said. "You won't believe what we have here. The Velez-Candiotti Braun family are old-time

Argentines but with a long tradition of marrying into British, German, French, and Italian families of wealth. If there were a royalty in Argentina, it would be this family. There is none more prominent or more important. They own half the country and that is not an exaggeration."

"How far back do their land deeds go?" Douglas queried.

"Back to the Spanish crown land-grant days!" Charles exclaimed. "The king of Spain gave them tremendous tracts of land the size of the British Isles, or bigger, for 'services rendered.' Their progenitor must have saved the life of the king or saved his whole kingdom—something like that. Over the centuries—they go back to the very beginning of the Spanish occupation of Latin America—they have learned to protect their land and their kingdom. It truly is that: a veritable kingdom."

"Jock," Douglas interjected. "You have to tell me about Fernando!"

"All in good time, dear fellow," said Charles with a smile. "Let me continue the background! The Braun family divided the land and companies among the descendants to make it look diversified. But the real power continues in the hands of whomever the family chooses to head up everything. It is all done legally. The consortium is divided into a number of holding companies, but, in fact, the real power is in the one genius who can keep the whole family working together and cooperating fully with each other."

"Let me guess," Douglas said. "Hugo?"

"Yes," Charles said, nodding. "This report says that Don Hugo, as they call him, is the top man of the family—the reigning chief. He is a financial wizard, a doctor of laws, and a polished diplomat. The report also adds that he's a fine person and extremely competent as the head of this multi- national conglomerate. It is a trust made up of the families and their common holdings. Hugo is called the 'King of the Gauchos' with respect. And before the disgrace, young Fernando was referred to as the 'Prince of the Gauchos.'"

"Just a moment here!" Charles exclaimed. "*What* disgrace? Come on, man, you're keeping me dangling out here—what happened?"

"Douglas, I am getting to that, but please be patient—stay with me,"

Charles insisted. "First, I have to tell you the rest of the information about their empire. They have huge *estancias*—enormous great working cattle and sheep ranches—several of them with over one million acres each, now divided into stock companies with family members holding shares to the companies, with some of them living overseas where they have other foreign investments to manage, so it functions like an international holding company."

Charles continued on with details about all the ranches, wool-export companies, meat-packing plants, sugar plantations and more, while Douglas grew more and more impatient. His friend, however, was still not through.

"The family is a kingdom right out of a fairy tale book. They live well but try to avoid the limelight. They are not ostentatious. According to the account, they try very hard to avoid spoiling their children, and are intent on raising them to be productive in one specialty or another. Those who get to the top positions in the family infrastructure are talented, well-educated, and seem to earn it. They are very close-mouthed about themselves and avoid any kind of publicity. They are afraid of kidnapping threats like the Lindbergh case here in the United States or extortion for any reason. They seek spouses for their children with good blood lines and established gene pools, but of course it doesn't always work out like those of the older generation in the family want it to—"

Douglas couldn't bear it any longer.

"Jock!" he exclaimed. "Get to it! Tell me about the disgraceful thing that happened!

"Here are some newspaper clippings, Douglas," the consul said, relenting. "I will let you read them, but let's be very careful about this. I have been warned by London not to get involved in the wrong way or it could affect my career. What I can tell you is that Fernando was the heir apparent to the entire family establishment. He was to take his father's place as soon as he settled down, married, learned all the many facets of the various companies, and proved himself. However, Fernando was quite a ladies' man, a drinker, gambler, and there was gossip and half a dozen scandals in France, England, and Boston. And then a disaster happened three years ago—a car accident after a big party with alcohol, and a girl died."

Douglas was listening to his friend while he scanned the newspaper articles and saw the gruesome photos.

"What did Don Hugo do?" he asked. "He must have been horrified and humiliated to have his name tarnished in such a public way."

"Indeed," Charles responded. "He disinherited Fernando, told him he was a disgrace to the family, and apparently told him to never return home to Argentina. The boy disappeared and apparently never learned that a police investigation of the accident exonerated Fernando because he had not been driving the car—it was his roommate, who had secretly taken Fernando's car."

Douglas considered all this information carefully. He had so many questions, but wanted to do some of his own research.

"Does anyone in his family know that he's here?" he asked.

"No, but they'll find out soon, now that I've been asking questions," Charles replied. "The family in Argentina has had private investigators trying to locate Fernando, but someone here at the university is protecting him. He writes to his family twice a year, but the letters are mailed from different cities all over the country. And he's been using his mother's last name."

Charles wagged a finger at his friend.

"I have orders, mind you, *orders*, not to intervene until Hugo contacts me," he warned Douglas. "The family in England is contacting the family in Argentina and will let us know what his desires are. Now, my friend, do you see what you have stirred up? What if Fernando really does not want to return to his family? I imagine he has a healthy dose of pride and is trying to change his life on his own, away from his family. And what if the family still does not want to have anything to do with him? Then what?"

Douglas had an idea.

"I owe him something for fixing my car," he said. "I am taking my yacht out to the island of Catalina next weekend. I have a nice sixty-foot sailboat that takes some real skill to handle well, and you said he once won a yacht race. Maybe if I invite him he will reveal something else so I can keep you out of trouble but still learn more."

Charles agreed that it was a clever plan, or at the very least a way to stall for time without too much risk. The two friends finished their dessert, argued jovially about who would pay the bill, then walked out into the California afternoon sunshine, unaware of all that their discovery and investigation was unraveling in faraway places.

CHAPTER 7

THE PARIS OF LATIN AMERICA

BUENOS AIRES IS deservedly called the "Paris of South America." Its broad, tree-lined boulevards with sidewalk restaurants under colorful awnings, heroic-size statues and spectacular fountains, grand architecture in public buildings, elegantly dressed citizens, the opera, ballet, symphonies, and art museums—all make it one of the world's most beautiful and cultured cities.

The similarity to Paris is not a coincidence—the engineer who planned the layout of Buenos Aires and who designed many of its principal landmarks is none other than the same Frenchman who created the city of Paris: Carlos Thays. For example, the height of the buildings lining the principal downtown boulevards of Buenos Aires are limited to the same height as the public buildings on the main streets in Paris.

In the 1930s, Argentina was a very prosperous country. It had more miles of railroad per capita than England, more automobiles per capita than the United States, more telephones per capita than France, more hospital beds per capita than Germany, and more baked pizzas per capita than Italy. Consumption of red meat and wine per capita was the highest in the world.

Behind this economic progress was the immense wealth of the fertile pampas—hundreds of thousands of square miles of rich, black, loam soil at least thirty feet deep—so rich that commercial fertilizer was never used or needed.

In addition, the famed pampas surrounding the city of Buenos Aires in three directions claim a benign climate that never freezes, seldom gets above 95°F, never suffers droughts severe enough to affect the whole area, and rains so regularly and evenly that irrigation is not needed. Floods are only sporadic in very low river bottom areas.

The pampas of Argentina are one of the greatest breadbaskets on Earth. In the 1930s, the production of grains and cattle so exceeded Argentina's consumption that the surplus for export could feed many of the world's nations in need.

The Buenos Aires residence of Don Hugo Velez-Candiotti Braun and his British-born wife, Dame Helen, was palatial. Located in the northern suburbs of the city, it overlooked the wide expanse of the Rio de la Plata. The river was forty miles wide at that point and on the opposite side of the river lay neighboring Uruguay. The Atlantic Ocean was about one hundred miles away to the east, yet the ocean tides affected the level of the river in front of the city.

The family estate, located on a high point of the bluff facing the river, sloped gently toward the shoreline for several blocks. The grounds included formal gardens on all sides around the mansion, two tennis courts of red-clay surface (crushed brick dust), and an Olympic-size swimming pool with diving boards and platforms. The expanse was further decorated with statuary by renowned sculptors, reflecting pools, and artistic flower beds carefully attended by professional gardeners.

The complex included a ten-car garage with live-in quarters for several chauffeurs and a full-time mechanic, several guest cottages, and security guard posts. An enclosed aviary full of colorful birds, a small zoo for the delight of children, and decorated pathways completed the estate. Large, full-foliaged trees planted in strategic places provided total privacy. In fact, from the streets surrounding the area nothing could be seen but dense vegetation. A very large, ornate main gate with a paved driveway curving out of sight was imposing enough that only invited guests would even dare approach it.

To see the place from a distance out in the river was to observe a green park of detailed perfection crowned by a multi-columned mansion with a large terrace where the family could watch yacht races, passing river barges and cargo ships, or just enjoy their meals in private splendor. It was indeed every bit a private park. For sheer size and elegance, the Velez-Candiotti Braun estate would rival the finest of Europe or the "Great Gatsby" estates facing Long Island Sound.

Inside the colonnaded and pillared great mansion, a grand staircase curved from both sides of the foyer leading up to the bedroom suites, lit by a domed skylight. The living room to the right of the large foyer was enormous and exquisitely furnished. The dining room beyond the living area could serve fifty sit-down guests or several hundred for smorgasbords. Imported crystal chandeliers hung in abundance in each room, and a palatial area hosted dancing or private concerts. Throughout the mansion hung museum-quality oil paintings, and ornate statuary were abundant.

To the left of the foyer lay the study, two stories high. The bookcases were on three sides from floor to ceiling and full of thousands of fine quality leather-bound original copies of the English- and Spanish-speaking worlds' best books. The fourth side was reserved for portraits of ancestors in carved, gold-leafed frames. It was considered to be the most complete private library in the entire country, if not in all of Latin America. Two full-time professional librarians supervised the collection and additions to it.

The immense fireplace in the study, large enough for a tall man to stand in without stooping, was framed in carved, imported Italian marble. Two heroic-sized statues of ancient Roman deities supported the wide mantelpiece. The furniture was massive and master-crafted. Most of the artifacts were fine antiques imported from European castles.

Don Hugo and Dame Helen had personal desks of matching mahogany brought from the West Indies and placed side by side. Each had their personal files for their work, research, correspondence, and personal matters, as well as a personal secretary to take care of their multiple interests. The staff was instructed that no one was to enter the study when Hugo or Helen were there except at their call, and it was off limits any time they were at home.

Relaxing in their study, the couple was discussing Hugo's latest trip. He had just returned from a sweeping tour of family interests in the southern part of Argentina, the Patagonia. Although Helen had long ago mastered Spanish, Hugo always spoke to her in her native English.

"*Querida*, you really should see Bariloche and the lakes this year!" he insisted. "The wildflowers are out in colorful profusion. The lakes are crystal clear and deep blue right to the edge of the forests coming down from the snow-covered peaks above. The Andes have never been more spectacular. I'm sorry you couldn't go this time. I really missed you."

He was very concerned about his wife's health. She had not been doing well lately and the doctors had not yet found the source of the problem.

"And I missed you, *mi amor*," she said, reaching over to squeeze his hand. "You know that I love the southern Andes—the beauty of the year-round snow on their peaks and the blue lakes and whitewater rivers always give me such joy. But tell me, how are the sheep? How are my little lambs?"

She loved the huge herds of sheep, and she worried about the yearly crop of lambs. Some lost their mothers to predators or illnesses, and she felt keenly responsible for their care whenever she could travel to the sheep camps.

"The sheep produced a good crop of lambs, and last spring's shearing has given us a record wool clip," Hugo responded. "Good quality, too—should bring a fine price in London. We'll have several shiploads to export after we take out what we need for our own mills. The pastures look like they will carry the flocks well throughout the year. Just enough rain in the valleys and sufficient snow up in the mountains."

Helen listened carefully. She was interested in all the operations of their various companies and kept herself up to date on their conditions. She loved Bariloche, a beautiful town on the edge of Nahuel Huapi, a glacial lake that sat at the foot of the Andes Mountains. The area reminded her of villages in the Swiss Alps. She also oversaw the upkeep of their several residences in Patagonia, and was very attentive to the needs of the staff who worked for them and their families.

"Hugo, how are the workers getting along?" Helen asked. "Do we have the remodeled schools and the additional hospital beds for them that we promised?"

Don Hugo took a report from his desk and brought it back to where they were seated by the fireplace. It was summer south of the equator, so no fire was needed, but the study's cozy environment made it one of their favorite places to talk.

"Here is the report on the schools and the hospitals," he said, handing it to her. "Richard prepared it. He is doing a good job looking after the social welfare of our people. The doctors have finished all the vaccinations and the dentists have checked all the children this year. Is there anything else I could tell you, my dear?"

Helen laid the papers aside without looking at them, knowing they were well prepared. She would get to them later, but right now she had other questions.

"Mi amor, how about the lodge at Bariloche? Did the flower beds get planted early enough and are the fruit trees looking good? I must get down there for the fruit harvest—I love picking the cherries in the orchard and the berries from the bushes. There is no place in all of Argentina that has such great fruit! The peaches and apples will come

on later, but I like the early fruit the best. And what about the lighting plant? Did they get the new diesel installed?"

Hugo was very proud of his wife. She had remained beautiful and feminine through the years and was always very interested in everything about the sheep and cattle ranches, the sugar operations, the businesses, and especially the people. She added her feminine touch to their many homes. It was also typical of her acute mind that she would remember such things as the fruit and the lighting plant.

"*Querida*, the lambs are all taken care of, the diesel generating plant is in and working, but it makes more noise than we thought it would, so we are moving it farther away from the main house. In fact, we used it this year to run new electric clippers in the shearing sheds instead of the old belt-driven mechanical clippers. We will leave the plant out there and just run long lines over to the house. And yes, the fruit will be abundant this year, according to old Jaime, our horticulturist. He is hoping you will come down and put up some bottled fruit like you did three years ago."

Hugo enjoyed visiting their various operations. He felt that it was the duty of the family members to travel frequently, not only to be familiar with the people and the operations but also because of an old Argentine saying, "The eye of the owner fattens the cattle." He knew that just having himself and his wife visit the places kept all the caretakers and supervisors on their toes trying to please them. She was always generous in her praise of everyone and that made them work even harder. He knew he didn't have to be a genius to be a manager, but he did have to go out and look around regularly to be able to make proper decisions and provide guidance and motivation to all the men.

Helen's favorite place of all was the Llao-Llao lodge at Bariloche. It was a huge German-type hunting lodge of varnished logs, high vaulted ceilings, and enormous rock fireplaces. It was the center of their sheep and wool operations and their other business interests in the southern part of the country.

In addition to the lodge at the foot of the Andes, they had a city home in the heartland plains of Córdoba, some eight hundred air miles to the north (over a thousand by surface), which was the focal point of their business interests in the heavy manufacturing sector: tractors and farm equipment, cars and trucks, and diesel engines for locomotives and river boats.

Another four hundred miles farther north from Córdoba, they had the sugar plantations, sugar mills, and another beautiful home.

For vacations they had their choice of homes at resorts in Brazil, Uruguay, and Chile, as well as in Europe. Some members of the family and their children were always traveling and using these various properties. Helen had the family assignment of looking after the maintenance and upkeep of all these residences.

Argentina is a relatively long and narrow country. If placed in the northern hemisphere across the United States, it would stretch from Cuba in the tropics north to the middle of Hudson Bay, with tropical climates similar to Central America in its extreme north, moderate climates like Oklahoma or Texas in the middle, and frigid climates like Canada in its extreme south. Consequently, the members of the extended family could vacation and do business at their own places according to the climate and scenery they wanted. There was even a secretary who scheduled the comings and goings of the family to all these homes.

Don Hugo knew that his wife's interest in Bariloche would only last a moment, and then she would lapse back into her personal and private worries and concerns. Helen had become very introverted. She had not been her usual self these last three years, and he knew the reason. He decided it was best to address the matter now rather than just talk about his trip.

"I know how you are suffering, my dear," he said, holding her hand. "On this trip down south I thought about Fernando every day while I was there. That was the last trip we made together—the three of us."

Just the mention of her beloved son caused tears to well up in Helen's eyes.

"I am sorry that I am such miserable company," she said. "I thought I was listening to the report of your trip, but I guess when my mind wanders, it always shows, doesn't it? I too was remembering that last trip, but you need me to be happy and excited and responsive, and all

I can do is feel depressed and so sad. I get so tired of just sitting here at home, but I don't feel like traveling and the doctors can't seem to help me get over this pain."

She had been suffering from internal pain for some time now, but the specialists had no diagnosis and no solution. At times the pain would become almost unbearable, but it would usually ease up after a while.

Hugo realized that, despite Helen's apparent interest in his trip, she probably had not paid much attention to what he was saying until he mentioned Fernando.

"Remember when he caught that big fish?" Hugo asked, trying to get her to smile. "A twenty-pound trout! And then he flew with me in the plane out to the sheep stations where we did some good, hard horse-back riding and spent a few nights under the stars with the gauchos. Do you remember he went back later alone with the plane to do that veterinary medicine study on our sheep? And when we came back through Bahia Blanca, he played polo with some of the men. They still ask about him a lot."

Instead of making Helen smile, the memories put her in a melancholy mood.

"What do you tell them, Hugo?" she asked. "I have been looking at the pictures we took of that trip—I have almost worn them thin. I keep wondering where Fernando is now—how he's doing. How long has it been since that last letter arrived?"

"Five months and two weeks," Hugo said. "The last one came from Wyoming in the western part of the United States. Perhaps he is on a ranch there or at least working with horses he loves so much. Maybe we will get another letter soon."

"He was such a dear boy," Helen said forlornly. "No matter where he was around the world, he always remembered our birthdays and anniversary. Now he doesn't ask anything about us. He just lets us know that he is alive and well and that we should not be concerned about him. At least he is thoughtful enough to do that."

She returned to the theme Hugo knew well and from which he

suffered deeply. Every time his wife brought it up it was like turning a knife inside him, cutting him clear to the core again. Maybe he deserved it, so he let her punish him over and over again.

"Hugo, Fernando must be suffering, too," she said, her voice breaking. "Isn't there something we can do that we haven't thought of to find him? It isn't like our son to leave us out of his life so totally. Couldn't we have done something differently?"

He sensed that, in reality, she was really saying, "Couldn't *you* have done something differently?" He knew she believed it was all his fault—that he had overreacted and had done more harm than good. He was certain that he had not been wrong to treat Fernando so sternly, and his mind went back over that situation for the millionth time. He was always so sure about his decisions, including this one.

Hugo sat in his leather chair in silence with his head bowed, his face between his hands. Their conversations on the subject always came to this point, both of them retreating into their memories—replaying those times over and over. Hugo remembered what an outstanding and talented son they had reared. Fernando was athletically gifted and well-coordinated in a way only one-in-a-million athletes are. Everything is easy for them, and it was that way for Fernando. They are stronger and bigger than their peers or siblings. They seem blessed with phenomenal hand-eye coordination and lightning-fast reflexes that make them superior in games and contests. They have an instinct for winning, and, for them, training is not a burden—it is part of their competitive spirit. But despite all his talents and privilege, Fernando had made serious mistakes and tarnished the family name.

With all these advantages, how could this boy have let us down so terribly? How could he have embarrassed us so much? he thought sadly.

Fernando had inherited qualities from his forefathers centuries before him: some had been part of King Arthur's Knights of the Round Table, some had cast the Moors out of Spain, some had erected stone castles in Bavaria. But Fernando's greatest love had not been passed down by his ancestors, but rather from his father. From the time he was a little boy, Fernando and his father had spent hours and hours together on horseback practicing different polo shots on the best horses in the world, raised on their own ranches.

At the same time that Hugo was reflecting on Fernando's horsemanship, Helen was remembering what an outstanding student their son had been. He could get the highest grades in the class anytime he tried to—which was not all that often, she had to admit. His problem was that his mind was so fast that teachers had to challenge him with extra work. Long before his classmates were ready, Fernando would shoot ahead into the advanced concepts of mathematics or science. His parents provided private tutors to develop his talents, but even with that, he had time left over to take flying lessons from an excellent German instructor who had come to Argentina following World War I.

The instructor had flown with the Red Baron himself, Manfred von Richthofen, and Fernando had progressed under his tutelage to commercial and instructor pilot licenses in multi-engine aircraft. Because of his knack for engines, he received permission to take the official Rolls Royce course required of the top mechanics at the dealership in Buenos Aires, which the family owned.

But when Fernando left for Cambridge to study aeronautical engineering, that's when the trouble started. After he was expelled for breaking serious rules, Hugo and Helen sent him to La Sorbonne in Paris. Fernando did get top grades the first year, but before the end of the second year he was expelled again. In frustration, his parents decided to send him to Harvard. After a few months without incident, Fernando's weaknesses for women, gambling, and alcohol surfaced again, and this time a tragedy occurred, leading to his being expelled once again under the cloud of a police investigation.

Perhaps the pressure was too much, thought Hugo. *He knew everyone expected him to take my place someday, but first he needed sterling grades and a university degree.*

Hugo was a doctor of laws, but other past leaders of the family had been men of letters, distinguished authors or university professors, or men of science. The leader of the family needed to establish his intellectual ability, intelligence, and competence in order to unify the family behind him. In addition, the future leader needed to show his dependability and character through advanced study, marrying well, and settling down to learn how to run all the many family interests with skill and profitability. The family leader needed to do what was best for the whole family, not just for himself. This was not unlike the preparation of members of royal families who were in line of succession for the crown.

In his thoughts, Don Hugo continued going back over the life of Fernando—reexamining his own relationship with his son.

He had the brilliance, skill, and personality to win the family's support. Why had he fallen to such a disappointing disgrace? With so much going for him, why would he turn to drinking and gambling? Fernando had no need for gambling to get money. He was naturally happy, so he didn't need the benefit of stimulants. No one in my own family had these weaknesses.

Don Hugo did not know the answers and maybe no one would ever figure it all out. But in his mind he was convinced that he had not overreacted from disappointment at Fernando's third major failure. He had been deeply depressed and distraught when the news hit Buenos Aires. It was in the American papers as well as all over Argentina. The headlines regarding the tragedy were burned into his mind:

"WEALTHY LATIN JAILED"

"HEIR INVOLVED IN DRUNKEN SCANDAL"

"GAMBLING AND ALCOHOL TRAGEDY"

Hugo was humiliated that the family's reputation, and even Argentina's, had been stained and besmirched by his own son. The punishment must be as drastic as the crime, he had determined angrily, so he had sent a curt cable soon after receiving the news. The message was still clear in his mind:

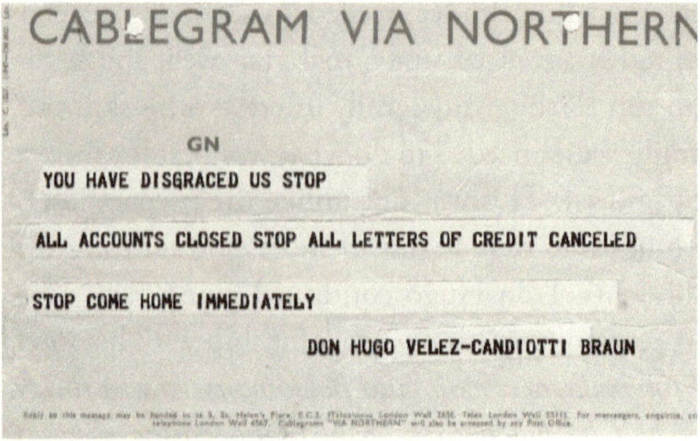
CABLEGRAM VIA NORTHERN

GN

YOU HAVE DISGRACED US STOP

ALL ACCOUNTS CLOSED STOP ALL LETTERS OF CREDIT CANCELED

STOP COME HOME IMMEDIATELY

DON HUGO VELEZ-CANDIOTTI BRAUN

He had not even signed it "your father."

Three years ago when Fernando received that cable, he assumed that the full use of the formal name without any familial softening meant that his father was disinheriting him, that he was being dropped from the line of possible succession to his father's position, and that his father no longer claimed him as his son. It was a family discipline—a means of censoring unacceptable behavior and conduct. Fernando interpreted "come home immediately" as "don't ever come home."

Disappearing with only part of his extensive wardrobe, Fernando had left no trace as to his route or his whereabouts. The only evidence that he was alive were the semi-annual letters. Although Fernando started each letter with "Dear Parents," Hugo knew they were actually directed to Helen. Hugo believed that Fernando instinctively knew that his mother was suffering, and that without letters from him she would have a mental breakdown. He also assumed that Fernando was hurting, but felt that the boy deserved to suffer. Hugo had wanted to punish his son for not living up to his expectations and dreams. He had once loved his only son but was no longer certain of that emotional devotion. Hugo did not want to forgive Fernando as Helen did. He was still a Latin man with a German mother, full of stubborn pride, determined to be strong-willed and unwavering as his parents had been with him.

During this meditation and reflection, the silence between these two suffering parents had drawn longer and darker until now it seemed like a thick, cold wall between them. Each was withdrawn into their own worlds, thinking of the past and of what might have been, what could have been, what should have been. Each was on opposite sides of the cause and the solution to the dilemma.

"Helen," he said, breaking the long silence, "before I left for Patagonia, I received a message from the British ambassador that he had heard a rumor that Fernando had been located in California. He asked what they should do if it proved to be him. I told the ambassador to visit with you. Have you talked to him?"

"Yes, but I didn't think the rumor was any different from all the other false leads we paid for," she responded sadly.

"Mi amor, I want to find Fernando," he said. "I don't think the family is ready to accept him back yet and maybe I'm not either, but I need to find him for *you.* Can you understand what I am trying to say?"

This last importuning was an effort to break through her silence. Helen felt that the only way to soften her husband's heart was to forgive him. She knew she could not challenge him or blame him; the only solution was to love him. She embraced her husband, and he held her tightly.

"Hugo, my dear, of course I forgive you," she said softly, pulling back to look at him. "I know that Fernando forgives you too. I am so sorry that I have been blaming you, because I too am at fault. I didn't know how to handle his obvious weaknesses. I should never have insinuated that it was your fault. I just wanted him back so much. We will pray and work until we find him and bring him home honorably. What the rest of the family thinks is of little importance right now. We will find him, I'm sure of that!"

Helen brushed away her tears and they embraced again, this time long and tenderly.

"Hugo, why don't you check with the ambassador about this latest report?" she asked. "Who knows, maybe this time it might turn out to be something."

Hugo agreed, and the couple strolled arm in arm out to the terrace overlooking the river. The day was balmy and beautiful—the kind of day that had given the city its name, Buenos Aires ("good breezes"), by the first Spanish sailors who had brought their ship into these waters. River boats and an occasional yacht sailed up and down the waterway in their view. Little puffy, white clouds formed above the wide river, a panorama any French painter would have loved to reproduce.

After a leisurely breakfast, they returned to the book-lined study to make the phone call. Hugo dialed the ambassador, whom he knew reasonably well, and after going through the telephone operator, the office secretary, and finally the private secretary, he eventually heard the ambassador's booming bass voice on the line.

"Don Hugo, what a pleasure!" the British dignitary exclaimed. "I have been expecting your call. You did get my second message that I urgently needed to see you personally, did you not?"

"Why no, Mr. Ambassador, I didn't," Hugo said, surprised. "I just returned from my trip to the Patagonia late last night. How long ago did you call?"

"Oh, it was only two days ago," the ambassador responded. "I could have called your wife again, but the last time I spoke to her it seemed she had little faith in these rumors. But now it seems it is more than just a rumor, so I felt it best to speak to you alone first. We have a confirmed report—rather a long report in fact—from London regarding your son. I think you ought to come by. It is a bit lengthy to discuss on the telephone. When could you come? Or should I bring it to your office?"

"I'll be downtown in about thirty minutes," Hugo said. "Is that a good time?"

The ambassador agreed, and Hugo hung up the telephone, not knowing whether to be excited or fearful. Helen looked at him expectantly, wanting to know what the ambassador had said.

"Well, he said he has a long report on Fernando," Hugo said cautiously. "He didn't give any details but he said it was not a rumor. Our son may be in worse trouble, or he might be all right."

Hugo paused, searching for a good way to express his fears. Right now, he felt that he wanted to share with her any good news by taking her with him, but what if the report contained something negative about Fernando? He decided to be totally candid with her.

"My lovely Helen, it is up to you to decide if you want to go with me or let me spare you in case it is bad news. What do you want to do?"

Even though the last three years had weakened her resolve considerably, Helen was a woman of character. She responded without any hesitation.

"Give me a moment to change and I will go with you," she said.

Hugo nodded, smiled lovingly at her, and gave her a kiss on the cheek.

Hugo and Helen were escorted to the top floor of the British embassy in downtown Buenos Aires, where they were ushered into the ambassador's oak-paneled office. He stood and came around his massive mahogany desk to greet them.

"Don Hugo, Dame Helen. So good to see you again."

He greeted them with a Continental-style embrace, touching cheeks, smacking soft kisses into the air.

"Please do sit down. Make yourselves comfortable. Will you have a spot of tea?"

Protocol would have called for small talk and *mate*, an Argentine tea, but Hugo was impatient, anxious to get to the purpose of their visit.

"Thanks, but not now," he said. "What news do you have of Fernando?

Understanding their concern and their hopes, the ambassador came right to the point.

"We feel that we have good news," he said with a smile. "The identification seems most positive. Fernando is in Southern California attending a prestigious private university there. He is soon to graduate with honors in aeronautical engineering. He is registered under your maiden name, Helen—Fernando Underwood. That would not have been hard to do since his passport, according to our records, is made out in good Argentine style, Fernando Hugo Velez-Candiotti Underwood, mother's maiden name last. Is that correct?"

They nodded in agreement, their hearts pounding with the good news.

"Our informants tell us he is working his way through school on a polo scholarship," the ambassador continued. "He is the team captain and he also teaches classes in polo. That covers his tuition, and he earns spending money and living expenses by managing the university stables and the staff there. Everyone speaks very highly of him. He has a marvelous reputation. The report says that his conduct is exemplary."

He picked up a large packet of papers and handed it to Hugo.

"Here is the written report. The only people involved in this private matter are our staff in London and the Earl of Wittingham, our new consul in California. You may remember him. He played polo about the same time you did. He was with the cavalry and also with Hurlingham Polo Club."

"Yes, I certainly do!" Hugo replied.

"There is also one other person there in California, a British actor, Sir Douglas Barrington," the ambassador continued. "He is now famous in Hollywood pictures, but at home he is one of our best Shakespearean actors. This Sir Douglas also played polo with members of the royal family, so he knows polo talent when he sees it. He and the consul saw Fernando play polo and declared he is playing at a ten-goal handicap level. Chip off the old block, eh, Hugo?"

Hugo smiled at the compliment.

"Anyone else involved at all?" he asked.

"Well, yes," the Ambassador admitted. "I hope you do not mind. We touched base with some of Helen's family for positive identification, but we have told the few we spoke with that this is a very private matter and is to be held in the closest of confidence. Our staff can be trusted, and Sir Douglas and the consul are also completely discreet. We did not know exactly what you wanted us to do. What are your instructions?"

"May we sit here alone for a few minutes to work this out between us?" Hugo said after a moment of thought. "Do you have another office we can retire to?"

The ambassador was on his feet immediately.

"No need to move," he said. "I have other things to do in the outer office. You will not be disturbed. We understand that you need discretion, and we are ready to cooperate to the fullest extent."

It was obvious that the ambassador was sincere and open. He was aware of Fernando's past problems and no one wanted to complicate the situation unnecessarily with such an influential family. Some parents might want to rush to their lost child, and others would prefer to wait until the prodigal son returned home, humbled and penitent, seeking nothing but to be a servant in his father's house.

The dignified diplomat stepped out of his office and closed the door, leaving the couple alone. It was a mark of sensitivity that they appreciated. Seldom would a top diplomat leave his office to anyone not of the royal family, but Hugo and Helen were as close to being a royal family as Argentina had, and Helen was part of British aristocracy. Hugo was especially touched by the older gentleman's diplomacy and his thoughtful gesture.

"Oh, Hugo, what an answer to our prayers!" Helen exclaimed, tears of joy in her eyes. "But there are so many unanswered questions. If he is playing good polo he must be healthy. And if he is graduating with honors that must mean that he is studying well, concentrating, and staying up with his class. But where has he been? What else has he been doing all this time? How did he get those letters to us from so many different places? Should we go to him or should we cable him? Hugo, what should we do?"

It was characteristic of Helen to scatter thoughts and questions like rockets shot into the air. Also, it was evident she had forgiven Fernando.

Hugo, on the other hand, was deliberate and cautious. He was not about to forgive Fernando nor could he forget. His position was rigid. He sorrowed for his wife, but it would take a long time to forgive the embarrassment Fernando had caused.

After a few moments, he spoke.

"I would like to find out from someone about Fernando's attitude toward us before we contact him. I would also like the university to cooperate with us a little. He could not be that close to graduation unless someone helped him get his transcripts and list of courses from other universities. He seems to be doing great without our money or communication. Maybe he needed to be on his own. Maybe the drinking and gambling was a reaction against our pressuring him to measure up to the expectations we set. We need some help on this before we jump in prematurely, perhaps doing more harm than good—"

"Hugo, you are right, but please go to California and observe him without him knowing you are there," Helen interjected. "That way you can find all these answers. I don't think I can travel. This is wonderful news, but I am still suffering from maladies that I fear are deeper and not at all related to this emotional stress. Fernando may need funds and in his pride he would not let anyone know. He may need encouragement to return to the family and to come back to Argentina. Maybe he doesn't know that the police exonerated him or that we know it was his roommate who was driving Fernando's car."

Don Hugo had to admit that his wife seemed too fragile to take the long ocean voyage, but someone from the family should go to California between now and the time Fernando was to graduate. They would decide what to do after that. In the meantime, no contact should be made, nor should anyone divulge that his parents now knew his whereabouts.

The logical person to travel now would be Hugo himself, but he was reluctant to take that voyage. They continued to discuss the pros and cons—what should be done, how to do it, and the implications. There were the other members of the family to consider. Should they be told, or should it be kept secret until Hugo could find out all the details? They opened the packet of papers to see if any answers to their questions could be found there.

They found the clue they were looking for. A regent by the name of

Dr. Rheinhart seemed to appear from time to time in the material. He played polo, had horses, and had high-level contacts at the university, but he had not told anyone about Fernando's true identity. Perhaps he was the confidante that Fernando needed; perhaps it was he who assisted Fernando to stay so invisible for over three years.

"You must go, my dear," Helen said, knowing that her husband needed a little push. "Only you can find the answers to our questions."

Hugo wished that she could accompany him. He did not like to make long trips alone. She had always traveled with him to Europe, either for business or pleasure. When he had important matters with Swiss banks, he always included some skiing there. She had accompanied him when he had to go to England to talk to the people who bought their frozen and canned meat and who brokered their shiploads of wool and other export products. They would visit with her relatives, attend the opera and plays, hunt with hounds, and go to the horse races. They usually spent three months abroad each year, but this time he would go alone to the West Coast of the United States. He had not been there in many years.

"Helen, I agree that I must go," he acknowledged. "I think I know how to handle this. If I calculate correctly, graduation is only a few weeks away. That would give me time to get to New York, do some business there, and take a train to Los Angeles. I have been to California only once before, but maybe the ambassador can have his consul there make the arrangements. I will need some bank connections and letters of credit in my name."

Hugo's mind was now functioning and marking off the details that needed to be taken care of before the trip. He and Helen stood up and embraced, and he saw a new light and enthusiasm in her eyes that he had not seen in many long months. She had really needed this good news.

The ambassador rejoined them and assured them that he would pass the messages on to London and from there to California. No one would contact Fernando or disclose that his secret had been found out. He would also arrange for Hugo to have the full use of all British consulate facilities and connections in California, since Argentina had no offices there.

Exiting the front entrance of the marbled embassy building, their chauffeured Rolls Royce limousine pulled up, having been signaled by the doorman. In silence, in the back seat of the big limo, they passed by flower-filled plazas with giant, heroic-size marble statues shooting long arcs of water sprays into the fountain pools. Flocks of semi-tame pigeons strutted the plaza pathways or rested on the statues. Well-dressed Argentines bustled by on their routine business affairs, unaware of the tense and tender drama going on inside the two passengers of the imposing limo.

CHAPTER 8

A WARNING FOR DON HUGO

TO FERNANDO AND MAGGIE, the flowering of their romance was totally exhilarating, although each was carefully avoiding out-of-control infatuation. They had been spurned in the past by others and each had hurt the feelings of someone else at some time. Young love makes many mistakes. Independently, they had vowed not to let such a situation happen again. They had begun seeing each other more and more frequently, at least as time and circumstances would allow.

They enjoyed strolling hand in hand along the paths between campus buildings, oblivious to the students rushing to or from classes. Spring was in the air and little attention was paid to the tall, attractive couple. Their interest was focused on each other, except when an occasional acquaintance greeted them.

As they entered a vine-covered old classroom building on the engineering side of campus, Maggie asked, "Fernando, am I really making any progress with polo? I am so discouraged! You make it look so easy, but I am just not connecting. It embarrasses me to think I'm your worst student. Is there any real hope for me?"

Maggie had never been so frustrated with anything in her life. She thought she had great horses and she had always been told that she was an outstanding horsewoman and a well-coordinated athlete, but today she just felt like giving up. She had attended Fernando's polo classes twice a week for over a month and she still could not master the fundamentals.

"Your only problem is that you are a perfectionist and too hard on yourself," Fernando told her. "Please don't get discouraged—you're progressing just fine. In fact, your slow-trot dribbling of the ball is coming along great. You are confused because you haven't had time to train your eye-hand-ball skill at a gallop speed yet. They are different and each takes more time to develop. But you will get there soon enough. You can't hurry it up at all, so just relax and practice. You'll make it. I promise."

They took seats next to each other just before the professor began his lecture on aircraft fuels and lubricants. He covered the latest discoveries regarding additives that could reduce "detonation" (pre-ignition or knocking) at maximum power settings. This affected airplanes on climb-out after takeoff or at full-throttle-to-the-firewall settings as in air racing. Both students were vitally interested in everything that would affect the performance and long-term reliability of an engine, especially in a race.

Maggie was increasingly obsessed with the hope of finding two planes and one or two sponsors so she could compete in the pylon race and especially in the coming cross-country air race. It was more than just a girlish dream or a youthful goal. Flying in the air races against the men was a longtime passion—even a compulsion—of hers since she first soloed a plane. Perhaps it went further back than that—maybe her competitive spirit developed by trying to keep up with her brother. In any case, the fixation was even more important to her than romance or Fernando or anything else.

Maggie had been influenced by a well-known aviatrix of the flying sorority. Mary Jane Carver, known affectionately to all her friends simply as "MJ" was an accomplished pilot, having accompanied her husband on flying adventures to many parts of the Americas, from Alaska all the way down to southern Argentina. She and her husband, Sam, didn't have children, so they flew, took pictures never seen by ordinary land-bound folks, wrote about their adventures, and were dedicated to furthering the science of aviation. They were able to travel so much because MJ had inherited money from her grandparents, and Sam had made his fortune in mining ventures all over the Western Hemisphere.

Two years ago, before Maggie met MJ, tragedy struck. Sam had been killed in a flying accident in the Andes. The Carvers had financed a new plane to participate in the pylon races, and MJ knew that Sam would have wanted her to fly it in the race. It was lightning-fast, highly maneuverable, and had new streamlining and engineering features. MJ was looking forward to the women being able to race again and hoped that she and the plane would do well, in honor of her husband. She had encouraged Maggie to try both pylon racing and long-distance racing.

That subject made Maggie's thoughts turn to an exchange with Luke Wilson a month before.

One day before a flying lesson, Luke had overheard Maggie and MJ whispering about something as though it were a military secret. They were discussing the new plane that MJ's friend Amy would race cross-country. It was all metal, twin engines, and big enough to have a very special feature.

"What's the feature?" Luke asked them.

"Oh, none of your business, Luke," MJ said playfully.

"Aw, c'mon, ladies," he said. "We're all in this together. Has Amy found a way to increase the power of the engines or reduce the induced drag to give her plane better speed or more endurance?"

MJ and Maggie looked at each other and started giggling.

"You guessed it, Luke," MJ said, trying to keep a straight face. "She found a way to really increase the endurance and long-range ability of her plane!"

The two friends kept laughing, and Luke could not understand what was so funny about a technical matter.

Finally, the girls confessed.

"Amy has a plane big enough to have what all female pilots want most," MJ said in a whisper. "She has an auto pilot installed and a toilet in the rear. She can leave the controls unattended for a few minutes, take care of her personal needs, and get back to her pilot's seat. It really increases the distance she can fly without landing."

Luke had laughed and agreed it was a secret worth keeping.

Maggie's attention returned to the lecture in time to catch the last part about the higher-octane rating. On their way out of the classroom, Maggie suddenly grabbed Fernando's arm and stopped.

"Do you realize what a higher-octane rating would mean in a long-distance race at full power?" she exclaimed. "Not just a few laps around a closed course, but all day long at full power—ten to twelve hours with every inch of manifold pressure the whole way. What a beating that engine would have to take—unless the fuel could be improved to stop the knocking!"

He nodded and smiled at her enthusiasm. She confused him a little. When he wanted to talk romance, she wanted to talk polo or air racing. She flitted between the interests of their lives like a hummingbird seeking nectar, going from flower to flower. Fernando, on the other hand, was more and more smitten with her, to the exclusion of all else.

"Maggie, why don't we take the horses down by the river this evening instead of having a polo lesson?" he said. "Bring your mallet but no balls. We'll just trot along and swing at leaves or clods. That will help you develop an automatic perception of exactly where the ground is at all times. Besides, I think we need a change of scenery. Okay?"

She smiled appreciatively, accepting the invitation, remembering how much she loved the bridle paths down by the river. But she switched subjects again, to his disappointment and consternation.

"Fernando, I am really worried about finding a sponsor who will provide me with both a good pylon race plane and a cross-country racer. Do you think it's an impossible dream?"

Fernando wondered if their romance would actually survive her air-racing obsessions. He was actually a little jealous of her love affair with air racing, but he was more worried about her competitive determination to beat the men in the air. Men had initially prohibited women from racing, and she took it as a personal affront.

Thousands of miles away, Don Hugo was flying north in the company airplane. He sat immediately behind his two corporate pilots, who were holding the plane at a level of seven thousand feet between loosely separated, fair-weather cumulus clouds.

The plane was a small, twin-engine British de Havilland biplane—a wooden-ribbed, wooden-spar wing with a welded tube steel fuselage. The whole structure was covered with cloth, and the wings were tied together with steel wires crisscrossing like bridge reinforcing. The twin engines were inverted, with in-line cylinders, and very efficient for that time. It had conventional landing gear with a tail wheel.

In addition to the two company pilots in the cockpit, there was space for five passengers in the cabin. The plane was not large or fast but was very dependable—it could make reasonably long cross-country trips in good weather. However, it carried only basic instruments and very short-range radio transmitter and receiver.

Hugo had not been able to depart for the United States as soon as he would have liked because of business and Helen's failing health. The business problems were related to union agitation over salaries, working conditions, and benefits. There seemed to be growing labor unrest, agitated by Marxist communists and European socialists infiltrating the ranks of the laborers of the meat-packing plants on the coast, at the tractor and farm implement factory in the middle of the country, and the sugar plantations and mills in the north. There was increasing discontent and higher demands. The government seemed powerless to keep order, and the union agitators were destroying morale and productivity.

At the same time that employee relations were disintegrating, inter-family relationships were also coming unraveled. Profits were down so dividends had been cut. Some family members were in favor of private, armed, bully troops to force pro-union workers out of their jobs and to hunt down the clandestine union organizers. Other family members felt that appeasement and compromise were best, but they were afraid this would cut profits further.

Part of the family was challenging Hugo's ability to coordinate all the various interests, noting that for the last three years he seemed far too much occupied with Helen's health and the "Fernando disgrace," as some called it. They felt that these distractions had led to his neglecting the business.

Hugo's brother, Roberto, was competent enough to take over for a few months, but Hugo did not even try to explain the hidden reason for his sudden trip. He feared that Roberto might try to take over in his absence if he knew that Fernando could be back in the scene again as Hugo's possible replacement.

Also, Roberto was in favor of breaking up the family holdings into several autonomous companies, each under a different family member, rather than continuing with Hugo as the chief executive officer for the entire family. This was a direct challenge to Hugo's leadership. Roberto felt that the conglomerate, though somewhat hidden behind various corporate walls, was so large that it could become a target for government expropriation or even international attention and intervention. Hugo, however, was afraid that some economies of scale might be lost, and that control would be sacrificed and the tradition of a united family would perish.

Will matters get out of control during my absence? Hugo wondered. *Should I have told Roberto about finding Fernando, that he was cleared by the police after his roommate confessed to everything, that Fernando is now graduating from a leading prestige university with no help from anyone?*

He resented having to make this trip at this particular time. It was all Fernando's fault. The boy deserved to be punished, not coddled. Not one of his letters had shown remorse or repentance.

Hugo had much on his mind as they flew over the flat, fertile land below them. They flew across pastoral Uruguay to a seaport on the southern coast of Brazil, where Hugo would take passage on a company freighter that had left Buenos Aires one week earlier.

As it was too noisy to talk, the pilot passed a written note back to his boss.

"We have crossed over Uruguay and are one and a half hours from landing at Porto Alegre, Brazil," the note read. "The last weather report is holding up. We expect to land on time. Any instructions?"

Hugo read the note, looked at the clear blue sky above, the green, rolling fields below, and around them the continued separation between puffy, white, non-threatening clouds at their altitude. He nodded his head and motioned with the flat of his hand held in the vertical toward the nose of the plane, saying in effect, "Continue course straight ahead."

He scribbled two short words on the bottom of the same paper, "Fuel supply?" The pilot checked his gauges again and wrote, "Two hours fuel at least plus one hour in the reserve tank. ETA one hour. Good tailwind."

Hugo smiled, leaned his head back on the headrest, closed his eyes, and returned to his thoughts. He had decided to let their flagship freighter leave the Buenos Aires port on schedule since he could catch up with it by plane. This allowed him an additional week in Buenos Aires because the freighter had to stop in Montevideo, Uruguay, and again in Porto Alegre, Brazil, for cargo. He was glad he had been able to spend the extra week at Helen's side.

His last visit with Roberto, his brother, had been pleasant despite their disagreement on future handling of the overall conglomerate strategy, and his brother had promised to make no major decisions without contacting Hugo on the ship's radio. Nevertheless, Roberto was not always predictable, so Hugo's concern persisted. They would stay in touch by ship-to-shore radio. It would be by Morse code, plus they had a few code words of their own to cover such things as financial transactions, union matters, and family names.

The shadows of the trees down by the river were long, and the breezes wafted the perfumes of spring flowers through the air. There were no other riders using the long, winding trail. Fernando and Maggie were riding her matched palominos, using English riding saddles. Wearing white polo riding breeches and bright blue polo shirts, they swung their polo mallets, or "tacos," as Fernando called the long-handled club.

Fernando had Maggie swinging at leaves, twigs, papers, clods, and anything else that would move. He wanted her to gauge her own height and the varying distance of the horse above the ground and swing the mallet head so it just brushed the dirt, lifting the target leaf or clod without digging into the dirt or missing it completely. He congratulated her when she lifted a pebble, knocking it twenty feet ahead of them without so much as raising any dust.

"Now that is precision, Maggie!" he exclaimed, beaming at her.

They spoke of horses, flying, polo, exams, their fast-approaching graduation, and the air races. Occasionally, Fernando would interrupt with some instructions, encouraging and coaching her as they rode along.

"Straighten your elbow—let the swing be a constant radius arc—shorten your back swing to half stroke for now—there you have it—a little harder than that—just right—perfect form—good."

At a secluded spot on the trail overlooking a place where the stream widened, a place concealed by the heavy vegetation around, they dismounted and hitched their horses to a tree limb. Maggie let Fernando take care of both horses while she went to the edge of the lookout spot to enjoy the view below. She stood with her back to him, quietly pensive. *This is so peaceful,* she thought, *but how long can it last?*

Fernando finished loosening the cinches and attending to the horses. He sneaked up behind Maggie and wrapped his arms around her waist, hopeful that she would accept the affectionate embrace. She not only welcomed it but leaned her head back on his shoulder for a moment, looking straight ahead. Then she turned her face toward his, slowly rubbed her nose against his cheek from side to side, and smacked a playful kiss on his cheek.

Fernando turned Maggie toward him and lifted her off the ground with a tight hug before setting her back down gently. He kissed her fully. His Latin passion was evident yet very much under control. Maggie responded with warmth and contentment that delighted them both. But only for a moment.

Again, she confused poor Fernando by pushing him away. She began talking about race planes again.

"Luke thinks one of the airplane manufacturers might lend me a factory demonstrator for the long race and pay the expenses," she said. "It's a new, small-cabin plane that is quite fast and has long-range tanks. It's a fabric-covered biplane but very aerodynamic, and is surprisingly fast even though it carries a big engine. Do you think it could be souped up with more power? I don't have to win, but I don't want to come in last and be laughed at, either."

Fernando was disappointed that the romantic mood had been interrupted so abruptly.

"Sure," he answered flatly. "Most planes can handle a bigger engine, or a supercharger, or cut a few feet off the end of each wing to reduce parasite drag, but you have to calculate the pros and cons of each modification. What factory is it?"

Fernando turned and walked toward the horses wondering, *Will there ever be room for me in that beautiful mind and tender heart of hers? Am I going to have to compete with an airplane for her love forever or just until this race thing is over?*

Roy looked at the drawings Oscar had brought him. He was impressed.

"This looks like a modern race plane, but it's just a bit fat behind the engine, don't ya think?" Roy asked.

"Yes, but remember we want four people in the cabin, two side by side in front, and two right behind, side by side," Oscar explained. "The businessmen need four places, or at least one for the pilot and three for the wheeler-dealers. You're thinking our usual one person in the front cockpit and one person behind."

He tapped his finger on Roy's head.

"Ya gotta think *modern* cabin," he said. "Now here are the figures on the load and the speed. But we do have a problem with the wings. They're too long, and they're not braced well enough. Any ideas?"

They went over the drawings and figures and discussed options and changes. They started with a low-wing monoplane but the landing gear didn't fit into the original low wing, so they had to make adjustments. The wing was too weak for high-speed stress in tight turns so it had to be strengthened. They needed extra space for larger fuel tanks. Each problem had various possible solutions, each with advantages and disadvantages, compromises and trade-offs.

Roy, the businessman, had his point of view, and Oscar, the engineer, had his slide rule and tables for calculations. They worked things backward and forward. No one remembered who suggested it—maybe both came up with it simultaneously—but they decided to go back to the biplane arrangement they were most familiar with.

"Yeah," Oscar said, nodding vigorously. "Give it two wings, one over and one under the cabin. That way the wings can be shorter and more efficiently braced with guy wires and struts."

In a biplane, the traditional placement is for the top wing to be forward, and the bottom wing staggered behind toward the tail. Oscar, however, noted that with the landing gear retracting into the lower wing, that weight moved the center of gravity too much to the rear. He would have to move the bottom wing forward to just behind the engine and right under the pilot's place in the cabin. He played with that a bit and then, penciling, he took the top wing and slid it back to where it rested right over the cabin. The reversed position of the two wings gave the drawings and the working model an appealing staggered appearance. It looked more streamlined than the traditional configuration.

Oscar also figured out that he could cause the lower wing to stall later than the top wing, giving better safety and control when stalling the plane intentionally at the point of landing. He made another engineering modification he had long wanted to try. He tapered the fuselage behind the cabin down to a wasp-like waist at the empennage where the rudder and elevator surfaces begin. The effect was innovative and spectacular.

"We need a name," Oscar said. "How about Staggerwing?"

"That's it!" Roy responded happily.

He was ecstatic with the resulting looks as well as the better-than-expected performance figures Oscar calculated. The plane would be fast, carry an excellent fuel load, carry two people in front and two or even three in back, fly in and out of short runways, and could be sold at an attractive price. Being responsible for marketing the new plane, he was concerned about how to make the biggest impact on the slow sales market with no money for a wide advertising campaign.

Enter Luke Whitney, the famous air-race pilot. Word was out in the flying community, and among the air-race pilots especially, that Luke had a female pilot who wanted to fly in the coming cross-country air race. He could vouch for her flying ability, but she needed a sponsor who could provide both the race plane and foot the bill for expenses. He also suggested that if any manufacturer had a demonstrator that they would like to use for some free publicity, they would surely get it with this woman as the pilot, because she was already in the news with a movie stunt now on the silver screen.

Roy and Oscar could see the benefits from this opportunity. Regardless of where the plane placed in the race, they would get free advertising, free exposure, and wide recognition that their executive-cabin plane was safe enough and easy enough that a lovely woman could fly it across the country.

The public would quickly appreciate that the cabin of this plane would be comfortable enough for a woman. The pilot would dress in an attractive, feminine outfit ready for any photo op. She would not have to wear a bulky flying suit with a fur collar and boots or need helmet and goggles. Her hair would be as well coiffed at the end of the race as at the beginning.

When Roy and Oscar saw Maggie's movie stunt and the studio's still pictures of her, they were doubly impressed—they had found their pilot!

Hugo was standing beside the captain on the bridge of his biggest ocean-going freighter, enjoying the smell of the sea. They were just entering the spectacular Rio de Janeiro harbor, one of the most dramatic harbor entrances in the world with Sugar Loaf Mountain rising abruptly from the sparkling azure sea. Behind it and inside the harbor was the famous Botafogo Yacht Club full of world-class yachts.

Hugo remembered the days when nineteen-year-old Fernando had captained their ocean-going racing yacht from Buenos Aires to Rio, nonstop, to win the coveted South American Cup race. Fernando was the youngest captain ever to win—the youngest to even enter. Just thinking about his son at that stage in his life with so much hope and promise ahead brought tears to his eyes. As the ship passed the yacht club, he looked up at the majestic Corcovado mountain crowned with the world's largest statue of Christ. He forced his thoughts back to the present and to his wayward son whom he was to meet for the first time in three years.

Hugo calculated that after discharging cargo and taking on new cargo they would be about twelve days from New York. He was booked into the Waldorf Astoria for a week to take care of export financing for their wool to Europe, their canned corned beef to England, their sugar to the United States, and import financing for various plant expansion projects where they would be bringing new equipment from Germany, France, and the United States.

Normally London banks would do this kind of financing for them, but with the effects of the Great Depression, Hugo had looked around and found better interest rates in New York. Now was a perfect time to finalize some business deals.

The seas had been calm off the southern Brazilian coast, but the news from California had not been so peaceful. A few hours before arriving at the Rio harbor, the radio operator had brought him a sealed envelope—the sealing being only symbolic, since the radio man had carefully copied each letter of each word as the Morse code signals came in over his earphones.

"Don Hugo," he had announced, "this just arrived for you from your New York offices."

Hugo opened the envelope, glancing to see who it was from. He realized it actually came from California but was relayed through the New York office.

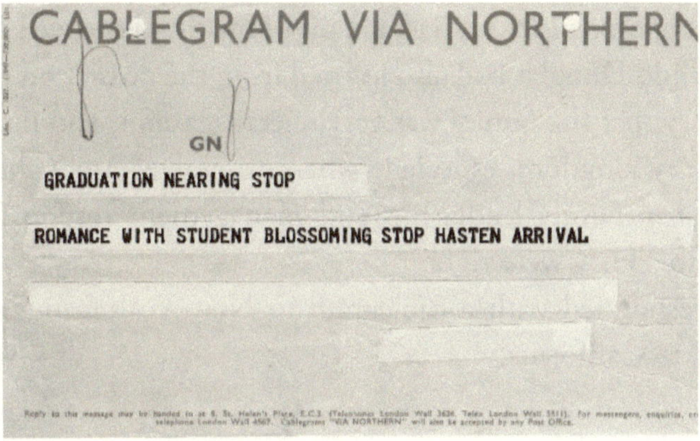
CABLEGRAM VIA NORTHERN

GN

GRADUATION NEARING STOP

ROMANCE WITH STUDENT BLOSSOMING STOP HASTEN ARRIVAL

Don Hugo could not know of the effort Charles and Douglas had made to work out the careful wording of the cable. They knew it was not their business to pry into this delicate family matter, but they also knew that Hugo had no other source besides themselves, and having initiated the whole thing they felt a sense of responsibility to help bring matters to the best possible conclusion. They had become aware that the relationship between Maggie and Fernando had grown like a brush fire, escalating far beyond what either of them had been led to expect from Fernando's virtual celibacy over the last three years. Neither knew

Maggie at all, but word went around the stables and through certain high circles at the university of this blossoming romantic interest between the mystery polo player and the movie stunt-cowgirl.

Charles and Douglas had never said anything before now to the British home office nor did they feel free to contact the Velez-Candiotti-Braun-Underwood families directly. But after they received Hugo's schedule and realized that he might want to know about the romance, they obtained permission to send the radio message to him over the ship radio using the veiled term "candidate." They had hoped that Hugo would arrive early enough to take care of matters himself, but now that he was arriving later and the romance was developing faster, they decided to give him some foreknowledge. They hoped he would guess that they were concerned about the tradition where graduating couples, very much in love, had a habit of making June wedding plans.

Charles and Douglas had also learned from the dossier on the Argentine dynasty that the family was very selective about who married into their wealthy kingdom, especially when it involved a possible heir apparent to top family leadership and management responsibilities in their empire. They were right.

Hugo responded with a cablegram to New York, requesting it be forwarded to California.

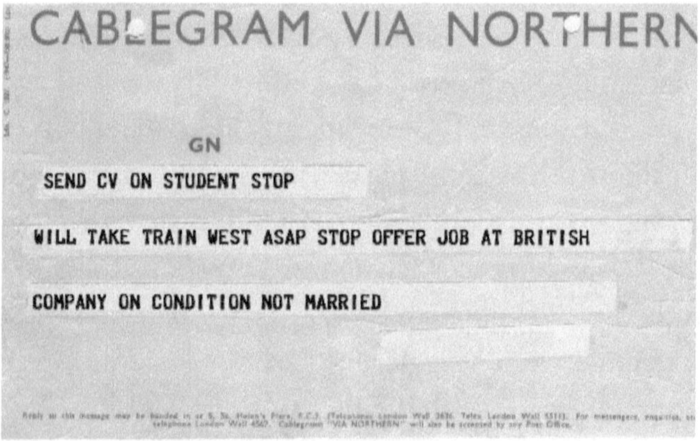
CABLEGRAM VIA NORTHERN

GN

SEND CV ON STUDENT STOP

WILL TAKE TRAIN WEST ASAP STOP OFFER JOB AT BRITISH

COMPANY ON CONDITION NOT MARRIED

While in Rio de Janeiro waiting for the ship to discharge and load cargo, Hugo visited the Brazil offices of his new international bankers from New York, hoping to take care of most of the business arrangements. With the new threat looming, he would cut his visit to New York short and take the first and fastest way west.

His ship cleared the busy, world-famous harbor with a sundown sailing. Hugo stood on the extension of the bridge just outside the command position in the balmy ocean breeze, watching the pink-colored evening clouds drifting above the city. Copacabana Beach streetlights and apartment lights twinkled, casting intricate shadows on the patterned tile sidewalks along the beach. He wished his beloved wife could be with him to enjoy the romance of this great city, now disappearing astern as they headed north.

Hugo had just settled down to enjoy his evening dinner with the captain and first officer when the radio man brought another bombshell message. It was from his brother, Roberto, back in Buenos Aires. After just a glance at the sealed envelope's contents he excused himself without touching his meal and retired to his private quarters. The news was not good at all. Hugo studied the text, his brow furrowing deeper and deeper.

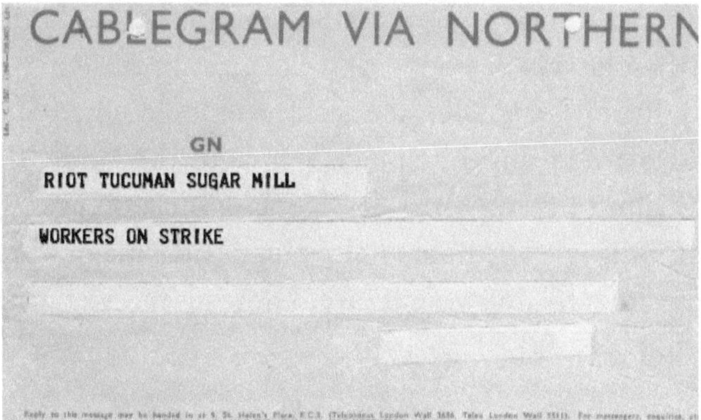
CABLEGRAM VIA NORTHERN

GN

RIOT TUCUMAN SUGAR MILL

WORKERS ON STRIKE

Hugo stared at the sea out the porthole of his suite and marveled that the sea could be so smooth while there was so much turbulence back home and in California. It became even more imperative that he break up a romance he didn't know anything about because Fernando might be their best hope in a major labor showdown in Argentina. Fernando had a special relationship with the workers throughout the entire family enterprises. They all loved the lad. Ever since he was a boy he had accompanied his father around to all the plants. He'd been quick to make friends, he'd played soccer with the workers' boys, and he had a gift for remembering names. But if he made a poor choice of a wife who would not fit into the family, they would never give him a chance to become a leader in family business affairs.

As a teenager, Fernando had worked the dirtiest jobs. He'd worked alongside the slaughterhouse butchers, the sugar plantations cane cutters, and the factory mechanics. He had ridden with gauchos on both cattle and sheep ranches. He'd been called "the Prince of the Gauchos" with great endearment even by those restless union agitators who looked down on the rest of the aristocracy. Fernando and his mother had long led the movement inside the family to improve conditions for workers and their families, and that too was known by the workers. On the other hand, Roberto's oldest son had spent most of his time in the city and had not become involved with the nuts, bolts, and people of the family interests.

Fernando's advantage and future usefulness in family leadership had been lost when he was dishonored in the press because of his conduct in England, Europe, and later, the accident in the United States. Now, if Fernando married someone unacceptable to the family they would never allow him to come back into family leadership even if his connections with the laborers might help. Hugo had a major burden trying to figure out how to stop young love, knowing full well that it might already be too late.

CHAPTER 9

CONFESSIONS

MAGGIE HAD INVITED Fernando to a Western rodeo weeks before, and now the perfect opportunity had come. To celebrate his twenty-eighth birthday, she bought him a pair of cowboy pants, Levi's, a leather belt with a Mexican silver buckle, a plaid shirt, and Western high-heeled boots to wear for the occasion. The gift was a source of embarrassment to him because he didn't have any way to reciprocate in kind. No girl he had ever known had given him a personal article of clothing. Nevertheless, he accepted the new wardrobe and wore them to the rodeo.

After arriving at the fairground and seeing everyone else dressed in similar gear, he felt somewhat more at home in his new duds, even though it was obvious that his outfit had never seen dirt or sweat. The high-heeled cowboy boots took a little getting used to. It was like trying to ice skate when you have only used roller skates. He wobbled a little at first but soon found his balance.

Fernando had ridden with the gauchos working cattle on the pampa, and he doubted there was much about cattle, sheep, and horses that he did not know. But Fernando had never tried bull riding Western style, and that event impressed him. Argentina had almost exclusively British breeds of cattle—Hereford, Angus, and Shorthorn. Fernando had heard of the huge Brahmas but had never seen them in a rodeo where they actually tried to maim their unwelcome riders.

The roping events were also fascinating to Fernando because of the very different approach as compared to Argentina. The gauchos did not "bulldog," jumping from horse to the steer and wrestling it to the ground. The roping of calves or steers was also very different.

"This is very interesting, Maggie," he said. "We train our roping horses to turn around when the cowboy dismounts and to pull away from the downed steer; you train yours to back up after the cowboy dismounts to keep the rope tight."

Maggie was astounded at the difference.

"Why in the world would you do that?" she inquired in surprise.

"Well, our way makes more sense," he responded good-naturedly. "Here, you anchor the rope to the horn of the saddle, which is up high on the shoulder of the horse, and make the horse back up. If the steer gets up on its feet again and is fast enough to run at an angle to the pony, a big steer could pull the pony over. We anchor the lariat down low to a ring in the rear cinch of the saddle, and have the horse pull away, which gives the horse much more traction and the steer less leverage."

With good humor they exchanged opposing points of view through all the events, remarking on how interesting it is that other cultures find different ways to get the same job done.

"We say 'there is more than one way to skin a cat,'" said Maggie.

"Hmm," Fernando responded. "We don't have a good translation for that in Spanish."

Finally, the last events of the rodeo came with the wild bronco riding, both bareback and with saddles. This is the most dramatic of rodeo events with a good share of the cowboys getting dumped, sometimes resulting in broken bones or worse. No one likes to see anyone get hurt, but the cowboys were testing their skills against the horses and competition can sometimes be vicious. The winners received good purses much prized in the Depression years when most cowboys had a hard time making ends meet.

"Do you break broncos in Argentina the same way we do, or do you have a different way to do that, too?" Maggie asked Fernando.

"The gauchos used to tame wild horses that way because it is faster," he responded, "but we did away with that practice on all our ranches at least fifty years ago."

"But how in the world do you break a horse for riding to show him who's boss?" Maggie asked him. "I can't see any other way than just jumping on and having it out with him. He throws you and you try again until you win and he gives in."

"Well, most of our horses are thoroughbreds and very valuable," Fernando explained. "We can't afford to run the risk of injuring an expensive animal in a fall. But more important is the concept that we do not want to break our animals' spirits. For polo, for the racetrack, or even just for ranch work or breeding, we value the courage, the boldness, and the spirit of our horses. We don't want to diminish any of their natural personality, which we have tried to breed into them."

"But how do you get them to obey you?" Maggie asked.

"They become obedient and well trained—*manso*, we call it—not through fear of the rider, but rather due to trust and confidence in the rider," Fernando said. "We train with love and tenderness precisely to nurture the independent spirit of the animal. Doing it that way makes them far easier to train, quicker to learn, and they love the game of polo or the challenge of the race, working harder to win for us. We never try to break the spirit of our horses."

Maggie had never heard a man talk so tenderly about his horses, and she was impressed—again—with Fernando's understanding and perspective. It made sense and it did seem more civilized than spurring or whipping a horse into submission. In fact, she and her dad had worked very gently with her palominos almost from the day they were born. They were never wild and never resisted the saddle or the rider.

Suddenly Maggie recalled that Fernando had just referred to their "ranches" plural and spoke as though he grew up with a lot of property and herds of horses. *When would he open up with the whole story of his life?* she wondered. She felt close to him but there was a great, dark secret area of his life into which he would not yet let her enter. She felt that the time was growing near, however, when he would have to tell her more or she would lose her trust in him. She didn't want to wait forever.

On their way out of the rodeo arena and into the parking lot a strange, awkward incident happened. Maggie had needed some subtle way to push or encourage Fernando into opening up with her and indicate what he was thinking concerning their future together. As if in answer to her unspoken request for help, an old acquaintance called out to her from across the crowd.

"Maggie!" he called. "Maggie! Wait up a jiff, will ya?"

Hurrying toward them came a lanky, suntanned cowboy who could have been from a Levi's commercial. He looked the part of a successful, young, professional cowboy, which he was. Tall and thin in a tough, wiry way with an infectious grin, he threw his arms around Maggie and gave her a big smack on the lips. His Western hat was tipped irreverently back on his curly head, he had a self-assured swagger, and his voice was low and mellow with a distinct Western drawl.

"Honey, I've had a hankerin' to see ya for a long time now. Where ya been hidin' out?" He ignored Fernando standing beside her as if he didn't even exist.

Maggie felt it best to not let that go on, so she interceded.

"Fernando, this is an old friend of mine, Curly Jackson," she said. "We used to do rodeos together, and he's one of the best on the circuit. He's the one I pointed out to you. He won the bull-riding and the bronc-busting events, remember?"

She continued without waiting for any response, hoping they would shake hands as gentlemen and not adversaries, even though she felt Fernando bristle when Curly kissed her impetuously.

Embarrassed and still blushing at his impulsive display of affection, Maggie stammered.

"Curly, this is Fernando Underwood. We're students together at the university."

Curly was a bit quicker than Fernando in courteously extending his hand.

"Well, Fernando, you're in the company of a great lady," he said with a huge smile. "I've been in love with her all my life, and as soon as I get some money I'm gonna propose to her again. Just have to give ya fair warnin'—all's fair in love and war, they say!"

Curly turned back to Maggie.

"Hey, seriously, where have ya been? And where's your brother, Scott? I haven't seen him around here neither. Don't ya do the rodeos anymore?"

Maggie really liked Curly; besides, it suited her just fine to have Fernando feel a little competition right now.

"Scott broke his hip and leg real bad in an accident sometime ago," she explained, "so he's back home and we dropped out of the circuit. I decided to go to school to finish my degree, and in the meantime I do a little stunt riding for the movies to earn some extra money. He's still recuperating, but he got married to his nurse there, so I don't think we'll ever get back to rodeo. How's it goin' with y'all?"

Maggie was unaware that she was slipping into a cowboy-type drawl, but it was something that Fernando noticed—perhaps because she was back in a familiar environment and with an old friend. Feeling more and more uncomfortable, Fernando said not a word.

Maggie and Curly visited a bit longer and then Curly, noticing the brand-new pants, boots, and shirt Fernando was wearing, leaned down to whisper in her ear.

"Where'd ya get the drugstore cowboy, honey? Aren't ya runnin' with us real cowboys anymore?"

Maggie desperately hoped Fernando didn't understand the insult, but decided she better put a stop to Curly's teasing, which was getting just a little out of hand. They had dated for a while, and he had asked her to marry him once. Curly did have a lot of good qualities, but he just wasn't the type she was looking for. He had no interest in an education, only in following rodeos. She liked him, but she could not let him insult Fernando, so she felt she should set the record straight.

"Curly, would you please watch your lip!" she said, frowning. "Fernando can hold his own with any of you on any horse any day! He's got a bigger outfit than you have ever seen."

She was guessing and exaggerating, but she thought she could get away with it.

Curly got the message and backed away quickly.

"Hey, okay, okay," he said, holding up his hands. "Just wanted to make sure ya wasn't lettin' us down. Ya know we are all in love with ya—especially me. It's been great to see ya again. Tell Scott hello and hope he gets back in the saddle real quick-like. Well, bye. Hey, it's good ta meet ya, big guy."

Maggie shook her head at his audacity. She apologized to Fernando for Curly's rudeness. He just shrugged his shoulders, gave a half smile, and wondered a bit about what the former relationship was with this cowboy. He realized that there was a lot about Maggie that he didn't know and had not dared ask because he himself was not ready to reveal his own past life and family.

"Curly did propose to me, but I broke it off," she explained. "All he wanted was for me to be a stay-at-home wife, barefoot, poor, and pregnant. I wanted a lot more out of life and out of a husband."

Don Hugo, again on the bridge of the *Star of the Patagonia*, had just looked at the charts showing they were a short way off the coast of New Jersey, just hours from docking at their pier in the New York harbor. The trip had been smooth all the way, but the messages certainly had not been. The company news had him worried and perhaps that aggravated his feelings and caused him to be more worried or concerned about Fernando and the possibility of a serious romance with the unknown girl than it should have.

The word from the consul in California was not bad, but it was not reassuring, either. He had read and reread the latest cablegram from the Earl of Wittingham, trying to read between the lines.

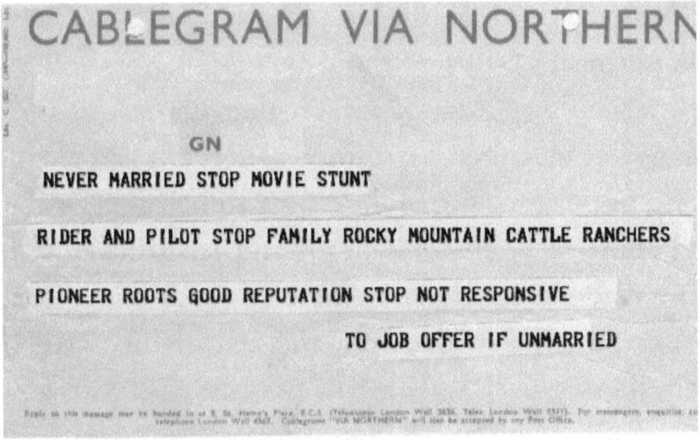
CABLEGRAM VIA NORTHERN

GN

NEVER MARRIED STOP MOVIE STUNT
RIDER AND PILOT STOP FAMILY ROCKY MOUNTAIN CATTLE RANCHERS
PIONEER ROOTS GOOD REPUTATION STOP NOT RESPONSIVE
TO JOB OFFER IF UNMARRIED

Don Hugo knew the Depression had hit U.S. cattle ranchers rather hard, and that the Western mountain ranchers were worse off than the Texas outfits. He also felt that there was no particular disgrace to have parents with financial problems not of the girl's doing.

The rest of the message indicated that the girl was intelligent, probably had ambitions, her reputation seemed to be intact since nothing negative was mentioned, but he could just see his family cringe at "rodeo stunt rider" and "part-time movie stuntrider." That would not add to her image at all. It was taken for granted that the family expected Fernando to marry a European princess of some royal family or a daughter of the Rockefeller or Ford fortunes.

There were also other serious problems that troubled Hugo. What if Fernando actually married this girl? Then what would they do? Could she possibly fit into the family? Hugo's thoughts swirled around in his head like a tornado. He had to set some priorities, or else he would just muddle about in confusion.

He shifted his focus toward Helen, his beloved wife. She was ailing mysteriously. Was it related to the tragedy of being alienated from their only son, or was it a serious physical illness? She had not been able to have other children, and perhaps that disappointment had affected her health.

As if a light turned on, everything became clearer to him. His first priority had to be to convince Fernando to return to Buenos Aires to see his mother—for her sake. Helen's health, both physically and emotionally, would never return without being able to see her son. If, or whom, he married was secondary. Whether the rest of the family accepted him or not was also of less importance. He had to find a way to get Fernando back home for enough time to be able to straighten him out, pound some sense into his head, and let him know how much damage he had done to his mother's emotional and physical health. Having re-confirmed that decision, the rest of his problems seemed easier to handle.

Maggie and Fernando drove into the polo stables with the convertible top down, even though the evening was cool. Fernando was driving with one hand, his right arm around Maggie's shoulders to keep her warm. He felt an uncommon stirring deep within him. Some kind of premortal instinct was encouraging him to override his natural cautions. Never before had he entered into this new and risky territory of true love.

He had come to realize that more than anything else in this world he wanted a permanent relationship with Maggie and he wanted to take care of her every need for the rest of her life. He could not tolerate the thought that after graduation he might lose this beautiful angel. She might go off to work somewhere, or she might run into another old friend like Curly. She might even fall in love with some pilot, or Luke himself. Luke was a bit older, but it was very obvious that he had a crush on Maggie. She might even go back home to her parents, who might try to keep her from an unknown like himself.

He was aware that she already had a steady job offer from the movie company, and he himself had that strange offer from some British company—only if he were unmarried.

Fernando felt that he did not have enough financial stability to be a suitable candidate for marriage, but he realized as they were driving home that he had better propose now or run the risk of losing this exceptional woman. He knew they were getting close to declaring their love for each other. But he also knew that he would have to tell her his whole story and, by the same token, he wanted to know more about her. This was his point of no return. He had to commit himself and accept whatever her reaction would be.

When they arrived at the stable complex, Fernando turned the machine off, and for a few moments they sat silently in the little convertible without speaking, their fingers intertwined. The soft glow of the lights under the arches of the office and stable complex gave only dim light to the area around them. It was late and all the stablehands were in bed; no one was in sight. A horse whinnied and was answered by another in the distance. Fernando wanted to be direct but sensitive; above all he wanted her to give him the answer he wished so much to hear.

"Maggie," Fernando said, looking down at her head on his shoulder, stroking her hair, "I think you know how I feel about you. Your coming into my life has caused me to change all my plans for the future. There is a lot of my life that I haven't told you, but I am convinced that now, tonight, I must tell you all you want to know. Before I do, though, I need to know how you feel about me. I can't risk going any further without receiving some positive indication from you."

Maggie sensed that this was the moment she had desired, but now she was frightened somewhat about the sudden risks and changes ahead. One thing she did know was her own heart. Never in her life had she felt such admiration and respect for a man. Here was a soulmate and true protector, just as she had always dreamed. She knew she wanted to make a home with Fernando and have children with him, and she had all the traditional hopes and aspirations of a young bride. She admitted to herself that she was in love, yet she still had some lingering doubts because there was a lot that Fernando had not told her.

It thrilled her to sense where Fernando was going, but there were things she needed to know before she made any permanent commitments. She thought of her family and their concerns about an unknown South American; she thought of Luke and his plans for her; and above all, she thought of her own longtime goal to fly in the big air races against the male pilots.

"My darling Fernando," she said tenderly, "I do love you. But as you have said, there are many things we need to talk about."

With that declaration, she quickly put the ball back in his court. Fernando was relieved and delighted.

"I love you and want to marry you," he said, embracing her. "I want you to know that I greatly appreciate your allowing me to wait until now to reveal everything about myself. Now let me tell you about my background. My family lives in Argentina, as you know. I am the only child of Hugo Velez-Candiotti Braun, Argentine-born of Spanish and German families. My mother, Helen Underwood, is British. The families would be considered well off. I was to have been the heir, but I made some serious mistakes. I don't know why—maybe just to prove my independence in a strange sort of way. I was young and foolish, and fell into bad habits and bad company. I was arrogant and selfish and egotistical. I thought of no one but myself. I began drinking and gambling. I made some wrong choices and was thrown out of school three times—in England, France, and New England."

He was silent for a minute, but Maggie didn't rush him. She could tell this was a lot for him to share.

"On the East Coast, there was an accident involving my car," he finally continued. "A girl was killed in the accident. I still don't know who was driving the car—my roommate or another classmate who had been drinking, but it was not me. The news hit the papers here and in Argentina. They printed that I was a drunken playboy of the most worthless kind. My father and my family—uncles and aunts and cousins with major stockholder positions in the family's companies—all decided I had brought too much dishonor on the family name. My father sent me a strong message about canceling all funds and ordering me home. I knew that I was being disinherited. The university expelled me."

Fernando paused to gather his thoughts. Maggie squeezed his hand and gave him a tender peck on the cheek. Somehow she had suspected some of this, but it was comforting to hear it directly from him.

Continuing with his confession, his voice was soft and repentant.

"I gathered a few of my clothes and left in the middle of the night. I had only the money in my wallet. I hitchhiked west with only a desire to get lost and perhaps reach California. I had no plans, no goals, just an awareness of how much I had thrown away. I rode a freight train a few hundred miles until I was discovered and thrown off. I hitchhiked and made it as far as Iowa, I believe it was. I had not eaten for days and I offered to work for food at a nice-looking farm. Luck was with me. The farmer had injured his back and couldn't work, and his wife was desperate. They had no money, but I was happy to work for just a bit of food. They let me stay there a few months until the husband improved. I was able to fix some things that even Mr. Gunther did not know how to repair—there was an old truck I was able to get running again, and I made one good tractor out of two that were out of commission. They talked me into getting back into school some way and proving that I could make a success of myself without outside help."

He paused again. He had wanted to share his story with Maggie for a long time, and it seemed like it was all rushing out.

"So I came out West a few miles at a time, working for food and rides," he said, wrapping up the story. "I ended up here and applied for a job as a stablehand. They took me on for board and room only—no money. Eventually, Dr. Rheinhart found me and offered the scholarship. You know the rest. Once I have that diploma in my hands, and once I have a job that will allow me to make a living, I want to go back to Argentina to see my parents and try to heal the wounds I caused. I don't know if I will be accepted, but I want to go back for just a short visit to see my parents, and to tell them that I love them—and then I'll return here to marry you, if you will have me."

Maggie had been afraid for a moment that his whole objective was to return to Argentina, seven thousand miles away, and remain there. She feared that he was more interested in justifying himself to his family than in marrying her. But he had made it sound like the need to go home was only for a brief visit, and that was a great relief to her.

Fernando had given a relatively short summary to a long and tragic history. He knew he had left out quite a bit.

"Maggie, do you have any questions you want to ask me?" he asked gently, preparing for the worst.

"Fernando, I believe you and I believe *in* you," she said, squeezing his hand. "You are good through and through. I have come to know that you are a man of good character. You are intelligent, and I'm sure that you will always make enough to support a family. Sure, I have a lot of questions. Do you want children? Do you want a home here in California? Will you settle down and provide the security I long for? I was really tired of the rodeo circuit traveling all over the West from one town to another. I love it here now and I love flying and the movie stunt work, but I know that raising a family isn't quite compatible with stunt work and air races. After these two races, I will be ready to settle down to my first priority of being a good wife and mother."

Fernando sensed she had more to say, so he remained silent.

"My faith and regular church worship are important to me and my family," Maggie continued, "and I believe parents should teach their children spiritual values and good manners. I feel the mother needs to be in the home, if possible, and it is best if the parents are of the same religion. And to me, the father, like my own father, needs to be the principal provider and the main spiritual leader of the family. Nevertheless, my parents are coequal in everything."

Maggie felt she had come on a bit strong about her own family values, so she turned the conversation back to Fernando.

"But tell me about your goals—what are they now that you are graduating?"

Her emotions and these questions had all been bottled up since they had met, and now they were spilling out one on top of another. She wanted answers so badly and all at once.

Fernando, like most men, had not been thinking about children and building a family and settling down. He just wanted to marry this woman and be with her forever. Just in these few minutes, though, he had discovered that women are oriented a bit differently than men, and that Maggie was certainly a lot different from all the other women he had ever known. He now realized that he had to offer security and stability to this woman he was in love with, as well as spiritual strength and leadership. This was new to him.

"I have always thought of myself living in Argentina and running part or all of the family businesses," he admitted. "Home was always going to be Argentina. But I have cut myself off from all that. Now my goals are your goals. I would like to be an aircraft engineer designing and flying fast airplanes, but I would also like to have a place where we can have a string of polo ponies with space to run them and practice and train them. And yes, I like the idea of a house full of children! I was not raised with siblings, but I have some uncles with eight to ten children and they seem to have a wonderful life. Religion has been strong in my mother's family but not so much in my father's. You know, perhaps we could have our own aircraft manufacturing company or our own air taxi company like Luke. I also like business and management. I will just look for the best opportunity and work like mad to earn enough to support you in the manner that you deserve."

Maggie was pleased with his response, and now she could feel more secure. However, her next question was full of uncertainty.

"How will your parents look at me?" she asked, her brow furrowed. "Do you think they will accept me? Tell me about your mother and father. What are they like?"

For the next hour or so, Fernando talked about the qualities of his parents, and also his father's negative attributes. He was honest with her. He did not exaggerate anything, but he never disclosed to her the extent of the family fortune. He acted as though the family business and interests were modest. No need to get her interested in what he had lost.

Far past midnight, they finally moved on to Maggie's family. She explained how they were a pioneer family who had been among the first settlers of southern Utah in the canyon and cattle country—beautiful Grand Canyon, Zion Canyon, and Bryce Canyon with brilliantly colored sandstone bluffs and acres of land to run cattle in. She talked about her parents, and she spoke of her grandparents and great-grandparents as though they were all still alive.

Fernando sensed that she had a love for past generations and their accomplishments and the heritage they had given her. She described their home, their ranch, her older brother, and the younger children of her family. She talked about Kanab and the scenic country where Hollywood directors had filmed movies on part of their ranch. She described to him the sights that were different from anything in Argentina.

Fernando wanted to visit her family and her homeland to see for himself where she was born and raised.

Suddenly Maggie remembered her passion for flying.

"Fernando, let's not even think of marriage until after the race," she pleaded. "Okay?"

She looked deep into his eyes in a way that was sobering, and he saw something in her demeanor that he didn't understand, but he nodded his head reluctantly, giving in. He wondered if her hesitation to talk about a more serious relationship was related to anticipation for the races and the possibility of accidents, disablement, or even death.

They shared a tender embrace, kissed briefly, and reluctantly said goodnight. Fernando walked to his quarters above the polo office and Maggie drove home to her apartment—both oblivious to the world about them.

In his room a nagging question bothered Fernando: *Could he handle her?* This magnificent woman he loved would never be happy with him if he tried to dictate what she could or could not do. She was like the thoroughbred racehorses they raised, born to run, not to be a brood mare or a plodding work horse. She could not be broken with harshness because that would break her spirit. He would have to handle her with persuasion, patience, tenderness, and pure love. Even though flying could be dangerous, he had to support her or she would bolt and run just like any frisky thoroughbred mare.

CHAPTER 10

PLOTTING BEHIND THE SCENES

DOUGLAS HAD FERNANDO on his mind while he sat waiting at a table reserved for him in a remote corner of an upscale restaurant. It was his favorite place to meet friends without being bothered by fans or other studio personnel. He had picked up the morning newspaper and it now lay open in front of him on the table. He appeared to be scanning it, but the truth was that he was not even reading it. It was a ruse to keep passersby from interrupting him to shake hands.

He knew a major showdown was imminent in Fernando's life and he worried about whether it was going to be good or bad for the sharp young polo player. Originally, Douglas had felt it might be a great idea to bring to light that one of the world's best polo players was hiding incognito at the local university. But since he and Jock had traced

Fernando's background, his thinking had taken a turn. Douglas had come to genuinely like and admire Fernando, especially since last week when they had sailed together out to Catalina Island and back on the actor's new sailboat—an international-class racing yacht.

The distinguished-looking British consul entered the dim interior of the posh restaurant. Knowing he was a little late, he waived the maître d' aside and strode directly to the familiar table in the back corner. Sure enough, Douglas was there, appearing to be absorbed in the newspaper.

"Good afternoon, old boy!" Jock's jovial greeting startled Douglas for an instant.

Douglas looked up, scowling at first, then, seeing it was Jock, smiled.

"G'day to ye, me lad," he said in a Scottish accent. "Just sit yerself down—I'm a-holdin' it fer ye. Got our usual drinks a-comin'. How've ye been?"

The old friends enjoyed lapsing in and out of different accents from various parts of London and the entire British Isles. They accurately mimicked the well-known idioms, idiosyncrasies, and expressions they were so familiar with from their homeland.

"What's in the paper this morning that interests you, Douglas?" Charles asked. "The headlines, the business news, the social gossip, or the movie news praising you?"

He was well aware of his friend's trick of pretending he was reading the paper to keep people away, but he still wondered if Douglas actually read any of the sheet spread out before him.

"Matter of fact," Douglas replied, "I couldn't tell you a thing of what's in this paper. You know me—just act like I'm scanning it, letting my thoughts drift off into me own private world . . ."

"Well, if you're not reading, where are your thoughts? You looked deep into something, I dare say!"

Charles had been right. He was pleased he could read his fine friend so well. Douglas hesitated a moment and decided to share his thoughts.

"I was just thinking about Fernando and wondering if things will be all right with him when his anonymity is suddenly stripped away and his true identity is disclosed," he said, looking concerned. "I sure hope he won't be hurt by all this. In my opinion, I think the family is doing the right thing by not interrupting at all until after the actual graduation takes place. You know, I have really taken a liking to him—especially since our cruise out to Catalina Island last week."

"Oh! I meant to ask you about that," Charles said. "How did it go?"

"Oh, we had a marvelous time!" Douglas responded. "He watched the crew sailing that new boat and making a frightful number of technical mistakes until the true sailor in him just could stand it no longer. He asked if he might help 'a bit.' That was an understatement! Since I was aware that he knew much more than I did, I asked him to take over for a while. In a jiffy he had a better set of sails up and the crew working together better than the captain could have."

Charles shook his head in amazement.

"Were any other yachts out?" he asked.

"Yes indeed!" Douglas said. "Another boat came by and challenged us to a race to a nearby channel buoy and back. Fernando asked if I wanted some fun so I agreed to it. We were running just a little ahead to the buoy, but when we did our turnaround, the other boat switched sails to a giant spinnaker for the run downwind. Fernando asked me if we had a spinnaker sail and pole down below in the sail compartment. I didn't even know, so quick as a flash he had me take the wheel while he went under deck to look. He found the spinnaker and the pole to set it in place. Then he taught the crew how to do a fast takedown of the Genoa jib and raise the balloon spinnaker while the captain kept the course straight. Soon we had the biggest full sail you have ever seen! We gained on the other boat and finally won the race!"

Charles was smiling widely, enjoying the enthusiastic and animated narrative.

"Do you remember the original dossier on Fernando from England and Argentina?" he asked. "It said that he had captained his family's offshore racing sailboat from Buenos Aires to Rio. If Fernando could sail that race as captain while still in his teens, in the challenging conditions of the Atlantic Ocean, I imagine he can sail anything!"

Charles was impressed with young Fernando, and also with what they had learned about the rest of the famous family. Now it was his turn to share some new information.

"Douglas, I received word from the London office today that all our plans for the graduation have been approved by the family in England and in Argentina," Charles reported. "They insist that Fernando not meet his father until after he receives his diploma. Strangely, they did not confirm that Don Hugo agrees. They may have checked with him—and they should have—but he is at sea and they may not have included him. In any case, that is their problem. We are committed. If things go well, they will get credit for great diplomacy and for healing a deep family wound. If things go poorly, we of course will get all the blame. Are you ready for the curtain to go up on our little conspiracy?"

"I'm as ready as we can get," Douglas responded. "No problem as far as I can see. Have I told you of the studio's new plans for me that involve both Fernando and his girl?"

"No! Tell me." Charles was eager for news

"This new film is about a cross-country air race," Douglas said. "A lot of planes and both male and female pilots. I am to be a race pilot—with a Yank accent to boot! There will be a romance between me and a female pilot and the excitement of crashes, fires, engine failures, getting lost in storms, the whole works! They've really pulled out all the stops for this one. But listen to this. The fellow who is providing all the planes, pilots, and stunt flying is a race winner by the name of Luke Whitney. He's the model for the role I am to take. He has a flying school connected with an aircraft sales office, hangars, and shops for maintenance on engines and planes, plus a charter service, and he provides stunt flying for the movies. When I went to meet this Luke at the hangars the other day—he happened to not be in—who do I run into right there in his office but our Fernando and Maggie, the girlfriend!"

Douglas interrupted his narrative to have a bit of his food, which was getting cold.

"Get on with it, man!" Charles insisted. "What happened then? What is the girl like?"

"We already knew she was graduating with Fernando in a few weeks with a full-fledged aeronautical engineering degree," Douglas said, dabbing his mouth with a napkin. "Which, by the way, is a new field for women. This girl is very pleasant and pretty. In fact, dressed up for a party I dare say she would be a real beauty. And she is sharp—a quick study, I hear. And on top of everything else, she is also a pilot. It's rumored that she is one of the best, although she doesn't have a lot of hours yet. But, Jock, get this. She is a movie stuntwoman for my own studio, doing Western cowboy stand-ins for the leading ladies who don't like to mess up their hair or get dusty. The studio says she did a great stunt in her last movie that's in the theaters right now. Since I will be working with her and other female pilots, they want me to be sure to see it. They want me to understand this new kind of woman."

The co-conspirators continued to talk about the details of both the air-race movie and their involvement in the mysterious plan for Fernando.

"Jock," Douglas continued, "it seems to me that if Don Hugo comes to town before the graduation, it would be best to just take him directly to the polo stables and let the two of them be alone. Why does London want to do it the other way—to meet after graduation?"

"I don't have the faintest idea, my friend, but this thought occurred to me," Charles responded. "It is possible that, since Don Hugo is at sea, the family in London contacted Helen in Buenos Aires and asked her what she would suggest. And perhaps she felt it best to let Fernando graduate on his own, so he can say he did it all with no reliance upon family connections or money. After graduation they can bring his father up to Fernando as he comes down off the stage to rejoin his class after receiving his diploma. His father is the one who cut him off—who disinherited his own son. That would be the best moment for them to meet."

Douglas absorbed the whole scenario that Charles had just outlined for him, nodding in agreement.

"You know, Jocko, old boy, you could have been a good Hollywood script writer!" Douglas said, delighted. "That is a splendid idea. It would be just like a happy ending for a movie."

They laughed together at the thought, but both knew there was plausible truth in the idea Charles had conjured up in his fertile imagination. They were truly trying to bring about a happy ending for the young man they both admired. Douglas pondered on that scenario as he sipped imported soda water, acknowledging again that it would certainly be a great solution.

"Yes, that idea could explain the instructions to try to keep them apart until after graduation," he agreed. "But what do we do if he insists on going right to Fernando?"

"We'll just have to think of something," Charles said. "You're the actor—just ad lib! Take him out on your new boat. Or, better still, hire Fernando to fly someone to Las Vegas or the Mexican border, getting back just in time for the graduation. I'm sure you'll think of something to keep Don Hugo busy or Fernando out of town so there would be no possibility of them meeting until after the graduation—as we have been instructed."

Don Hugo had to be at the Wall Street offices of his international bankers to sign loan agreements at nine o'clock the morning after he arrived. He had hoped to leave for the West Coast immediately upon docking, but now he had no option. The bankers insisted that they had to have him personally sign the papers—not his brother in Buenos Aires or his assistants anywhere else. This delay would cost him two days, but he hoped to still be able to arrive in California one day before Fernando's graduation. His telegram to the consul explained the altered schedule.

Reclining in his large leather chair in his consulate office, Charles read the incoming telegram to Douglas over the telephone.

"This delay in his arrival reduces our problem of distracting Hugo by a couple of days," Charles said, "but we still have to think of some diversions to keep him away from Fernando the afternoon he arrives, and that whole evening and the next morning before the graduation ceremony."

"We can bluff our way through that problem, can't we, old boy?" Douglas said with a laugh.

"We certainly can," answered the consul with self-assurance. "The university president has other commitments, and regrets that he cannot meet Fernando's father until after the graduation. But both Dr. Rheinhart and the registrar are very cooperative and could stall Hugo for as long as need be. Oh, and Douglas, I am still counting on you to have some kind of party at your place with a few celebrities to honor Don Hugo. Please invite people so important that Hugo will feel that he cannot afford to offend them and will be obliged to attend. My driver and I will bring him, of course. Hopefully, by the time he has met all the guests he will be exhausted enough from the long trip that he will want to retire early without seeing Fernando, and—"

Douglas interrupted his friend with a thought.

"But, Jock, Hugo himself said he only wanted to see Fernando from a distance and remain unseen. Do you still think we need to try so hard to keep them apart until after the graduation?"

Charles was ready with an answer for this kind of debatable question.

"I think we better be prepared for anything," he responded. "Just be ready to come up with something innovative and fascinating at any time in case a problem develops."

The two comrades discussed details and options further. Before dropping off the line, Douglas remembered something important.

"Oh one more thing, Jock. I met with studio people today at Luke's hangar to discuss that upcoming air-race movie, you know, and found Fernando and Maggie there again. They were very helpful to the writers there trying to develop background material for the script. They stood so close to each other that they were almost always touching hands without seeming to be doing so."

It was late. All the lights were out except for those under the arches of the corridors just off the horse stalls and the office lights that were always left on at night. In the shadows, a couple could be seen sitting very close together in a convertible parked in front of the offices. Maggie cuddled in Fernando's arms, enjoying the feeling of safety and strength he emanated.

"Sweet Maggie, it is all working out just perfect for us!" Fernando said happily. "I've got Luke's firm offer of a job on this air race movie deal, plus an offer that my university advisor found with an aircraft manufacturer back East. Also, there is that other offer from a British company that pays better than anything else—but *only* if I remain single. I would not consider the last one, but I might be able to talk them into taking both of us. You could travel with me like Anne and Charles Lindbergh did on their trip to the Orient. So it looks to me like we have enough job security to get married now. How about it, Maggie?"

She knew it was not in Fernando's nature to wait very long for her to make up her mind about marriage. She had been cautious—that was not her own nature either. Not too long ago she had hoped for something to cause Fernando to open up, trust her, reveal his past, and propose to her.

Unexpectedly, that old cowboy boyfriend had appeared out of her past. That relationship had never been anything serious. He just wasn't her type.

And poor Luke, she thought, even he has been acting more like a suitor than an instructor lately.

Now it was Maggie who was pleading for time, not Fernando. Maggie wanted time to introduce Fernando to her parents in Kanab and time to do this movie. Above all, she wanted time to fly the cross-country race if she could find a sponsor. When that dream was fulfilled, maybe she would be ready for marriage.

"Fernando, let's not talk marriage right now," she finally said. "It's too fast for me to rush into marriage this soon, even though I do love you. I had always thought of myself marrying someone from my own kind of life with my family all around. I want my family to be a big part of the most important day of my life. To me, marriage is for always, not just 'till death do us part.' I am the first daughter to marry in my parent's family. I know they will want a big party at home on the ranch, and my family would need time to adjust to different cultures and customs. Besides, we have some family problems of our own to solve."

Fernando was taken aback and wounded, but he needed to focus on Maggie right now. She was clearly distraught.

"Maggie, what is it?" he asked. "What's happened?"

"It looks like we might lose the ranch," Maggie said. "I didn't want to tell you because I didn't want you worrying about me. Dad is way behind on the mortgage and the bank is threatening him. I can't help much. I have sent money home, but not enough to do any good. Fernando, please don't be concerned. I do love you. You are the finest man I have ever met. Just let us hold off being engaged. Please?"

Maggie started teasing Fernando with playful kisses until he gave up on talk of marriage for now. In spite of this setback, he was feeling a new kind of freedom he had never had. Not only did he have his engineering degree virtually in his pocket, but he had job offers to prove that he could determine his own destiny. If his family did not want to claim him anymore, he could hold his head high again anyway. With such a promising future, his self-esteem would be restored.

Most importantly, this wonderful, remarkable Maggie had become a symbol to him. Not only did he love her, and not only did he truly want to marry her, but it seemed now that marrying a good woman of talent, character, skills, and beauty because he loved her and she loved him proved that he had matured far beyond his old family tradition of marrying for titles and financial position. She had neither, yet he wanted her.

Luke had come to see the writing on the wall. He recognized that he had probably lost Maggie to Fernando. He was still very fond of her, although now more in the role of a "favorite uncle" to her. He had also come to admire Fernando. Learning of the young man's dilemma, Luke had offered to loan him the money to buy an engagement ring as soon as the studio check cleared.

But this was complicated with a feeling Fernando did not understand. There was some kind of prompting warning him that the longer it took to get Maggie to the altar, the greater were the risks, threats, or uncertainties that might keep her from being his. Waiting until after the races to talk marriage seemed too far away, considering those persistent dark, uncertain feelings that kept looming in front of him.

"Maggie, why don't we go looking at diamond rings tomorrow—just for fun?" Fernando suggested.

In his mind, a three-carat diamond like the one his father had given his mother would be appropriate, even though he had no idea what that might cost. His family had jewels handed down from prior generations, he remembered. In fact, if he had not been disinherited he might have asked for one of the heirloom diamonds to give to Maggie.

But Maggie was thinking of something simpler, like the no-diamond gold band her father had given her mother. Fernando and Maggie had not talked about anything as insignificant as the size of a diamond. Their backgrounds were so very far apart that they would surely find many such wide differences in each other's expectations in the future. But for now, all Fernando wanted to do was gently encourage Maggie to commit to marrying him.

"No. Not yet," Maggie said with a serious look. Fernando recognized the firmness and gave up for the time being.

"Maggie, let's not talk anymore about anything serious. I'll get the phonograph, and we'll play our favorite tango and dance like we did the first time."

They both knew that the sensuous steps of the tango they had first danced on the office veranda under the arches would bring them close to each other like nothing else would. She waited patiently, knowing that after dancing, Fernando would give in to her request to wait. Fernando, on the other hand, was hoping that after dancing, Maggie would give in to his desire to not delay their engagement.

They danced and they talked, the sensuous music weaving its magic. Maggie, softening, agreed upon a kind of compromise. They wouldn't announce any engagement but they would have a more definite understanding. Her reluctance to commit kept rearing its ugly head—some premonition, perhaps, but she just knew she had to wait, and asked Fernando once again to be patient.

CHAPTER 11

AN UNEXPECTED VISIT

THE COUNTRY'S FASTEST passenger train snaked its way through the switching yards a few minutes from the station. Don Hugo had his hard-sided leather luggage, monogrammed with his initials, all packed and ready for the red caps to carry from his private suite out to the platform. Hugo did not know if the British consul would meet him personally or just send a secretary and chauffeured limousine. He hoped it would be only a staff member so he could get out to the university as soon as possible.

During the long journey across the broad expanse of America, Hugo's mind had been flooded with flashbacks of the life of his only child. He remembered when his son was born and what he was like as an infant. The strong, endearing personality traits began to show up in his toddler years. Hugo's fondest memories were of Fernando's first grades in school up through about age twelve. When Fernando became a teenager there were mixed memories—mixed in the sense that Fernando was proving to be an outstanding athlete and good student, but with strong signs of independence. His mind was quick, and he was so argumentative that it was a challenge to stay ahead of him. He was brilliant but always trying to prove his wings like a young bird, not content to stay in the nest where safety and food can be found.

Though always loveable and a source of great pride, young Fernando constantly pushed his parents and all other adults to the limit. He wanted to drive before he had the coordination to do so safely; he wanted to play polo before he had the skills to avoid dangerous spills; he wanted to fly airplanes long before he had the judgment to stay away from danger. He even wanted to sail out of sight of land long before he had the ability or experience to get back to a safe harbor should a storm overtake him.

Hugo was lost in reverie the whole crossing, barely noticing the fruited plains, the purple mountains' majesty, and the magnificent beauty of America in early summer. His thoughts were on a young Fernando and the many girlfriends who had always swarmed around him. It had been difficult to keep Fernando under control with all his romances. In desperation, Hugo and Helen had moved him around from place to place under the guise of training and education.

They took him to the far south of Argentina to study sheep ranching and the wool business. They sent him to the far northern section of the country to learn everything about the sugar plantations, the sugar mills, and the marketing of sugar both domestically and for export abroad. They had him spend many months on the cattle ranches and in the meat-packing plants. And with Fernando's interest in mechanics, he was a natural to learn the Rolls Royce agency business and maintenance. He had not spent any time with the ocean freighters but later on he'd have to learn the details of the shipping business.

Finally, they had found a solution that caused their son to forget all about girls: flying lessons. That pulled him away for a time, but in Fernando's late teens the polo bug bit harder, and he quickly became a leader in the local polo circles. The training required to prepare for local and international matches was so intense and time-consuming that women were relegated to the bottom of his list of priorities.

Hugo and Helen thought they had been quite successful in raising a son who had no interest in alcohol or other vices, so they had no hesitation about sending him abroad to get a university degree. They first became aware that something wrong was happening with their son when her family in England warned them that Fernando's professors were not pleased with his progress. They knew that he was bright and intelligent enough, but they learned, much to their horror, that his social life and drinking were interfering with his studies. Also, much to their disappointment, there came word of gambling and then losing large amounts of money. Hugo and Helen were heartsick. Where had they failed?

Fernando was soon expelled from that school, to the embarrassment and chagrin of the family. Hugo had expected his son to take his own position at the head of the family conglomerate, or empire, as some called it. Certainly, he had the personality and talent for the job. The rest of the family did not have anyone quite the right age or ability to handle it. With this failure in England, something had to be done.

As the train sped across the Midwest and down into the southwestern part of the country, Hugo continued reviewing the whole history of his son's downward spiral in his mind. He recalled that, with some influence, they were able to get Fernando accepted to the Sorbonne, one of the greatest French universities. Fernando promised he would change his ways, but he slipped again and quickly fell in with the wrong sort of crowd.

Perhaps to impress new friends or maybe still trying to demonstrate his independence of parents, family, professors, and the rest of the adult world, Fernando continued to gamble while drinking heavily, which again led to large losses. Once more, he was expelled for conduct unbecoming a student and for failure to pass the required tests. A complete disgrace was in the making.

Fernando eventually returned to Argentina, spent time playing polo, took advance flight training from a German instructor, and sailed again in the race to Rio de Janeiro. A few girls came in and out of his life, but he seemed to be cured of the lure of alcohol and gambling. As a diversion from all his hobbies, he did some work at the meat-packing plant involving the labor union because some of his boyhood friends were now leaders in the radical labor movement. Some of the most intellectual youth of the Argentine aristocracy had become caught up in socialism, communism, workers' rights movements, and similar issues, and had turned their backs on their families and traditions. They tried to convert Fernando to their revolutionary philosophy, and long nights were spent discussing, debating, and pleading for better treatment of workers and their families.

In the midst of all this, his interest in a degree in industrial engineering was beginning to grow. Hugo shared Fernando's desire with a friend in Boston. That friend was instrumental in getting Fernando admitted to a prestigious technical university in New England, but only on probation. Tragically, once away from home he fell again into the same old habits. It seemed he just could not handle the load of academic studies together with trying to impress friends with his independence and unlimited funding. Again there were major losses, especially with gambling, so Hugo was forced to tighten up the bank account. But that just seemed to make matters worse.

Reflecting on all that had transpired, the whole series of incidents sickened Hugo anew. Now, in a short few hours, he might face Fernando again after more than three years. First, Hugo wanted to meet the university authorities who had taken Fernando in and protected him. In some way they had obtained his credits from other previous universities, financed him, and now would see him graduate with honors. Hugo had a debt of gratitude to these men he knew he could never repay. They had brought about a miracle no one else had been able to achieve, but would it last?

He was anxious to know what their secret was, how they had succeeded where he had failed as a parent; however, he would never be able to trust Fernando again. He wanted to see the prodigal son he had once trusted and loved, partly out of curiosity, partly because he felt Helen could not recover without some favorable information, and partly to shame Fernando for his past conduct.

With priority status, all switches were opened to the train that pulled slowly into the area where the platform was cleared in preparation for its arrival. The Earl of Wittingham was standing right where Hugo's train car was to stop, Douglas and the vice-consul beside him. Charles and Douglas, both wearing grey homburg hats, were dressed in double-breasted suits, the most advanced style from the Continent. The chauffeur had remained with the huge silver and black limousine outside the station platform.

The train came to a stop with a hiss of air brakes. The door opened and Hugo stepped out to greet his reception committee. He recognized both gentlemen immediately. He had played polo a few times with the consul many years ago, and he knew Douglas's face from the movies. The red caps promptly brought the luggage, packed tightly on a platform dolly, and the procession moved directly to the VIP reserved parking area. The group caused a bit of a fuss with photographers, who were rapidly converging on them. Invariably, the press spots celebrities like piranha fish going for blood. Reporters shouted out for information and interviews, but Douglas just smiled and waved them away.

The big Rolls Royce with the British colors flying from both front fenders also caused some commotion. Southern Californians were used to celebrities, but somehow this seemed to be different. Who were the foreigners, they wondered? Douglas and Charles hoped nothing would appear in the papers for Fernando to see.

After settling down inside the limo, Hugo was the first to speak.

"Your Excellency, I truly appreciate the honor of being met personally, but you need not have bothered. I know my visit must be an imposition; nonetheless, I welcome your assistance. I suspect that you know a good deal about my purpose in coming here. The main reason I accepted your kind hospitality is that I may need some special help to break through the university's barrier of silence and convince my son that he should see me."

It was obvious that the whole situation was difficult for Hugo to verbalize, especially in front of the consul, whom he knew only slightly. The movie actor and the vice-consul were virtual strangers.

"Dr. Velez-Candiotti, please call me Jock," Charles said warmly. "You are among friends, and you need have no fear regarding confidentiality or discretion. Now, there are things we can do immediately and some might take a bit longer. What is your pleasure?"

"Jock, I like your openness," Hugo said, smiling. "For a career diplomat, you cut through the protocol very quickly. Both of you, please call me Hugo. Now, please tell me about my son. I'm anxious to know about Fernando."

It was evident that his every thought was directed toward his son. The story resembled the faithful father and the prodigal son in the Bible, except that it was the father who was unrepentant and not the son.

"I saw your son a few days ago," Douglas said, eager to share his opinions. "We have become quite close friends, and he is giving me flying lessons. I am to play a pilot in a movie about air racing, and Fernando was recommended as both an aeronautical engineer and a flying instructor. He is an excellent teacher. Besides that, we have gone sailing together. I own an international-class racing sloop, and I discovered that Fernando knows more about it than I do! But the first thing that impressed me about him is that he plays the best polo I have ever seen. As you can tell, I am a fan of your son!"

Hugo was surprised but pleased that a famous movie star was paying tribute to his wayward boy. *Yes,* he thought, *Fernando could have been all that he is describing, but he did not live up to that before. How in the world did my son get through a demanding and prestigious university without the old problems recurring? Has he really changed, or is it a front?*

"I have stayed out of the way on purpose," Charles said. "Fernando does not know me, but I know him by reputation and I have watched him play polo. He is spectacular! I don't know at what level he was playing when he left Argentina, but right now he is in top form. I dare say that Fernando plus the three of us could take on any foursome in the world and do quite well! Of course, he might have to do it alone—none of us are as good as we used to be."

The men laughed at the thought of them playing polo together after so many years.

Hugo was almost speechless hearing this gratifying and welcome news. Fernando had shown great promise, but he was far from a ten-goaler three years ago. He was completely unaware of the transformation that had come over his son, brought about through self-discipline, sacrifice, and self-control. As he listened to Douglas and Charles reveal more about this changed son of his and the circumstances that brought this about, Hugo learned that Fernando had become a mature, serious, focused, dedicated student. Hugo remained skeptical, not yet realizing that his son's new single-minded dedication to regain his family's respect on his own merits had brought about a total reformation. In reality, every aspect of Fernando's life had been altered by going through a crucible of adversity and practicing disciplined self-control. It appeared, from these reports, that his son had indeed become a new person, a different person—but he had to see him in person to be sure.

During ensuing conversations, Hugo came to see that the limitations and the discipline imposed by having almost no spare funds had been good for Fernando, who evidently had come to appreciate the value of hard-earned money. He also learned that his son had gone without the pleasures of a car, comfortable quarters, prestige, new clothes, or well-to-do friends.

Perhaps now he has recognized that many of his past friends were only fair-weather friends as long as he had money, Don Hugo reasoned to himself.

In reality, Fernando had matured in ways his father could not yet even begin to imagine.

Before arriving at the residence and during a brief rest there to unload the luggage and to enjoy a glass of delicious, freshly squeezed

California orange juice, their conversation continued to center on Fernando and his present situation. When the consul and Hugo were ready to leave, Douglas left to go back to the studio and Mr. Williams returned to the consulate, leaving Hugo and Jock alone to meet with the university officials.

Dr. Rheinhart waited for them in the president's office made available to them for this occasion, where he was joined by the registrar. The president had business elsewhere. After introductions, Hugo explained that he was there to pay a debt of gratitude to the university and to those who had helped his son so much.

"Dr. Rheinhart," he said, "I understand that you are the one who offered Fernando the position in the polo stables that led to his playing for the university. It seems to me that Fernando must have told you about his past history and the family's reaction to what happened three years ago. I understand he is using the Underwood name so I'm curious, how did you get his credits from other universities, which are in his full name?"

"Fernando was very reticent at first," Dr. Rheinhart answered. "He would not open up to me or anyone else. But finally I won his trust and he told me about his past. He still loves and respects you and his mother very much, Dr. Velez-Candiotti. He is desperately striving to regain your confidence and to prove himself to you and others in the family. He values your family traditions and standards. He loves you, and he knows he has let you down. We all have come to love this great son of yours, no matter what the past might have been, and we now want to protect him. To us, the important thing is how *you* feel about him."

This was a completely unexpected turn of events for Hugo. He'd assumed that he would be the one in control. He felt that Fernando and the university should do some explaining to him, but now the tables were turned. Here this prestigious member of the University Board of Regents was putting Hugo on the defensive. Dr. Rheinhart had praised Fernando and now was asking if *he*, Hugo, was worthy to meet his own son!

At first, somewhat insulted by the regent's question, his face colored. But he thought of his wife at home—sick, lonesome, and terribly concerned over her only son. Tears came to his eyes at the thought, and his rigid face softened.

"I don't think you have the right to question my attitude toward my son," Hugo said without anger. "Yet you say you love him, which touches my heart deeply. You have hit me where I am the most vulnerable. Therefore, I accept your right to question my feelings toward Fernando. My son hurt me greatly—not once, but several times. Now, however, I see that something has happened in a most remarkable way, and he has won your loyalty and affection. I respect that, sir, and I thank you. You deserve to know that before I left Buenos Aires and my ailing wife, I promised her that I would give him her love and invite him to return to her bedside. You need not worry about my attitude. There are some things, however, especially in the family, that may be irreversible. I don't know how all the others will react. They may not want him back."

It had been a long confession and a partial disclosure of his feelings. He had not admitted to them that he still held strong feelings against Fernando's conduct, but the attitude of these men had humbled Hugo beyond any experience of his life. He said nothing for a long time.

"As a father myself, I think I understand what you are feeling," Dr. Rheinhart said, breaking the silence.

"You should know, Hugo," Charles said, "that the registrar here has done a great service to your son. He is the one, with the guidance of Dr. Rheinhart, who worked out the transfer of credits, the name change, the funding, the scholarship, and everything else. The two of them have been like parents hovering over Fernando, without him ever suspecting how much they were doing. They controlled his funding so he had just enough but not one cent extra to spend. They helped work out his academic scheduling together with his work schedule. They made sure he had understanding professors, supervisors, and friends in the right places at the right times. They have done a masterful job, and Fernando is not even aware that anyone other than Dr. Rheinhart did anything out of the ordinary. But we have had one unusual surprise of late."

Don Hugo suspected that there might be some kind of a hitch somewhere in this marvelous story.

"What is that?" Hugo asked, concern written on his face, fearing that there had been a relapse to old problems.

"Well, despite our efforts to the contrary," Charles explained, "Fernando seems to have fallen in love with a young lady. We are afraid you are going to have a marriage on your hands."

Hugo already knew about this development. After a moment, he stood up and crossed the large office to look out a window at the students walking past while he gathered his thoughts. He could see attractive, suntanned young people hurrying this way and that going to classes. He could also see some holding hands with spring love shining in their bright faces. *Fernando and this girl must be like that,* he thought.

"Gentlemen," he said, returning to his seat, "I hope I am regaining a son, and if it means gaining a daughter I have never had, I only hope she is strong enough to hold her own in our formidable family. Please tell me about her. What is she like? What is her background?"

Dr. Rheinhart felt that Hugo was handling the situation precisely as he and the consul had hoped for, not sensing the contradictory turmoil going on inside this prideful father. Now he was willing to be candid and open in explaining everything they knew about Maggie.

Dr. Rheinhart was ready to oblige. He had a dossier containing Maggie's transcript of grades, every class she had ever taken, a few pages of notes, and photos of her family. There were pictures of the ranch in Kanab, Utah, and sheets of her genealogy back a few generations, photos of her rodeo days and others of movie stunts. Hugo eagerly looked through everything.

"If you will allow me to turn off the lights," Dr. Rheinhart said after several minutes, "I'd like to show you some film clips of Maggie doing the stunt she's most famous for."

He pulled the drapes and turned the lights off. A large projector started to whir and a black-and-white film appeared on the office's white wall. There she was, Maggie at a dead run leaning way out trying to catch the rope ladder, missing it, and falling into the dirt in a huge ball of dust. Then the second attempt: Maggie jumping successfully from her horse to the ladder, climbing up the ladder into the cockpit. The sequence of aerobatics with the vertical four-point roll, the plane diving back on the director who flung himself into the dirt to duck the propeller. The plane picking up the top of a bush in its wheels before pulling up into a victory roll. Maggie getting out of the plane with the help of Luke, to the applause of the crew. Fernando approaching Maggie as she beckoned him over to meet Luke.

The film clip ended. Lights came on and Dr. Rheinhart pulled open the drapes. Hugo was speechless.

"I show you this so you will know she is not just some pretty face," the regent said. "Here is a skilled woman, strong-willed, and determined. No one better get in her way! And, as you can see from her class reports, very intelligent. I don't know what you have in mind for Fernando, Dr. Velez-Candiotti, but she is as impressive a woman as I have ever seen. Not only does she have a reputation as a virtuous and modest young woman, those who know her say she is kind and generous—she even sends money home to help her parents."

Don Hugo suddenly realized that he had been set up. This group was ready for him. The consul and the movie star had defended Fernando, and now the regent had defended Maggie. He was a bit overwhelmed and taken aback.

"Hugo," Charles said, "we have a reception in your honor over at Douglas's home tonight. Half of Hollywood will be there to meet you. They have been told you are a great Argentine polo player, horse breeder, industrialist, and businessman from the pampas. You know, what with a boxer called the 'Bull of the Pampas' who wants to beat our heavyweight Joe Lewis, and the tango that is sweeping the night clubs and dance floors here, everyone wants to know more about your great country—and they want to meet you. Also, the president of the university has learned of your Oxford doctorate degree. He insists that you accompany us on the stand tomorrow with the other dignitaries. We have located the appropriate robes for you. Will that be all right?"

Don Hugo, shocked, only nodded at matters moving so fast.

Things are going along okay, thought Charles, *but I sure hope that Douglas found a way to pull off this cocktail party and keep Fernando out of sight at the same time.*

Charles wasn't aware that Douglas was ready with an excuse that Fernando was out of town. Luke had asked him to make a legitimate flight to Las Vegas overnight. Fernando would return tomorrow morning well in advance of the graduation. Luke offered Fernando good money to pilot the charter flight—a studio official who needed to be in Vegas. It appeared that things were under control.

Everyone said their goodbyes and the consul and Hugo returned to their waiting limo, discussing the planned activities ahead.

Though Hugo was exhausted from all that had transpired in the last few hours, he showered, dressed for the reception and dinner, and left with Charles for Douglas's home, fully expecting to meet Fernando there.

When they arrived, Hugo was duly impressed with the spectacular setting and the lavishly furnished home, and he thought, *This might be an enjoyable evening after all. Now where is Fernando?*

The guest list was a Who's Who of Hollywood, but as luck would have it, one uninvited guest—Maggie—showed up unexpectedly just as the first guests were arriving. She had come looking for Dr. Rheinhart. At the entrance, the butler would not have let her in had it not been for Douglas spotting her from across the hall. He gasped in astonishment and, waving and motioning to Charles, rushed to the vaulted entrance where Maggie was frantically insisting that she be received.

"Miss Maggie!" Douglas greeted her warmly. "You remember me from the studio meeting at Luke's? I'm the cohost for this dinner, and we would love to have you join us."

Maggie was nicely dressed but not appropriately so for a party of this magnitude, and it was evident that she immediately felt uncomfortable being there. She started talking rapidly, agitation in her very bearing.

"Forgive me for bursting in like this, but I have an urgent message for Dr. Rheinhart," she said quickly. "It is an emergency involving Fernando Underwood. Could I just see him to pass the information on? It really is very important!"

Charles immediately left to find the regent and returned with him in just a minute.

"Fernando called me from Las Vegas," she told him, speaking rapidly. "The plane started heating up over the desert on the way there, and by the time he landed in that heat of Vegas the oil temperature was into the red line. He's coming back tonight on the train so he can be here in time for the graduation tomorrow, but he'll barely make it. I'll meet him at the train station with his clothes and graduation cap and gown. He didn't want you to worry—it'll be close, but he'll be here!"

Dr. Rheinhart insisted that his chauffeur would pick Fernando up from the station. Maggie, grateful, declined their offer to come in and rushed away.

All three men were delighted to hear that Fernando was unable to get back for the party, as they now would have a legitimate situation to explain to Don Hugo. The conspiracy was working so far.

They looked forward to the graduation tomorrow and the meeting at long last between the father and his prodigal son.

CHAPTER 12

EMBRACING THE PRODIGAL SON

MAGGIE'S PARENTS WERE staying with relatives and had arrived the day before. She had been visiting with them when the urgent call came in from Fernando. She felt disappointed about the sudden Las Vegas trip because she had wanted Fernando to meet her family before graduation, but now that would have to wait until after the ceremonies.

The university campus was filled with flowering trees, shrubs neatly trimmed, and a profusion of summer flowers. The university groundkeepers had worked hard trimming, cleaning, sweeping, and painting, and the campus looked better than ever. The visitors matched the beautiful grounds. The ladies wore wide-brimmed hats and colorful dresses, and the men were in their best summer suits and elegant panama hats, providing a stunning, colorful picture to equal the environment. The day was sunny and the graduation would take place in the football stadium.

The members of the graduating class were required to sit in alphabetical order, so Maggie Rockwell was assigned close to the end. Fernando Underwood would normally be farther back and somewhat close, but he was receiving special honors, so he would be seated at the front of the regular class members.

Seating for the graduates was on chairs placed in rows on the grass. Family members and spectators were seated in the bleachers. The dignitaries and faculty, wearing colorful robes representing the universities from which they had received their doctorate degrees, had a reserved area on a raised platform facing the graduates.

The procession, led by the university president, distinguished visitors, and high-ranking faculty members, and followed by those to receive honorary doctorates, filed in as the university's large marching band played. Next came the graduates who were receiving their doctorates and master's degrees, and finally, the students who were graduating with bachelor of science or bachelor of arts degrees. The latter group was less picturesque in their black robes trimmed with crimson, but nonetheless they added to the traditional pageantry of the occasion.

Anxiously, Maggie looked around for Fernando. She spotted her parents up in the bleachers with their backs to the sun, and was sad that Fernando had no family there to cheer for him. But where was he? She hoped that someone would save a place for him if he came in late. She walked in with her group and sat down in her assigned place.

Looking at the program for the first time, she found the line with her name and then looked for Fernando's name. To her surprise and delight, she noticed that he was graduating with honors. The program read, under the section "magna cum laude," Fernando Velez-Candiotti Braun Underwood. Maggie was overwhelmed—she had no idea that Fernando was an honors graduate.

Just as she was starting to panic, she saw him coming in with the other honors graduates. He looked so handsome in his formal attire.

She wished she could catch his eye, but there was no way.

As Maggie watched him sit down, she noticed that from behind the built-up platform an usher was bringing Dr. Rheinhart, the British consul, and another distinguished-looking gentleman to the back row of the dignitaries' section under a large covering. As they sat down, the impression struck her that there was something familiar about the tall, handsome man, but she could not put her finger on it. Was he in the movie business some way, or part of the university?

Music heralded the beginning of the ceremonies. With a deep, resonant voice, the university president announced the program exactly as it was printed. Her day had finally arrived, and so had the time come for Fernando to get his treasured engineering degree. The customary short speeches, the usual honorary degree presentations, and the established protocol of the occasion plodded along. At last, the moment came for Fernando to march up the steps to receive his special honor. He did so with great dignity, looking very princely and thoroughly the part of a new professional engineer in aeronautical science.

Even with such an unusually long name, the announcer seemed to pronounce every word of it with significant emphasis as though he had been coached. It appeared to have an electrifying effect on Fernando. He seemed to stand taller, his face more chiseled in classic features. When the announcer read his full name as printed in the program, Maggie was very proud of Fernando for being part of this select group of graduates but felt a little left out that he had not told her.

Fernando walked down off the platform and took his seat again. Those around him gave a congratulatory slap on the back or shook his hand as he passed them going to his seat. He smiled and nodded, but Maggie didn't think he said a word to anyone.

Finally the time came for all to file by to receive their diplomas from the president and to shake hands with the other dignitaries.

When Maggie approached the gentlemen, she smiled pleasantly but was taken aback when the president continued to hold her hand, turned to the keynote speaker standing next to him, and introduced her.

"This is one of our most famous students," the president said. "Margaret is an accomplished pilot and has performed some of the greatest flying and horseback stunts the movies have ever filmed. Her latest picture is being shown around the country."

Then turning to her, he said, "Margaret, we are all proud to know you."

Maggie was speechless. She had never said one word to the president before, yet he spoke of her as if she were an intimate friend. As far as she knew, no one on campus had paid even the slightest attention to her movie connections. She had tried to protect her anonymity, but somehow word had reached as far as the president of the university. Maggie did not want to delay the line, so she thanked the president graciously and moved on.

As she came down the steps, an usher took her by the arm.

"The president would like you to wait here for a few moments until Fernando Underwood receives his diploma," he whispered. "After that you can walk back to a seat reserved for you by him. Is that all right?"

So that's it, she surmised. Fernando must have requested for her to sit by him at the end of the graduation ceremonies. He must have told the president about her stunt work.

She waited patiently in the shade of the platform for the alphabet to work down through the students to Fernando Underwood with the long name. Just as the students were getting close to "U," Maggie noticed that another usher was bringing some other people up behind her. She turned and noticed the British consul, Dr. Rheinhart, and the other gentleman, all dressed in their ceremonial doctoral robes. They had been brought down from the back row of the dignitaries and now stood beside her.

She was aware that Dr. Rheinhart had visited Fernando frequently at the polo stables. He was usually there when Fernando played polo, and Fernando took personal care of Dr. Rheinhart's horses, so Maggie had met him on a number of occasions. He normally seemed reserved and only interested in Fernando, but now he took her by the elbow.

"We thought you might want to congratulate Fernando personally," he whispered, "and we have someone here who also wants to greet him. If you don't mind, would you let this gentleman greet Fernando first when he comes down the stairs?"

Maggie had no other choice. Something strange was happening over which she had no control.

Fernando's full name was read over the public address system as he received his diploma. It resounded and echoed throughout the stadium. She wondered again if it was her imagination or whether the announcer was doing something special for him?

Fernando took the diploma from the president.

"Congratulations again, Fernando," he said, shaking his hand with both of his. "We are very proud of you. Now, we have a surprise waiting for you at the foot of the platform before you return to your seat."

This statement puzzled Fernando, but he automatically moved on as all had been instructed to do so as not to slow up the procession.

Fernando, tall and handsome, the treasured sheepskin in his hand, walked the width of the platform to the stairs and started down. He glanced at the small group near the foot of the steps, but paid little attention to them. His thoughts were on his mother and his father over seven thousand miles away. How much he wanted them to share this moment with them!

As soon as his foot touched the grass on the playing field he sensed that the small group in the shadows, the tops of whose heads he had seen below him as he descended the stairs, moved forward, and he heard his name called out by Dr. Rheinhart. Fernando turned and—could it be? Yes, it was his father standing next to Dr. Rheinhart! The unexpected shock froze him in place with one foot on the grass and the other behind him on the last step.

Incredulous, his heart beating fast and hard, Fernando thought, *Could it be possible? Is this really Father? Where is Mother?* A million thoughts and questions raced through his mind like rockets whizzing by. Who would move first?

Don Hugo was close to tears, his emotions rising to the surface. He was so proud of his son, but afraid that their relationship had been damaged forever.

Is Fernando still my loving son or is he a stranger now? Doubts and concerns plagued his mind just as they did Fernando's.

In that same stunning instant, Hugo realized that his pent-up love for his son was greater than his long-held pride, and suddenly he comprehended that he was guilty of a greater sin than Fernando's.

Hugo moved first. With one quick step forward, long arms outstretched widely, tears now freely streaming down his face, he wrapped Fernando in his arms.

"Oh my dear son," he said, sobbing. "We are so proud of you. Please forgive me. Forgive me, Fernando. *Perdóname, mi querido hijo.*"

Fernando was thrilled beyond any adequate expression. He responded to the fatherly embrace and wet kisses on both cheeks with an equally firm hug. He fully understood how difficult every single word must have been for his father to express. He also comprehended what it meant.

"Congratulations, my son," meant that he was no longer an outcast. His father was calling him "son." And "we are very proud of you" was a tribute to Fernando having worked out his own education and graduation with no help. Somehow they had learned of his accomplishments, and they were proud of him.

"Your mother sends much love," Hugo said, pulling back so he could see Fernando's face. "A kiss from her and one from me."

He kissed him again on both cheeks, which were now wet with tears.

Kisses from his father, as though he were a little boy just found after being lost in the trackless expanse of the pampas, was a tender touch full of familial meaning. But the most significant expression of all was the pleading, "Forgive me," which seemed to come from deep within his father's soul.

Fernando responded eagerly by wrapping up his father again in a tight *abrazo*, and his father slapped his son affectionately on the back, his repentant tears changing to tears of joy. At long last, they stopped and looked deep into each other's eyes without saying a word.

Fernando, gaining control over his emotions, finding his voice, and clearing his throat, looked into his father's eyes.

"No, Papá," he said softly. "It is I who must ask forgiveness from you. I disgraced myself and our family. I have worked hard to regain your trust in me, and I will spend the rest of my life proving it."

Hugo understood and caressed his son's cheeks with his hands.

With these tender words, the wounds of recent years were miraculously healed and the two were united in mutual forgiveness. The prodigal had returned, the proud father was humbled, and with their love there was no challenge that could not be overcome.

Dr. Rheinhart cleared his throat officiously to signal that they needed to let the rest of the proceedings finish appropriately. He led them around behind the platform out of sight of the graduates and the people in the stands. Some had noticed the little drama unfolding down below.

Hugo was standing beside his son, arm in arm, uncontrollable tears streaming down his face. The long wait had been difficult for him. The trip had been tiring, but most of all this traumatic experience was almost more than he could bear. Finally he gained control and wiped away his tears.

"I apologize for the show of emotions," he said. "It must be the Latin in me—certainly it's not the German. My thoughts are now on Helen, whose health did not allow her to accompany me."

Fernando was visibly shaken, but Hugo quickly reassured him.

"She is doing better," he said. "I received a cable from her last night telling me that the doctors have found the right medications for her pains. She is very anxious to see you."

Maggie had been waiting for the right moment to come join them. When he saw her, Fernando pulled her toward him and put one arm tightly around her waist.

"Papá, this is Margaret Rockwell, my future wife," he said. "I love her deeply and have proposed to her. Maggie, this is my father. I know you will love him."

Maggie started to put out her hand to shake Hugo's, but she couldn't resist the impulse to wrap her arms fondly around him instead and plant a sweet kiss on his cheek.

"How absolutely wonderful to have you come to our graduation!" she exclaimed.

Maggie's spontaneous show of affection startled Hugo, but he loved it and squeezed her back. *Family be damned!* he thought. *She is a wonderful girl. She will fit in just fine!*

Maggie was now anxious to find her parents and introduce them to Fernando and his father. She caught their eyes and waved them over, then introduced them.

Hugo and Fernando did not know quite what to expect from Maggie's parents. It had occurred to each that her rancher father and mother might turn out to be ragged-looking, uneducated, country bumpkins from the Rocky Mountain valleys. Instead they encountered a well-dressed, well-spoken, handsome couple. Maggie's mother was still very attractive, possessing the natural grace and composure of a former beauty queen. They learned that she was a university graduate, had taught school, and was a leader in community affairs, including politics.

"My mother's mother was a sheriff in our county," Maggie said, explaining their background. "She carried a gun and nabbed the toughest horse thieves and bank robbers of the area. She put up with no nonsense. Mother is from the same mold, and they tell me I have some of both their traits."

When she introduced her father, they learned that he too was an educated man and active in politics, the president of the regional cattlemen's association, and a lay leader in their church.

Fernando now clearly understood a lot more about Maggie's character, stubbornness, and heritage. And Maggie could plainly see that Fernando's family was very respected. University presidents, consuls, famous movie actors, and regents would not be involved for just an average student.

There was much for Maggie to think about and sort out in her mind. All she could see right now was conflict ahead. She wanted to marry

Fernando, but she didn't want to go off to some faraway place in South America. She wanted her family to have time to come to know Fernando and for his family to get to know and accept her.

The biggest obstacle looming in front of her, big as all outdoors, was that she still wanted to fly both races and prove herself before getting married. *Yes,* she admitted, *I know I'm as stubborn as Grandmother was, out tracking down a horse thief in the red rock canyons of southern Utah! I'll marry Fernando, but on my terms!*

CHAPTER 13

FERNANDO ANNOUNCES THEIR FUTURE PLANS

THE CONSUL RODE with Douglas in the actor's convertible so that Hugo, Fernando, and Maggie could be alone in the consulate limo as they returned to the residence. Maggie noticed that everyone seemed to take it for granted that she belonged to Fernando, and that marriage was just around the corner. She liked being included yet was a bit reticent because she was still not ready to wear a ring or even set a date until after the race, which was a little over two months away.

As Fernando and his father talked about family matters, her thoughts turned to her parents, who were following the limo in their car through the heavy traffic.

She thought that her mother looked so lovely in the new dress she had made for the graduation. She still continued to make all her own clothes on the family Singer sewing machine. Maggie remembered many peaceful hours as a youngster playing at the feet of her mother as she sewed or mended the family's clothes. Last Christmas, Maggie had given her mother a new electric motor attachment so she didn't have to use the treadle. Cattle prices being what they were, she knew her mother would never buy one for herself, and it seemed the perfect way to express her love for her dear mother in a practical way.

Dad looks great too, she thought, smiling to herself as memories of him on the ranch filled her mind.

Maggie looked over at Fernando, but he and his father were still so engrossed in each other, catching up on the past three years. It was as though she was not even there. She considered joining their conversation, but they were focused on each other and oblivious to her. Besides, the intimacy of their reunion caused them to slip unconsciously into their native Spanish from time to time. She felt left out, so she turned her thoughts to her own parents again.

Dad looks so suntanned and handsome and athletic! Maggie thought. *I'm really impressed with his new outfit!* Her dad's new suit had a slight Western cut to the pockets and trim. He wore his best black boots, highly polished, with a handcrafted design on the upper part of the boot. The artistic design was hidden discreetly by his pant leg but was partly revealed whenever he sat down and crossed his leg.

I bet he does that on purpose—pulling up his pants just a mite—so that people can see the unique pattern on his boots! Maggie surmised. It was one of her dad's many little idiosyncrasies that she loved. He liked to appear conservative and modest, but hidden away were these little flashy touches that told her he had a wild streak in him just like she did.

Her father also had on a new Stetson that shaded his face from the sun. The hat was very traditional and had a low crown and narrow brim.

"It's called the Stockman," he had told her when she was a little girl, "and it's for a cattleman to wear to town."

She had asked to hold it and noticed that while the felt was a delicate gray, the inside lining, which was hidden from view, was a brilliant red satin.

She almost giggled out loud, just thinking of it. *Dad likes his exotic touch.*

She was very proud of her family and happy to have them meet Fernando and Don Hugo, as everyone seemed to call him with great respect. Her musings were interrupted right at that moment as she overheard part of the conversation between Fernando and his father.

". . . and the bank will take care of all the details," Hugo was saying. "Your account is now open, and I have established your letter of credit. I suggest that you replenish your wardrobe, and pick out a couple of cars that you can use while you remain here."

She had never heard of anyone buying a "couple of cars" as though they were a couple of tires! She must have squeezed Fernando's hand at the expression because he quickly looked over at her, tried to figure out the meaning of the squeeze, and, a little confused, changed the subject immediately.

"My father has given me some very good news, Maggie!" Fernando exclaimed. "He says that Mother's condition is serious but not life-threatening. You will love her. She is such a wonderful person. And we were just saying how pleased we are to meet your parents. They are great people, just like you said."

He suddenly realized that he had not included Maggie in their conversation and tentative decisions.

"Forgive me for seeming to ignore you, my dear, but Father tells me that there is a serious problem back in Argentina with some of the companies," he explained. "It looks like he wants me to return there as soon as possible, both because of Mother and also a labor problem with the unions. But first I have to travel to New York to finish some business that Father wants me to wrap up for him. I'll tell you all about the details later. It might just bore you now."

Maggie glanced at him and looked away quickly, not being able to hide her deep disappointment, but said nothing. Was his family more important than her races? Was he going to New York and to Argentina without talking to her about it? Was he walking out on her? Now that he had his old life back, would he have any need for this new life with her? She was suddenly confused and afraid.

The limousine, followed by Maggie's family, pulled into the estate marked by large stone pillars at either side of the entrance. A guard opened the ornate wrought-iron gates. Polished brass shields on each pillar announced that it was the consul's residence, representative of His Majesty the King of England. The landscaping up to the lovely mansion was immaculate, with flowers and plants adorning each side of the long, curved driveway.

Charles and Douglas had arrived just a few minutes earlier and were waiting on the marble porch just outside the large double doors that opened into a wide marbled entry. The guests were ushered inside the spacious residence, where drinks were being served by uniformed waiters. Dinner was already prepared and waiting to be served.

At dinner, Hugo and Maggie's father had a lively discussion about cattle and horses and found that each was as well-informed and educated as the other. But when her father indiscreetly asked how many head of cattle Hugo ran on his ranch, Maggie would have kicked him under the table if she had been closer! She herself had no idea, but she was afraid that the Argentine ranches were probably much bigger than their Utah spread. She was absolutely right. All ranchers like to brag a bit, but Hugo did not consider it bragging to give the facts. But he did try to soften the comparison by explaining at length the differences between the two countries.

"Things are a lot different down there from here," Hugo said. "We have land that has come down to us from old Spanish land grants given by the king over four hundred years ago. We have some ranches of half a million acres that carry a hundred thousand head of cattle. We also have some good tracts of land of only twenty thousand acres that can carry ten thousand head."

Mr. Rockwell had no idea anyone in the world held property so large that they could talk numbers like that. His face showed shocked amazement. Not even the cattle barons of the last century ran outfits that big! Hugo realized that Maggie's father was trying hard to grasp the size of the Argentine ranches.

"Please understand me, Señor Rockwell," he said apologetically, realizing his mistake. "Values are different down there. A thousand acres here might be worth more than one hundred thousand acres down there. But let me tell you a family story that is well known in our nation's history. Fernando's great-great-grandfather gave half a million head of cattle to Gen. José de San Martín, the liberator of our country and our equivalent to your Gen. George Washington, to feed his army. Of course, some were sold to raise money and some were kept in reserve if needed. It was San Martín's army of Argentines and Chileans that conquered the Spaniards and achieved our independence and that of several other neighboring countries. But that wasn't enough. The general also asked for and received twenty thousand head of horses for his cavalry!"

Maggie and her parents were overwhelmed by those numbers and were speechless.

"We have split the original large tracts of land into a number of smaller properties now," Hugo said, "each as its own profit center and each as a separate corporation."

The small group recognized that Fernando and his father represented a culture and a society that was little understood and little appreciated in the United States. Even so, they were profoundly impressed with a family that had such a long and illustrious history and which apparently had made major contributions to the foundation of their Latin American country.

Maggie felt absolutely numb. Her world was being shaken. She knew Fernando as simply a solid, talented, and intelligent man with a flawless character. When they met, he was disinherited from all his family's wealth and was almost penniless. But now, all this affluence—with huge ranches bigger than whole counties back home and enough money to buy a couple of cars at a time—threatened her to the core. Before, he had needed her. Now she felt he did not need her for anything. She sensed a change in their relationship, and it was quickly turning into an insecurity that she had never experienced and could not understand.

While the men talked cattle and ranching, Maggie's mother kept up her end of the conversation speaking interestingly and animatedly with the consul's wife and Douglas's wife and others who were there.

After dessert, Maggie and Fernando had a chance to slip away into the paneled study out of sight of the others. He gave her a tender kiss, oblivious to the rather cold and impersonal response Maggie gave him. He asked her to sit down beside him where he could look into her face and share his feelings with her.

"Maggie, my love, you have no idea how happy I am or what a burden has been lifted from me," he said, with a joy she had never seen before. "You seemed to be resting in the car while we drove here, but Father brought me up to date on so many important happenings. He has reassured me that all is forgiven and forgotten. He calls me 'son' easily again, and he told me that he will open enough bank and credit lines that I will be able to do anything you and I need to do."

Maggie didn't say anything, so Fernando barreled on. Maggie had a million questions to ask and some important issues to settle, but he hadn't even noticed.

"Father told the university president he wanted to endow a chair in our family name and make some other contributions. It's a little embarrassing, and probably intimidating to you, but he wants me to move immediately to a hotel suite. He says to buy a couple of cars for you and me. Oh, and he wants to send one of the family heirloom diamonds up on the next company freighter. That will be about a month from now. I'm sure that all of this is overwhelming right now for you, but I hope in time you'll come to accept everything."

Maggie was baffled and hurt that he didn't stop to ask if that was all right with her. Everything was all mixed up in her mind. Was she really in love with this new Fernando? This was a rich Fernando who didn't need her like the modest and humble Fernando had needed her.

Now her car was not even necessary for him to use for transportation. Apparently, he could buy a fleet of cars if he wanted to. And company ships? Fernando had never said anything about a shipping company! That was beyond her wildest imagination. And rent a hotel suite? That would be unthinkably expensive. Her head was spinning like a wild desert dust devil kicking up tumble weeds and throwing loam in all directions.

Not even aware that Maggie had not responded to his generous offerings of a car or a large diamond ring, Fernando went on talking faster and faster, excitement ringing in his words, bulldozing her over with all his plans, believing all this would impress her. He did not realize he was treading on delicate ground with an independent woman like Maggie. Fernando was wound up like a spinning top. He jumped from one thing to another.

"This business matter in New York that Father wants me to finish is very important," he continued. "It involves some major financing for the family through a Wall Street bank consortium. He signed most of the papers, but now they have some others that need to be signed by me, with Father's power of attorney. Maggie, this might mean that the rest of the family could accept me back into good graces! That would be a major miracle. It would mean that I could be back in line to take my father's place whenever he and the family consider me ready for it. We can have such a wonderful time, you and I, in Argentina."

Maggie had to break in and stop all this madness. She could not contain herself any longer, trying her very best to keep her frustration under control.

"Fernando, I don't want to do anything or say anything that would dim the luster of this day for you," she said, measuring her words carefully. "But I have learned a lot about you in a very short amount of time, and you need to slow down. First, you graduated magna cum laude and I didn't even know about it. You've been reconciled with your father and that's wonderful also, but you never told me about the millions of acres and millions of head of cattle and sheep that your family owns. Nor did you even mention the shipping company or that there was unlimited money to buy 'a couple of cars' and heirloom diamonds that I can't even choose for myself!"

She became more and more indignant just thinking of all he had said.

"Fernando, you haven't once said a single thing about my plans—only yours," she said, her voice quivering and pitched higher than normal. "You just expect me to jump when you say jump and to go off to

South America because you have money there!"

Fernando was at a loss for words. He was shocked by this unexpected outburst.

"And now I don't even know if I still know you!" she continued with a sob. "I loved the Fernando I knew who had to watch every penny and who didn't have a car or any of these worldly trappings. I was drawn to the man who was always thinking about the horses in the stables and whether they were healthy, who was concerned about the stablehands and if they were being paid enough and working hard enough. Fernando, you were different then. You seemed to be my kind of man. We—at least I—thought we understood each other. But now that I see you in a different light, I'm frightened and so unsure of our future together."

Fernando tried to protest, but it was Maggie's turn to continue like a runaway train.

"I don't know if I can fit into your society kind of life with consuls and famous movie actors and presidents of universities making a fuss over you and your father. Fernando, let's just go back to the stables and dance the tango in the dark—or ride down by the river and talk about us. Just you and me. This day has gone too fast and so much has happened that I can't understand or even catch my breath."

She paused for a breath. Fernando was smart enough to remain silent until she had run down a bit. But she wasn't quite through yet.

"Fernando, aside from all this, even though I might love you, I have wanted to have time alone to spend with my parents. They need to know that I love them and that I'm not deserting them. Can you possibly understand that this is getting bigger than I am able to handle so suddenly?"

Maggie started to sob. She was crumbling inside and her world was crumbling outside. She turned away from him.

Fernando was sensitive enough to realize that he had not prepared Maggie for all this and smart enough to know that she was absolutely right. Frankly, after so long a time, he himself wondered whether he was just going along with his father's wishes or if he was truly excited about being put back into his family relationships and complications so suddenly. Deep down, he had to admit that all those material trappings he had been used to before had been just that: trappings. Was he *truly* prepared to step back in so soon and so quickly? He had best back off a bit for both their sakes.

Now he too was afraid of what this could potentially do to this precious relationship he and Maggie had. *Are our ties of love strong enough to overcome the differences of our two worlds?* he wondered. At the same time, he rationalized, *This is not my fault. I did not set this up. It just happened all by itself—at least without my knowledge. Father arriving unexpectedly and all the attention from important people is a total surprise to me. Maggie can't blame me, but I can understand that she is confused.* His thoughts boiled and tumbled, producing some mixed feelings of his own.

They sat there in awkward silence, mired in thought, their backs to each other. Maggie shed quiet tears of apprehension. Fernando sat pensively, chiseled resolve setting into his strong face.

Maggie broke the silence.

"Let's call the whole thing off," she sobbed. "I don't think I can handle it all."

Without knocking, the consul entered the study looking for them, oblivious to the emotional tenseness that permeated the room.

"Oh, there you two are," he said jovially. "Forgive my intrusion, will you? But we need you. Your father is looking for you, Fernando, and Maggie, your parents would like to leave so they are looking for you too. Can you rejoin the group?"

Maggie wiped her tears away, paused a moment to gain control, put a smile on her face, and they walked out to rejoin the guests. As they entered the room, Hugo came quickly over to them with a concerned look on his face, apparently very shook up over something.

"Fernando, Maggie, I have just received this cable from home," he said urgently. "It's just as I feared might happen. You need to read it."

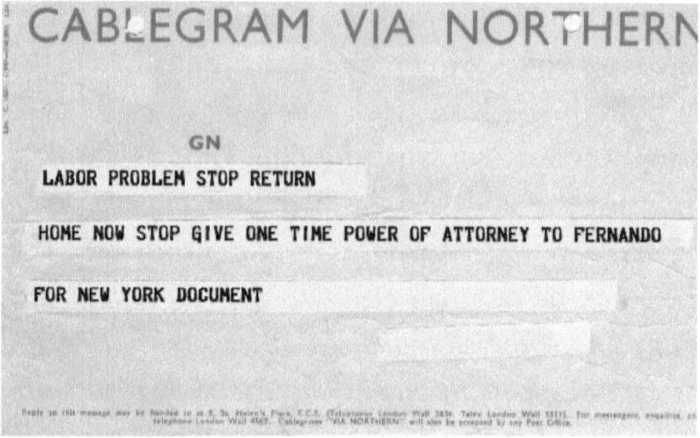
CABLEGRAM VIA NORTHERN

GN

LABOR PROBLEM STOP RETURN

HOME NOW STOP GIVE ONE TIME POWER OF ATTORNEY TO FERNANDO

FOR NEW YORK DOCUMENT

Hugo explained the nature of the emergency and expressed his regrets.

"I had planned on spending some time here," he said, "but I was afraid this might happen so I am prepared. I think it would be appropriate that we have one last toast to Fernando and Maggie and their graduation."

The consul signaled his head waiter, and the trays filled with champagne, juices, and other drinks were brought in quickly. He paused to make certain that all had their respective glasses with the desired drinks and offered an eloquent toast to the future of the graduates, individually and together. Then he toasted his guests, Fernando's father and Maggie's family, and others, saying something kind and gracious about each. At last, lingering goodbyes were said, with promises made to visit each other's ranches, and the caravan of cars moved off to their individual destinations. Despite the offer to use the limousine, Maggie left with her parents, while Fernando remained at the residency to spend the last evening with his father.

Troubled by their first disagreement, both strongly shaken by circumstances out of their control that threatened their entire future together, the couple had a long conversation by phone later that night.

"Please forgive me for taking your feelings and your opinions for granted," Fernando pleaded. "I really want our marriage to be a partnership. I love you too much to lose you over this. I know you have a lot of thinking to do, but I need to give my father a wedding date so they can have time to make plans. Could you please talk it over with your parents and see what they think?"

Maggie sighed and said she would. Despite the drama earlier, she did not want to lose him.

Fernando picked Maggie up the next morning in a big new roadster so they could bid Hugo bon voyage at the port. After hugs and kisses, reflecting some degree of reconciliation reached during their telephone conversation the night before, they got in the car. Maggie slid over close to Fernando and rested her arm on his leg, so as to leave his hand free to shift gears.

"Have you given some thought about my request?" he asked, as soon as they were out of the driveway and on their way.

"Yes," she said with a smile. "My parents and I stayed up most of the night after my conversation with you, discussing everything that had transpired. They have helped me see that my reaction yesterday was mostly one of accumulated stress, exhaustion, surprise, fatigue, and everything else that was no fault of yours. They helped me put things in proper perspective. So I accept your proposal, and I would like the date of our marriage to be one month after the races—that is, *if* I can somehow find a way to enter and fulfill that big dream of mine. So, you can tell your father of the tentative date. And I would like for our wedding to take place in Kanab, my home."

Without giving any indication of disappointment, since he was hoping for a lavish wedding Argentine style, Fernando simply smiled and squeezed her hand.

"Whatever you want, *mi amor*!"

Before she could say anything else about that, he immediately changed the subject to the one he was dying to share with her.

"My dear, there's some exciting news I want to share with you," he said. "I begged Luke to let me tell you first, and he is anxious to talk to you. I wish I had a drum roll right about now—he has a sponsor and a plane for you to race, and they will pay all expenses for the cross-country race!"

Maggie squealed and laughed with joy, bouncing up and down on the leather seat.

"Hold on, hold on!" Fernando said, laughing. "Let me continue with the rest of the plan. Luke will arrange all the details. I will go East. There I will take care of my family business matters—if you feel good about my doing that."

He paused to make sure that she was following him and that he was not pushing her. They had talked about having this kind of communication the night before. She nodded in agreement with a huge grin on her face.

Fernando continued, reassured by her smile, the squeeze of her hand, and her closeness.

"I will finish my New York bank business for my father, but I won't go to Argentina," he said. "Instead, I will stay here and do background work for Luke and your studio, getting cameras and equipment ready for a crew to film the start of the race in New York. When that is completed I will fly out to the Midwest for the filming of refueling at Wichita of the various race planes stopping there, including you."

He paused again, glancing over at her. Maggie nodded silently, almost in a daze.

"If you want," he continued, "I will help get your plane ready before I leave for Wichita. I'll finance whatever needs to be financed, and I will help you plan your route through the weather, taking into account the last-minute reports."

Maggie impulsively leaned over and gave him a big kiss on his cheek.

"Yes, please!" Maggie responded excitedly. "Thank you! Thank you!"

Maggie felt a new sense of fulfillment of a long-held dream come true at last. She had felt deep in her heart that somewhere there was a perfect airplane waiting for her to fly. She knew it would be just as good as the other race planes, and she knew she was just as good as the other pilots.

The perfect plane would somehow be symbolic of her own unique self, and she was thrilled beyond words. And she recognized that Fernando was making a sacrifice for her by not going home to Argentina, even with his mother's health and family business matters. This was truly a sign of his commitment to her.

CHAPTER 14

MAGGIE FINDS A SPONSOR

YESTERDAY HAD BEEN an eventful day. Fernando and Maggie had said goodbye to Don Hugo at the gang plank leading up to the enormous freighter, the biggest and the newest flagship of the family fleet. The news of Helen's sickness cast a cloud over the parting, but Hugo was irrepressibly demonstrative of his pride and affection for Fernando and Maggie. He also said he understood and supported Fernando's decision to not travel to Argentina yet. They waved goodbye, shedding tears as churning tugboats slowly towed the giant freighter from her berth at the pier.

Hugo stood on the bridge alongside the uniformed ship captain, waving to them on the dock until the ship moved out of sight. On the way home, Maggie and Fernando rejoiced together as they discussed their marriage plans as well as the upcoming race. They talked of the miracle news that Luke had finally found a sponsor with a plane for her to fly. Things were falling into place.

Earlier that morning, however, the mood had been very different. Maggie had called to say she urgently needed to meet with Fernando and Luke.

"New developments," she just said.

Fernando could sense from the tone of her voice that there was trouble brewing. Just when he thought he had everything under control, her call indicated a different kind of nervousness or tenseness in her.

Why does she want Luke to join us? Fernando wondered. He was aware that Luke was both Maggie's flying instructor as well as a mentor in the flying community. But aside from that, Fernando felt that Luke had some ulterior romantic motives. Luke was twenty years older than Maggie but was still a very dashing and handsome man. Maggie had assured Fernando that she had no romantic interest in Luke, only gratitude and fondness for him. She had also talked of Curly, the rodeo cowboy who had once proposed to her. Yet Fernando had a lurking insecurity regarding his position with Maggie, and he admitted to himself that he was jealous of Luke.

She had run both hot and cold on their upcoming marriage, but had finally agreed to his proposal with the proviso that it would take place one month after the cross-country race. He also feared that she still was reacting negatively to his newly established position of affluence and the family duties that would take him away to New York just when she might need him the most. What could these "new developments" be? Fernando turned the options over in his mind, somewhat concerned.

He entered Luke's office at the airport, noting that Maggie and Luke were sitting very close, in deep conversation. The sleek lioness lying on the floor beside the desk accepted Fernando with only a sniff and a look of recognition, then slumped down again.

"We were just discussing a problem we might have," Luke said, standing up quickly.

Maggie gave Fernando a half smile but remained seated. He had been ready to give her a hug and a kiss but she didn't meet his eyes. Jealousy reared its head again, and Fernando, aware that these two had been meeting before he arrived, stood there feeling very uncomfortable. It was an awkward moment.

"Fernando, Maggie and I have been talking about the race," Luke explained. "Now that I have found a sponsor with a fine plane to fly in the cross-country race, she has come up with another idea—a very dangerous one potentially. She has always wanted to fly in both races, but I thought she would be content to fly in just the cross-country race. Now she insists on *also* flying my old racer in the short pylon race. I don't agree, and I have been trying to convince this stubborn fiancée of yours of the dangers of this kind of flying, especially for a novice. But I'm not the one who is marrying her. It's up to you to talk her out of this. I know we had talked a bit about getting a new engine for my plane, and she has flown my old racer, but this is up to you two."

Fernando was stunned. He knew about pylon racing, of course, and Maggie had talked about her desire to race against male pilots in both types of racing, but he never took her seriously. He always assumed that she realized there was no way to get two airplanes to race. He certainly was not in favor of her flying the more dangerous pylon race either, and at this late date it seemed totally unreasonable for her to even bring the subject up.

Fernando looked at Maggie incredulously, then at Luke, realizing that he and Luke, a one-time competitor for Maggie's affections, were now both on the same side. How in the world could he handle this impetuous and headstrong girl he loved? He turned to face her expectant gaze. He was going to be tough and strong and mean if he had to in order to talk her out of this foolish and absurd idea, but he didn't want to lose her, either.

"Maggie . . . ," he began, then trailed off as he collected his thoughts. "Maggie, don't you remember that the reason the women were grounded from racing was because of the accidents and deaths of two good, young female aviators?"

His voice wasn't as strong and demanding as he wanted it to be. He tried again, this time with more emotion.

"Maggie, I don't want to attend a funeral before our wedding," he said firmly. "I am against it totally and completely. I agree with Luke."

Maggie stood up, her back straight, and faced Fernando. She smiled engagingly enough, but there was a bit of reserve in her body language.

"My dear macho-gaucho-man, don't you think I'm a good enough pilot?" she questioned, a bit defiantly. "You're an aeronautical engineer, so you of all people should know the progress and the better construction of the airframes and engines compared to those of just a few years ago. Don't you know that the new rules are safer in the pylon races? You know that the engines are safer and more reliable than three years ago and that the planes' wings are stronger and can handle the tight, high-G turns better. You know I'm capable of doing this! All I need is a chance."

She had hit them with a barrage of questions and implied statements that put them on the defensive. Fernando was not usually at a loss for words in a technical, aviation-related conversation, but with this determined woman who was defending her passion, he could not find a quick response.

"Hey, you are right on a lot of things," Luke interrupted. "But perhaps I have made the mistake of letting you fly my high-performance planes."

"I had always thought she would do well in the cross-country race," he said, turning to address Fernando. "She has a good head for navigation, on instruments as well as under visual conditions, and with a dependable plane she can fly as well as anyone. One day I let her fly my old pylon racer over there, that yellow one in the hangar hanging from the rafters. She flew it as a chase plane to follow me in my new long-range racer that we had just finished building. The idea was to let her watch for any signs of engine smoke and to give her a little bit of experience in something different. I did some simulated pylon turns and she followed me through very well. I stepped up the speed and tried some more vertical turns down on the ground around a couple of tall grain silos. She stayed right with me. I went up to altitude and did some aerobatics and again she stuck with me like a true fighter pilot."

Maggie gave Fernando an "I told you so" look.

"I believe that she will be able to pass any of the flight tests required of new first-time pylon racers," Luke continued. "In my opinion, she is good enough and capable enough. But that is not the question, Maggie. Anything can go wrong in those pylon races down close to the ground and there is just no time to jump, no time to make a planned emergency landing. If anything goes wrong, you just come down and 'buy a piece of ground' right there."

Fernando smiled wryly. The reference to "buying a piece of ground" was an old cowboy term that meant a horse had bucked you off, but in the flying community, it meant something gravely different.

"*Mi amor*, please listen to us both," Fernando pleaded. "You know I love you and look forward to many years of being together. Luke and I are only thinking of your safety. Look, one race is enough. One flight is enough investment of time and money and attention. A prior race will only distract you from your preparation for the big race. Please reconsider. We can talk more about this later. It just doesn't seem to fit together."

Fernando thought he had made enough points, and with Luke's support he hoped that would be enough to dissuade her. Again, he was wrong. Maggie asked them both to sit down. They obeyed meekly, resigned to listening to her arguments.

She petted the lioness, looked out the window at the beautiful planes on the flight line, then she looked through the interior window between the office and the hangar and saw Luke's big, new cross-country racer on the floor. Above it was the much smaller old, yellow, pylon racer that Luke had referred to. She took it all in. She faced her two closest friends and began a monologue she had practiced in her mind for a long time.

Fernando and Luke saw her jaw tighten, her back stiffen, her head held high, and her gaze was piercing. Maggie launched into her defense like a trial lawyer at summation.

"You may not remember my family history but let me tell you about it," Maggie started. "My great-grandparents were pioneers. They won the West the hard way. When they crossed the plains there were no roads, no towns, no civilization at all. They built our ranch from scratch against all odds. Nature sent floods and drought, bugs, and plagues, but they kept clearing the land, bringing in irrigation water from the mountains, raising crops, building their herd of cattle, breeding horses, making peace with the Indians, fighting off cattle rustlers—the whole bit. They were partners in everything. It was a coequal partnership. My great-grandmother was just as tough as my great-grandfather."

Fernando did not quite get where she was going, but he did not dare lose eye contact with her and he was fascinated by her grit and boldness.

"My grandparents were the same way," Maggie continued. "However, Grandpa died young, leaving Grandma with two young children. She could have given up and moved into what was now a town and maybe been a schoolteacher, but she chose to take care of the place. She ran the ranch. She dug down deep and decided she could be both a mother as well as the boss of the ranch. She knew how to ride, how to shoot, how to raise hay, and how to raise cattle. She knew how to protect her property. The Indians were a problem for a while, but she helped deliver their babies, nurse their sick, feed them when they ran out of food, and they in turn defended her place against any wandering tribes. She carried both a six-shooter on her hip and a carbine in her saddle scabbard. Cattle rustlers found her more than a match for them. Her feminine intuition prompted her to put out Indian scouts to watch for rustlers."

By this time, Fernando and Luke knew exactly where Maggie was going with this.

"She figured out how to drive her cattle to the best market at the best time," she went on. "She managed her money well, bought more land wisely, increased her herds, came to the attention of the people in town, and when they needed the toughest person around to be the new sheriff, they chose her. With Indian help, she tracked down bank robbers and cattle thieves and brought them to jail. She was handy with her guns and out-shot and out-witted the bad guys. She was an original Annie Oakley: a gun-totin' frontier woman. And in time she was elected to be the first female mayor. No one ever got in her way without paying a price for it. I know that I inherited some of her qualities."

She paused to take a deep breath. Fernando was learning something about Maggie. He leaned back, looked over at Luke, smiled, and turned back to face her, making himself comfortable and settling down as if for a long time. Maggie continued telling her history.

"In time, Father took over the place. He married Mother, who also grew up on a large ranch doing everything that was needed when they were short-handed. My brother and I are twins. I grew up on the place expected to work just as hard as he did. I could drive a tractor at the same time he could. I could milk a cow the same time he could. I could rope just as well as him, but he was better at bronc breaking than I was. We raced each other, we competed against each other in everything, and both of us are wild competitors, giving no chance to the other. Sometimes he beat me and sometimes I beat him. We got into rodeo stuff trying to be better trick riders than the people we saw in the rodeos. We finally started working together instead of against each other. We worked up a successful routine for show riding, but my brother entered some competition bronc riding and was hurt. I was offered some movie stunt jobs and from that got interested in flying and in aeronautical engineering. I was making enough money to send some home because the ranch fell upon hard times during the Depression and Dad had to mortgage the place, plus cattle prices fell even more, unfortunately, and he had to sell off part of his herd to avoid bankruptcy."

Fernando thought Maggie might be running down, but she kept going. He had found out a lot about the fighting spirit hidden within this woman he had come to love and admire.

"Somewhere along the way I fell in love with flying," she said. "I loved the ranch but flying was an adventure on a higher level, no pun intended. I loved the mental science of it, the freedom of flight in three dimensions, and the beauty of the colors of sky and earth. As you both know, from the air you cannot see mud or weeds or garbage down below. Everything is organized and beautiful. The shapes of the clouds above and the patchwork of the land below is painted in beautiful colors in artistic designs arranged by God. A pilot can fly like the birds at treetop level, leap across valleys and rivers, wander over to see the other side of a mountain, or explore the cloud canyons into which children ride on imaginary steeds."

Maggie paused. Both Luke and Fernando knew they were looking into the heart of a unique individual who had an inspired ability to explain her passion for flying.

"I know flying can be dangerous," she said, shifting her tone of voice. "I accept that. Riding a horse across a flat field can also turn dangerous the moment he steps into a gopher hole, stumbles, and goes down, throwing you on the ground and rolling over you. I have done that, I've been there. Sometimes bones get broken; sometimes you end up paralyzed; sometimes you die. But I have a quote here from Luke's friend, Charles Lindbergh. I knew this might come up so I have it with me. Let me share it with you."

She began to read: "I lived on a higher plane than the skeptics of the ground; one that was richer because of its very association with the element of danger they dreaded, because it was freer of the earth to which they were bound. In flying, I tasted a wine of the Gods of which they could know nothing. Who valued life more highly, the aviators who spent it on the art they loved, or these misers who doled it out like pennies through their ant-like days? I decided that if I could fly for ten years before I was killed in a crash, it would be a worthwhile trade for an ordinary lifetime."

When she looked at their faces, Maggie knew she had won. She had touched their aviator hearts. Their eyes glistened with both understanding and admiration. They too had chosen to fly in spite of the dangers of pioneering a new and glorious science. Their opposition evaporated with the words from a pilot they admired and revered. Both sat in stunned silence. There was no getting around her reasoning. Now they both understood more clearly than ever before and were convinced of her passion and her determination.

"I know there are risks," she said again. "But I am proud to be part of the pioneering adventure of this grand new science."

She was a competitor by nature and just had to race. She was like a thoroughbred racehorse born to run in the Derby or die trying. She had a pioneer spirit to win against nature at all odds. And she had it in her head that she could race against the men and maybe win or perhaps lose, but she had to try.

Maggie sat down, wrung out with all her talking. She waited for the men to find their tongues and words.

"Okay, you win," Luke said first. "But what do you want me to do? I found you a sponsor and a long-distance race plane. Do you expect me to come up with another miracle?"

"Yep, I certainly do!" Maggie exclaimed. "All I want is for you to give me some more practice in your little yellow pylon racer. I know it needs a new engine. You don't have the money for one, but maybe you could trade that little roadster . . ."

She looked at Fernando, who was jolted back into reality. Now she had floored him again. Did she actually want him to trade his brand-new fancy car in for an airplane engine? Was she really serious? He waited for what seemed an eternity before he continued.

"Okay, Maggie," he said, giving in. "You need an engine. I think I can find the money without trading my car back in. Would that help?"

"Oh, yes, yes!" she exclaimed quick as a flash. "And I want you to know that I appreciate your support more than just the money. We will pay it back to your father. And then we can get married and go to South America or wherever you want to go! Now, how do we do all of this?"

For the next few hours the three of them worked out the details of the coming weeks. Luke had to get his own new cross-country plane ready to fly. It needed a short-range radio and basic instruments. They also had to get his old pylon race plane ready, and he had to give Maggie more practice in low-level, high-speed pylon turns. And then the three of them had to get the planes to New York. New information from the factory was that they could have Maggie's cross-country plane delivered to New York, so that solved one problem. Their heads were reeling thinking of all these details.

The pylon race would be held on Long Island, New York, two days before the cross-country race would start. Fernando had to sign papers on Wall Street and take care of business matters in New York for his father. It was not complicated—just time-consuming. But working together, they finally figured out how to fit it all in.

Maggie was on cloud nine, even without being in an airplane. Both of her greatest flying dreams were being fulfilled, and her joy and enthusiasm were boundless. She hugged Fernando. She hugged Luke. She kissed Fernando. She leaned in to kiss Luke but then thought better of it and just gave him another hug. She beamed and thanked them over and over again. She was as giddy as a little girl at Christmastime!

Maggie asked the motion picture company to help set up a press conference for her at the studio, and requested assistance from their public relations department. This publicity was going to help their big movie project along.

At the studio, the press gathered for the important announcement. It was a large room, with multiple microphones installed at the podium. The room was full. The reporters wore felt fedoras and looked a bit unkempt, as reporters often do. The head of the studio called them to order, introduced Maggie, and told them that she had an announcement to make.

Moving gracefully to the podium, Maggie's smile dazzled.

"As you all know, I have just graduated with my aeronautical engineering degree," she began. "You've also heard that I have a sponsor and a new plane to fly in the great cross-country race from New York to Los Angeles. What you don't know is that I now have a second plane to fly, so I am also entering the pylon race, which will take place before the cross-country race."

A surprised murmur rippled through the audience as the reporters took notes.

"I have the support of my future husband, Fernando Underwood, who is helping the studio with the forthcoming movie about cross-country racing," she continued. "He is also financing a new engine for the pylon racer I will fly. I also have the support of my mentor and instructor, the incomparable Luke Whitney, who will be flying in the cross-country race but has decided not to fly this year in the pylon races. He is allowing me to fly his pylon racer that you saw him fly last year. Now, any questions?"

The unruly reporters started shouting questions at the pretty aviatrix before them. For a moment it seemed that pandemonium reigned. The studio people were startled. Usually the reporters behaved with more respect, but they sensed something really newsworthy, leading to them behaving like spoiled children all trying to get the same piece of candy. Since no one stepped forward to call the meeting back into order, Maggie raised both hands and called for them to be quiet. Everyone hushed.

"Now please sit down," she said, taking charge like a schoolmarm. "If you have a question, raise your hands and I will call on you one at a time!"

In awe, reporters turned to one another and murmured their admiration.

Maggie singled out a hand in the middle. The reporter stood up with his pad and pen poised to write.

"For our readers, could you explain the difference between the pylon race and the cross-country race?" he asked.

"There are several differences," she responded, eager to explain. "First, the cross-country race is 2,450 miles long, flown coast to coast in almost a straight line. The pylon race is only a hundred miles, flown around a three-sided course of ten miles each for ten laps. Second, the cross-country race is flown at high altitude and the pylon race is flown right down on the deck. And third, the cross-country is usually flown in bigger planes carrying a big load of gas, whereas the pylon race is usually flown in smaller planes carrying only enough gas for half an hour. There are other differences as well."

The reporters were furiously taking notes. Maggie called on one.

"Miss Rockwell, why are women being allowed to fly again in both races?" he said. "Isn't it too dangerous for young ladies? You can't win anyway."

Maggie was expecting this question also. She had answered it many times, and it always bothered her.

"Sir, your question offends me and offends all the women who read what you write," she said sternly. "At least half your readers are women. Are you going to tell them you think we're inferior to the male pilots and can't win? Last year, with no women flying, two men lost their lives. Men were not prohibited from flying. We think we have a right to fly and to compete as equals. You ask, 'Why are women being allowed to fly now?' Because we complained and the public put pressure on the race promoters. The media joined our side, so I thank you all. With your support, the ban was lifted by popular acclaim. Next question, over there."

"Why is pylon racing so popular as a spectator sport?" another reporter questioned.

"The closed-course race around pylons is right in front of the grandstands," Maggie explained. "The public can see the planes take off from a runway in front of them and then circle the course fighting for the lead all down low at eye level, again right in front of them. Some planes are flying lower than the people at the top of the stands. And the noise is exciting. The place rumbles and vibrates as the roaring planes flash by, jockeying for position, just like in a horse race. It is really exciting. And there will be not just one race but five preliminary races, two semifinal races, and one final Gold Cup race for the overall winner. In a cross-country race you cannot watch the planes. They take off and disappear into the distance quickly."

The next reporter asked a related and important question.

"Then why do you fly a race from coast to coast if no one can watch you fly?"

Maggie had a answer for every question but needed a break from speaking. She nodded her head at Luke.

"We have here one of the best-known race pilots in the world," she said. "Let's have him answer that question."

Luke was flattered; he stepped to the podium and answered with precision.

"Both types of races are really to promote scientific progress in the development of engines, air frames, aerodynamic streamlining, higher speeds, longer endurance, strength of new materials such as the use of aluminum in place of fabric or welded steel in place of wood, new types of fuels and lubricants, and so on. We know that in Germany, Italy, Russia, Japan, and other countries the governments are paying for the development of new and faster aircraft, but here in the United States everything is being left up to the private companies to do the developing. Promoting air races is one form of stimulating progress. We have new engines and new airplanes on the drawing boards for the races that will meet or surpass all military planes of our own and other countries. On the other hand, we do not have the factories set to mass-produce large numbers for military use in case of war. We will need government help and contracts in order to do that if war ever comes. We have the know-how, but other countries are already far ahead of us in production facilities. Through air races, private industry can make sure we stay up with them at least in design and technology."

The reporters continued to ask questions, and Maggie and Luke handled them all with exactness and a pleasing demeanor. She was a professional engineer defending her discipline with style. Fernando was very proud of her and thought how much his extended family and the workers throughout the family businesses were going to fall in love with this tough, intelligent, and beautiful woman he loved so dearly.

At the end of the press conference the studio publicity people, taking advantage of having such a large press corps in attendance, announced their upcoming new air-racing movie. The movie would do a great job of making the air races even more popular in the years to come. With that, the press conference was over.

CHAPTER 15

THE STAGGERWING

"The Staggerwing cleaves its way through the air as a shark slices through waves, seemingly unconscious of the effort, beautiful as a water-nymph. The takeoff is a moment of simple, glorious joy. There is this gigantic, thundering, clattering roar as you push the throttle forward, a brief moment of directional uncertainty, an overwhelming aroma of warm oil, and then she leaps, bounds into the air as though all the wolves in Siberia were baying at her heels."

—James Gilbert, 1996

IT WAS LOVE at first sight when Maggie met her new cross-country race plane—the new, larger, faster executive-cabin airplane. Maggie, Fernando, and Luke had been summoned to the airport hangar by Roy Butterfield, the president of the company.

Luke had negotiated the contract in which the company agreed to provide Maggie Rockwell with their new model to fly in the cross-country air race, as well as to cover all expenses. In the contract, Maggie, as pilot, agreed to fly the race to the best of her ability with intent to win the race for prize money. In exchange, Maggie would allow the factory to use her name and photograph for their advertising and publicity for one year from the day of the race.

Roy had flown the plane to New York and was waiting at the designated airport hangar when the pilots arrived. Maggie signed the papers, and he handed her the pilot's manual. Afterward there was a formal presentation to the public outside. Roy presented his and Oscar's pride and joy, their newly designed airplane they had named "Staggerwing" because of the negative, or "staggered," placement of the wings.

Maggie, Fernando, and Luke stood in front of the middle of the hangar on the cement apron that was wider than the hangar itself. Several company executives and employees came out of the building to watch, as a number of reporters, photographers, and a few potential customers had been invited to the Staggerwing's unveiling.

Interest was high because the ship was rumored to be a new type of cabin plane that would be easy to fly, comfortable to travel in, fast, long-range, equipped with blind-flying instruments, short-range radio transmitter and receiver, and safe for VIP executives. It could cross the country in less than a day. It could fly higher than any mountains in the United States. In the hands of a competent pilot, it would be safe to fly in weather and at night.

The company owners astutely recognized that having an attractive young woman fly their plane in a major race being covered by newspapers and radio across the entire country would give them and their plane immediate favorable publicity. The press would emphasize every feature as well as the problems each feature was designed to solve. The Staggerwing would be the first production-line executive-cabin plane that was fast enough to enter a major race with expectations of placing high at the finish line.

It certainly helped to have Maggie as the pilot, since her new movie was in theaters. Instead of the actors being the top news items, it was Maggie and her stunt—jumping from a running horse to a ladder dangling from a plane passing overhead—that received all the attention.

At this point it no longer really mattered how well she finished in the race because the papers were already full of information on the Staggerwing, market curiosity was exploding, and orders were beginning to come in. The factory was located in the oil country area of Middle America and executives in that business were potential sales prospects.

The suspense was building as the excited throng gathered behind the controlled barriers where Maggie, Fernando, and Luke waited for the tall hangar doors to open. Then, with a flair for the dramatic not common in the aviation industry, a drum roll sounded from inside the giant hangar and the doors began to open. Men were pushing the tall panels to the left and to the right. The interior was dark and nothing could be seen by those standing in the bright sunlight. Quickly, four young boys, wearing their high school band uniforms, stepped forward and with their shiny trumpets proudly blasted out a heraldic fanfare.

The brightly painted Staggerwing emerged from the dark background, regal and majestic. Two line boys and two mechanics pushed it out slowly. Its oversize chrome spinner hit the sun's rays first with a dazzling sparkle. They kept pushing the plane forward and the round cowling covering the radial engine slid into view, followed by the windshield slanted backward and upward. The bottom wing's leading edge appeared, and then the leading edge of the top wing glowed in the sunlight.

Soon the whole plane was exposed and stood there gleaming and shining, to the enthusiastic applause of the onlookers. The fabric skin had been shrunk to form-fit the stringers and frames. Many coats of airplane dope had been spray-applied and then hand-polished with jeweler's rouge to a mirror finish, making it look like it had been carved from Jell-O.

The tail sat low on a very short tail wheel so the plane had a jaunty angle to it. The main landing gear was quite tall, but after takeoff it would fold into the belly of the plane, transforming the whole into a very streamlined craft.

The unveiling had an electric effect on the pilots standing by. Each one wished he could get in, fire up that big round engine, and take to the skies. The Staggerwing seduced every pilot in view. She was so attractive just sitting there that those pilots' minds were flooded with dreams of faraway places they'd now be able to visit in style. She instantly became the prized chariot of its day—a magnificent flying carpet.

Maggie was transfixed and somewhat breathless. She was honored to be trusted with command of such a beautiful, aerodynamic creation.

"I have never seen such a beautiful plane in all my life!" she exclaimed. "She's gorgeous! I never imagined that a cabin plane could look so fast just parked on the ground!"

Roy smiled and, with a flair, proudly handed her the keys.

"She's all yours to fly, miss," he said. "We may own her, but she's yours until you arrive in Los Angeles. Why don't you walk all the way around her more carefully and then climb up the wing walk and step into the spacious cabin. While you walk, we'll point out a few things you'll need to check on before every flight."

Maggie, Roy, Fernando, and Luke all approached the silent, poised plane as if she were a sculpted work of art. They were respectful of her position and status but wanted to look at her more closely. Maggie carefully ran her hand along the leading edge of the lower wing all the way from the tip to the junction with the fuselage. She patted it affectionately like she patted her horses. She kicked the exposed tire like all pilots do. There was no reason for it because she could see if it was flat or not, but it seemed to be a gesture of ownership—and Maggie felt like a proud owner. For a while, anyway.

Fernando and Luke got down on their haunches and peered up into the wheel wells and into the engine compartment. Roy showed Maggie where to drain the sumps of each fuel tank and how to inspect the fairings that covered the retracted wheels for possible damage.

At the nose of the plane, Maggie took out a handkerchief and patted the chrome spinner with the cloth, so as to not leave any fingerprints. She looked into the finned cylinders and the chromed pushrod covers.

"Allow me to show you how to check the oil level and look for signs of oil drips," Roy said, pointing to the engine.

"Have you got some rags in case the radial throws some oil?" she asked.

"You bet," Roy responded. "They're stacked away neatly in the baggage compartment in a small box with a screwdriver and other tools."

Fernando thumped the chrome guy wires bracing the wings to see if they sounded tight enough. Luke commented on the remarkably fine finish evident everywhere. Maggie was all the way around the plane to the tail on the far side when she just could not contain herself any longer. Where the fuselage narrowed down to a very slim waist just before the tail surfaces of the rudder and the elevators, she bent down and kissed the taut fabric surface and impulsively wrapped her arms around it in an affectionate embrace.

"Oh, you beautiful doll—you great big beautiful doll!" she exclaimed.

She had fallen in love with her airplane. She found herself already bonding with the Staggerwing. The tail passed her inspection and she came around to the door. With the key the president had given her she unlocked the cabin door, climbed up on the wing walk, and poked her head inside. Maggie felt like her eyes were deceiving her at first glance into the elegant interior of her Staggerwing. *Am I dreaming or is this magnificent creation for real?* she asked herself.

She was used to the rather austere appointments of most planes she had flown. Planes usually had only basic essentials, partly to reduce weight and partly to reduce cost. There was typically no upholstery, no padding, no flooring, no heat or air vents, and even the seat was usually just a metal bucket-type pan a little larger than the parachute pack that pilots sat on. Even instruments were usually stuck into round holes in a flat sheet of metal. There was no attempt to make it look nice—just functional.

The Staggerwing, on the other hand, was an enormous step up in creature comforts. It was designed for the affluent corporate executive who needed to get to another city fast to take care of important business and thereafter return to his office or home in the most comfortable manner.

Gasping and smiling and *oohing* all at the same time, Maggie stepped inside the cabin, carefully caressing the fine pleated leather seats and side trim as though they were covered in ermine, allowing her fingers to linger and enjoy the feel. She reached up and stroked the soft headliner that hid the thick insulating materials between the cabin and the outer skin. It was plush, smooth, and first-class limousine quality. She didn't know whether to trust her sense of touch or not—it was oh, so delicious!

She noticed to her delight that care had been taken to make the instrument panel look finished and professional. There were no gaps, holes, dangling wires, or roughshod items. She smiled with approval when she saw that the cabin had a heater for altitude or winter flying, as well as air vents for every passenger. The flooring could have come right out of a Packard or Rolls Royce, and, not being able to resist, she slipped off one shoe to feel the luxuriousness of the carpet.

"I could even place a crystal vase with flowers between the pilot and copilot seats and it would look right at home!" she exclaimed to the men outside. "Hey, I could even wear silk stockings and high heels instead of my cowgirl outfit and not be the least bit out of place!"

Feeling like a queen, she took the left seat gracefully, locked her hands around the pilot's control wheel, leaned back, closed her eyes, sighed contentedly, and dreamed of the magic and wonder and drama she would experience as captain and commander of this marvelous flying machine that would be her home in the coming days.

Not wanting to disturb her reverie, Roy climbed in and quietly sat down in the copilot's seat, Fernando and Luke right behind, anxious to hear all the checkout procedures.

When Maggie came back to reality, they went over all controls, knobs, instruments, gadgets, switches, valves, locks, and procedures. It was a very complete checkout, but Maggie could see that she would need to spend most of the night reading the pilot's manual to get it all down so she could pass a blindfold test as well as a shakedown flight the next day.

Fernando and Luke sat on the wide, comfortable back seat and watched wistfully, each wanting to be in Maggie's place. The most uncomfortable place in a plane for a pilot is the back seat, but they were happy for Maggie and the fulfilling of her dream.

After that, there would be a few familiarization flights, then the day of the pylon race in Luke's plane—and two days later, the big cross-country race in this beautiful Staggerwing! Maggie could hardly wait.

CHAPTER 16

A DANGEROUS PYLON RACE

THE DAY OF the pylon race was perfect summer weather on Long Island. The sky was a warm blue color with floating fair-weather cumulus drifting like fat white sheep across the sky. An enthusiastic throng filled the bleachers to capacity. Animated conversations rippled throughout the crowd of spectators. The weeks of publicity had built up popular interest in the race, in the pilots themselves, in the planes they would fly, and in the movie—soon to be in the theaters—that would include footage from the actual race.

Everyone present knew the actor pilots by name, but they also knew the real pilots by name. There was great speculation as to who would win and who would lose. The fact that the women were racing again in force to challenge the men in the most macho and dangerous of all sports had added a lot of fuel to the fire of speculation. Some expected the women to do well, while others thought they would fall apart under the pressure. Speeds had increased significantly in the past three years since women had last raced. Did the women have the muscle to handle the controls at high speeds and high-G loads? Would this year's pylon racers hold together better than last year's? Last year one racer's wing had fallen off and another's engine blew up. Reporters actively sought answers to these questions.

The pylon race would be under new rules for greater safety. Instead of a large field of twenty racers bunched together like horses in the Kentucky Derby, the first part of the race would be in small groups of four planes per "heat." This would lead to safer traffic in the turns around the pylons. It also meant five preliminary races, one right after the other. Then the top two planes of each heat would be matched in two heats of five planes each per race for the semifinals. Finally, the top two planes of each semifinal heat, a total of four planes, would race in the final or Gold Cup race. This would produce a lot of action, eight races, and be a real crowd-pleaser.

Down on the flight line, assistants and mechanics readied planes and Maggie posed for pictures. Luke was occupied fixing the fuel system and carburetor so it would run richer, adjusting the ignition system for more accurate firing of the spark plugs, and tweaking the cooling baffles on Maggie's plane. It had a new engine but it was running hot. It was a slightly bigger engine in cylinder displacement but the engine mounts were the same size as the previous one—this made for a tighter fit under the cowling. It was putting out more power, but the cooling seemed to be less effective so the cylinder head temperatures were running very high. The baffles must have been different, but there was no time now to experiment with changes to eliminate the problem. Luke hoped that the short race would not cause Maggie any major engine problems.

Fernando had his own opinion, but Luke had not asked for help nor had Maggie, so he just stood to the side, feeling very much like a fifth wheel, watching things happen, left out of all the action. True, he had been absent and busy in New York on family business, but still he felt awkward and useless. He did have time to share the success of his visit with the Wall Street bankers with Maggie. He told her how he had explained his last three years studying out West to the financiers. It was also important to help the bankers understand that the labor problems and political unrest in Argentina could be solved. In the end, they had expressed confidence in Don Hugo, in Fernando, and in the family businesses. Although she didn't understand much, Maggie was pleased with the news.

Maggie was scheduled to fly in the second heat of four planes. She had looked at her competition and liked what she saw. She knew the pilots of the other three planes, and they were all seasoned, expert pilots. She had walked along the flight line and saw that some had retractable landing gear and some had fixed gear. The fixed-gear planes would have more drag and would therefore be slower. Maggie's plane, Luke's old racer, had retractable landing gear, but Luke had had some problems with the wheels hanging up and not dropping down and locking in place to land, which concerned him.

"Now Maggie," Luke had reminded her, "if the gear doesn't go down when you get ready to land, all you have to do is slow down to about 100 mph indicated airspeed, pull the nose up a bit, then take your feet off the rudder pedals and kick down on the wheels. You can see the wheels right under your rudder pedals when they are retracted. I've had to kick it down several times so it's no big deal. If that doesn't do the trick, go ahead and land flat on her belly, but stop the prop crosswise so you don't bend it."

Maggie had heard this several times in prior checkouts, but Luke was repeating it because when an emergency hits, you need to react fast and automatically. You don't have time to think things through.

Her competition's planes had different kinds of engines: round or radial engines, in-line engines that were right side up with the spark plugs on top, and others that were inverted with the spark plugs on the bottom. There were both air-cooled and liquid-cooled engines. Some had one wing and others had two. Several planes had a single wing with the wing on top like birds, and others had a bottom wing only.

Maggie was comfortable with Luke's old pylon race plane. It was a tried and proven design, easy to fly, very maneuverable, quite fast, looked sharp, was air-cooled, and had retractable gear. Her only worry was the overheating engine, but since the flight was a hundred miles, at over 200 mph it would only be a thirty-minute flight. She figured it should handle the stress.

An announcer would provide ongoing commentary of the action to the crowd over a giant public address system during the eight races of the day. Using high-powered binoculars, the excited spectators were ready to follow the race planes as they flashed around the course. Those who had attended these races before knew the drama that would unfold, punctuated throughout by the roar of powerful engines, the vibrations felt in the gut from the high revolutions of the slicing propeller blades, and the play-by-play announcer over a very powerful public address system booming out the details:

"Watch the action on Pylon #2 . . ."

"Oh, oh, look, the red biplane has a smoking engine, watch that . . ."

"Oops, the silver monoplane is pulling out of the race . . ."

The first heat of brightly painted planes took off individually on the runway in front of the stands, and the capacity crowd was treated to a noisy spectacle right before their eyes. Then the planes caught up and grouped together in a planned formation as they flew off into the distance and joined up with a pace plane that had taken off first.

When the pace plane had all four planes abreast, he led them back toward the first leg of the race, which was the pylon in front of the stands on the right-hand side, perpendicular to the runway from which they had just taken off, and going away from the crowd.

The pace-plane pilot brought the speed of the formation up to 200 mph, and as he crossed the pylon he pulled up in a vertical climb, signaling to the formation that they had a race.

Each pilot firewalled his throttle to reach maximum power. They had exactly 3.3 miles before reaching the far pylon. The crowd could see the planes trying to get ahead and turn inside, forcing the slower planes to drop back or ease outside the turn for safety. Another 3.3 miles, and they rounded the third pylon to come flying back in front of the cheering spectators. Of course, the pilots could not hear a thing above their own engine so the effort was lost on them. By this time, the fastest plane had taken the lead and the next one was close behind. The third and fourth planes seemed evenly matched and were racing neck and neck.

As the formation came past the crowd, again at breakneck speed and almost down on the ground, the two leaders were still slightly separated, but three and four had traded places at a back pylon because one pilot had been more aggressive and cut inside, forcing the last one to drop behind.

The next lap around, the lead plane was showing some smoke but he kept his engine going full bore, trying to squeeze every bit of power out of it to stay ahead. Maybe the pilot didn't even know he was showing smoke from his exhaust. Perhaps it was just the rings out of kilter and passing a bit of oil into the cylinder, or even a valve going bad. It could be that he had a high temperature signal.

The last plane was doing something different. The pilot seemed to be climbing a little higher. He could not get inside his opponent, but he was staying even with him while climbing slightly.

Maggie, Fernando, and Luke were standing side by side as spectators of the first heat. Luke pointed out to Maggie the technique the last pilot most likely was going to try.

"Watch what he does," he said. "It'll be dangerous but he might get ahead of his rival. He'll wait until the last lap and then using his altitude as an advantage he'll suddenly dive down, picking up extra speed and maybe slide inside or under the other guy and pull ahead right at the pylon. Watch him. It might work, but don't you try it. It's easy for the other guy to accidentally chop off your tail with his prop and you'll both go down."

As the first heat came around for the tenth lap, the first plane was still showing smoke, but he was not slowing down. The second was right on his tail, but unable to move ahead. Suddenly, the last plane made his move. He dove down just as Luke had anticipated, pulled slightly under and in front of the plane previously ahead of him and beat him to the last pylon, then turned quickly to take third place. It was a gutsy trick, dangerously low and in the other pilot's blind spot, but it paid off. Since only the first two planes would qualify for the semifinals, it only served to show the audience the tricks the pilots might have up their sleeves.

Maggie's heat was called. Her heart raced. She kissed Luke, as he was closest to her, and whispered, "Wish me luck." In her nervousness she forgot to kiss Fernando standing just a little back of Luke. She climbed in her plane, pulled her goggles down, and then remembered Fernando. She looked for him, saw him, and all she could do was blow him a kiss. Fernando felt color rise to his face in a moment of jealousy at her overlooking him.

She started her engine and, when signaled, pulled into her place on the runway. The flag went down and off they started. After liftoff, Maggie pulled her landing gear up, and it closed without a hitch. She hoped it would come down as easy as it had gone up. She caught up with and followed the pace plane and then drew into the line-abreast formation.

Each knew who was placed inside on the pole, second next, then third, and finally the outside racer at fourth. They knew the pace plane would set a pace of 200 mph and then zoom up to start the race. When he disappeared overhead, Maggie pushed her throttle all the way and felt the power increase. All gauges read in the green; no problems yet. One plane was ahead of her, but she was ahead of the other two when they hit the first pylon turn.

She felt the rough turbulence caused by the pilot in front of her. The two behind her had a rougher ride still. She was surprised by all the bouncing, somewhat like being in a fast boat bashing against the tops of the waves. It was harder to fly smooth turns than she expected. Even at full power, Maggie could not quite catch up with the plane ahead. Maybe he had a bigger engine, because she didn't think he was flying any better than she was. She had to be careful not to cut a pylon because if she did, the penalty was to turn around, go back, do the turn again the right way, or receive a penalty.

On the fourth lap, one of the racers behind tried to get ahead of her, but she held her course and didn't let him scare her and cause her to move outside the turn. But now she knew he had the power to try to pass her, so she had to fly a perfect track around the course. Then she noticed her temperature gauge. It had started to climb.

Maggie was the only woman in her heat. She had to beat the men. She had to hold it together until she was one of the two winners of her heat. She tried enriching the mixture, which would put more gasoline into the engine to help cool it. Luke had adjusted the carburetor for this purpose so she had a little more room for cooling, even though it would burn a lot more fuel. She had plenty of fuel so it was worth trying. It seemed to help.

The turbulence was worse each time around the circuit. All four planes were really churning the place up. It was bumpy but exciting. Maggie managed to hold her place in the race and not let either of the two behind her get ahead. Then at the last lap the pilot in front just dropped out. There was no sign of fire or smoke or anything, but he pulled outside and the other three passed him like bullets. She hoped he would get down okay. One of the planes behind her managed to get ahead on the straightaway at the last minute but she still placed second in the race.

She would qualify, but she did not win the heat outright as she had hoped to do. When she tried to put the gear down it didn't work, so she followed Luke's instructions to the letter. She slowed way down, pulled the nose up, put both feet on the tops of the exposed wheels and pushed down hard. The wheel covers opened, allowing the wheels to drop down and lock. It had worked just like Luke said it would.

Maggie came around for the landing and noticed that the plane that had been ahead of her but had pulled out of the race was off to the side of the runway—so the pilot had made it safely to the strip. Apparently, the engine had quit before being able to taxi in. It seemed to be intact, and she was relieved for him.

Fernando and Luke helped her climb out of the cockpit, congratulating her on being a qualifier for the semifinals. The third and fourth heats had some moments of suspense but no wrecks, no fires, no tragedies. There were some close calls juggling for position on some of the pylon turns, but from the distance of the crowd to the farthest pylon it was hard to see. It looked like very near misses with the group batched together, but maybe in the air they had more room between them than it looked like from the ground.

When all twenty planes had completed the five heats, there were ten qualifiers for the semifinals. Maggie was a qualifier, which thrilled her immensely. But now she was flying in a heat of five planes. The other four might be as fast as she was, maybe faster. Now she had to fly better than before, in addition to avoiding the tricks of the others.

There were only two women among the ten qualifiers—Maggie and Mary Jane. All the other female pilots had opted out of the pylon race. Maggie was thrilled to know that her mentor—her inspiration—was one of the qualifiers.

MJ was an experienced pilot, having been in racing before the edict banning the women. She was a competent pilot working for a government agency. Maggie liked and respected her and enjoyed the association with such an expert pilot. Her plane was new and she handled it very well. Maggie was in the first heat and Mary Jane was in the second.

Maggie was ready to go. The same drill for takeoff, climb, follow the pace plane, watch it zoom up, then push that throttle all the way to the firewall, squeeze a few more rpms while saying a prayer, and the race was on. She was in the middle of the pack at the first turn around the pylon. Two planes were ahead of her and two behind. Although all of them were at about the same speed, she felt boxed in. She could not tell whether anyone had an advantage except that the first ones to make the first pylon had the smoothest ride. Around and around the pylon racecourse they went—like race cars at Indianapolis Speedway, except that it was a triangle course instead of an oval brickyard.

Maggie was not winning, but she was not losing, either. If one of the planes ahead of her had engine trouble she would move into that place and make the Gold Cup finals. Then disaster struck. The cylinder head temperature moved above the red mark and into the danger area. Then the oil temperature started to move up. All of a sudden, the engine began to shake and run erratically. The plane slowed down to the point that the planes behind were able to get ahead of her. Now it was a matter of trying to nurse the engine along to just complete the final laps or abandon the race. She decided she had better abandon the race.

She was coming down the far side of the course. At the same instant that she took that safer decision, a piston blew off the connecting rod and right out through the engine case and out through the cowling like a bullet. The solid piston mass ripped through the cylinder head, sending shattered pieces of metal like shrapnel in all directions. It was a cannon-like explosion. Scalding hot oil spewed out covering the windshield, preventing her from seeing anything forward. She knew the runway was somewhere out in front of her about two miles ahead, but she could not see it clearly. Then she spotted the next colored pylon out past the left side of the blackened windshield. If she could make the pylon, she knew the unseen runway was just beyond it. She was now trailing a streak of black oil and dense smoke across the sky and flying by instinct.

The startled crowd were on their feet, sensing an ugly crash unfolding. Maggie tried to remain cool and professional.

Best to leave the landing gear tucked inside, she thought. *Better to pancake this mess than flip over. At least there's flat land between me and the pylon, and the runway is just on the other side.*

She hit the quick-release latch, ejecting the cockpit cover. That would allow her to jump out faster once she had the plane on the ground. Again she had a glimpse of the pylon but she was dropping fast.

Seeing what was happening, Luke and Fernando had begun to run toward what was going to be the accident area. They were both praying that she would be able to get the plane on the ground safely. At least she seemed to sense where the flat area around the pylon was, but they knew she could not see anything clearly. They hoped there would not be a fire or a flip-over crash. The fire trucks with sirens blowing had already started toward the estimated crash site even though the race planes were still zipping around the course. The crowd was on its feet hoping for the best outcome but fearing that the accident could end in tragedy. The press and photographers were also scurrying to the crash site.

Maggie fought the now-soft controls. She had to keep her speed up so as to not stall, yet get as slow as possible to reduce the ground skid. She aimed to the right of the pylon she could only see dimly now and then through the oil and smoke. She tried to wipe the oil off her goggles but that just smeared them worse. The cockpit and her clothes were a mess, all oil-soaked. The oil was hot and she was glad she had worn leather gloves and a thick flying suit for just this kind of protection. She rode the stricken plane toward the ground, leveled off, guessing she was at the right height, and let the airspeed bleed off.

Then she banged into the ground prematurely. Miraculously she held the plane flat but it skipped into the air again.

"Oh, noooo!" she moaned. By instinct she held the plane level, not letting the nose drop and dig in, but also not letting it stall either because then the nose would drop straight down. She held it just right, expertly. It hit hard but flat and started to slide. The engine tore through a mound of dirt, which raised a cloud of dust. Then she hit the pylon tower. Her wing sheared it off clean at the base. It was made of lightweight aluminum pipe bolted together to form a stiff structure fifty feet high, but she went through it like a hot knife through butter. It was covered with brightly colored red-and-white checkered squares. She not only cut the base off but the whole gaudy thing toppled down on top of her plane. As crashes go, it was a mighty spectacular one. The crowd was hushed in dreaded expectation.

The crash trucks with sirens and flashing red lights were at the crash site immediately, in addition to an ambulance, accompanied by a few motorcycle policemen and the running reporters. It was pandemonium and circus all mixed together.

Maggie had shut off all switches and valves but she could smell gas leaking from the wing tanks. Fortunately, there was no fire at first. She was stunned by the impact against the windshield, but there were no obvious cuts, no broken bones, just shock and disappointment. Aware that fire might follow any second, she undid her belts and tried to stand up on the cockpit seat. Red-and-white banners covered with dust and oil surrounded her. She was pinned in by the pylon lying on top of her. The plane was a mess and ready to burn. Maggie thought, *Well, this is it!*

The first person to reach her was Fernando, who had outraced Luke. He dug through all the bunting and aluminum framework to get to her. She was struggling, covered in oil, looking for a way out. Any sign of panic was replaced by disappointment at losing the race and wiping out Luke's plane. She was mad and frustrated and frantically trying to free herself.

Very much relieved to see that she was in one piece and not unconscious, Fernando fought desperately to get her out. Using all his strength, he bent rods out of the way and ripped the bunting apart. She managed to stand up and he quickly pulled her away from the plane, dashing through the smoke and wreckage to get to safety.

Luke, out of breath, arrived at their side, then spotted a flickering flame.

"It's going to blow up," he yelled. "Get away from it!"

They all dashed to a safer distance and the men checked Maggie to see if she'd been injured.

"*Mi amor*, are you okay?" Fernando asked, trying not to let the panic in his voice show. He knew it was an inappropriate question at a time like this.

"No, I'm *not* okay!" exclaimed Maggie, exhausted and very chagrined. "I'm out of the race and I've destroyed Luke's plane and your new engine! I never swear, but there are times where if I spit, the grass will never grow again!" He laughed heartily, relief coursing through him. What a woman!

At that moment, the wreckage erupted in flames and then exploded. The firefighters backed away—there was the danger of a second explosion—and let it burn. Maggie pulled off her helmet and goggles, and shook her head to free her matted hair. The doctors checked her, cleaned the oil off her as best they could, and wiped away the smoke and smudges from her face.

Maggie tried composing herself. But when she turned to Fernando who embraced her with his waiting arms, she began to sob. Luke stood nearby, watching and waiting, while she regained control.

The hushed crowd, still standing, expected a signal that she was either alive or dead. From the distance and with the dust, the collapsed tower, and the fire and explosion, they could not get a clear view of what was happening.

The race planes continued their last lap, and just as they landed one last flaming eruption ended the tragic wreck of Luke's airplane and the crumpled pylon.

Maggie insisted she was all right and had to let the crowd know. She was limping slightly, so Luke and Fernando borrowed a stretcher from the ambulance, laid her on it, and carried her back toward the crowd. Before they neared the stands, Maggie sat up partially, and as they passed in front of the crowd she gave two thumbs up. The fans went wild.

The two men took her into the infirmary for a more thorough check by the doctors and so she could change to clean clothes.

A new temporary pylon was erected so the race could go on for the finals.

Maggie's friend, Mary Jane, was now the only female finalist in the Gold Cup competing for the winner's purse and trophy. From twenty pilots at the beginning, they had narrowed it down to ten. Then from ten, it was now down to four.

MJ was flying a perfect race and her plane was performing very well, but on the sixth lap disaster struck again. At the second pylon, a plane following Mary Jane edged in too closely. For just an instant she was in his blind spot, below and under his nose. His prop cut off the rudder and elevator of her plane. Both planes crashed. The other pilot managed to land his almost-uncontrollable plane on the flat area inside the three pylons. Mary Jane had no way to control hers. It dove into the ground, nose down. Instant death—no fire.

Fortunately, Maggie did not see the accident. She heard the crash and the audience's screams and the sirens' wail. Fernando and Luke were still inside the building with her, but all three sensed there had been a fatality. Others came running to give them the bad news—it was her beloved friend MJ.

Shocked and stunned, Maggie just could not believe it. Both of them had felt they would be able to race with no accidents. Now both had suffered the unexpected and the unfathomable. Maggie had survived to fly again, but now . . . Mary Jane was gone. Maggie broke into uncontrollable tears.

The president of the race committee came immediately to see Maggie. His face was grave and shaken.

"Maggie, I'm *so* grateful you are all right," he said. "On behalf of the committee, I want to express our condolences and sorrow about Mary Jane. We felt that you might be her closest friend here. I have a big favor to ask of you, and I realize this is very difficult for you right now. But would you be able to call her parents and express our deepest sorrow and regrets on behalf of the race committee and all the pilots? She was flying such a great race. That new plane her husband designed was not at fault. It was just one of those accidents that is no one's fault—it is just the risk of the race. We know you will be able to give them some comfort—you will know what to say for all of us. It will be hard but we feel it should be another woman who talks to them at a time like this."

Through her sobbing, Maggie nodded.

"Yes," she said in a whisper. "I'll try to do what she would want me to do."

She understood. She had never had to do anything like this before but somehow she felt spiritual strength and the obligation to do it.

The great cross-country race was now two days away. Would she fly again? *Could* she fly again? Would she ever get over this tragedy? Did she dare get into an airplane again? Would she be able to control her tender emotions enough to start up an engine, taxi out, and fly off into the wild blue yonder? Doubts and uncertainties flooded her mind, and she expressed them verbally to the two men she knew would understand.

Fernando and Luke could empathize completely with what she was feeling. They gave her all the support they could but still felt quite helpless. Maggie would have to shoulder the burden. Talking to MJ's parents could break her or make her stronger. Then a thought came to her mind as if from her grandmother. Her pioneer forefathers had faced death by horse accidents, wagon rollovers, plague and fever, flood and fire, even Indian attacks. They trusted God and put their faith in Him. Now she knew what to do and how to do it.

Maggie's strength of character and spiritual depth were amply demonstrated by the fact that she had been able to shake off the effect of her own near-death accident and MJ's fatal accident in the pylon race as well. The press coverage of the pylon races and the accidents there had added greatly to the public awareness of this race and her own place among the female pilots of the time.

Maggie's self-confidence and professional boldness had been high, anticipating her lifelong dream. But now, waiting nervously in her hotel room early on the morning of the big day, still grief-stricken over the loss of her friend, she suddenly felt like a little girl, insecure and afraid. Was it a premonition? Would she crash on takeoff like the overloaded planes in Luke's stories? Would she suffer a fuel-line leak with a subsequent fire or an oil-line leak throwing black, hot oil all over her windscreen, leaving her blind like in the pylon race? Would she make it to her destination or would something tragic happen to her or to any of the other racers?

Her thoughts were as dark as the cloud-laden sky. Should she drop out?

No!

Mary Jane would not want that. Fernando had asked her if she would want to drop out because of her accident and MJ's sudden death.

"Not on your life!" she had exclaimed. "I've been waiting to take on the men in this cross-country race ever since I started flying. My accident was an engine failure, and MJ's accident was a no-fault situation. She was just in the other pilot's blind spot. We both were willing to run that kind of risk. I hope and pray that everything does go all right for me and for everyone else, and that the fastest plane wins, but if not . . . but if not, I still want the privilege of saying that I did my best."

Maggie wished she could have Fernando beside her in the plane to reassure her and replace her fear with confidence. He was such a rock and had been so supportive. He had bought her a new parachute with quick-attach buckles so she didn't have to wear it in the cockpit, and he had shown her how to wear only the harness, leaving the pack in the back by the door. The parachute bottom was very hard compared to the softness of the pilot's seat.

"You can't use that old seat pack chute," he had said to her. "It is too uncomfortable for over twelve hours in one day. Just leave the chest pack here by the door. If you have to bail out, just trim the plane for level flying and then get back to the door fast, clip the chute pack on, and jump."

He had said it so matter-of-factly that she thought maybe he was feeling that she would have to jump at some point on the trip to escape death.

"Oh, if only he had not gone on before just to get ready for the filming of the mid-continent refueling stop!" she lamented aloud.

Maggie knew that after finishing his work on Wall Street and after taking care of setting up the filming of the early-morning takeoffs, Fernando had to take off in the chartered Stinson to make it to Wichita. There he would supervise the filming of the landings, refueling, and takeoffs at that midway point across the country. This included Maggie's plane. They had worked on her maps and headings and navigation. The weather report was not complete by the time he had to leave, but they had discussed the probable options.

Now, just sitting here waiting, waiting, waiting for her turn, Maggie compartmentalized her thoughts, blocked out the tragic pylon race day, and replayed all the technical events of the day before her. She wished that Fernando could have been there the previous night at the promoters' meeting for the pilots, followed by the final weather briefing and the last press conference.

She had especially needed his consoling and comforting words to help her cope with the sudden loss of her friend. They had talked openly about the great spiritual reunion on the other side between Mary Jane and her husband. They had been separated by his death, but now through her demise they were united again in the life beyond.

There had been several decisions she had to make, and she needed his input. Normally she would have taken such matters in stride, being the professional engineer and pilot she thought she was, but at the beginning of the first of the three meetings there were decisions she had to make all alone that could affect the outcome of her standing in the race. At this moment, Luke was totally absorbed in his own race, as she knew he should be, and Fernando had gone ahead to Wichita, leaving her alone.

The drawing for takeoff slots had been the day before. Each pilot drew a number and then, depending upon which number they drew, they took their choice of the various available takeoff times spaced fifteen minutes apart. The race would start two hours before sunup.

The air race was not like a horse race—the air race was against the clock. The winner would be the one with the shortest elapsed time from takeoff in New York until flashing over the center of the field in Los Angeles at one thousand feet, which would mark the finish line.

Maggie drew number five, right in the middle of the nine racers. There were five women and four men in the race. Two men had dropped out at the last minute. One dropout was a wealthy oil man; his plane's gear-retraction mechanism was not working. The other plane was reportedly pulled out by order of the military. They insisted on protecting some potential military secrets incorporated in that race plane. There were no unexpected last-minute entries to take their places. Maggie was actually pleased not to be racing against either one of the supposedly incredibly fast mystery racers because now it would be a much closer race. Perhaps she had a chance after all!

Maggie had talked to Luke's friend Joe after he drew number one and chose to start at 4:30 a.m., the earliest takeoff time possible. She asked him why he chose such an early time.

"I'm comfortable flying night instruments," he told her, "and besides, I think everyone will be on the gauges for a good while with that dismal weather report all across the Appalachians. I've decided to go a bit north of Luke's preferred course. The headwinds are lighter up north, I believe, so even though I fly a longer ground track I think I'll make it up in faster groundspeed and will hit good weather sooner."

Joe's assessment had confused Maggie. Luke had assured her that the straight-line course would be best, but now here was Joe taking a slightly longer north route.

"How far north do you think you'll go for your first fuel stop?" she asked him.

"Well, I'll have to stop for fuel three times and I figure my first stop will be Fort Wayne, Indiana," Joe answered. "That's only a hundred miles north of Luke's course, but I calculated it to make a difference. Besides, I have a friend there who promises a ten-minute turnaround and he'll pay for the gas, so it's worth it."

"How come your big Northrop needs so many stops?" Maggie asked. "I thought you would have extra tanks."

"Well, we made a tank to fit in the back cockpit," Joe said, "but before installing it in the plane we put gas in to test, and it had a tiny crack. The welder thought he had washed out all the gas, but when he put the torch on it to repair the crack, the tank blew up on him. The plane is fine because the tank was not in it, but now we have no auxiliary tank. A little bit of gasoline will emit enough fumes to make quite an explosion! The welder is okay, but it scared us all and we didn't have time to start from scratch, so I decided to forget the custom-built tank and make an extra stop instead."

Her friend Betty, who pulled number two, made 6:00 a.m. her takeoff choice.

"I just love the early light," she explained. "I love the glow of the sunrise, especially when I climb through the overcast and break out on top."

Maggie thought to herself, *That is a woman's perspective, all right. She wants to fly the prettiest flight she can as if there were a camera plane flying beside her!*

"Do you have a supercharger on your plane to get up above the cloud layer?" Maggie asked Betty.

"Yep," she replied, nodding. "I got the engine with the impeller on it. It's gear-driven, not exhaust-driven, and gives me best efficiency up at fourteen thousand feet. The tops are forecast at ten to eleven thousand, so I'll go on up through and just fly on top."

Yeah, but the headwinds are stronger the higher you go, Maggie thought. *I wonder if it's wise to go that high.* But she decided not to challenge her friend on that since Betty had many more thousands of hours and cross-country experience than she herself did.

Maggie could just see in her mind Betty's single-engine, low-wing Lockheed Orion with the pretty paint job zooming up through the dark clouds out into the morning sunshine with blue sky overhead. Betty's plane had retractable gear, and although a bit slow for this race it did have long-range tanks from her recent South American flight, and in the air it was a pretty bird.

Amy and her twin-engine, all-metal Lockheed with the twin rudders on the tail was the number three pick. It was a long-range, sturdy-looking aircraft, and in Amy's hands, Maggie knew it would be a difficult plane to beat. She was sure her own Staggerwing was the faster of the two with that new "secret" engine, but a lot still depended on the details—winds aloft, accurate navigation, fast refueling, and so on. Amy chose to fly off at 5:30 a.m.

Maggie hadn't asked her opinion on anything in particular, but had heard that Amy would fly the same route Luke had planned last year and again this year. It was slightly different from Maggie's route.

The number four pick was Buddy with his home-designed high-wing cabin plane that looked so dumpy. Maggie could not believe his plane could fly as fast as Luke said it had flown last year. Bud called his plane a "DGA."

When a reporter had asked him what the acronym stood for, without hesitation he had replied, “Damn good airplane!” That quip was repeated in all the newspapers. They liked to have some quotes that were different and catchy. The public loved reading about the pilots and their exploits.

No one knew which route Bud would take, but rumor had it he would take the northern route. It was not a lot to the north of Luke’s, but Buddy’s choice had some disadvantages as well as some advantages. Each pilot had to decide their takeoff time and course for themselves. Bud chose to take off at 7:00 a.m. Maggie thought she knew why he would take off later than the others. Buddy had a lot of airline flying in this part of the East, and she guessed that from past experience he knew that this storm was weakening and that the headwinds might be calmer if he took off later.

In Maggie’s judgment, pulling out number five was good luck for her. She had lots of choices, being in the middle of the pack. She could take off as late as 8:00 and still make Los Angeles before the 6:00 p.m. deadline. She felt that would give her the best possible winds all the way across. That would not leave much margin for error, but using her intuition, Maggie chose 8:00 a.m.

She wasn’t near Luke when he chose his time. He had picked number six, which meant he followed Maggie in choosing the time to take off. She thought he might take 7:30 or 7:45. She was right. He chose 7:45 and winked across the room at her. She took that to mean she had made a good choice because it was close to what he thought was best.

Maggie desperately wished Fernando had been by her side to help her choose the time, especially since the others went for earlier times. Barbara took 5:00 and Lolita chose 6:30. The oil company DC-2 transport was thought to be the slowest of all, but they had planned three gas stops mostly for the benefit of local dealers who wanted publicity photos of them with the crew in front of the company “race” plane. It was more of a promotional project than anything else. They chose 5:45 a.m., and that left Maggie as the last one to take off.

“Hey Maggie,” Lottie called, walking over. “Is your plane so fast you can make it by the deadline? I think you ought to move it up a bit, but it's your call—just a thought."

Maggie began to worry. Did everybody else know something she didn't? Why were they all leaving so early? Soon Luke came over.

"Say, Luke, Fernando and I looked at the pattern of this storm that's now lying across the Appalachian Mountains," she said, pointing to her weather readout. "We think that its groundspeed is slowing and maybe it might even go stagnant by eight o'clock. Are we right? What's your feeling about that?"

"Maggie, you have a point and I agree," he said, reassuring her. "That's why Buddy went for 7:00 and I chose 7:45. So don't you worry. I made some mental calculations and you should do just great if you don't drift off your course line. I'll be just fifteen minutes ahead and faster than you are so my refueling team will be waiting for you as agreed upon at Indianapolis, Wichita, and Albuquerque."

Maggie had been told originally that she might need three refueling stops. Now, however, when she took delivery of the plane, the president, wanting to keep it a surprise until the very last moment, informed her that a bigger engine and larger wing tanks had been installed so she could fly faster and make only one gas stop instead of three.

Fernando, knowing the additional horsepower and fuel capacity, had agreed that from Wichita he would phone Indianapolis and Albuquerque to tell them not to count on Maggie for refueling because of last-minute route changes.

Maggie expected less headwind than was forecast to give her an extra hour advantage off the total flying time cross-country, but it was hard to not tell her friend and instructor the factory secrets.

Their university professor had helped her and Fernando analyze winds aloft with the latest techniques. The way she and Fernando figured it, on the race day the winds aloft out of the west—headwinds to the racers—would die down as the day progressed. Her late start should help by giving her weaker headwinds to fight. On the other hand, lots of experienced pilots had chosen to take off early, and the weather was notoriously capricious.

Maggie was a bit uncertain about her route and again wished that Fernando had been with her at the briefing last night. She was sure he would have agreed with Joe and opted for swinging more to the north of the straight-line route they all called the "Luke path."

There was one dip in Luke's line and that was in New Mexico. He insisted on dropping down to Albuquerque, as he had done last year, and had urged Maggie to follow that track.

"The route north of Albuquerque is over the Sangre de Cristo Mountains, some of the most barren country you can imagine," Luke had warned her. "If anything went wrong, it would take days to find you. And if you do get over the rough New Mexico country, your line of flight from there to Los Angeles would still take you across northern Arizona between the San Francisco peaks and the Grand Canyon. It's beautiful country, but there are no emergency airports, rough country underneath, and always, *always* there are big cloud buildups. You have to dodge around them because one of those big babies can tear the wings off racers like ours—a desert cumulonimbus has vertical winds of up to a hundred miles per hour, so stay out of them. And some are so big you lose half an hour going around one. If you fly over Albuquerque, you will have good old Route 66 highway close to the remaining straight line to Los Angeles. It's just safer."

Maggie had listened intently, knowing his years of experience. Now that they had the benefit of the latest weather briefing, she could fine-tune her exact route.

Maggie had also wanted Fernando to be with her at the publicity and photograph session the previous night. He was so handsome and stood out in any group, making her look better. She had worn her freshly laundered cowgirl outfit with the red-checkered shirt and a red scarf tied at her neck. With her boots, she stood taller than some of the male pilots. She had noticed that the short ones tried to stand away from her in the group picture.

At the promoters' request, everyone had gone outside to shoot photos. Seeing all the planes lined up just before sundown had been a thrilling moment for Maggie. All nine racers in a line with each pilot standing just to one side of the nose of their aircraft. The two twins were on either end—the oil company's and Amy's ship. Maggie's Staggerwing was not the smallest, but it was not as large as some of the others either. The lineup was an assortment of aircraft types that really demonstrated the progress of the aeronautical art of the day.

Maggie had paid particular attention to the two all-metal twins, the huge Douglas DC-2 and the solid, faster-looking but smaller Lockheed of Amy's. She thought that Buddy's high-wing, fabric-covered cabin job next to the Douglas DC-2 made his white "DGA" look rather small. Next was Joe's Northrop Gamma, a large aluminum plane with a long fuselage and fixed-gear enclosed in giant wheel pants to provide streamlining.

Shoulder to shoulder with Joe was Luke's racer, a medium-sized, all-aluminum, retractable gear, low-wing plane. It was made distinctive by the large cowl on the engine with teardrop bumps to streamline the rocker-arm covers.

Alongside Luke's was Maggie's brightly polished Staggerwing. Then next to her was Lolita, standing by her rather radical racer with the inverted in-line engine, the smallest of all the planes.

Next came Betty with her big Lockheed Orion, sporting a cockpit up on top just behind the engine. It had retractable gear but was big and heavy for the engine.

Between Betty and Amy on the end were Barbara and her long-range racer, a barrel-shaped and low-winged configuration. The cockpit sat way back toward the tail and seemed to be part of the rudder itself.

The night before the race, Luke told Maggie that Joe had lost his parachute.

"I think he hocked it to get gas money," Luke surmised.

"Hey, I brought my other chute," Maggie said. "I'll run and get it. I just feel that he needs a chute. No one should fly at full power across the country without one—just in case."

She went to her corner of the hangar where her belongings were in a locker, pulled out the chute, which was older but still in good condition, and took it over to Joe's plane.

"Hey, Joe, I understand you've misplaced your chute," she said, handing it to him. "I won't let you fly without one! Besides, you need to sit on it to see over that tall panel."

"Nah, you need it just as much as I do," he said, thanking her, but putting up a hand. "I'm taller than you."

"Oh this is my other chute," Maggie said. "I don't need it. Fernando bought me a new chest pack that has quick snaps on it."

"Maggie," Joe replied with a chuckle. "I've flown this plane for over three years and never had to use a chute. I have a soft pillow to sit on. What makes you think I oughta have a chute now? Besides, how old is this 'other' chute you want me to take?"

"Joe, just take it," Maggie insisted, putting it in his hands. "It's like new. Never used, but it was repacked just a month ago. You can just give it back to me when we all get to Los Angeles, okay?"

Joe accepted somewhat reluctantly and thanked her. But he admitted to himself, *In this business, you never turn down an offer of a chute.*

CHAPTER 17

THE BENDIX RACE BEGINS

JOE'S 4:30 A.M. takeoff awakened Maggie. It was so dark she could only see the blue flame of his exhaust and the lights on the plane. It was impossible to go to sleep now, so she got up and got dressed.

Maggie's thoughts drifted back to Mary Jane. What a sweet and lovely friend. How tragic to have her life snuffed out by the aviation she loved! Maggie believed in the peace and beauty of the next life and was comforted by those thoughts. She must close that door for now and move on.

"I'll fly this race in your honor, MJ," she said aloud, her voice breaking.

She listened carefully as each plane took off. Since she was the last one in line, she didn't want to go over to the airport until it was absolutely necessary. Waiting in her room, nervous yet impatient, she heard the rough, powerful rumble of Barbara's long-range "GB" racer warm up.

She watched from the window as Bab's plane trundled down the runway.

The engine was turning high rpms, but it was so heavy with fuel that Maggie worried about the slow acceleration. The engine was laboring and the prop was biting the air, but it wasn't increasing the movement of mass like it should. Maggie could see and hear that midfield was not a good place for an easy takeoff. It would either be a squeaker or a ball of fire. She tensed and prayed for her, knowing that Babs had calculated everything very closely.

Off in the distance the fire trucks stood at the ready, their engines running. At the last moment, Barbara eased the heavy plane into the air. Maggie couldn't really see if she was off due to a slight dip in the runway, but since she couldn't hear sirens and didn't see red lights flashing, she knew Barbara was safely airborne. As soon as the distant plane became visible, Maggie could tell that the rate of climb was painfully slow. Surprisingly, the plane kept flying straight out to sea.

"I didn't dare turn for fear of losing some lift," Babs explained later. "I knew it was clear on out to sea with no rising terrain so I just held my course straight ahead for ten minutes or so before I risked turning. By then I had inched up to a thousand feet and felt it safe to come around in a very gentle 'grandma' turn. It was a close one, all right!"

Maggie had finished breakfast by the time she heard Amy's twin engines throbbing smoothly. They sounded solid to her. Maggie had her bags packed and was almost ready to go downstairs to check out of the small hotel when Amy lined up for the starter's flag. She didn't worry about the load-lifting capacity of Amy's plane and there weren't any other causes for concern Maggie could think of for this accomplished and experienced pilot. Maggie didn't even look out the window to watch the most famous of the female pilots take off. She knew it would be a professional and routine departure, as, in fact, it was.

The DC-2 must have been starting its 1200 hp engines while Amy was taking off, but Maggie didn't hear it until fifteen minutes later when her taxi arrived at the hangar. The big twin-engine transport took off sedately with minimum fuss. It just bored ahead and lifted off like a big, slow freighter. Douglas had a newer model called a DC-3 that was faster and bigger, but the first ones off the factory line were going to the major airlines due to prior commitments.

The sky was now light enough to be able to watch Betty taxi out. She waited for the starter's signal to get ready, held the brakes hard, and then wound up her engine to maximum rpms. The engine screamed, the brakes strained, and the plane shook, dust devils whipping up like a whirlwind. A stream of dirt and pebbles broke loose behind her plane. Betty had lined up right at the end of the pavement off the runway with only soil and grass and the airport fence behind her. When the starter's flag dropped, Betty was ready and her plane fairly leaped ahead.

Maggie knew that Betty would get off well before she reached the end of the runway by the way her plane accelerated. She had the tail of her plane up easily and lifted shortly after the midpoint down the runway. The plane was silhouetted against the gray of the sky, but the sun was close enough to rising that there was substantial light. Maggie tingled with excitement, as any pilot does, watching the landing gear fold into the pockets in the belly and clean the plane up aerodynamically before immediately increasing its speed. It is one of those little satisfactions that pleases all pilots. Maggie felt good about Betty and her chances, even though her plane was not known as "fast."

At 6:30, as Maggie was beginning her check of every aspect of her plane, she heard Lolita's racer turning over. She was the only one flying an in-line engine. She had argued with Luke about the relative merits of in-line vs. radial. Every other plane in the race including the two non-starter mystery ships had radials of different sizes, but Lolita had held out for an in-line engine, saying it was more streamlined and had less frontal area to cause drag—less "front plate area"—and that she had found a way to solve the overheating problems. Curious about the contrast between the two engines, Maggie had asked Lolita to show her.

"Look, honey, have you ever seen a bigger oil radiator?" Lolita had asked her proudly, pointing it out. "And I have shutters on it so I can vary the cooling effect."

Maggie knew that some European engine manufacturers were cooling their in-line engines with both a large oil radiator to care for the engine oil as well as a circulating coolant system with jackets around the cylinders, much like a car engine. Instead of water, however, the coolant was a special non-boiling, non-freezing liquid. Water was useless to cool an airplane engine, since it would boil at altitude as well as freeze easily. Maggie had to admit that it sounded reasonable enough to work. Lolita's engine had a bark to it, very different from the radials that kind of rumbled. The exhaust stacks were direct from each cylinder into the air stream, so each one spit fire in the dim morning light.

The sun was up now, but just barely, and the sky was overcast. Maggie and the mechanic Fernando had hired rolled her plane out of the hangar. While they were draining a small sample of fuel from each tank just to make sure that there was no sediment or water in the fuel, they heard Lolita take the starter's flag. Her engine changed in tone from barking to a great roar and the little racer sped down the runway and climbed into the air in record time. Lolita didn't carry as much fuel as others so she would have to make quite a few stops for gas. The plane was super light, fabric covering on a steel frame. She climbed easily and quickly disappeared from view.

Maggie had finished checking her plane when Buddy took off in his unlikely high-wing cabin racer with the all-white paint job. His takeoff was normal, as was Luke's, who took off just before Maggie. She hurried over to the run-up spot at the end of the runway to wave Luke off at 7:45. She blew him a kiss and he smiled broadly, waving to her before looking back at his instruments to check the engine gauges. Then he focused on the race starter with the flag in front of him.

Just before the starter gave the alert, Luke adjusted his flying helmet and pulled down his goggles. He had a closed canopy over his cockpit, but he always flew like an old military pilot and racer, using helmet and goggles. He explained that it was part habit and part safety. Once, a long time ago, a windshield panel of his had blown off in a race and his sturdy goggles had allowed him to see in the wind.

With the preparatory signal, Luke raised his engine to the peak roar, brakes held, airframe trembling with the same excitement that the pilot was feeling, and then the flag went down. Brakes off, accelerating, Luke sped down the runway straight as an arrow into the now colorful, brighter sky. Maggie expected nothing but a perfect flight from Luke.

Joe was a good-looking man, early thirties, athletic in appearance, and well-dressed. In fact, most people were surprised to find out that he was a commercial pilot. He had been educated as an accountant, but he couldn't handle the long hours in an office crunching numbers, percentages, ratios, and tax tables. He had started keeping books for a company that used airplanes for business purposes, eventually learned to fly, and moved up to a commercial license. He still did bookkeeping but was also managing the flight department of the company without being a corporate pilot. He enjoyed flying, loved the wind and the weather, machinery and engines, and the challenge of flight far more than the drudgery of a desk.

The Northrup factory had produced a unique airplane that had valuable and interesting characteristics. It was a big single-engine plane that could carry a good load at a fairly decent speed. A few years ago, Joe had purchased one secondhand for his own use with his inherited money and the last of his savings. He wanted to race for personal publicity and experience.

However, Joe had two problems. First, he wanted to move up in corporate management, yet remain flying. Second, he had fallen in love and wanted to get married, but he didn't have enough income or job stability to duly impress his future in-laws.

Luck or proper preparation broke in Joe's favor. Another company had a job opening for "corporate pilot and aviation department manager." They wanted someone who could move up in management, who had a commercial pilot's license, and who had a business or management degree of some sort. Joe had come to their attention, and they told him that if he did reasonably well in the race, and if his name became a little better known in flying circles, they might offer him the job, at double his present salary, to both manage and fly. He would achieve both goals of marriage and a better flying job if he did okay in the race.

Joe made his first fuel stop at Fort Wayne, Indiana. He landed straight in, braked hard, spun around, and taxied fast back to the gas pit where his friend was waiting. There were no cameras waiting for him. His friend had two trucks ready and they filled the tanks while he grabbed a sandwich and a bottle of pop. Afterwards, hurrying, he jumped back into the cockpit, hit the engine's start button, and took off into the wild blue yonder. The weather had been just like he expected. By going north he had picked up some better winds and had avoided a heavy rainstorm.

Joe was letting down toward Kansas City when bad luck hit. First, there was a vibration that only an experienced pilot would notice. He checked his instruments for anything out of order. All seemed to be okay. Then the vibration occurred again, but worse this time. Something was going on, but what was it? Fuel? Magneto spark? A crack in a spark plug perhaps? He was only about thirty minutes out, and at nine thousand feet descending at full race speed when big problems erupted.

A flash of flame like an explosion came out of the engine up front and was whipped back at him by the slipstream. It enveloped the plane in flames. He immediately switched the fuel tank off so no fuel would get to the engine compartment to feed the fire. Of course, that also stopped the engine. The explosion had apparently ruptured an oil line because the fire continued to burn. Joe knew he had a reserve oil tank about where the flames seemed to originate that would feed the fire for a while, and then perhaps blow up. Also, he feared that the fire might get to a fuel tank or to the carburetor to cause another explosion. The fierce blaze stubbornly refused to go out.

Joe tightened the belts on the chute Maggie insisted he borrow. He undid his lap and shoulder belts from the seat when the fire did not go out as fast as it should have. He threw the plane into a sharp dive to try to blow the fire out, but the heat was getting into the cockpit. The smoke and the heat were both getting to him, and it was hard for him to breathe. His only option was to jump. He couldn't get it on the ground in time, so he better hit the silk to save his life.

He opened the cockpit cover, pulled the plane up to slow down, rolled it over, pushed the stick forward, and gravity plopped him out like a pit from a cherry. He pulled his ripcord as the tail flashed by. He thanked the good Lord and Maggie for insisting he take her other chute. The canopy blossomed open. Suddenly, the plane, diving again, blew up in a yellowish red ball of fire. Joe had never seen anything like that before. It defied all normal analysis. It should have gone out when he cut the fuel off. He had escaped certain death by only two or three seconds!

As Joe glided slowly down in the midwestern summer morning, he lamented the loss of all his dreams. No race, no job, and probably no marriage. The explosion caught the attention of onlookers on the ground. The authorities were notified, as were the Kansas City press. All came to see the accident site and to interview the heroic survivor of the in-air explosion. In hardly any time at all, he was being interviewed on the radio, and the news media flashed word all across the country by telegraph. He was the first casualty of the race.

To his surprise, Joe had become an instant celebrity. He tried to keep the explanation simple, but the press jumped to wild speculation about the terrors of fire in the air—no way to escape except to jump!—and treated Joe with great respect. His face and clothing were seared and burn-marked, but he had been protected from further injury by the extra heavy clothing he always wore. The dramatic and frightening accident, as reported in the press, enhanced his image and reputation. Before he could arrive home, the job was his, the marriage was scheduled—and, well, he had only lost a plane.

Barbara was an intelligent, attractive businesswoman. She was happily married, two children, both in college, and had started a business that had exploded with unexpected success. She was famous as an entrepreneur across the country. She was an outstanding pilot and had stayed up to date on new airplanes equipped with the latest radios and instruments. She flew herself to business meetings because it was easier, and she made news wherever she went. Barbara's husband was very supportive but busy with his own interests and seldom seen in public.

Because of her image, outgoing personality, and numerous connections in business and politics, Barbara was one of the women who had exerted every pressure she could think of to be permitted to fly again in the races. She was a close friend of Mary Jane and her husband's, both of whom were involved in aviation and air racing. Together, Barbara and Mary Jane had visited most of the major newspaper and magazine owners in the country. Finally, public opinion turned in favor of the women, and the race promoters decided to lift the ban.

Barbara was offered the chance to fly a very fast but somewhat tricky plane in the races. She opted to stay out of the closed-circuit pylon race, but relished the idea of flying what could be the fastest ship in the cross-country race. It was an unusual airplane. It had a very large radial engine attached to a short fuselage, which made it look ridiculously fat. It was light, but the short fuselage and small control surfaces made it hard to handle. It was designed to fly fast, but that also made it stall out at high speed, so she had to come in hot every landing. The plane had a reputation of being difficult to fly, so she felt both honored to fly it at no cost to her and challenged to prove she could fly with the best of the men.

Barbara had her big racer flying like a rocket. She was boring a long hole in the sky at good speed with no problems until she sprang a fuel leak on the last leg of the race. It did not catch fire but her cockpit filled with wet gasoline, soaking her flying suit. She was flying a bomb ready to detonate if the gas got close to a spark or anything hot. Barbara shut off her radio and all electrical systems except the magnetos to the plugs, which are well insulated against sparks.

She reduced power and searched her gasoline-soaked map for a place to land. She considered jumping but she wanted to get her racer down in one piece rather than sacrificing it. She hoped she could do it. With marvelous skill and phenomenal luck, she glided down to an airfield. With the assistance of an expert mechanic, they had the leak fixed quickly with new tubing, completely dried out the cockpit, and sprayed the plane with a noncombustible solvent so she was safe to take off again. Barbara only lost about one hour, so she was still hopeful. She had seen racers bounce back from similar problems and situations and still win the race in other years.

Amy was an adventurous pilot with a number of international flights to her credit. She had set records for both speed and distance between various points in the United States and destinations abroad, and had acquired commercial sponsors who benefited greatly from her remarkable success. She was competent, thorough, and dedicated to the cause of advancing aeronautical science through air races as well as setting new records, frequently replacing those set by men before her. Her sponsors pushed her to ever greater efforts and higher risks in exchange for the publicity she generated.

Amy's husband was not a pilot but supported her enthusiastically. He seemed to enjoy being married to a celebrity and encouraged her activities. He helped manage her affairs, but he did not mix well with the pilots who admired his wife so much. Amy was getting tired of all the attention and hoped to get out of the racing and record-setting high-pressure environment. In fact, she said her new plane was going to be her last. She wanted to fly in the cross-country race and afterward one more record-setting jaunt around South America.

Her new plane was a beauty. It was a medium-size, twin-engine, all-aluminum job with retractable wheels, and a feature all women envied—an enclosed potty. It was not as fast as some of the other planes but it had long-distance tanks. As a result, for the coming race she was going to make only one stop halfway to the West Coast.

The magnificent performance of Amy's plane was assuring her of an outstanding race. She had flown a bit farther north than the "Luke" course line and had found better weather than Betty had a bit to the south. Neither knew how the other was doing nor could they communicate back and forth. Long-range radios existed but were much heavier than the lighter short-range radios in use by most planes of the day. It was each pilot on their own, relying on personal ingenuity and resourcefulness.

Amy had always been blessed with unusual luck to go along with her competency. Her new plane was flying well and she expected to finish very high in the race. She knew exactly where she was all the time, and her equipment was functioning perfectly.

She really enjoyed this kind of flying—a new plane with state-of-the-art equipment and weather she could handle easily, although head-winds were heavier than expected. But any other early takeoff would have had the same problem. Perhaps she should have tried taking off later like Maggie and Luke, but still, she was making good time when a freak accident occurred.

The cockpit of this particular big twin had an escape hatch over the pilot's head, hinged at the back side. The hatch was to provide cool air for the pilots when the plane was on the ground, and it was an escape route in case the back door was blocked. Amy had complained to the manufacturer that the pilot's compartment up front was like a green-house—it was sweltering in the summertime. A long taxi from the flight line to take off would cause the pilot to perspire greatly because the little side windows did not scoop in enough air. If the plane was not moving very fast while taxiing there was no breeze in the pilot's area, and no way to cool off. The factory obliged by adding a hinged top hatch to the compartment.

Singing to herself, Amy was cruising along happily without a worry in the world when the vibration of the plane jiggled the latch. With a loud *swoosh*, the hatch opened and tore loose, taking the radio antenna with it. The wind roared. The screech was deafening, but the suction was worse. The wind took all of Amy's maps and navigation notes—courses to follow and radio frequencies. She had no other option but to land. The next city was Wichita straight ahead.

Maybe there'll be a mechanic who can rebuild a new hatch, she hoped. Later the newspapers would say she "wrestled with the controls to get her ship down." That "she was terrified," and other such exaggerated comments. Actually, she handled it like any other in-flight emergency. She was cool and calm and made a perfect landing. She knew exactly what had happened and why.

Fernando was in the air with the Stinson and a cameraman when they spotted the big twin coming in for a landing. They were able to get excellent footage of the plane touching down. Fernando wondered why Amy had the hatch missing, and he also questioned why she had come in without calling the tower to ask for a straight-in approach. After he landed, he got the whole story from Amy herself as she hovered anxiously over two craftsmen, experts in working with aluminum, who were cutting and riveting metal to make a new hatch and fix it in place. A radio man was jury-rigging a temporary antenna so her radio would work again. She was back in the air quickly, with a new set of maps, and still a major factor in the race despite the incident.

A major midwest oil company was very aviation-minded and had widespread operations across the country. These included oil wells, a chain of service stations, pipeline interests, wildcat drilling sites, and regional offices to handle all of this in their districts. Top management had found that they needed a fleet of airplanes to meet their needs. The cost accountants had discovered that airplanes more than paid their way, and the executives enjoyed getting around faster as well as being home more often.

Their newest aircraft was a big twin-engine passenger plane with a cabin for up to twenty passengers. The seats could be removed in order to load freight that might be needed to handle an emergency somewhere. It was not a race plane by any standard, yet top management was very image-conscious. Simply flying this plane in the race, with their corporate logo visible in newsreels at the movie theaters or newspaper photos on the streets and in the homes of America, was profitable advertising.

Their aviation department had a number of competent pilots flying smaller Stinsons and Bellancas, but the DC-2 was the company's flagship. The two pilots assigned to operate the big plane had been acquired from an airline that went bankrupt. They were ex-military pilots with valuable training and experience in multi-engine airplanes. They were both family men with children, so they did not take chances; they were serious and dedicated to their profession, conservative in everything they did. They wore their spotless uniforms and would stand at attention while executives loaded or unloaded.

Flying in an air race was a new experience for these seasoned pilots, but instructions were just to show how modern and up to date their company was. It was all for corporate publicity and creating a favorable image.

Air racing was an uncertain science, and the number of strange mishaps had slowed some of the race planes. But one of the most unexpected delays was with the DC-2. At Wichita, taxiing in to load fuel, the plane got stuck in the mud. The weight of the big twin-engine transport was borne up by the pavement, but in a turn off the runway, the pilot cut a turn too close and allowed one wheel to drop off into the mud. It sank to the axle. The pilot tried to gun his engines enough to break free, but all he did was pivot around to where the other wheel also dropped into the mud.

Fernando came up with a solution. He found two tractors and some strong ropes to pull the plane to firmer ground. At first, the wheels stayed deep in the mud like embedded plows. Fernando had to make a ramp out of wooden planks and steel bars he found alongside a hangar construction site to support the weight of the plane. Finally, the heavy aircraft was pulled up the homemade ramp and then back over onto the pavement.

The pilots appreciated Fernando's help and offered to give him a ride to Los Angeles. He accepted, since Maggie had already arrived and departed before the DC-2 had landed in Wichita. Besides, his filming duties were under control, so the crew could finish without him.

Betty had a lot of flying experience, but she never tired of the beauty, the excitement, and the challenge. She always felt like a bit of an outcast among the flying fraternity. She liked them all, but many were a bit coarse in their culture, lacking the refinement and training that she had received. She had the money to do what she wanted and did not need sponsors or connections for favors. She was entirely independent, and, though courteous, was somewhat of a loner.

Her flight plan was to follow the shortest, most direct route all the way to Wichita for a one-stop race across the country. The beauty of her flight was marred by unexpected severe weather. Her somewhat early takeoff and direct route put her right into the heaviest weather across the mountains. She had climbed to cruise altitude, but found it to be solid instrument conditions. She tried going higher but did not break through into the clear as she had expected. She attempted a lower altitude between layers, but there was steady rain. She moved back to her original cruise altitude, and that's when her problems started.

First, her navigation radio went out. It had never failed her before, but the precipitation must have leaked into the system some way and shorted it. She found herself on instruments that indicate which way is up, but she had no way of knowing if her navigation was even close to the ground course she wanted to fly.

Betty was not nervous about the radio failure; it was only an inconvenience for the time being. But after hours of droning along in the soup, she calculated from the maps on her lap that she must be about one hundred miles east of St. Louis. She noted that the terrain was such that it was safe to try a let-down through the clouds so she could see the ground and get her bearings. The storm she was flying in might have winds from a different direction and with a different force than she had calculated. She broke through the lower level at a good altitude and searched for landmarks to locate her position. She could see a railroad but that was not enough. A highway was not enough. At last, she spotted a lake and river in the distance with the combination of railroad and highway needed for positive identification. That pinpointed her position. To her dismay, she had been slowed down by unexpected headwinds at her altitude, plus she had burned more fuel than expected when she changed altitudes trying to find the best level.

She decided to stop at St. Louis for fuel even though she had not planned a stop there. She had made no arrangements for fuel, but assumed that a city that big would have a gas pump attended at this time of day. Betty tried to make up some time in her descent by using full power. She could tell from the ground she was passing over that there had been a lot of rain during the night and water seemed to be in surface ponds on the farmers' fields even now.

She spotted what she thought was the airport and aimed toward it, but when she was almost there she realized it was not an airport at all. She looked farther and found what looked like the municipal airport—a huge grass field with hangars along two edges of the field. In a city this large she had expected a paved runway, but no. There was no apparent traffic and she had no radio so she landed straight in. The field was muddy and her gear splashed mud all over her pretty airplane, which exasperated her. She taxied toward what looked like a gas pump area and shut down, hoping that someone would appear to service her plane, but no one came out to greet her.

Betty climbed down from her tall cockpit onto the wing and from there jumped down to the ground. Her shoes sank in the mud. Disgusted, she rolled up the bottoms of her slacks and slopped through the murky, gooey stuff replete with oil to a small building. She knocked on several doors, and she hollered out, but could find no one. Looking over to the other side of the field, Betty saw a bearded man peering at her.

"Can you get any gas for me?" she shouted over to him.

"Don't think I can," the man shouted back slowly.

Impatiently, Betty called again, cupping her hands around her mouth like a megaphone.

"Where can I find some gas quickly?"

Strolling nonchalantly across the field to Betty, the fellow answered.

"Don't rightly know, miss," he said, uninterested in helping.

"Hey, I'm in a race and I need fuel—right now!" Betty ordered impatiently, as though she were speaking to a servant. "Is there a gas truck or someone with the keys to that pump over where I am parked? The pump has a big padlock on it or I would pump it myself!"

"Well, we've got a holiday here and a parade downtown so no one came to open up this morning," the farmer said, shrugging.

His drawl was beginning to really infuriate her. "Petite" Betty (as she had become known because of her small stature) started showing signs of losing her temper all together. She took a deep breath and calmed down a bit.

"Can't you help me some way, mister?" she pleaded.

The less-than-energetic old man didn't have any idea how to get the gas she so desperately needed, nor was he inclined to go looking for help.

Almost reduced to tears, Betty heaved a huge sigh, turned with a flair and, disgusted, stomped back toward her plane. Retracing her steps through the muddy field, she tried to stay on patches of grass to reduce getting more of that sticky mess on her new leather shoes—she had chosen to wear these low-heeled pumps so she would look presentable for photos at the finish line.

"Grrrrr," Betty muttered out loud. "I should have worn the boots!"

When she got to her plane, she shouted loudly trying to get someone's attention—*anyone*! She walked over to a nearby hangar door and kicked the metal side of the hangar, all to no avail. Already she had lost half an hour!

Suddenly, an idea popped into her head. Maybe it was a bad idea, but she was desperate. Back in her plane she had a survival kit from her trip flying over the jungles of South America. Inside the kit was a pistol she carried to ward off natives, charging alligators, or some such emergency. She knew how to shoot and thought that if she had to put her plane down somewhere with no food, the .38 revolver would help her find something to eat. She pulled it out of the kit, took the fire extinguisher from the cockpit, and walked over to the gas pump. "Petite" Betty sighted with the gun to blow the padlock off without starting a fire, knowing full well that it was a dangerous thing to do. She had the fire extinguisher at her leg, ready to use. She pulled the trigger and the padlock shattered. The pump handle worked, so she stretched the hose to the wing tank closest to her. She pumped furiously. The process was slow. First she had to pump to fill the glass tank on the top of the pump and then release the nozzle so the gas would flow into her wing tank.

She was aware that the fellow had come over to watch when she shot the padlock off the pump. *I wonder if I can get him to help me move the plane so the hose can reach to the other wing!* she thought. Betty pulled out some green backs and offered to pay him if he would help.

"Shucks, lady," he said in that maddening drawl, "I don't need no money to help someone as desperate as you, and I don't want you to shoot me with that gun. Just tell me what you want me to do."

Fortunately, he pushed better than he talked and they managed to get the other tank filled. But now they had to push the plane back farther away from the pump so that Betty could have room to start her engine, taxi forward, and then brake to pivot on one wheel and get back to where she could take off.

Sweaty, tired, unhappy, disgusted, muddy little Betty finally got her plane off the ground and on her way again. She knew she had lost valuable time, but with luck and by forcing her engine a bit more she might pick up some of the wasted minutes.

Lolita had learned to fly from her father. They had a barn on the farm large enough to hangar a plane, a tractor, farm equipment, and their truck. They owned an older, open-cockpit biplane that they used to fly the fifty miles to the closest town for spare parts and other small items. They also used it for daytime social events, including Sunday church, weather permitting. The family had a two-and-a-half-ton truck with cattle racks to move animals to market or to bring large supplies back home, but with a bad road the trip by truck was over two hours. By plane it was only half an hour. Lolita and her mother would squeeze into the front cockpit and her dad flew the plane from the back cockpit. Their home strip was part of the pasture closest to the large house.

Her parents died young, leaving her the large property. Keeping the plane for herself, Lolita sold everything else to a relative for a little bit down and a large balance to be paid off each fall until the account was clear. It was enough money for her to buy a home and a small business in town and indulge in aviation, her passion. Soon she upgraded to a faster plane and flew to events within a five-hundred-mile radius of her home.

Things went well enough for her in business, but not in love. Lolita never found a husband. She became a somewhat irreverent member of the flying circles, famous for her caustic humor and sunshine-happy personality. She wore pants all the time, smoked like a chimney except when around aircraft, and drank with the boys except when flying the same day. Some people thought that she had an inferiority complex that she covered up with her outrageous behavior.

Before the ban against women flying in the air races, she had flown borrowed planes. Now she had acquired her own cross-country racer that was small, fast, and unusual, just like its owner. She would have to make extra gas stops, but her many friends would help her refuel at out-of-the-way airports all along the route.

Not really caring whether she won or not, Lolita was flying for the sheer joy and exhilaration of piloting a fast ship against the men. She also wanted to prove the in-line engine, which she thought had been much maligned. Her crew had modified a good racer, installing the new engine with a big oil-cooling radiator to cool the engine.

Her race was proceeding as expected until, all of a sudden, her engine coughed and stopped in flight. She tried everything to get it started again. She had a lot of altitude so she experimented with a few things. She finally found she could get it started by flying with the left wing low and running the electric fuel pump to transfer fuel from the right wing to the left low wing. There was some strange obstruction in the system.

She landed with one wing low at an airport where there were mechanics available. They emptied the tanks and checked them with mirrors and flashlights. They blew compressed air through all the lines. Finally, they found a little piece of a rag left in one tank that had caused the fuel starvation, and she was back in the air faster than she had thought possible. Maybe she still had a chance after all.

Buddy was an old-time barnstorming pilot who had done every kind of flying possible. He had flown air shows, dropped parachutists, flown freight to the mines, performed mercy missions, and flown for an airline that had gone out of business. He loved flying and had a passion and talent for designing new planes to fit the better, more reliable, and more powerful engines coming out of the factories. He had supervised several builds of his own designs and flown and sold them. He flew part-time for a new struggling airline for a living.

With no engineering background but a good eye and a lot of experience, Buddy had gone to a welder to explain his concept: a new cabin plane that could also be fast enough to race. He had no engineering drawings, just some sketches. The welder was confused a bit so Buddy drew his fuselage design in chalk on the welding shop cement floor. Then he drew a rough outline of the single wing that would go on top of the fuselage. It was a fast high-wing monoplane with a fixed landing gear. It would be fabric-covered for lightness and fast, easy construction. The cost of building such a plane was relatively modest. The engine would be a newly available 700 hp radial with a constant speed propeller.

When finished and rigged, Buddy flew the plane and found it to be surprisingly fast and easy on the controls.

Luke and Buddy liked and respected each other, but there was a friendly rivalry between them. The previous year, Luke had lost to Buddy only because he let Buddy refuel first just out of courtesy, not thinking it would affect the outcome of the race. At the finish line, Buddy was ahead by less than one minute. Luke came in second, having lost by being a gentleman. This year again there would be an intense yet friendly competition. Buddy probably needed the money more than Luke, but both were flying because of dedication to the science.

Unless Luke developed some kind of difficulty, Buddy knew he had to fly a perfect race again to beat him, but right now Buddy was thinking about other problems. He had put a lot of money into getting his racer ready for this competition and he was in debt. He was counting on the race winnings to keep this business sideline of his going.

The race went well until tragedy struck him also. He had refueled twice, each time in just less than fifteen minutes. He was on the course that took him over the northern part of New Mexico and would have taken him over northern Arizona. Luke, on the other hand, had always felt that the route was dangerous there, so he swung south to be over more populated areas. As Buddy was tooling along over northern New Mexico, the plane suddenly went crazy. It gyrated and thrashed around the sky like a top winding down and then falling over.

"I think I lost a prop blade," he explained after the race. "One blade must have broken off at least halfway down between the hub and the tip. That caused a wild vibration that shook the plane so bad that I couldn't keep it under control. I tried to get my hand on the throttle to pull the power back when the engine must have seized, because I think we must have snap-rolled so violently hard that I hit my head on the cabin post and was knocked unconscious. The plane is so strong that it survived the twisting, wrenching, and spinning in the sky, plus it is so stable that when the engine quit and the plane finally smoothed out it kind of glided by itself down to almost ground level, which is when, fortunately, I came to and tried to dead-stick it into a flat piece of desert."

Buddy overshot the area he was aiming for and ran off into a ravine. He ended up a pile of junk, nose down in the bottom of a deep ravine of the high mountain desert.

"'Oh, boy, I bet there's no one for miles,' I thought, but luckily an Indian had seen me go down," he recounted. "He came galloping up on his horse. I was pinned inside the wreckage. Thankfully, there was no fire. The Indian peered in, saw that I was alive, tried to pull me free but could not, so he left. I hoped he had gone to get help, which he had, but it took him several hours to get back. I guess I drifted in and out of consciousness several times from the loss of blood and the pain. But the Indians brought some tools, cut me out, and took me by horse and then pickup truck to their closest nurse and from there to a hospital."

Regrettably, his dreams of winning were shattered, but more importantly, his life had been spared.

Luke was probably the most experienced pilot in the race, and everyone recognized his superior piloting skills. He was also a gentleman and a friend to everyone in the flying fraternity, lending airplanes, money, or support to any who needed it and all who requested it. His background was as varied as his own multifaceted personality. He had signed on with a circus as a teenager, learned to be a lion tamer, and then joined the military to fly at the end of WWI in France. After the Great War he had done the usual bush flying, barnstorming, border crossing, international adventuring, and now charter work and movie stunt flying. He had once flown for an airline, but did not like flying daily scheduled routes.

"Too much like being a bus driver," he had explained.

Luke had been married but was long divorced. He seemed to have an inner sadness that he covered with a flashy persona. For a while he had found that flying jobs came his way because of his flamboyant personality, good looks, sharp military bearing and uniform, and all the publicity from winning air races. Now with his reputation well established, he continued to dress in a military uniform of the now nonexistent Nevada Air Force with rank of full colonel and ten brass emblems of wings and propeller on it.

To further this image, which made him unforgettable to the news reporters and the public, was his hobby of raising pet lions. Most were carefully secured in cages at a farm for movie animals, but at least one old, tame lioness was always in his hangar office "protecting" her caretaker.

Even with the bizarre image touches, no one doubted Luke Whitney's flying ability. In spite of that, his history was full of a string of bad-luck race incidents like missing out on first place by only seconds last year—less than one minute. Luke's comments were only, "Oh well, Buddy needed the money more than I did last year. This year it's my turn to win."

As Maggie predicted, Luke was flying a perfect race. He was sure to win this time. Every fuel stop was a perfect precision drill. He didn't like pouring in gasoline—especially the high-octane volatile stuff—while the engine was hot and still running, but leaving it idling eliminated the risk of starter problems. His navigation had been precise and the weather and winds aloft had obeyed just like he and Maggie had expected. He was happy to see Fernando at Wichita—it's always a pleasure to be assisted by another pilot when you're in a great hurry. Fernando climbed up on the wing so they could talk over the noise of the idling engine. They spoke about the great movie shots they were getting while the planes had come through for refueling.

"I sure got some great movie footage of that fast gas crew working on your plane," Fernando said. "I'm sure the studio will be able to use a lot of what I filmed with those three cameras running simultaneously."

Luke's next gas stop was Albuquerque, where he landed hot,

blistering the runway with a wheel landing. Running down the runway, he kept the tail up on his racer at part throttle to get to a place where he could turn off to the taxiway faster. He fast-taxied back to where the gas trucks were waiting to do the fueling. The authorities had cooperated, but they had him use a far corner of the field so that if there were a fire it would not burn up anything but cactus. While his propeller ticked slowly over at idle, Luke sat in the cockpit drinking a soda pop the crew gave him. He marveled that the engine could run so many hours with no bad signs of any kind on the temperature or pressure gauges.

The boys had him ready in a record nine minutes and fifteen seconds. When he started to taxi back, the tower advised him that the wind had changed. They wanted him to taxi all the way to the other end of the field and take off in the opposite direction of his landing. He argued with them about that, but they had already changed other planes and would not reverse their traffic pattern again for the one racer.

Unhappy about that, Luke turned around and did a high-speed taxi toward the opposite end, tail up blasting along the taxi strip. When he came to the far end he dropped his tail and applied his brakes to slow down to turn, but his brakes did not take hold. Emergency! Luke had two choices facing him. He could go straight ahead out into the desert cactus and possibly nose over in the soft New Mexico sand, or he could try to turn and run the risk of causing his gear to fold. He decided to try to make the turn. It did not work. The centrifugal force on the slender gear leg plus the heavy gas load caused the outboard gear leg to buckle inward. Ground loop! The wing tip dug into the dirt and spun the plane around.

In that instant he knew he was out of the race. There was no fire, fortunately, and it could be fixed in a couple of days, he hoped. What a tragedy! Luke was always Luke, typically philosophical about dropping out of the race.

"It was my fault," he explained later. "I just drove it too fast and had the bad luck of the brakes fading for some crazy reason. This race is all about reliable equipment. I never had brake problems before. I guess I should have installed new brake linings before the race."

CHAPTER 18

MAGGIE SOARS INTO THE SKY AND WINS THE RACE

MAGGIE HOPED SHE hadn't been unwise in choosing the last starting slot. It made her feel all alone to watch the other racers fire up and take off into the wild blue yonder. One last time she went over her list of items to take with her in the cabin: water thermos, cookies, maps, navigation notes with plotter and pencils, her E6-B round slide rule, a list of power settings from the factory, and other personal incidentals.

She did a pre-start checklist for the umpteenth time: fuel gauges, fuel selector switch in the right position, flaps up, controls free, brakes set, prop control full forward, mixture control full rich, carburetor heat off, trim tabs set, door locked firmly from the inside, parachute pack by the door with the attach rings facing up, test master battery switch, test instrument lights and all other lights, make sure the pitot cover was removed and inside the cockpit—the list seemed endless.

She had her side window open, and now was the moment for which she had waited so long. She smiled appreciatively at the two-man crew standing by to assist in watching for fires on starting and to pull the wheel blocks when she was ready to taxi.

"Clear front!" she hollered, giving the crew a thumbs-up signal.

"All clear!" the crew chief responded, holding up a fire extinguisher.

Maggie built up her fuel pressure with a few strokes of the wobble hand-pump, hit the primer to inject a small amount of raw fuel into the carburetor, turned on the master switch, and hit the starter button. One blade, two blades, three blades, and she turned the magnetos to "both." The dual sparks ignited the first cylinder on compression and fired with a bang, blowing smoke and flame out the exhaust. The prop spun, but no other cylinders fired. Maggie pumped the throttle expertly, and other cylinders started to fire roughly, long flames shooting out the exhaust stack with a lot of black smoke. Maggie knew it was normal with this engine and adjusted the throttle a little bit more. Then all nine cylinders caught with a roar. She backed the throttle off a tad, and the big radial settled down into a steady, throaty rumble. It was a drill she enjoyed every time she fired this engine up.

The engine started without a hitch, which was a big relief. It was always an embarrassing possibility for an engine to be balky, to get over-primed and flooded, or to wear down the battery with the heavy drain from the starter just when she needed to start it the fastest. Lady Luck was with her. It was a good start and the oil pressure came up immediately. Maggie enjoyed the feeling of knowing exactly what the engine was doing by watching all the instruments intently.

She had earned her right to be in the select group of female aviators flying this prestigious cross-country air race. Maggie felt she could take care of the engine and the aircraft as well as any man. Now she had the chance to prove just that in the race ahead. Everyone in the flying community had congratulated her on handling her emergency crash in the pylon race so well. The accident was in the back of her mind, but she was determined to push it out.

As soon as things had settled down, she gave a thumbs-outward signal to the crew chief. He and the other crewman ducked down and ran behind the propeller to pull out the wheel chocks. Soon each one held up a wooden chock by a rope handle to show Maggie she was free to roll. She added an inch of throttle for more rpms. The engine growled a little. More importantly, she started to roll forward. Maggie hit her right wheel brake, pivoted smartly on the spot, and when the nose was pointed toward the taxiway she released the brake and rolled in a straight line to the run-up position just off the end of the runway.

She turned onto the paved circle, pointed the nose into the wind for better cooling, and braked to a full stop. Now she was ready for the final pre-takeoff check list. Maggie brought the engine up to 1800 rpms, just shy of full power, and then cycled the constant speed propeller to make sure it was functioning perfectly. She pulled the prop control all the way back twice, noticing each time the rpms dropped correctly, then pushed it full forward. Next came the check of the mixture control and carburetor heat. After that, she checked the magneto systems again, first the left system and then the right before returning to "both."

Maggie tried the carburetor heat again to make sure the early-morning humidity had not allowed some late-forming ice to restrict the throat of the big Stromberg-Carlson carburetor. Immediately, rpms dropped. She took the heat off and rpms came back up. That protection was working and no ice was present. She moved the controls in all directions to make sure there were no restrictions affecting ailerons, rudder, and elevator. She lowered and raised her flaps, watching the indicator for movement since they were underneath the belly and lower wing where she could not see them, and she checked the trim-tab indicator again for takeoff position. All gauges were correct. Radio frequency was set and the tower responded on 3023.5. Pleased that everything checked out, Maggie was now ready.

She looked around her cabin to see that all was secure one last time before rolling out to the very end of the runway and pivoting so that she could see straight down the center line of the longest paved strip at the airport. She had positioned herself so that her tailwheel was in the dirt but her propeller was over the runway's pavement—that way she could use every inch of the runway if needed, but the prop would not get nicked from picking up little rocks from the ground.

The plane was fully ready, and so was Maggie. The camera crew was in place, all prepared to begin filming her takeoff.

She didn't see the flag man. *Where has the starter gone?* she thought.

Her watch showed one minute to takeoff, and she wanted to start exactly on the nose. With some impatience, she said again, this time loudly, "Where is that starter?!" She became agitated.

As she looked around for the missing man, who had apparently gone into the line shack under the tower, she noticed that there seemed to be more people standing in front of the hangars and lining the runway than there had been when the others were taking off. It was probably just because the hour was more reasonable and the light more conducive to taking pictures, but she hoped they were also wishing her well—not just bloodthirsty people hoping to have the thrill of a takeoff accident.

At the very last second, the starter came running from the tower, but without the checkered flag. He waved at her and shouted something she couldn't understand. Finally she could read his lips screaming, "I've lost my flag! I've lost my flag!"

In a panic, he thought of a solution: he pulled his handkerchief out of his back pocket and waved it at her. He circled it over his head, meaning, "Rev up your engine and get ready to start!" Maggie started to giggle, and then laughed out loud. She put the throttle to the firewall, slowly and deliberately. The engine screamed, the plane shook, her palms began to sweat, and long clouds of dust, dirt, and small rocks streamed out behind her rudder like a comet's tail.

Down fluttered the hankie. How appropriate, Maggie thought, grinning widely and nodding approval. A lady gets a handkerchief instead of a flag. But if that's the way you want it, that's the way you get it. Here we go!

She released her hard-set brakes. The plane jumped forward instantly, pushing her back into the seat. The polished prop blades grabbed whole fistfuls of air, flinging them behind as they clawed forward, eager to get to flying speed. The crowd edged closer to the runway borders to take pictures of her flashing by. She was exhilarated by the growing acceleration. She had to strain to keep her head forward to see over the round engine.

Maggie noticed the plane was drifting leftward in spite of having full right rudder all the way in. Suddenly she remembered—the factory had told her that the souped-up engine would give her more torque so it would tend to rotate the opposite way. She was not supposed to use full power at the start of takeoff! Maggie came back a notch on the throttle, causing the screaming of the thundering engine to suddenly lessen in pitch. The pilots watching were startled by the unexpected sound, since no one ever reduces power on takeoff unless it is to abort. They all gawked intently as she continued racing straight ahead. Those alongside the runway noticed the swerve and the correction and did not know what to make of it.

Two old-timers stood at the entrance to a hangar. Both had flying helmets on with the ear flaps propped up so they could hear better, and their goggles were pushed up high on their brow.

"Hey, Zack, that doesn't sound like an R-985 engine to me!" said one to the other. "What in tarnation does she have installed in that plane?!"

"You're right!" Zack responded. "Whatever it is, it's got a lot more horses in it than the factory advertises. No wonder she came back on the power! Torque was pulling her off line and she couldn't hold it. And did you notice the plane seemed to lean a bit to the right? I'll bet she had the left wheel strut pumped up more than the other to help correct the torque, but it wasn't enough."

While the two speculated about what, if anything, might be wrong, Maggie wrestled her overpowered plane past them, brought the tail up when she had enough slipstream over the rudder to hold it straight, and then eased the heavy but strong-climbing plane into the air, adding the rest of the throttle as her airspeed increased.

The crowd cheered. They were all aware that the youngest and prettiest of the race pilots and the one who had narrowly escaped death two days before had chosen to be the last one off.

Maggie focused on the business at hand. First, she retracted the landing gear into the wheel wells in the belly of the plane. Those on the ground noticed that the plane went through a metamorphosis. With its wheels down it looked like an old-fashioned, awkward biplane, but the moment the gear disappeared up into the belly, the plane took on a new look. It was utterly streamlined and seemed to be more in its element. It took on a sleekness enhanced by the mirror polish on the skin. The lower wing jutted jauntily ahead of the top wing with a negative stagger—thus the "Staggerwing" nickname. This change in the plane's appearance could be compared to a perfectly proportioned wet dolphin resting at the water's edge, but propped up on funny-looking wheels. Then somehow the dolphin miraculously sheds the ungainly wheels and becomes a sleek and beautiful denizen of the deep like it was designed to be. On the ground, the Staggerwing is impressive machinery that only a pilot would love it. But once in the air and with its wheels sucked up inside, it was a sleek work of art to behold. Now Maggie's baby stretched for the sky like a streamlined, homesick angel, climbing sharply to where it longed to be.

Okay, now, let's see, thought Maggie. *Next item of business is to reset the power for cruise climb.*

She came back on the manifold pressure by pulling the throttle, watching the instrument carefully, and then twisted the propeller control to reduce the rpms on that instrument to her predetermined best setting. She had to do things in that exact order to avoid building up the pressure in the cylinders with the supercharger. She turned off the electric fuel pump that she used only on takeoff and landing. She also had a wobble hand-pump in case both the engine-driven fuel pump and the electric standby pump failed. Finally, she turned the fuel selector valve to the one tank she wanted to run for the next hour.

She banked the plane toward her climb course with precision. She was going to fly a straight route just as Fernando and Luke had instructed her to do. Now in the climb, her eyes scanned from instrument to instrument as she monitored her power settings and all engine instruments: oil pressure, oil temperature, exhaust gas temperature, cylinder head temperature, fuel pressure, then her navigation instruments. Magnetic compass checked against gyro compass—rate of climb, airspeed, altimeter climbing—then back to engine instruments through the navigation instruments again. Maggie's eyes darted back and forth, watching to see that every indicator was reporting all was well.

She had "bonded" with the plane when she flew it the day before on a shakedown flight, so her instincts told her that the vibration from the engine and the propeller were right on. The engineers had warned her that the bigger engine would cause major torque on takeoff, and they had set the wheel struts to help compensate for it. She was already used to it, but it did require more adjustment and attention than usual.

The controls were so sweet and balanced that the plane responded to her slightest touch. The engine just growled along, pulling them up and up to the altitude she wanted. She couldn't help giving a self-satisfied grin of exuberant joy. She took her left hand off the wheel she had been gripping, lifted her right hand off the engine controls she had been adjusting, and with the flat palms of both hands she patted the instrument panel in front of her.

"Congratulations, you beautiful doll!" she exclaimed out loud. "You've got us off to a great start. Now just take us to Los Angeles at full race speed!"

The sky was overcast but rays of sunshine came through from time to time, lighting the ground and the city below. New York was awake and bustling, but she noticed the traffic was not as heavy as the day before since it was Labor Day. Long Island Sound and the rivers in view looked inviting in the warm days of summer. A few pleasure boats were plowing the water this early in the morning and leaving long streaks of frothy wake etched in the textured surface behind. She saw very few sails but knew they would be out soon.

Maggie was on course and still climbing. The cylinder head temperature seemed to be creeping up. She had made the mixture a bit leaner for more power, so now she added a touch more of rich mixture back in to bring the temperature down to normal. The oil temperature was also notching up a bit too high, so she lowered her nose to pick up fifteen more miles of airspeed.

"Both measures should cool down their respective areas," Maggie said, as if talking to an imaginary companion.

She remembered that when she was with Fernando she talked to him while flying, even when concentrating on flying instruments. Now, all alone, she still liked talking out loud. She explained verbally what she was doing and why she was making the change. Hearing her voice seemed to keep her company, and it was reassuring to speak as though she were talking every decision through with a copilot or instructor.

A little more than an hour after takeoff, she climbed through the first clouds of the storm she had expected. She was on instruments and going over her well-learned instrument scan. Because of the way her instruments were placed on the panel in front of her, she had to scan six important dials in a fixed, clockwise pattern. There were three gyro instruments: the directional gyro compass, gyro horizon indicator, and gyro turn-and-bank indicator. The other three essential instruments for blind flying were the airspeed indicator, sensitive altimeter, and rate-of-climb indicator. Her regular magnetic compass was located up above the panel in the middle of the wind screen. Maggie glanced at that occasionally.

She also had a large clock with a sweep second hand for timed turns mounted close to the gyro instruments. In the panel, she had her two radios. The first was a receiver to hear the tower for takeoff and landing clearance; it also received the radio-range broadcast so she could know if she was on the "beam" or to one side of it. The other radio was a short-range transmitter to talk to the tower when she was less than twenty miles away. Bigger and longer-range equipment was available, but it was all too big and too heavy for the Staggerwing.

Now she was on instruments, and it was like patting her head and rubbing her tummy at the same time. It required practice and coordination and constant attention, although once in the routine it seemed easier. She had to keep her mind alert, as she was flying the ship while simultaneously monitoring navigation and engine instruments.

At exactly one hour after liftoff, Maggie switched to a gas tank on the opposite side to balance the plane. Once both tanks were down a bit she would transfer fuel to improve balance again so that the plane would fly a few miles per hour faster. She had six fuel tanks to manage. She was so busy trying to keep on top of all these duties, she found little time to think about Fernando.

After she had been flying for about three hours, Maggie's routine chores were memorized and so familiar that she had moments in between scans to actually enjoy what she was doing. At high-speed cruise, the "music" she had been waiting for began to penetrate her body. The plane had a beautiful, harmonic sound to it.

The wind rushing by could be the string sections of a symphony orchestra! she thought joyfully. *And the rumble of the engine could be the kettle drums together with the bass viols, way down deep. The brass is the sound in my head from the vibration of the skin of the plane stretched tightly over the frame. Everything together is a harmonic chord!*

Her imagination carried her to a different, exotic world in the sky.

Maggie was surprised at her own creative, artistic expressions, likening the sounds at cruise to a beautiful symphonic melody. She had read or heard of the phenomena only once. Some famous pilot— *Was it Karen Blixen or Beryl Markham or Anne Morrow Lindbergh?* she thought— had commented that during long flights at steady power settings, if you fiddle just a little for perfect synchronization you will hear a kind of celestial music replace the rumble of the engine and the rush of the wind. It is a lost chord that you can find if you listen for it and pay attention.

Suddenly, a strange sound interrupted her symphony. It was a staccato sound she quickly recognized as big, splattering rain drops. The clouds were thicker and darker than she had expected.

“So here it is,” she said with a deep, long sigh.

Maggie had climbed through wide openings between scattered, puffy blossoms of white fair-weather cumulus clouds on her route, then cruised between thickening layers of gray stratus clouds. The solid front she had to fly through next changed color to dark, threatening black, and soon became a boiling charcoal thickness. She was now on instruments, as she had anticipated. She had to avoid the worst areas marked by lightning strikes, and Luke and Fernando had both prepared her for this type of flying in rain, hail, turbulence, and zero visibility.

Comparing ordinary, clear-weather flying to instrument flying is like comparing Sunday driving in the country to 200 mph Indianapolis race driving. Being able to fly blind is a skill acquired by many hours of hard practice—much like how a virtuoso violinist learns to play with her eyes closed.

With no visual reference to the horizon or the ground, pilots can suffer spatial disorientation or vertigo. A pilot with vertigo cannot tell if he is banked or level-winged, turning or flying straight, climbing or diving. Gyro instruments keep a pilot oriented, but it takes a lot of training. Without the instruments and the training it is easy to end up in a descending graveyard spiral, ever faster and ever tighter, that ends in a high-speed crash.

Maggie felt she was prepared for any eventuality, but to stay calm as much as possible she returned to her musical musings, trying to talk over the noise the rain was making to keep that feeling in the pit of her stomach from turning to big-time panic and fear.

“That beating sound from the raindrops is like snare drummers beating a long roll with their drum sticks on the leading edges of the wings,” she said nervously in a loud voice.

The clatter on the front of the plane grew louder and heavier. At first the rain drops were being whipped to spray by the propeller, but now they were so heavy they were getting through and hitting the windshield with a wilder sound. The big drops seemed like lead shot being thrown at the plexiglass in front of her. She hoped it would not shatter.

Instinctively, Maggie reached for her old flying helmet and goggles to make sure that if the plexiglass did break she could protect her eyes. She could see the rain streaking past her between the two wings, like tracer bullets zipping past from an unseen machine gun.

The sound became so deafening that it drowned out the roar of the engine. Maggie was alarmed. She had never been in rain so heavy before.

Will the engine run in this rain? Will it drown out the carburetor? Will the water short out the two magneto systems? she worried.

In the midst of her increasing anxiety about the engine, leaks started to develop in the cabin. First, water came dripping through the ventilation system. She needed fresh air, but she shut most of the system off because her maps were getting wet. Then water began seeping through minuscule cracks around the windshield. It was supposed to be carefully caulked and watertight, but some moisture was coming through.

Suddenly she saw a lightning flash to her left.

An embedded thunderstorm, she thought. *I'd better turn thirty degrees to the right and go around it.*

But soon after the change in course to avoid extra turbulence, she spotted more lightning in the darkest area to her right. Luckily, her instrument lights were working well in the darkness. She was glad she had tested them.

"Better come back ten degrees and fly in between the two cells," she said, but the din was so deafening she couldn't hear her voice, and wouldn't have been able to even if she had shouted.

Suddenly, her composure was put to the acid test. Lightning flashed closer than before with a crash of sound and blinding light. The turbulence seemed to be wrenching the wings off the plane. An unseen force catapulted the plane upward and a high-g jolt, dropped her head to her chin. Maggie fought to keep the wings level and the nose boring straight ahead. She noticed that the rate-of-climb indicator was pegged at the maximum reading straight up on the dial—over *three thousand* feet per minute. Her altimeter had gone crazy and showed her zooming upward although she was flying with her nose level. She knew logically that she had entered a violent updraft, but she felt like she was being sucked upward by a giant vacuum cloud.

Then, just as suddenly, the little plane, still enmeshed in roaring rain and some small hail, dropped like a car going off a vertical cliff. The wings twisted and creaked. The fuselage bucked like a wild horse and groaned under the giant stress. Maggie's head was thrown back and forth, and she couldn't read the instruments clearly. She was flying by gut instinct more than by instruments now. She knew she had to let the plane bounce and float without trying to resist because if she horsed the controls around, that could damage the structure. It was best to ride it out, but the downdraft was like being in an elevator in freefall.

Now the instrument was pegged at a power dive of *three thousand* feet per minute, but was probably worse. The engine was not screaming as loud as it would have in a dive, and the airspeed was dropping off instead of increasing. What was happening? Was she losing control of the plane? Was the plane being torn apart by the violent updrafts and downdrafts? Maggie came back on power to reduce the strain on the structure. She fought to keep the wings reasonably level and the nose from climbing too much or diving too much, no matter what the altimeter said.

She feared over-controlling under these circumstances and resisted any sharp or violent movement of the controls. Luke and Fernando had said that coming back on the power would reduce the tendency to over-control. She wished they were with her, but this had been her choice and she knew it was her test. All the other planes had to fly through this storm. Had they survived? There was no way for her to know. Would *she* survive? She didn't know that either. The plane creaked and groaned from the stress. She was talking less audibly now out of fear and worry, her heart racing, her mouth dry.

If she could keep her airspeed from getting too low and stalling, and from getting too high where the wind would rip the wings off, and if she could keep enough control so she could fly out of the writhing tentacles of the octopus-like storm, she and this beautiful machine would survive. She was convinced now more than ever that her pretty ship was built stouter and tougher than she had ever imagined.

As soon as they could get out of the storm, she could regain her navigation control. Right now she just had to survive. Usually by going in between two cells she would be out of the most violent part in about fifteen minutes, but this storm front was much wider and deeper than the weather report had led her to expect. She hoped she would fly out of it soon—she had already been in it for what seemed like hours.

It was like being inside a cement mixer with a hundred hammers beating on the sides. The lightning flashed all around her. She kept one eye closed so as to not become totally blinded from the brightness. Just as she thought it couldn't possibly get worse, her hair stood on end—not from fright but from static electricity! The wings took on an eerie luminescence, the struts and chrome brace wires glowing weirdly. She couldn't see the cowling in front of her because of the rain pelting the windshield, but the propeller blur seemed florescent through the blinding rain. She had no windshield wipers on this little plane; the blast of the air and water in the raging slipstream would have ripped them off anyway.

Then she became aware of something behind her. She glanced back for just an instant and saw what she first thought was a glowing ball of fire inside the cabin by the back bulkhead. She worried that the gas tanks might explode. Then just as suddenly, the glowing ball disappeared, the static electricity evaporated, and the glowing wings and the florescent propeller whirl ceased. The rain had stopped!

She could hear the noble engine still pulling steadily.

"Attagirl!" Maggie exclaimed with a big grin. "Keep running smoothly, okay?"

She caressed the panel in front of her as though she were stroking a baby.

Her altitude was four thousand feet higher than when the storm had started. Paint had been peeled from the leading edge of her wings. A few spots in the cabin seemed wet, but she was okay—just tired and perspiring.

"Now I just need to find out where I am!" she said.

Maggie tried her radio. Nothing but static, as she expected. She was still in between the cloud layers. She decided to let down through the strata below her and hopefully find the ground at some safe place. She returned to her previous compass heading, hoping that she wasn't more than fifty miles off course. Fifteen minutes off would put her about fifty miles away from where she was supposed to be, but had she flown north or south? Maggie would have to drop down through the overcast to find out. But first she made some rough calculations. She figured she was now about an hour east of Wichita.

Suddenly, her engine quit.

The prop was still windmilling, but it was not pulling any power. Then Maggie remembered—just before the lightning, she was planning on switching tanks, but in the frightening crisis she had forgotten to do it. She must have run the upper left wing tank dry. She switched to the upper right tank, hit the electric fuel pump, and started pumping the wobble pump, all at the same time. She had to let go of the controls and use both hands to get it done. Her arms and hands were moving in a blur so fast that she looked like a human octopus. The necessary fuel pressure came up as the starved engine coughed, caught, and surged back to full power. Maggie breathed a big sigh of relief.

"Boy, that was close!" she exclaimed. "This race business is not for the faint-hearted, that's for sure! But now what can happen next? I'd better get back to the maps and calculations to find where I am, don't you think?"

Maggie was confident that her "companion" nodded in agreement.

In the turbulence, the parachute chest pack had bumped up front and had lodged down by the copilot seat's rudder pedals. The flashlight was missing, the sandwiches were strewn around, and the pencils were nowhere to be seen, but the rest of the things were within reach. She would have to find every single article because they were dangerous just being loose. They could get lodged in some control cable pulley, jam it, and cause a serious or even fatal accident.

"One more worry," she complained out loud.

The rain started again and then cleared up. The sky lightened considerably, and just as suddenly as she had flown into the clouds, she found herself flying in the midst of a beautiful midwest summer day with blue sky above, white clouds behind, and stretching off in both directions. She had made it through the embedded squall line and the entire wide front. She could clearly see the rain-washed countryside below her. She opened the air vents again, a bit of moisture still dripping from them, and smelled the sweet fragrance of recent rains on green farmlands below. She relaxed and enjoyed the let-down to a lower altitude.

By setting her nose down just a little and leaving the power high, she picked up thirty more miles per hour. She was a streaking bullet boring westward, but she still hadn't found out exactly where she was, and she needed that information to chart a course to the fuel stop in Wichita, Kansas. She spotted a lake and a railroad and then the highway. But the city she saw was not in the right place.

"Darn it!" she exclaimed, frustrated.

She pinpointed her position and found the storm had moved her off track about the fifty miles she expected and to the north. That was not too bad. The time on instruments had also been a time of headwinds, but not as bad as the forecast, so her theory that the storm was slowing down was correct. She had not anticipated so strong a squall line, so perhaps she should have flown at a different altitude, but that was all behind her. Now she had to correct her course and barrel on down to Wichita—and to Fernando.

Fernando! Maggie surprised herself at how often she was thinking of him. She missed having him wave her off back in New York this morning when she started this great race. It was as if he was now an essential part of her heart and her whole soul. Even though she understood that he had promised Luke and the studio that he would help them with the filming in Wichita, she still wanted him to be there watching her takeoff. Also, during her hours in the air, her yearning thoughts returned to him every time her routine chores allowed her to. She would monitor the instruments, check her navigation, and then think of Fernando. Again and again her eyes would scan the glass-covered engine gauges, then look at the compass, mark off each fifteen-minute, sixty-mile distance covered, and then think of Fernando. She really loved him and wanted him near her every minute.

Maggie saw what must be Wichita in the distance and, according to the map, she knew the field was to the south of the city. It was almost exactly halfway in the 2,450-mile race. She had enough fuel to fly another hour but was happy she didn't need to. She monitored instruments and found everything in perfect shape. She did not want the engine to cool too much. She still was in a race after all, so she left power on and just blasted downhill in seeking to arrive short of the field at a thousand feet, call the tower for a straight-in approach, and land as fast as possible.

At the appropriate distance she tried hailing the tower. At first, she only heard static, but eventually they responded.

"Staggerwing cleared for straight-in approach to runway 27, wind fifteen from two six zero."

"Roger!" Maggie exclaimed, relieved.

She pulled up sharply to kill off speed so she could drop her wheels, dropped flaps to kill more speed, and settled in for a smooth wheel landing. She made the first turnoff, and taxied as fast as she dared back to the gas trucks. She was hoping Fernando was on the ground and not up in the sky filming her landing. The crew signaled her over to the fuel trucks where she shut the engine down, and the men ran hoses to her tanks and immediately started pumping on both sides. A mechanic opened the engine compartment to check oil and look for leaks.

Maggie opened the door and stiffly climbed out. She did not see Fernando anywhere, but by the time she was on the ground, there he was, waiting anxiously with open arms. She fell into his embrace, and they kissed in spite of cameras on them.

Who cares? she thought. *He is mine, all mine!*

"Fernando, you didn't tell me about the dragons in that line squall!" she said, punching him playfully in the shoulder. "I thought they were going to eat me alive. And the front was much deeper than expected. And the rain peeled the paint off the leading edges of the wings! Will the factory think I did the wrong thing with their plane? Did you have to fly through that yesterday?"

"Hey, I flew under it," Fernando responded with a grin. "I didn't have as full a panel as you do and I couldn't fly as high as you so we dodged around it, but down low. It was not as bad yesterday as today, but some of the pilots have told us that it was pretty heavy stuff earlier this morning and getting worse. Did you have any real problem?"

"Oh, no, not at all!" she lied, smiling. "The engine performed beautifully, and the plane doesn't seem to be bent. No, seriously, it was a tooth-rattler and a head-shaker! I have never seen so much heavy rain! Part of the inside of the cabin is still soaked. And that noise from the rain and hail! I couldn't hear myself think! It drowned out the sound of the engine and I thought it would flood the engine with water, but it kept running—that is, until I ran a tank dry. That sure woke me up! But it restarted immediately as soon as I changed tanks and hit the pumps."

At that moment she remembered something.

"Fernando, I lost my flashlight and pencils and several other things," she told him. "Could you help me find them? Oh—and I heard the music! Glorious, symphonic chords. Heavenly!"

"I had hoped you would," Fernando responded with a smile. "I'm really happy for you, *querida.* And I'll find your lost items!"

In a flash, Maggie was back to reality.

"By the way, how am I doing in the race?"

Fernando had been keeping tabs on pilots who had reported in by long-distance radio. He told her that Luke was arriving in Albuquerque soon, that Buddy had not been heard from recently, and Joe was out of the race. He also said that the hatch on Amy's plane had blown off, had just been worked on, and that she was probably about even with her in speed. The DC-2 just radioed in. They were twenty minutes out making a straight-in approach.

"Maggie, you'll be able to save a few minutes if you could get off the runway before the DC-2 is lined up for final approach," Fernando said. "Otherwise, you'll have to wait until after they land, because there's only one runway long enough for these heavily loaded racers."

They walked with their arms around each other while Maggie stretched her legs. The Staggerwing factory president saw them, but waited until they had turned around and were headed back to the plane.

"Maggie, you're doing a great job!" Mr. Butterfield said with a big smile, walking over. "Is everything going all right for you? How's our plane behaving?"

"Oh, it sure is!" Maggie said, glowing. "It's still a dream boat. Sorry about peeling some paint back there in that rain and hailstorm. She doesn't look quite so sharp with the leading edge all exposed down to the primer. I didn't know an engine could keep running with all that water splashing over it. I even got wet inside the cabin!"

"Oh goodness, don't worry about that!" Mr. Butterfield responded. "When I flew the plane to New York I plowed through a small rain squall, but it wasn't enough to do any damage. While they're topping the tanks I'll tighten the plexiglass seal. In any case, it looks like clear sailing from here to the West Coast, except for some slight buildups over northern Arizona near the Grand Canyon. Be sure to stay south of there and you'll not get wet—I promise."

Maggie laughed good-naturedly, waved goodbye, and turned back to Fernando.

"My dear gaucho, please get to California as soon as you can, will you?" Maggie said, patting his cheek. "I miss you terribly! When I'm flying along I talk out loud to you just as if you were right there in the cabin with me. It seems to help a little. Sure wish it were possible for you to arrive for the big party tonight!"

They hugged tightly. She couldn't delay her departure any longer—every minute lost was three to four miles she would have to make up. Maggie put one cowboy boot on the step and swung the other into the cabin. She turned to close the door behind her, and blew a kiss to Fernando first. After closing and locking the door, she slipped forward into her left-hand seat. She fastened her belts quickly, and noticed that the lost items had been found and were now in a paper sack.

She looked out the window at Fernando and shouted "thank you!"

while waving the paper sack.

She began her start-up procedures.

"Clear front!" she called out her open side window.

Fernando repeated the signal and the crew had fire extinguishers at the ready. Maggie fired up quickly and started taxiing immediately. She called the tower, advising them she was ready to depart.

"There's a DC-2 on long final about five miles out," the controller said. "Can you beat him with ample margin?"

"Roger!" Maggie exclaimed.

"Staggerwing cleared onto the active runway and cleared for immediate takeoff," the tower said.

Maggie wasted no time and bolted down the runway. Once again she found that she could not hold the plane straight. The torque twisted her to the left, even though the left gear strut was pumped higher than the right one. She pulled the throttle back slightly, kept control, and soon was off and climbing into the blue western sky.

Fernando watched as she tucked the gear in and climbed straight west. The slight crosswind had been no problem; in fact, it had helped.

Maggie had no trouble adding the rest of her remaining power as soon as she reached over 130 mph airspeed. That was also a good climb speed, so she let it sit there and just watched the altimeter wind up through eight thousand, nine thousand, ten thousand feet, up to her cruising altitude, twelve thousand feet. She had excellent efficiency at that elevation, but it soon became evident that she would need to go on up to thirteen thousand if she wanted to clear the tops of the fluffy fair-weather cumulus clouds spread across the horizon in front of her.

She loved the artistic effect of white, curly, cottony clouds against the blue sky, but she did not want to bump her way through them, nor did she want to fly around them. It was easier to just climb a bit and slide over the top. Once set up for cruise, no mountains bothering her and the engine behaving perfectly, Maggie just could not resist the temptation to fly a direct line despite Fernando and Luke's insistence to take the southern route over Albuquerque. She knew it was vacant land, but from thirteen thousand feet she could glide fifteen miles in any direction even if she had total engine failure. She took the chance to shorten her route slightly.

The flight settled down into boredom. No instruments to fly and no radio range to fly out here in the golden West. The government had installed the radio-range system only close to her destination and in the more populated eastern part of the country. Someday, they would have it coast to coast. All she had to do right now was tend to the engine instruments and fly her westerly magnetic course.

Maggie, like all pilots, was always mentally prepared for an unexpected emergency, even when everything seemed to be going just fine. She was continually looking for the best place to land if needed. Usually engine problems develop slowly with some warning, but occasionally an engine can just quit. She knew that her emergency protocol dictated that her best course of action with a dead engine was ninety miles per hour and a descent rate of nine hundred feet per minute. In a no-wind condition, that worked out to about ten minutes of gliding time in any direction, or fifteen miles. That's a circle of thirty miles diameter. Usually there's a reasonable place to land as long as the pilot is alert and noticing good places just flown over or out in front on the map. Maggie was constantly looking, calculating, and remembering, even when thinking about celestial music, Fernando, and Mary Jane.

After the first half of her flight, when she had been busy flying on instruments and navigating and penetrating the storm, this was a cakewalk. She remembered the longtime flying quote, "Flying cross-country is hour after hour of boredom, punctuated from time to time with moments of sheer terror."

She smiled as she thought of Fernando, who had told her that. She loved to hear him talk about flying down in Argentina. One evening, while they had sat on the bottom bleachers of the vacant polo field, he had entertained her with fascinating stories about his country. He had flown their slow, old cabin plane from Buenos Aires down to the Patagonia and back. He had gone around to every family cattle ranch in the pampas and to every family sheep ranch in the southern Patagonia one summer. He had been checking on the effects of some new medicines the company vets had recommended the year before to reduce illnesses in their cattle and sheep. He was sent to get the reports and to look at the herds as well as to notice if there were any differences in their appearance and statistics.

While Fernando described his activities there, Maggie saw the vast cattle ranches stretching across thousands of acres of flat pastureland in her mind's eye. But Fernando had told her something about his country she found almost unbelievable.

"The pampa is the richest area in the whole world," he had claimed. "It is thirty feet deep of dark, rich loam. The natural rainfall is around sixty inches per year, spread almost evenly, so there is seldom major flooding or drought. The temperature rarely gets above ninety-five degrees Fahrenheit nor does it really freeze, although there are some frosty mornings in the winter. So with that rainfall, moderate temperature, and rich soil, we can raise wheat, corn, barley, or alfalfa, or just leave the ground in natural grasses that grow belly-deep for the cattle. There are almost no rocks and very few groves of trees except those planted for wind breaks and shade."

Maggie was impressed with the picture Fernando had painted of thousands of head of Hereford cows with their calves on one ranch and thousands of head of Black Angus cows on another ranch. There were, in addition, other ranches where they fed the calves after they were weaned from their mothers and until they were ready for market.

This is too amazing to even be true! Maggie had thought, picturing in her mind her own family ranch in mountain and desert country where natural grass pastures were hard to find.

"You need to see our ranch houses at Venado Tuerto, Trenque Lauquen, and Tandil," Fernando had gone continued. "They are real showplaces. But I like the old-fashioned working ranches better. One of my two personal favorites is south of Santa Fe, and the other one is situated just north of Bahia Blanca."

The faraway places with strange-sounding names intrigued Maggie.

In her heart she felt certain that someday she would see all of them.

Fernando had described their particular enchantments, the buildings, the corrals, the prize bulls and blue ribbon-winning rams with their lineage, and the trophies they had won at the annual cattle show at Palermo. He especially loved the horses they had at each ranch.

As she flew along over the western part of the United States, smiling to herself, reflecting on their many conversations, she remembered Fernando talking about his ancestors with pride.

"It started way back with one of my great-great-grandfathers," he had said once. "He thought it best that each individual ranch have the same markings on their horses. That way whenever he had gauchos together he could tell by their horses which ranch they were from. That developed into a competition to raise better and better animals on each ranch, which led us into breeding and training racehorses and polo ponies. It has grown over the generations into what is now the best group of ranches in the world, thanks to my hard-working forefathers."

She marveled that he didn't seem to be bragging at all—it was just a matter of fact for him. He said that the family felt it was a gift from above and that they had a responsibility to manage those gifts wisely. They felt they were stewards more than owners of such fruitful and abundant territories. Maggie worried that Fernando's family would turn out much more impressive than she imagined, but she looked forward to seeing this incredible land of the gauchos for herself.

The plane bored a hole in the sky, on and on, everything going very smoothly and uneventfully. Her scan of engine and navigation instruments was by habit, so her mind drifted back to reflecting on her conversations with Fernando about his family and homeland.

On another occasion, while they were riding, he had told her about the sheep ranches he visited on that long flight.

"Down in the Patagonia—which corresponds by latitude to an area from Kentucky north to the middle of Hudson Bay if placed in the Northern Hemisphere—it is cold and windswept, but there is enough grass for the sheep to graze if it is controlled carefully enough. The wind and the cold make the sheep grow a thick, long, staple wool highly prized in the British and European market. We have ten different sheep ranches down there plus a lot of other installations to buy and wash and prepare the wool for export."

"What's your favorite place there?" Maggie had asked.

"Our ranch just outside San Carlos de Bariloche in the Andes Mountains," he had responded immediately. "Our central sheep-ranching and wool-buying office is in Bariloche, and my favorite home of all is down there on Lake Nahuel Huapi. It is like your Jackson Hole in the Tetons or Banff in Canada—steep mountains deeply forested from their timberline right down into the brightest blue lakes you have ever seen. It is much prettier than Lake Tahoe, much more dramatic than the Rockies, and much more picturesque than Colorado. In fact, Bariloche is called the Switzerland of South America. There are thousands of lakes, not just one or two. And the lakes, the rivers, and the mountains stretch for over a thousand miles. You must let me take you there, Maggie."

She was flying as if on autopilot while these memories of Fernando and his descriptions of his homeland flowed through her mind. But suddenly it happened—that instance of "punctuated from time to time with moments of sheer panic." First, she had a sinking feeling that something was wrong. She looked at engine instruments she had neglected for a while and spotted the drop in manifold pressure. What could cause that? Had the throttle vibrated back from its setting? She checked and found it to be in place. Could it be ice in her carburetor at this altitude? She applied carb heat by pulling out the control that would blast hot air into the throat of the carburetor. Sure enough, the manifold pressure slowly climbed back up; the engine surged and began running smoothly again.

She had her confirmation. She had never encountered ice in the carburetor at this high altitude before, but, she reasoned, she was just skimming the tops of the clouds. If there was enough visible moisture to make a cloud, there was enough to form some ice in the throat of the carburetor. If left unattended, this ice could strangle the engine, cause it to quit, and make it impossible to get it started again. Since she had caught it in time she could breathe a heavy sigh of relief.

The plane droned on for what seemed like hours. Maggie checked her course. She was still north of Highway 66 per Luke's instructions, so she decided to let the northern crosswind push her a bit south. Besides, this was her country. Luke and others considered the western desert to be terribly barren and dangerous, but this was home to Maggie. She could see ahead to towering buildups going on—up to thirty thousand feet. That would be over the Grand Canyon and the Kaibab Plateau. Her childhood home was just north of the Grand Canyon rim.

Another philosophical thought came into her mind. Maggie remembered reading that the French pilot-author Antoine de Saint-Exupéry likened the whirring of his plane's engine to the beating of his heart. He saw both as machines so perfect that he became unconscious about their existence and thus more aware of the realities of the natural world outside him or his cockpit.

> It is not with the metal that the pilot is in contact . . . it is thanks to the metal, and by virtue of it, that the pilot rediscovers nature. [. . .] The machine which at first blush seems a means of isolating man from the great problems of nature, actually plunges him more deeply into them.[1]

Maggie realized that she was flying over the Arizona painted desert area of the Navajo nation south of the Grand Canyon, country she had visited frequently. She could spend days alone in desert like this and never feel lonesome. She had no fear of this rugged backcountry, knowing as she did how to find water and live off the land. She also knew a few landing strips that weren't on any maps. Even though she was strongly tempted to stay north toward the Grand Canyon, she decided to follow her course past the San Francisco peaks and down into the Los Angeles area.

---

[1] Antoine de Saint-Exupéry, *Wind, Sand and Stars* (New York: Houghton Mifflin Harcourt Publishing Co., 1992), 19–20.

Her line of flight would take her south of the tip of southern Nevada.

She spotted the familiar Colorado River crossing her route. She had driven through and flown over this area many times and had watched filming of cowboy movies in the country now behind her in the Grand Canyon and Painted Valley areas.

She heard the symphony music once again. The plane had burned off a lot of fuel and was lighter now, flying a little bit faster and smoother. The angels were with her.

Soon she was flying over the Mojave Desert into the low afternoon sun. She put the visor down and her sunglasses on. At last, she could begin her let-down into Los Angeles. She was so close!

Her thoughts turned back to Fernando and Luke and the other racers. How were they doing? Where were they? She turned on her radio—nothing but static. Reception was too poor, but soon she would pick up the beam leading over the San Bernardino Mountains into the valley. She knew she was right on course. The engine was performing perfectly, and again she heard the music. Everything seemed to be in tune.

The flight had been absolutely magnificent, and she felt she could conquer the world with this fast, powerful airplane. The factory hope of adding 30 mph to the cruising speed had been met. All systems had been totally dependable. Nothing had failed or given her any major problem except for the line squall earlier in the day. She had a slight headache, but that must have come from being at high altitude for longer than she had expected without oxygen. Maybe next time she ought to bring one of those newfangled pressure bottles with a tube and a mask to breathe oxygen whenever she was over twelve thousand feet.

Maggie found her thoughts flitting back and forth, now returning to her parents and to Fernando and wondering how things were going to work out. She realized there were going to be a lot of questions to ask and to answer. She had put them off on purpose so she could concentrate on the race. Now she would have to confront them all, including the details of the wedding and the future. Could she keep Fernando in the West? Would he want to stay? Did his family really need him in

Argentina? Would it be better for both of them if he returned and took his place in his family businesses? Would his uncles and aunts accept him?

Maggie and Fernando had discussed all the pros and cons. Fernando was obviously torn between his love for his parents and his homeland, and his love for Maggie. His new opportunities in the United States, and being able to use his engineering degree, did make him lean toward Maggie's homeland and family.

Maggie started her let-down from high altitude. Dropping her nose slightly increased her airspeed, exactly like she wanted. The increased velocity changed the sound slightly, and suddenly, Maggie heard the music again. It was a celestial harmony like giant choirs humming with a huge symphony orchestra full of strings, woodwinds, brass, and percussion instruments holding the chord in the background. The rhythmic throbbing of the explosions in each cylinder driving the pistons up and down, together with the scream of the wind streaming by and the vibration of the propeller tips whipping around at near supersonic speed, all combined to form a beautiful, musical chord that thrilled her. Her heart swelled with absolute joy and happiness, and she wanted to share this moment with Fernando. That thought caused her heart to speed up. Yes, she was in love. No doubt about it.

Maggie passionately wanted Fernando to be at the finish line to receive her, but he was a thousand miles and many hours of travel behind her. She wanted so much to have him at her side, to fly with her through blue skies, threading their way through billowing, cottony, cumulus-cloud valleys. She wanted to ride her horses with him at sunset when the shadows are long and the creek burbles softly and the breeze in the cottonwoods is just right.

Maggie's thoughts and passions made her oblivious to the plane and the race. Her let-down from altitude, her navigation into the Los Angeles valley, and her manipulation of the controls were all by instinct. She missed Fernando's touch, his kiss, his cologne, and his new, wonderful self-confidence. He had changed, she had changed, their circumstances had changed, and now closing fast upon the end of the race it did not seem to matter if she won or lost. She had flown the two races she wanted to fly, and now all she wanted was Fernando.

While Maggie was about thirty minutes from the finish line, the anxious media pressured the race committee into issuing the following:

Press Release from the Race Committee
Los Angeles Mines Field 4:30 p.m.

The Race Committee estimates of race results are based upon three race planes on the ground in Los Angeles, all female pilots, one known midair explosion with pilot safe after parachuting, two planes far overdue, and three educated guesses of possible locations of those still unheard from. Our estimated ranking of planes including those still in the air and based on their mid-continent speeds are as follows:

Pilot situation known or estimated by the committee:

Joe: Known crash north of Kansas City
Barbara: Landed 3rd place so far
Amy: Landed 2nd place so far
DC-2: Expected in last place
Betty: Position unknown, expected 4th
Lolita: Landed 1st place so far
Buddy: Overdue, search parties alerted
Luke: Overdue, unconfirmed accident
Maggie: Position unknown, expected 5th

Maggie's streamlined teardrop of an airplane with the lower wing jutting out in front of the top wing was knifing through the air at tremendous speed. Maggie had left full race power on, and with the higher airspeed the controls stiffened and kept it going on a rock-steady course. She drilled an arrow-straight line in the sky right for the airfield finish line in Los Angeles. She let down over the San Bernardino mountain range into the valley, the slight afternoon haze reducing her visibility. It was clear enough to follow highways and population centers below, but forward visibility was less than desirable. She knew she was on course, the radio range was working now and she was on the beam, but she could not see the airport until she was almost on top of it.

She had been in the air for over five hours since Wichita, and over ten hours total since departing New York that morning. She had flown into headwinds the whole way, yet her groundspeed was still higher than she had estimated it would be.

"This plane is a bullet!" Maggie exclaimed delightedly, affectionately patting the top of the instrument panel with her right hand. "Good race, *mi amor.*"

She giggled at having said a couple of words in Spanish that Fernando had taught her.

She peered intently into the afternoon sun, trying to spot the pylon in the middle of the airport. She let down so she would have a thousand feet as she flashed over the pylon, according to race instructions. Just before leveling out at her traffic altitude, Maggie spotted the pylon in the haze. She could see no other planes in the traffic and no one else was on the radio announcing their position. She keyed her mike to report that she was right over the pylon.

Then she blanched.

Out of nowhere, at her same altitude, the sky seemed full of airplanes coming right at her—a whole military squadron of planes. Maggie had looked up from locating the pylon underneath her just in time to face, head on, at full speed, a gaggle of about ten planes flying right at her. They scattered like a flock of geese. Some broke right, others left, and one went straight up as she wove in between them. Fortunately, they were expert at evasive combat maneuvers. They were gone as fast as they had appeared.

Maggie called the tower in startled language instead of usual radio procedure.

"Hey Race Tower down there, what's going on!" she demanded. "I thought this area was closed to all traffic except for race planes coming in. What in the world was that formation doing here? We almost had a bunch of midair collisions! Over."

The tower came back immediately with an apology.

"Staggerwing Racer, sorry about that. We saw them the same instant you did or we would have warned you. They are not on our frequency. You did a good job of flying in between them. We will report them, of course. They were military planes, obviously off course. Their base is five miles away from us. Over."

"Race Tower, thanks," Maggie responded, trying to calm down. "In the commotion, did you mark my time of crossing the pylon? Request clearance to land on runway two seven. Over."

"Roger, Staggerwing. We gotcha. We heard you approach, marked your time, and were looking up for you when those other planes blasted in here. You are now cleared for runway two seven. Call on final."

Maggie banked sharply to kill off speed, lowered her gear and flaps, and came back to landing power settings. She turned on final, called the tower, kept fifteen inches of manifold pressure, ran through her landing check list again—gas, undercarriage down, mixture rich, prop pitch, carb heat—100, 90, 80, touch down at 75 mph in a grease job of a wheel landing.

The moment Maggie had flashed over the pylon, the official timer had hit the button on the stopwatch that had been started when she began her takeoff roll from the New York airport. He looked at the time shown and gave a shout of alarm.

"Hey, you guys, we either have an error or a new winner!" he exclaimed. "Look at this time! Are you sure we have positive identification on that woman in the Staggerwing?"

Another official quickly rechecked the figures.

"Wow, she sure burned up the airways!" the man said in awe. "There can't possibly be another Staggerwing in the air. Did she call the tower?"

"It's that Maggie girl, all right," another official said. "I heard her call the tower a few minutes ago. She didn't give her name, but I heard her call and say she was a Staggerwing with the race pylon in sight. The tower cleared her across the pylon and into a downwind leg for landing."

"We've got a lot of action!" the first man exclaimed. "A Lockheed Orion just reported approaching the race pylon. That would be Betty. She's only five minutes behind the Staggerwing, but get busy making those calculations on elapsed times from New York."

The president of the committee spoke up, his voice full of excitement.

"It looks to me like we have a major upset," he exclaimed with delight. "The Staggerwing left New York two hours after the Lockheed Orion, yet it beat the Lockheed! Get me those numbers. The press will be wild with this news. Get it out on the loudspeakers, too, before those ladies shut their engines down."

The official calculations came out quickly. There were no speculations as to the causes of the delays of some planes nor were there explanations for Maggie's surprising win. She had come out of nowhere. They just reported the facts—the stories would come out later.

The question mark regarding Maggie's estimated top speed was the only way the committee could reflect their confusion. They knew the plane was supposed to do about 200 mph, but it had obviously flown much faster than that. Her airspeed from New York to Wichita was in the 230 mph range, and from Wichita to Los Angeles it had to be around 240 mph. However, like the rest, Maggie was flying into a headwind that caused a lower groundspeed. Also, the others had suffered serious delays, which dropped their calculated groundspeed.

The breaking news was that there were two major surprises: first, the women had soundly beaten the men, and second, Maggie in her Staggerwing had come from relative obscurity to take first place, and she didn't even know it yet.

Maggie dropped her speed until she could no longer hold the pert little tail in the air. She made a perfect wheel landing, and as she slowed down she let the tail sink and began to steer with the tailwheel more than the rudder. As she turned off the runway onto the taxiway, she saw and followed the truck with the "FOLLOW ME" sign painted on the back into the parking area for the race planes. She noticed the crowd waving wildly and was surprised they were welcoming her so enthusiastically.

She shut the engine down by cutting the mixture, and turned all electrical circuits off. The engine quit firing but the prop kept swinging until, at last, the blades stopped in a perfect horizontal position. The engine made the familiar crackling, creaking noises of hot metal cooling off. Maggie tidied up everything, set the control lock and the brakes, made sure all was secure, and undid her own straps, feeling very tired and stiff. She'd been frozen to the controls a long time—all day long, except for the brief stop at Wichita. She could barely hear wild chanting outside, but since her ears still hadn't popped from the letdown she couldn't understand what they were shouting.

She slid back to the door and yawned widely just before she opened it. Now she could hear the shouting more clearly. She opened the cabin door at the insistence of someone who was pounding on it.

"You won! You won! You won!" the fellow at the door shouted with an enormous grin. "You won it, Maggie! You women took on the men and you won! Congratulations! Great job!"

Maggie was in a state of shocked surprise. *How could I win?* she thought incredulously. *That must mean that others had accidents.*

Photographers crowded around. They had to have their chance to shoot the winner climbing out and down the step to the ground. Lines of policemen stood between the planes and the public, but the press was allowed alongside the plane.

"Hey, Maggie, pose on the wing for us, please!" one cameraman shouted.

She didn't want to put her foot through the fabric wing covering, but she could stand on the wing root walk strip up by the windshield and the engine because it was reinforced there to let mechanics stand on it. So up on the wing she climbed and motioned them around in front. They got their pictures, and she waved at the crowd behind the ropes that cordoned off the parking area from the people who had come to watch and welcome the winner of this race.

"How did I win?" she asked a race official incredulously. "Where's Luke? Is he okay?"

"Oh he's fine, but his plane is damaged," he responded. "He wiped out his gear in Albuquerque."

"And what about Buddy?" she questioned him, dismayed but relieved that Luke was all right.

The official frowned and looked less reassuring.

"Well, we don't know about Buddy," he admitted. "He is way overdue. He should have landed in New Mexico or Arizona for fuel, but no one has heard from him. He's down someplace because his fuel would have run out, but in that high-desert country it can take a long time to find a stranded aviator."

This report worried Maggie deeply. Concerned, she inquired about the others.

"How did the girls do?"

"Oh, they are all okay," the official answered. "Some are in, but their elapsed time is not as low as yours. Each one had a delay of one type or another that cost them the race. You are the only one we know of with no incident of any kind to slow you down."

Maggie was euphoric over her unexpected victory, but it began to sink in that her success was perhaps at the expense or the misfortune of others. Unfortunately, that was the way it always had to be in a race. They were not flying so much against each other as against the cutting edge of aeronautical science. Until every part could be built to last longer and be more dependable, and until every pilot made no mistakes, they would be pushing the limits of science through failure and error.

Pushing through the crowd, Lord Jockham and Douglas managed to get to her.

"Maggie!" they shouted over the heads of the press and race officials milling about.

She turned and grinned widely at them.

"Congratulations, young lady!" Douglas exclaimed. "You really did it! What a race you have flown! It's too bad about Luke and Buddy, but that is the risk you pilots all run."

"What do you know about them?" Maggie asked, furrowing her brow.

"Well, all we know is that Luke broke his landing gear at Albuquerque and that Fernando stopped to pick him up to bring him here," Jock said. "They will all be here before sundown."

"What's that? Fernando and Luke here this afternoon? But how?" she cried excitedly.

"It seems that Fernando helped the oil company get their plane out of the mud at Wichita, so they invited him to ride west with them. In the air, they heard about Luke being stranded at Albuquerque, so they landed there to pick him up. That's all we know."

Maggie was exultant.

"Fernando back in time for the celebration? That makes it all complete!" she exclaimed giddily. "He needs to be with me when they present the trophy. And Luke, too. They deserve to be part of all this. It was because of them that I'm even here—they made it all possible!"

Jock, shielding Maggie from the crowd with his tall frame and broad shoulders, pulled her aside.

"Maggie, there is a cable here for Fernando from his father," he said in a grave voice. "It is confidential, but Douglas and I think you need to be prepared. It is not good news. We don't think Fernando would mind if we show it to you before he arrives. It came to him at my office. Here it is, but keep it to yourself until Fernando has had a chance to read it a couple of times and digest its significance."

It isn't fair, Maggie thought, crestfallen. *This moment of joy is not supposed to be interrupted with any sadness or any crisis. This is our moment to share with joy and happiness.*

With deep fear and trepidation she opened the envelope and read the cable.

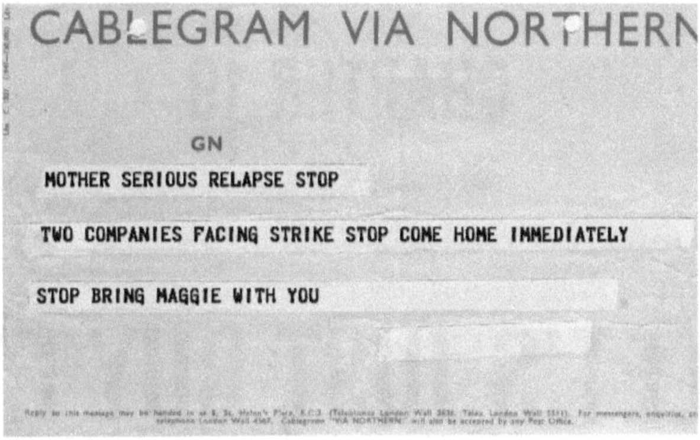

CABLEGRAM VIA NORTHERN

GN

MOTHER SERIOUS RELAPSE STOP

TWO COMPANIES FACING STRIKE STOP COME HOME IMMEDIATELY

STOP BRING MAGGIE WITH YOU

CHAPTER 19

LET'S JUST BUY IT

THE CABLE BROUGHT tears to Maggie's eyes. She knew how dear Fernando's mother was to him and how much he loved his father and the family despite the unfortunate misunderstanding and the disinheritance. Now it seemed that in the midst of crisis they were all turning to Fernando for help and were willing to heal all wounds. This would please him greatly in the midst of his grief. Fernando had delayed returning to his ailing mother and the family matters only because of Maggie and his desire to marry her on her conditions—after the race.

With this news Maggie could see her plans being shattered into little pieces like a mirror thrown against a wall. She wanted a formal wedding with all the trimmings, and that needed time to plan—at least several weeks. Should she send Fernando ahead to Argentina and follow later? Or should she send him home and ask him to return to the States as soon as possible, and postpone the wedding until then? What was the right thing to do?

She felt her head was in a spin. This day wasn't supposed to end this way either. The movie screenwriters were supposed to prepare a perfect ending for the race—and for our romance, she cried to herself, broken-hearted.

With her plans in a shambles of uncertainty on the very moment of a great victory, Maggie found her feelings in a jumble of contradictions. She was near tears of frustration.

She turned and looked up into Lord Jockham's face. He reminded her of her father at that moment, wise and mature, and she buried her head in his chest and began to sob. The very dignified diplomat had not expected this reaction from such a composed and competent young lady, but his instinctive response was to comfort her.

"There, there, my dear—be calm," he said kindly. "Fernando will arrive shortly. He will know what to do."

Maggie composed herself, wiped away her tears, forced a smile, and apologized for breaking down.

"I just needed a good cry, I guess," she said, sniffling. "I was feeling sorry for myself. I think I know what Fernando will do, but I'll wait until he reads the message and let him make his own decision. Do you know when he's landing?"

Douglas and Jock told her that the big oil company transport would be on the ground considerably ahead of their expected arrival. The three went over to where it was assigned to park so they could be the first to greet the crew and the passengers when the door opened. They visited while Maggie stretched her legs, her mind worrying about the cable and its implications.

In due time, the unmistakable drone of the two synchronized engines pulling full power could be heard through the haze even before anyone spotted the plane. It flashed over the pylon for the timers to note their official arrival. Immediately, the big ship banked around in a vertical turn the same way Maggie had done, and the pilot began to hydraulically extend the landing gear. The onlookers applauded this flashy move, although the plane was too far away for the crew to appreciate the gesture.

Expertly, the giant twin came in on short final, and to impress the gathering, especially the pilots in the crowd, they did a full stall three-point landing to perfection right on the numbers. Small planes do it easily, but to plant a big transport on the bull's eye at the head of a runway in full stall, three points, squeaking in best-grease-job style, is a major accomplishment. The people applauded wildly, enjoying the show. The DC-2 exited the runway at the first turnoff and followed the truck into the parking area to shut down.

Maggie, Douglas, and Lord Jockham managed to get through the throng and were at the side of the big silver plane just as Luke and Fernando were coming down the steps. Maggie threw herself into Fernando's arms, almost knocking him off balance, and gave him a big kiss.

"Thank you so much for coming to me," she whispered in his ear.

He gave her an extra tight hug, lifted her in the air, and swung her around.

"Congratulations on a great race, *mi amor!*" he exclaimed. "We were told on the radio that you won the race!"

He set her down and let her turn to Luke, who was waiting impatiently to congratulate her too.

"Luke, I am so sorry about your accident!" she said, giving him a hug. "Were you hurt? Can your plane be fixed?"

"First, my dear Mag, congratulations to you on a great race!" he said. "Fernando told me about your big engine and large tanks, so you only needed one fuel stop. It was a wonderful surprise to learn that! So . . . how does it feel to win your first big race, and in a factory demonstrator instead of in a custom-built race plane? How about that?"

Maggie accepted his praise modestly, but prodded him again.

"Really, are you okay?" she said, pulling on his elbow. "And how bad is your racer? Can it be fixed?"

"Thanks for worrying about me and the ship, Maggie, my girl," Luke said with a smile. "I don't have a scratch. I just lost my brakes for some unknown reason, and when I turned to stay on the taxiway the centrifugal force was too much, what with the overload of fuel, and the right gear just gave way. The wing settled down to the ground with just a bump. I think it can be fixed. There was no fire and the prop didn't dig into the dirt. We'll jack it up and fix it one way or another."

Maggie was relieved to receive Luke's favorable report, but she was still worried about the others.

"What news is there on Buddy?" she asked, concerned.

"We had a call on the radio saying they had located him and he is alive, but the plane is totally washed out," Luke responded. "We don't know what happened. They said he was in bad shape and in a hospital where he would have to stay for a while. He was sure lucky there was no fire."

Luke didn't tell her the full story. Buddy had serious injuries, and it would be a long time before he would fly again.

"And what about the girls?" Maggie queried. "Are they all okay?"

He did have news on them and shared it willingly. The pilot of the oil company plane had long-range radio on board so they were able to pick up quite a bit of news about the other competitors while coming into L.A.

"The men were the only ones with the accidents today," he reported. "Joe's plane blew up outside Kansas City, Buddy went down over northern New Mexico in the high desert, I wiped out my gear after my brakes failed in Albuquerque, and the DC-2 was delayed by getting stuck in the mud. The women had delays of one sort or another—with the exception of our champ here, of course. All are in but Betty, and she is expected shortly. The DC-2 flew a perfect flight before the mud incident, and afterward flew a rescue mission to pick me up and then bring Fernando here to Maggie."

Everyone laughed at the upbeat, positive attitude of the famous Luke, suffering bad luck once again.

Lord Jockham stepped forward and pulled Fernando aside.

"I have an urgent cable from your father," he said in a low voice. "You had better read it quickly while we have a calm moment. I had permission from your father to read it, assuming you might not be in until tomorrow."

Fernando knew it was bad news, judging from the serious expression on the consul's face. Concerned, he opened the envelope that contained the cable and read it through. Deeply troubled, he turned away to reread it. He looked over at Maggie and motioned for her to come to his side.

"You need to read this," he said soberly, handing her the cable.

Fernando read it a third time with Maggie. He had a very difficult decision to make. He knew how Maggie must feel about their wedding plans, but it looked like there was a life-and-death emergency regarding his mother that he had to take into consideration. Fortunately, his mind worked swiftly in a crisis. He had been well trained for leadership, and a true leader rises to his finest level in the most demanding of circumstances.

"Maggie, my dear sweet Maggie," he said, holding both her hands. "I wanted to marry you two months ago, but you wanted to wait. I considered the matter and felt that I should give in to your wishes because I felt that you had every right to fly your race. Now, my dear, we have another matter to consider. My mother, my father, my family all need me—and I need *you*. Now, I'm afraid that I have to ask you to give in to me for the good of others, even at your own sacrifice."

Fernando looked deeply into her eyes. They loved each other dearly, but here was a crisis that could divide them if it were not handled properly.

"I cannot stand the thought of leaving you behind," he said. "I honestly feel that I cannot live without you."

Maggie didn't interrupt him, and suddenly a solution popped into Fernando's head.

"Maggie Rockwell, will you please fly with me tomorrow to Acapulco where we can be married and continue on to Buenos Aires afterwards?" he said eagerly, still holding on to her hands. "I know it takes two days to get a marriage license in California, waiting for blood tests and so on. But in your plane, and stopping in Mexico to get married tomorrow, we can make Buenos Aires in about four days! I just need to talk to the factory rep."

Before Maggie could collect her thoughts and consider this kind of spontaneous proposal, Luke, overhearing Fernando's query, announced that he knew where to find the gentleman who represented the factory and offered to bring him over. When he returned a moment later with the representative in tow, Fernando asked Maggie to excuse them and he took the man and Luke to one side.

After a few minutes of hushed conversation, Fernando returned to Maggie's side.

"I have a deal to propose to you, *mi amor*," he said happily. "I have just bought your Staggerwing!"

Maggie gasped.

"With the long-range tanks and speed, we can make about two thousand miles per day," Fernando said with excitement. "It is a little over seven thousand air miles from here to Buenos Aires. We can go to our homes right after the presentation of the winning trophies and pack one light suitcase tonight. We'll sleep a few hours, and I'll have cars pick us each up and bring us back here an hour before sunrise. We'll make Acapulco in eight hours or so with one gas stop. We'll have a Mexican wedding with mariachis and all the trimmings!"

Maggie, still reeling from Fernando's proposal and his purchase of the Staggerwing, was speechless.

"We can fly on down the west coast to Santiago, Chile," he continued quickly, before she could say no. "From there we cross the Andes to Buenos Aires. It should take us three more days. You have already proven that this plane can make a long trip like that and also reach the high altitude necessary to cross the Andes safely. Maggie, I will apologize to your parents and I promise to make it up to them. What about it, *mi amor*?"

It appeared that Fernando had taken charge of the situation with such decisiveness, strong leadership, and positive direction that Maggie, her head spinning, almost had no choice but to accept his bold proposal on the spot. Her plans and desires were being swept aside by his audacious but understandable moves. Still, it was too fast for her to handle. She just had to talk to her parents. There are times and situations where there is no substitute for a loving and experienced parent's perspective.

Maggie found a telephone at the airport and called her parents. First she told them about her miraculous race and how she beat the men and all the other pilots. They were delighted. But then she shared the unfortunate news from Argentina that caused Fernando to buy her Staggerwing on the spot and ask her to fly with him to South America as his bride. They were as speechless as she had been just five minutes earlier.

"He wants us to fly tomorrow to Acapulco and be married there, since there is no two-day legal delay like in California," she said, ignoring their silence. "From there, we would fly on down to Argentina. What do you think, Mom and Dad? I want to go with Fernando, but it's a bit frightening."

This was all impossibly startling and unsettling. Fernando could tell a crisis was brewing. He asked for the phone and implored Maggie's parents to consider his side of the dilemma.

"I am the only son of a dying mother," he explained gently. "My duty, I feel, is to be at her side if at all possible. In addition, a terrible crisis at our family businesses has caused union leaders to insist that I personally negotiate matters because I went to school with them. With Maggie's plane we can get there in four days or less. If we went by ship, it would take almost four weeks. I must get there as soon as possible. We cannot live without each other. Please give Maggie and me your support and blessings. I will take care of her and bring her back as soon as we can."

Fernando's voice was authoritative and commanding yet kind and loving, his arguments reasonable, and his promise to take care of Maggie so reassuring that Maggie's father was the first to give in, although reluctantly. Quietly, with resignation, her mother agreed.

"We are not very happy about this sudden change in wedding plans," Mr. Rockwell said, "nor are we happy about you taking our daughter so far away from us so fast, but we do understand and we sympathize with you, Fernando. We also pray for your mother. My wife is nodding her head and I can tell she needs to talk to Maggie."

In a few seconds, Mrs. Rockwell, trying hard to control her tears, was on the phone with Maggie. They talked. They sobbed. Maggie told her about her narrow escape from the military planes, and they laughed.

When they said goodbye, they cried some more.

With sudden inspiration, Fernando asked to talk to Maggie's father again.

"Mr. Rockwell, thank you for giving me your daughter," he said. "Now, as a future son-in-law I have an offer to make. As soon as we get to Argentina I would like to telex your bank and offer a guarantee on your loan. Maggie and I will make your payments until prices improve here. Please don't sell off any more of your herd, especially your mother cows and heifers. We'll work out the details later. To proceed, I will need the name of your lead banker and his telex address so we can contact him."

Mr. Rockwell was dumbfounded and stammered the information, quite in shock, but he expressed his heartfelt gratitude for the generous offer. Fernando thanked him and said goodbye, again promising to take good care of their daughter.

The Rockwells never imagined their daughter would be swept off her feet by a handsome Argentine, a "prince of the gauchos," who had already bought the winning cross-country plane to fly her off to a movie-style wedding in glamorous Acapulco, and now had offered to guarantee their loan at the bank. They knew they should not interfere with true love or ignore a real crisis in Fernando's family circumstances. Besides, with their brief contact at the graduation festivities, they had come to like Fernando and trust him. Love for their future son-in-law would come in time, they were certain, but for now, it was more important that they were able to trust him.

At the airport, the movie director and crews came by for some final footage they needed to complete their movie.

"Luke, we have had to rewrite the story a bit," the director explained. "Instead of you—played by Douglas—winning the race, we will have Monica, the actress, play the part of the real Maggie, who wins the race. In the movie, you and Monica will fall in love, but in real life it looks like Fernando gets the girl!"

Everyone had a good chuckle.

"Luke, do you think we can fix your racer enough to stage that landing-gear failure for the cameras?" the director asked. "That would be a nice touch of realism."

It didn't take long for Luke to recognize an opportunity to recoup his losses.

"Oh sure!" he replied with a grin. "All I need is for you to buy that plane from me. We'll not only wipe the gear out again, we can stage it—it'll either just lie down and die in the dust, or we can make it look like it's going up in an explosion and a ball of fire. After I get out, of course, we use trick photography!"

"Deal!" the director said, laughing.

The plan was in place now. After the dinner in the huge hangar at which Maggie would receive the coveted trophy and the congratulations from the entire flying community, she and Fernando, with the help of Jock and Douglas's chauffeurs and cars, would both be taken to their individual homes to prepare for their long journey.

During the night, company mechanics would inspect the Staggerwing, fill the tanks, and get new maps of the entire route.

Suddenly, Fernando's remark about "packing only one light suitcase" registered with Maggie.

"Fernando, you said *one* suitcase?" Maggie exclaimed. "You've got to be kidding! No way can I travel with only one suitcase! You men just don't understand!"

"*Mi amor*, I'll buy you a whole new trousseau in Buenos Aires," Fernando replied, putting both arms around her waist. "We have shops that put Paris and London to shame. I promise you a mink coat, the finest cashmere suits and sweaters, and anything else you want. Silks, pearls—it's all yours! Just don't overload this plane right now."

He chuckled and gave her a kiss on the cheek.

Maggie understood what any pilot means about keeping weight down, so she promised she'd be prudent in what she packed, but she was not going to spend her honeymoon in western cowgirl attire, if she had anything to say about it!

An hour before sunrise they both returned, ready to begin their greatest adventure.

CHAPTER 20

OFF TO ARGENTINA

FRIENDS, ADMIRERS, AND the press had gathered to see them off. That lovely morning, the pre-sunrise sky and clouds were more colorful and photogenic than the famous sunsets off the Pacific coast. The whole sky was alive with brilliant colors, streaks of high cirrus clouds lit up with vibrant highlights. The rays of the sun rising behind the mountain peaks and some tall clouds on the far horizon spread out like spokes of a wheel in a bright sunburst.

Fernando and Maggie had loaded their two pieces of luggage, and waving to the crowd, climbed into the now-famous Staggerwing. The plane had been thoroughly prepared, but Fernando and Maggie had carefully walked around the ship, checking each area themselves.

Finally, settling in their seats, Fernando went through the pre-start checklist with Maggie, turned on the master switch, let the booster pump build up fuel pressure, and hit the starter button. He counted the blades of the propeller as they passed by until five and then turned on both magnetos, opening the throttle slightly at the same time.

The big radial engine started, one cylinder firing at a time, roughly, belching smoke, until all nine were firing smoothly. All gauges came to life on cue. The sleeping Staggerwing was now awake and ready.

As they were warming up the engine and preparing to taxi out, Fernando, in the left-hand pilot's seat, turned to Maggie, sitting in the right-hand copilot seat.

"My lovely flygirl, what made you agree to come with me so readily?" he asked.

He was truly amazed at how flexible and submissive she was after all the many times of hard-headed obstinacy he had encountered during their courtship.

"Don't flatter yourself too much, my gaucho prince," she said, teasing. "I happen to have bonded with this plane you just bought out from under me. No way was I going to let you fly this dreamboat of mine anywhere without me in it too!"

Fernando laughed heartedly, but inside he was convinced of something that was very special to him. He had a real thoroughbred racehorse of a woman—not any flighty filly, but a real thoroughbred. They were going to have quite an adventurous life together.

But Fernando and Maggie knew something that went deeper. Each loved the other with true devotion and a sense of duty and commitment to their destiny together, forever. They had now proven their willingness to make any sacrifice for the other. Fernando had said that he was willing to give up fortune, family, and country for his Maggie. She, in turn, had now shown that she was willing to leave parents and country for Fernando.

Fernando looked out at the line boy, motioned with his thumbs to pull both wheel chocks away, knowing that on Maggie's side another line boy would pull his side out simultaneously. Fernando pushed the button on the mike and asked the tower for permission to taxi to the run-up area at the head of the runway in use. He was cleared to taxi.

As the plane slowly inched forward, Maggie noticed a commotion among the crowd out her window. Someone was breaking through, waving his arms, and running right toward the whirling propeller.

"Stop! Stop! Wait!" she shouted to Fernando. "A man and a woman are running toward us shouting something!"

Fernando hit the brakes, bringing the plane to a full stop, and shut down the engine.

As the couple got closer, to her amazement Maggie could see they were her parents.

"Fernando, that's Mom and Dad! What in the world!"

She quickly undid her seat belt, jumped back between the seats, and opened the door before the prop had even stopped. She stepped out onto the wing walk of the plane, jumped to the ground, and ran toward them.

"How did you get here so fast?" Maggie cried, embracing them. "What an absolutely wonderful surprise! I was feeling so bad that we were leaving before we could really say goodbye!"

As fast as he could, Fernando stepped onto the wing walk and jumped down, excited and just as surprised to see them there.

Mr. Rockwell broke in as everyone was talking animatedly at the same time.

"Well, we decided to leave the convention after you called and drove through the night," he explained. "How lucky we made it just in time to see you!"

They all embraced, laughing and crying at the same time. Maggie jumped up and down with uninhibited delight like a little toddler.

"Oh, I'm so thrilled to see you!" she exclaimed happily. "I sure wish you could fly to Mexico for our wedding, and on to Argentina, too. Maybe one day, huh?"

With a flash of inspiration, Fernando spoke up, his arm around Maggie's waist.

"Maggie has just given me a wonderful idea. There is no more beautiful time than December—early summer—to visit Argentina. I can't think of a more appropriate Christmas gift for my darling bride than to bring her parents down for the holidays. The guest suite on our company ships is better than first class on the cruise ships. You'll enjoy the best service you can imagine—all courtesy of the company. That's only a little more than three short months away. Besides, I pray you'll be able to meet my mother and that I'll be able to show you our country and introduce you to my culture. How about it?"

For a few seconds Maggie's parents looked at each other in stunned silence. Squealing with ecstasy, Maggie wrapped her arms around Fernando and kissed him on the cheek. The Rockwells both broke into big smiles of happy anticipation. What an exciting adventure had just opened up for them!

"No one in Kanab is going to believe this!" Maggie's father said, laughing.

With the air ringing with joy, and giving one last hug and goodbye, Maggie and Fernando climbed back into their Staggerwing, finished their takeoff preparations, taxied down the runway, and climbed smoothly into the rosy morning sky, the landing gear disappearing into the belly of the plane. The transformation from a wheeled machine into a streamlined, flying, dolphin-like bird, now in its intended element, was both beautiful and magical.

A Los Angeles newspaper reporter waxed eloquent in his column the next day, telling the tale of the departure of Maggie and Fernando for Latin America. He included the surprise arrival of Maggie's parents to wish the couple—soon to be married in Acapulco—a safe trip and a romantic honeymoon.

Maggie Rockwell, winning aviatrix of

yesterday's accident-prone yet exciting cross-country air race, was shocked to learn that her fiancé, Fernando Velez-Candiotti Braun Underwood, bought her race plane—the now-famous "Staggerwing"—in order to fly home to Argentina to attend to family emergencies there. Mr. Underwood convinced Miss Rockwell to move their coming wedding up a full month to be married in Mexico on their way south.

The Staggerwing airplane not only carried Miss Rockwell to victory in the highly contested race, this flying machine remarkably matches her pert and spunky personality. It is streamlined, curvaceous, tapered where an airplane should be tapered, aerodynamic, travels with remarkable speed, and is very maneuverable in capable hands. In other words, it is just like a perfect female pilot, an aviatrix of renown, which Miss Rockwell has proven herself to be.

The airplane sits high on its front wheels, tail low, in a jaunty attitude. It looks fast just parked on the tarmac. But after takeoff, when the wheels retract into the bottom of the lower wing, a dramatic metamorphosis takes place. The plane now seems to leap forward with added speed. It climbs out at an impossibly steep angle like a homesick angel. The big engine roars, the propeller grabs at the air, and all heads in the crowd turn to admire the sleek, powerful, machine fly by.

In a similar way, Miss Rockwell herself causes heads to turn as she strides by with purposeful intent. She is the aviatrix of the century. This new kind of race plane has proven itself a winner in the midst of a depression that has affected the aviation business as well as all other parts of our national economy.

Likewise, Miss Rockwell has proven herself a winner of historic proportions by taking on the men in the most dangerous of all sports, air racing, and has beaten the best of them. What a brilliant combination: a fabulous new kind of airplane in the hands of a fabulous new kind of woman.

The winning aviatrix is university-educated, sophisticated, and competent, yet she has overcome many obstacles. To pay for her own education, she worked as a stunt woman for the movies. She comes from hard-working western cattlemen. We have a new role model, folks!

Miss Rockwell's Staggerwing likewise comes from hard-working people at a small midwest factory, trying to survive the Depression by making a new kind of plane, one that is better, faster, more comfortable, and more dependable for efficiency-seeking executives.

Now Miss Rockwell and Mr. Underwood are flying that same race plane off to Argentina, thousands of miles away, across jungles, deserts, the high Andes mountains, and fertile coastal plains. What a demonstration of the capability of these adventurous young people and this one-of-a-kind airplane. These are world travelers both at their best. Los Angeles—and the world, no doubt—wish them Godspeed and good luck.

The Staggerwing became the most enduring airplane of the 1930s and the most loved by all pilots for the next fifty years. But this one—Maggie's beautiful doll—flew off into historical oblivion.

But you and I know that it really went "Down Argentine Way," as the song goes, on a honeymoon trip for two young pilots madly in love.

Louise Thaden's original pilot license, No. 6850, issued by the National Aeronautic Association and signed by Orville Wright. (The Central Arkansas Library System)

Amelia Earhart, Ruth Nichols, and Louise Thaden

Louise McPhetridge-Thaden in her Staggerwing at the start of the Bendix Air Race.

Pilot Louise Thaden waves from her Beechcraft Travel Air Model B-400 after winning the first Women's National Air Derby in 1929

Louise Thaden (sixth from the left) poses with some flyers including Amelia Earhart (right) and Florence Barnes (left) while waiting for the fog to lift in St. Louis.

Thaden and Noyes win the Bendix Trophy

ABOUT THE AUTHOR

Robert E. Wells, a native of Nevada, is a former executive for Citibank and emeritus General Authority of The Church of Jesus Christ of Latter-day Saints. After serving in the U.S. Navy in World War II, he graduated in accounting and economics from Brigham Young University, then served a mission for the LDS Church in Argentina. He married the former Meryl Leavitt in 1952 and directed Citibank operations in Argentina, Uruguay, Brazil, Paraguay, and Ecuador. He and his family later lived in Mexico, Chile, and Guatemala, where he supervised thousands of missionaries and Church members. After Meryl passed away in 1960, he married the former Helen Walser, who died in 2023. They have a blended family of seven children, along with twenty-seven grandchildren and forty great-grandchildren. At age ninety-seven, he still lives by his motto: "I love the spirit of adventure and adventures of the spirit!" Wells is currently the second-oldest living General Authority for the LDS Church, after Pres. Russell M. Nelson.